MW01487932

A Lake Most Deep

By Rob Howell

ISBN: 978-0-9961259-1-8 (First Edition, Print Version)
ISBN: 978-0-9961259-0-1 (First Edition, Electronic Version)
ISBN: 978-0-9961259-6-3 (Second Edition, Print Version)
ISBN: 978-0-9961259-5-6 (Second Edition, Electronic Version)

Cover art copyright © 2015 by Patrick McEvoy,
www.megaflowgraphics.com

Lyrics on page 144 used with permission from the song *Measure of a Man*, by Heather Dale, www.heatherdale.com.

Works by Rob Howell

World of Shijuren

The Adventures of Edward Aethelredson
A Lake Most Deep
The Eyes of a Doll
Where Now the Rider

The Kreisens
I Am a Wondrous Thing
Brief Is My Flame (Forthcoming)
None Call Me Mother (Forthcoming)

Dedication

To my grandparents Edward, Irene, Bob, and Doris.
You have each made your mark in Shijuren.

Table of Contents

Foreword and Acknowledgments

If you are reading this, thank you for purchasing my first novel. I hope you like Edward, Piri, Ragnar, and the rest. I also hope you enjoy the world around them, especially since *A Lake Most Deep* is the first of many novels I will write in this world.

I am a historian and a language geek, and those parts of me clearly show through in the novel. I add bits of my world creation throughout the novel, even if they are not necessarily important for *A Lake Most Deep*. We all talk about things that are relevant to our personal context, and my characters do as well. Call these my homage to J. R. R. Tolkien's "cats of Queen Berúthiel." Many of these will become more relevant as more novels set in Shijuren come out.

While I tend to enjoy complex and detailed world-making, it can get confusing. To make things easier I have added several appendices. I have listed the people and places. There's a glossary and a calendar. I also included some notes detailing how magic works and how deities come into being in Shijuren. These last two items are there because I am always curious about the magic systems of other authors, and I assume many of you would be curious about mine.

One does not complete a novel by oneself. There are too many contributors to properly thank them all, but I want to point out a few in particular. Patrick McEvoy, the cover artist, put up with my nitpicking at his work. Susan Howell essentially funded this novel and served as an editor. Beth Agejew served as my primary editor. Jenn Nemec, Traci Austin, and Sam Strickland helped edit this as well. Jeff Fox helped ensure the body mechanics of the fight scenes that existed in my mind actually worked. Nina Hansberry helped me with languages. Michael and Neathery Fuller confirmed that a vessel carrying water from fountains to homes could be called an *amphora*, a question I never thought to ask. Jason Cordova helped me write the blurb, which is a surprisingly challenging task.

I want to thank Heather Dale for graciously allowing me to use lyrics from one of her songs in chapter 20. If you have not yet listened to her music, do yourself a favor and go to www.heatherdale.com. The song "Measure of a Man" is on her CD *The Trial of Lancelot*. Get that album, but only if you want something to listen to over and over, because you will.

I would also like to thank a few authors whose support was invaluable. Sarah Hoyt has never met me, but her blog commentary on the writing process and industry helped tremendously. Chris Kennedy taught me several important details about self-publishing and patiently put up with my ignorance. One author who inspired *A Lake Most Deep* is not around for me to appreciate properly. I will, however, send a signed copy of the cover art to the first person who finds my homage to Raymond Chandler.

A Lake Most Deep now belongs in the past. The future in Shijuren starts with a novel centered on Irina. She was once the Velikomat, or Great Mother, of Periaslavl. As the ruler of a kingdom, she has lived a long life handling great matters of state. We shall see how she handles the loss of her position and much of her power as she faces cold exile from her home.

Edward will return later in 2015, as a small favor for Honker Harald turns into something deadly. Who knew a little girl's doll could be involved in so many murders?

Feel free to email comments and suggestions to rob@robhowell.org. My Facebook page is at https://www.facebook.com/robhowell.org, and my blog, Howell's Howls, is at www.robhowell.org/blog. Finally, you can get all the information about the World of Shijuren, its history, people, and places at www.robhowell.org/shijuren. Eventually, this will hold all of my notes about the world of Shijuren, including hints of possible things to come.

Again, thank you for reading *A Lake Most Deep*.

—Rob Howell

Foreword to the Second Edition

Welcome to the First Anniversary, Second Edition version of *A Lake Most Deep*. This year has flown by and I have so many people to thank for helping me learn so much.

First, I should probably talk about what has changed here in the Second Edition. I believe that my production values and methods should be consistent throughout my body of works, and so the most important changes make *A Lake Most Deep* much more like *The Eyes of a Doll*.

Patrick McEvoy updated the cover to include a more professional spine and to change the size and placement of my name. The first edition only had my name in small letters on the front. Now, it is in big, bold letters on the front and also on the spine. Thanks to all the critics and friends who laughed at, I mean, pointed out my horrible self-promotion skills.

One thing I discovered is that each editor has a flavor, if you will, or a method all of their own, just like a producer can remix a song. My first editor, Beth Agejew, did a fine job, but I decided to have Kellie Hultgren re-edit *A Lake Most Deep* so it would be more consistent. As in the case of *The Eyes of a Doll*, there are things that Kellie pointed out were incorrect, but I decided to leave as they were. If you find a grammatical error, it is my decision and not a reflection of her editing. More importantly for the Second Edition in my mind is that Kellie remixed it to match the sound in *The Eyes of a Doll*.

I have also made a few continuity fixes to match *The Eyes of a Doll*. I am trying to stamp out these errors as much as I can now, rather than in the future. To that end, I have built a wiki for the Shijuren series at: www.robhowell.org/shijuren. I am using the wiki both to keep track of all the things I have already put in the books, but also things that have not yet been mentioned, including things that may never been mentioned. If you are an avid reader of the series, you will find hints of my future novels as I add to it. The wiki is nowhere near complete, nor do I ever anticipate it will be complete, but it is something I work on consistently. In truth, it provides a nice diversion for me, as the world-building is one of my favorite aspects of this job.

I had to fix one mistake in the story. Romaine Spence pointed out a significant plot hole. I have patched that hole. It did not change the mystery or arrangement of the story, merely the conclusion. Nevertheless, he was right to point out that I had not answered one of the central questions of the story. For that, Romaine earned a signed copy of the Second Edition and a place amongst my alpha readers.

The big addition to this edition is the map. Initially, Peter von Groote was going to create the map. Unfortunately, he suffered an injury and was unable to continue. Fortunately, I have many skilled friends and Adam Hale stepped forward and created the map in record time. I had wanted a map all along, and there will be other maps, including one of the world of Shijuren and other cities in regions as time goes by. Still, it is exciting to have another part of my vision in a medium we all can look at.

All that remains in this Foreword is to thank some additional people. I cannot possibly list all of the authors, fans, and publishing people who have helped me in this past year. There are just so many who have given their time and wisdom to help me get better and offer places to sell my books. Nevertheless, I would like to point out a few.

Steven Boyd, known as Master Andrixos in the Society for Creative Anachronism (www.sca.org), has sold my books at events. So, go to Calontir Trim (www.calontirtrim.com), buy my book, and a few dozen yards of cool trim while you are at it. He has also given me a place to meet readers at larger SCA events.

Another person of note is Deb Keller, known in the SCA as Antonia Stefani, https://www.facebook.com/thistlewoodsoap/?fref=ts. She has not only provided a place to sell my books, but also helped some with other small details. She is often there when I need another pair of eyes.

I would like to thank Cedar Sanderson, www.cedarlili.com, for both her kind review of *A Lake Most Deep* and her helpful suggestions. She is one of the people who pointed out that I needed to change the cover. She's both a talented author and artist, which you will see when you look at her stuff.

I cannot fully express my appreciation of LibertyCon. Uncle Timmy and his daughter, Brandy Spraker, have created a convention where people really are family. I have been to several conventions in the past two years, but none feel as comfortable at LibertyCon. I will be participating on panels for the first time in 2016, and I cannot express my excitement about the opportunity. Without the confidence LibertyCon has given me, I would not have pushed for other opportunities, such as applying for panels at Ad-Astra in Toronto and WorldCon 2016, here in Kansas City.

Again, I welcome comments and suggestions sent to rob@robhowell.org. You can find my Facebook page at https://www.facebook.com/robhowell.org, and my blog, Howell's Howls, is at www.robhowell.org/blog. Finally, you can get all the information about the World of Shijuren, its history, people, and places at www.robhowell.org/shijuren. Eventually, this will hold all of my notes about the world of Shijuren, including hints of possible things to come.

Thanks again, and here is hoping for a great second year.

—Rob Howell

Note About Links

I have linked each name, place, and new word to its entry on the World of Shijuren wiki at www.robhowell.org/shijuren when it is first used in *A Lake Most Deep* and also in its entry in the appendices.

My hope is that most reading devices used to read the e-book will have web access, allowing the reader to click on the item if they wish, have it show them the information about the item, and then allow the reader to return to the same page. In other words, I hope you can look things up as you wish without losing the flow of the story.

It is an idea that may or may not be a good one. Please tell me whether you like the idea or if the links themselves are distracting.

Thank you.

Map of Achrida
Drawn by Reader Anastasius

Prologue
Late Morning, 16 Foarmoanne, 1713 MG

Reader Veikko of Haapavesa
Library of Basilopolis

A man, a horse, and a vicious kidnapping and murder saved me.

Since you're a Reader, I know that's not enough of the story to satisfy you. That's especially true, no doubt, since you've told me that the "Gropa Crisis of 1712" is something that historians will want to read about in years to come. It did not seem that way to me at the time, but I suppose that's probably true for all who are involved in the events remembered as "history."

Though I have gained a home here in Achrida, and those events helped make that happen, I really did not want to sift through all those details. You knew that, but you are right, I do owe Bedarth and his memory, for he is the man who saved me. A more scrupulous person would have known not to play upon that memory.

You knew him much better than I did, though I was his apprentice for three years and you've always lived hundreds of leagues away from him. He was much more infuriating in person, almost as much as all you Readers are, and for the same reason. You all think you know everything. The fact that you usually do makes you more annoying, not less.

As for the horse, you'll have to ask Deor himself. Watch your fingers, he bites.

For the other, I suppose I should start my recollection by admitting that I don't really know if the initial kidnappings and murders were vicious. Bedarth taught me to be precise, after all. I wasn't there, and we'll never find the bodies.

You are welcome to ask Katarina the particular details of how she captured and killed Marija and her escort. She'll tell you, but she charges. I've paid her for information a number of times now, and I've regretted the cost each time, though she always fulfills her agreements. She just does so in her own way.

Of course, we know now she was merely a willing ally for the person behind the "Crisis." Tool is probably the wrong word, because it implies that she wasn't in charge. She only does what she wants, and acting as the catalyst for the crisis appealed to her, especially since she got to kill people while doing it.

But I'm getting ahead of myself, I suppose. Here are my memories from the moment I came to Achrida. Do with these what you will.

Edward Aethelredson

Chapter 1
Midday, 4 Gersmoanne, 1712 MG

The spring sun had soared by the time we reached the crest opening out to the city's valley. The vibrant colors made us take a moment to enjoy them. In many places, the contrast of the emerald evergreens against the sharp white of the mountain limestone would have halted us. Here, however, the deep blue of the lake that stretched out of sight to the east overwhelmed even that contrast.

The city gleamed below us. It stretched along the west side of the lake, curving like an amphitheater up from the shoreline to a large keep on the highest hill. Clearly, the inhabitants had quarried the limestone extensively to build that keep, the walls that surrounded the city, and most of its buildings. The bright red ceramic tiles used to roof most of the buildings made the city even more vibrant.

I could see another road coming from the west, intersecting this road from the north before reaching a city gate. The city matched the description I had been given of Achrida, and that meant there would be another road leading farther southward to Basil's City, the heart of the Empire, and my future.

That future could wait, though, since we had been on the road for many weeks to get here and it would be at least three more weeks from Achrida to the Great City. This was a place to rest, if one was in no great hurry.

"It's not like the Emperor knows we're coming. What do you think about staying here a few days?"

Deor snorted and started downward.

"By Falhofnir, horses are supposed to be led, not have their riders chase them."

I sighed and followed him. He cared as much as ever, and anyway, who was I to argue with an eighty-some stone stallion that was smarter than most of my cousins?

It took us about an hour to approach the gate and join the crowd waiting to be allowed in. Those in line spoke a babble of languages. I recognized some, such as the Kreisic that reminded me of home, the harsh sharp speech similar to what I had learned in Ivan Yevgenich's izba the previous winter, and even the Old Imperial I had pored over in so many of Bedarth's books. There was also a variety of others I had never heard before. Fortunately, Imperial seemed to be the most common.

"I admit it, Bedarth." I looked up at the sky, "You were right to make me learn Imperial. As usual."

As we got closer, I noticed a broad powerful woman managing the entry process. Her dark hair peeked out from a steel cap, and a short, riveted chainmail shirt protected her body. She and the rest of the gate guards had covered their armor with belted blue tabards bearing a yellow fortress amongst mountains. Her greaves and vambraces gleamed, unblemished despite the dust, mud, and droppings of the travelers and their horses.

Her bearing matched the precision of her equipment, and she only shifted when she saw me. She leaned over and whispered to the guard standing next to her, who quickly went into the gatehouse. I noticed a flicker of movement on the battlements and then saw the small half-smile of a perfectly balanced warrior on the woman's face.

I gave a half-smile of my own, slowly lifted my scabbarded sword, and slid it into Deor's pack. She gave a small nod but flicked her eyes to the uncovered point of my greatspear. I affixed a leather peace-bond upon the point. Her half-smile reached her eyes, but she never lost her balance.

Soon after, a guard came out with a small scrap of parchment. She flicked her eyes over the note and nodded. A large caravan that had slowed entry into and exit from the city finally left, led by a loudly cursing master who everyone ignored.

Presently, my turn arrived and the woman stepped forward.

"Milord, please state your name and why you come to Achrida."

"Edward Aethelredson from the Middlemarch of the Seven Kingdoms. Passing through to the Great City, though I will rest for some days before continuing."

"Know anyone here?"

I shook my head, her curtness contagious.

"There's a northerner who keeps an inn here. The Frank Faerie. Down Trade Road to the Square of Legends. Take Medusa's Way and follow the Fourth Serpent up the hill." She glanced at the greatspear calmly. "Keep the peace-bond."

She let me pass with another half-smile, though I noticed that two members of her squad had pressing business in the city that, oddly enough, seemed to coincide with my route.

I ignored them, though I did follow her advice.

The Square of Legends bustled and screamed. Vendors at kiosks hawked their wares. Teamsters yelled for people to get out of their way. The fountain in the center burbled as people filled amphorae. Dogs barked as they hunted for any interesting scrap amongst the moving feet. Most people ignored those around them and pushed through to one of the many roads that led out of the square, each marked with a large marble statue.

A statue of a woman with hair of asps glared at all before her, marking Medusa's Way. Its main route circled underneath the ridge and from it a number of smaller alleys and roadways snaked up to the base of the hill. I took what seemed to be the fourth one and soon wound up in front of a large, rambling building built into the hillside. Many feet above it, the battlements of the northeastern castle tower loomed, casting a shadow across the roadway.

A sign painted with a saucy winged figure leered happily over the main door. I tried to take a moment to appreciate the artistry, but Deor had other ideas and started walking into what was clearly the stable area. He whinnied his approval, and I could see why, as the stables looked clean and the hay fresh.

The whinny summoned a boy with dark hair spiking in many directions. The gaps of his clothing at his ankles and wrists suggested he had just grown a few inches.

"Apologies, good sir, I was cleaning the back stall."

"Stables always need something," I said, waving the apology away. "I might be staying here, but I need to speak to the landlord. Deor here would appreciate some oats and a place to relax..."

Before I could finish, the boy and Deor were in motion to a stable bay.

"Oh, you'll stay here, everyone always does," he said happily as he grabbed a bag of oats.

A black-and-white cat at the top of a stall yawned at me and fell back to sleep. Well. I had clearly been dismissed by boy, horse, and cat, so I walked into the Frank Faerie's taproom. The noise abated briefly as the patrons took a moment to assess the newcomer.

"Pick any damn place you want," came a rough voice from the gloom.

"Now, Karah, at least be lettin' the lad be havin' a pint before yer rude to him."

My eyes had adjusted by now, so I could tell the second voice came from a large and wild-bearded man behind the bar.

"Yes, Da," shouted a solidly built, blond-haired girl, "but sure as the lake is cold I'll need to."

The crowd barked the comfortable, knowing laughter of tavern regulars, and the bartender motioned me over.

"You've the look of someone from the Seven Kingdoms, meanin' you'll be wantin' ale or mead, and I've never been havin' any success with mead, and more's the pity since it's me own choice, so be wrappin' yerself around this here pint, which even them as doesn't care for me are to be allowin' is the best in the entire Empire, if I do be sayin' so myself."

"The pint will do, and how do you have time to brew when you don't even have the time to breathe when you talk?"

The regulars barked again and even Karah flashed a smile at her father's expense.

"I can see you'll be doin' just fine here." The bartender grinned. "I'm to be called Ragnar, and my family in the north were to be namin' me Longtongue for some reason, but that was bein' better than some of the things that my brothers were bein' called."

He pointed towards one of the doors, adding, "Me wife Zoe is bein' in the back. For some reason she prefers to be doin' the cookin' whilst I be doin' the greetin', which is bein' just as well as she's havin' the touch in

23

a kitchen and I don't, and with the dust of the road bein' on that fine tunic, if you had a horse you'll be meetin' me boy Eirik, and that there's me daughter Karah who'll surely be findin' some reason to be sharp, especially if ya pats her bottom, eh, Marko?"

Amidst another round of laughter, a regular glared over his mug showing off a splendid black eye.

My first sip confirmed that the ale matched Ragnar's claim, being rich and brown with hints of flavors new to me. Looking around, I immediately felt comfortable.

The large interior held three lines of tables with a great fireplace at one end and the long bar at the other. The bar served Ragnar almost as his throne. A couple of dozen people lounged around the tables, mostly tradesmen but also several women, including a few who probably spent late evenings offering comfort, or something like it, to men who thought they were lonely. On this early afternoon, though, all happily boasted and bantered loudly as Karah wove nimbly amongst them. A fat gray tabby jumped from a table and came over, demanding to be petted.

"That there is Melia who is after bein' the true ruler of the Faerie. Akantha is usually to be sleepin' in the stables with Eirik." Melia insistently butted my shins as Ragnar introduced her.

"Now I'm to be guessin' yer to be wantin' a room, and mine are bein' clean and sturdy, though not all of them fit for any proud nobleman or arrogant mage. I'm to be seein' from the rings on your arm yer not poor, but yer havin' the look of one of those damned carls whose shields wouldn't let me kin be raidin' your shores. Not me a'course, I was to be comin' south for the Emperor's gold." He grinned innocently and quoted a price that seemed reasonable.

"It's bein' a mite early for dinner and whilst me Zoe isn't havin' Karah's tongue, wherever that be comin' from, she'll still be speakin' most smartly if I was to tell you it was bein' ready, but I'm sure we can be comin' up with something to ease yer stomach a mite until she's to be willin' to part with tonight's fare which is the goat she's been roastin' all of the day."

"Yes to a room, and I can wait for dinner, though a bit of bread now would not go amiss," I said, petting Melia. "But give me a moment to check on my horse, and then I'll settle in."

"Tell Eirik you're to be stayin' in the top, back room over the stables."

I went back to the stables where Eirik had started brushing Deor down.

"You'll be wanting your packs, right? Da always convinces them. Anyway, I can help you upstairs with them."

The black-and-white cat celebrated my decision to stay by rolling over and draping her left paw instead of the right over the railing. Her eyes never opened.

I took my weapons and shield, and we split the remaining bags. He led me through the maze of corridors and up two flights of stairs to a rather large room. Clearly Ragnar had judged me well. The room was plain but, from my viewpoint, luxurious. While merely a simple rope bed, it was an actual bed. A dark wool blanket covered a fairly thick pine-smelling pallet. A sideboard holding several plain, red ceramic bowls ran along the window side of the room. Eirik placed my bags on the bed and opened the window.

"Me ma loves her baths, and we almost always have water heated, if you wish. Or we can bring some up and fill the bowls." He motioned at the pottery. "Oh, and before I forget, here, come and touch the keystone."

I glanced up at the top of the door arch, but he was pointing at a piece of sharp black stone that was placed in the door and matched a notch in the door- frame.

"There's a stonelord that likes me Da's beer," he said expectantly. When I didn't move, he continued, "These are keystones—they keep the doors locked for some of our rooms. Only the family and a guest it knows can open the door."

I placed my hands around the keystone, which briefly warmed to my touch. Bedarth undoubtedly sat laughing at my confusion in One-Eye's Great Hall at that moment. Years of his tutoring, and yet I had forgotten so quickly how common magic is in the Empire.

I shook my head and turned to Eirik. "I'll take the water up here for today, though I'm going to want a full bath tomorrow."

He nodded and left.

I went to the window and looked out. The top of the stable, which backed into the cliff face, blocked most of the view, but the opening let the cool lake air curl back from the rock wall into the room.

In but a few minutes, Eirik returned with a pitcher of scalding-hot water and a small loaf of bread that had been put back into the oven with some salty white cheese I did not recognize to melt inside it. I thanked him, and he left to finish grooming Deor. I stood at the window, watching people walk on the little piece of the Fourth Serpent that I could see, and waited for the water to cool a bit.

I ate the bread and cheese, washed the dust of the road off of my face and arms, and laid back on the bed to stare at the beams of the ceiling.

Aetheling no more, I thought. *What am I now?* It was a question I had had years to answer, but the answer still eluded me.

After resting for a while, I arose and went through my pack. I changed into a relatively fresh undertunic, which I covered with a green herringbone linen tunic trimmed with white embroidery that had stayed in my pack most of the trip, and a pair of sturdy brown linen pants. I had one pair of winingas that I had not used often, woven in a subtle red and brown pattern, and I let the simple yet precise process of wrapping them around my legs calm my mind a bit.

This was probably a good time to clean and mend the stains and tears that happen on long roads, so I bundled up much of the rest. The trip had also left its mark on my turnshoes, but my negotiations with Ragnar had given me hope that my hacksilver would exchange well and, in any case, I had seen too many skilled swordsmen slain from something as simple as their shoes slipping or tearing. Surely in Achrida I could find another pair.

Thus armed with the hint of a plan, I ventured to the common taproom. Ragnar, again, seemed to read my mind.

"You'll be wantin' some of the dust washed off them clothes, and you've no doubt ripped some seams here and there. Just be handin' them here, and I'll be gettin' our washerwomen to be carin' for them, and it's a good thing we're to be knowin' them as none of the women in the Empire be knowin' how to make good simple clothes for men—" He paused for a moment as he placed several filled mugs on a tray. "—as they keep wantin' to add pearls and beads and those things aren't bein' naught but a nuisance when one is havin' to do somethin', and besides I'm not to be doubtin' that you've been havin' yers touched up a bit and made to be pretty anyway, so they'd just be addin' somethin' that you'll not be needin' and they get annoyed when ya be sayin' not to add these fopperies but that's their way…"

Ragnar actually stopped as a woman leaned her head out of the kitchens with a raised eyebrow.

"Yes, cleaning and mending, please," I said after smothering a chuckle.

Smiling at me, she came out of the kitchen and introduced herself. "I'm Zoe, and I can take those for you."

The small, slim woman wore a brown dress trimmed with strips of a patterned fabric sewn vertically, and stained with the day's cooking. Flour mixed with the gray that had started to lighten her black hair. However, she was a woman for whom the gray and the stains on the dress simply made her more beautiful, not less. She reached for my bundle of clothes and primly took them away.

"Thank you." I turned back to Ragnar as she left. "Also, I need a new pair of shoes. Is there a good cobbler?"

Ragnar obligingly provided directions, with his normal commentary. I followed them, quickly contracted for a pair to be ready in three days, and returned to the Faerie in time for dinner.

It was delicious. Zoe had roasted a goat with some herb I had never tasted before. She served the goat with onion and leek soup and more of that bread covered in the salty cheese. While he might not have been able to brew mead, Ragnar clearly had access to honey, and he served it for dessert over some small, flaky pastries that would have let me conquer the Seven Kingdoms if I brought back the recipe.

After dinner I strolled around a bit, stopping to check on Deor. The stables cat had moved to one of the walls overlooking his stall. Eirik had shown me where they kept a basket for older apples, and Deor munched one happily as I checked his legs and hooves.

He had no immediate problems, so I started to examine all of our tack and harness, but Deor nudged me to stop. He was right, of course. It could wait until tomorrow when I could check and oil it all at once. He flipped his head meaningfully in the direction of the apple basket, and I got him another.

"Sleep well, my friend," I said. Deor actually left off eating the second apple to nudge me once more as I left him.

I went back into the tavern area and sat along the wall, drinking three pints while ignoring Ragnar's torrential speeches, Karah's scalding wrath, the various drinking songs of the scop, and the regulars' liquid laughter. Sleep approached, and I needed to rest.

Chapter 2
Morning, 5 Gersmoanne, 1712 MG

I woke up that morning exhausted, despite sleeping far later than normal. My fatigue made me grouchy and restless, and I got my just reward when Deor nipped me in frustration while I oiled his tack.

Rubbing my shoulder, I asked, "Would you like to ride around the city today?"

I was quick enough to get my fingers away from his teeth this time.

"Ah, so you just want to stay in the stable and eat all day."

A contented neigh was my response. The cat perched above him yawned and even glanced at me with heavy eyes. Well, that was clear enough.

"Fine, I'll leave you to it."

Unfortunately, Deor's contentment did not cure my restlessness. I went into the Faerie's taproom and up to Ragnar, who was cleaning mugs behind the bar.

"Ragnar, I need to hit something." At his raised eyebrows, I added, "Preferably a pell or a sparring partner."

"Ah, a'course, yer not the type to be wastin' the day lazin' about like some of these lackeys." He waved at a pair of men who had been there the previous night and had either stayed all night or come back already. "Now, I'm to be havin' my little pell under the hill that I sometimes be practicin' on, and givin' Eirik a bit of work so he's not completely useless, though he'd never match up to his cousins, I'm sure. I'm to be thinkin' it's this easy city livin', to be sure, that he's no good with a sword."

He gave a sigh so large that only a Svellheimer accustomed to long, cold nights filled with poetry of doomed gods could fully appreciate it.

"But I'm also to be thinkin' ya might be wantin' more, and iffin' ya do, maybe ya should be checkin' at the Pathfinder barracks. Piri herself might be there, and you'd be likin' that I think, given that you'd learn somethin' you've not seen, I'm to be sure—"

"That sounds perfect," I cut him off. "How do I get there?"

He followed the directions with a relatively short comment, "Now,

I've been seein' ya move, and I'm not to be doubtin' ya, but ya might just be needin' all of that fine shiny scale o'yers."

Something far too jovial hid behind that grin. He made sense, though, and I did want more than simple pell work. If some of the guards, even this mythical hero Piri, were willing to spar, I needed the practice. It had been months since I had last seriously trained. A few raids did not count.

Armor is made to be worn, not carried, so I threw it on, buckling the side straps. I then belted on my sword and saex, slung my shield around my back, and grabbed my spear with its peace-bond. I petted Melia as I left the Faerie and followed Ragnar's directions.

This morning held a slight rain, too light to wash the mud down to the lake. It did little but make the cobblestones slippery and irritating, especially in armor.

Nevertheless, I arrived at the barracks without falling. The guards were less than impressed to see me.

"Yeah?" one asked, shifting balance when he saw me approach fully armed.

"Ragnar of the Frank Faerie said you might allow me to practice with you."

"He did?"

"He especially suggested I should see if someone named Piri was around."

That caused a bit of a smile. "Hmmm. I'll ask the hecantontarch and see what she says."

He took a step back and called for another Pathfinder, who took the message, and returned to his post.

The same short, powerful woman who had let me in the gate yesterday arrived quickly.

She noted my armor and the sword at my belt and smiled slightly at the peace-bond. "I am Hecatontarch Piriska Mrnjavcevic. I expected you tomorrow, but today will work."

"Expected me?"

"Yes. You had the look, and Ragnar would suggest me. I expected tomorrow because you looked to have traveled far. You still don't look rested," she concluded critically.

"I felt the need to hit something."

"Hmmm." She paused, examining my kit. "Dmitri, show him around. He'll need some pell work to warm up, I've no doubt. After that, Arkady will start with him first."

One of the guards showed me the pell, the blunted weapons, and the various practice areas of the barracks.

For some reason, Piri's efficiency and Ragnar's jovial humor turned my tired restlessness into anger. I began my routine with a spear, shifting around the pell, and thrusting from a variety of ranges.

I tried to start slowly, but I simply could not get my feet to stay properly balanced and I moved faster to compensate. I could have blamed the wet stones, but it was my anger and frustration that really pulled me off balance.

I had only completed my first pattern when I realized Piri had come out to watch me. She had marched out to where she could observe me closely instead of staying under the portico, out of the rain. I would learn that little things like mud or rain never affected her. She said nothing, merely watched my technique.

She had the same calm, knowing look as Hlodowic, who had served as armsman for my father and had helped train me as a boy. It made me even angrier.

Nevertheless, I tried to refocus on my weapon and footwork. I let my eyes relax, seeing all that was around me, and let myself flow into my strikes. I completed my normal set of patterns with the spear.

Neither Piri nor I said anything as I chose a training sword. I started without a shield, again working as slowly as my irritation would let me. I could feel my sword striking too solidly as anger added to my technique. I switched weapons, completing my routines but never properly gaining my balance.

Piri simply stood there throughout the whole thing. Behind her, one of her Pathfinders came up in full armor, carrying a mug. Piri handed me the mug, and I drank thirstily. I might have done everything wrong, but at least the blood was flowing.

"This is Arkady. You will spar with him. Start with mace and shield."

Several Pathfinders rotated in and out to face me, switching weapons as Piri instructed. My anger, rust, and pride were left in the mud on that field, though I had some success.

"You leave when?" she asked.

"I was thinking of two more days, but my horse might prefer three."

"Make it three. Be here the day after tomorrow."

"Yes, Hecatontarch." What else could I say?

"And clean off your armor properly before then."

My glare slid off of her much as the rain had.

Two hours later I sat in the Faerie with a late lunch and one of Ragnar's ales before me. Melia lay on the table, rolled on her back, purring while I scratched her belly. I had cleaned both my equipment and myself, and the soreness of a good day filled my body. Nothing helps anger and restlessness like hitting someone.

The tavern did not seem particularly busy, though several of the regulars had returned to their normal spots. A few other travelers arrived: a singularly ugly, squat, round man and a group that included a lady with her maidservant and groom. The scop who had been here the previous evening fussed with something that had strings similar to those of a lyre but arranged much differently.

Another normal afternoon at the Faerie, I supposed. For the first time in months, I settled in for a long, relaxing evening, though I knew I would have to periodically banish the memories of many nights with my shield-kin.

Yes, I thought, stretching out at my table, the smell of Zoe's dinner and the stack of Ragnar's ale casks promised a very relaxing evening.

Chapter 3
Evening, 5 Gersmoanne, 1712 MG

I blame myself. I knew from the moment they walked in the Faerie that they came not for the ale. The day and the dinner had relaxed me too much, though, and I let it happen.

People had filled the Faerie to eat Zoe's cooking. Roast lamb, again seasoned with herbs new to me. Some green vegetable with a weird name that had been cut into strips and buttered with a hot spice that I also did not know. Fresh dark bread, steaming as it melted the butter atop it. Both cats roamed around, getting scraps. Interrupting that dinner was a crime in itself.

I saw them enter, four men and a woman, none looking particularly hungry or thirsty. With no warning, one of the men flicked something to the middle of the room. The room went completely dark, and the mayhem ensued.

Land magic, I thought. It happened too quickly to be Life magic. Not that it really mattered.

At least I was not frozen in place. I grabbed my saex and moved to the other side of the fire, whose heat I could feel at my back. I wanted to slide to the front door and cut them off. Not a bad plan, though I had to move slowly in the darkness.

I heard a scream, a sharp smack, and a variety of grunts and shouts, but in the dark the sounds simply added to the confusion.

The darkness only lasted a few moments, but that is an age sometimes, and when it relented all we could do was assess the aftermath. Some of the regulars had earned a few bruises and a couple of small cuts. However, the attackers had clearly aimed at the lady, maidservant, and groom, for they had disappeared from their table.

I took a quick breath and looked for any more immediate threats. With none apparent, I sheathed my saex.

Ragnar was doing the same thing with the large sword he apparently kept behind the bar. The Thunder God's rage filled his eyes.

Zoe and Eirik rushed in, which relieved his tension somewhat, though he waved them back. Karah had been knocked over in the darkness, and he moved over to help her up. The cats remained hidden under tables.

"I'm fine, Da, leave me be," she snapped, shaking her hand a bit. *At least one of us did something*, I thought, for a print of her hand surely marked someone's face right now.

I went to the door, looking for any hint of the attackers, but they had been too quick, and the Serpent was empty by the time I looked out.

I went back into the Faerie. "Ragnar, should I call the city guards?"

He snorted and fussed over his daughter, much to her annoyance.

With nothing better to do, and frustrated that I had not done anything in the first place, I went over to examine the table before Karah could clean it up. Two of the plates had been upended but remained on the table, and the third had been knocked off. It seemed clear each of the targets had been yanked up out of their chairs. I saw a small scrap of cloth in a small nick of the table, perhaps where a sleeve had been caught.

"Karah, don't clean this table yet."

"And why should I not?"

"I see something on the table I'd like to keep. Maybe take to a Reader. I presume there are Readers here…?" I cocked my eye questioningly.

"Of course," she sniffed. "Can I at least clean up the wine?"

"Be my guest, but don't let anyone touch the table."

I had listened to enough of Bedarth's teaching to recall that everyone who touches an item leaves their imprint upon it. Some zokurioi could read that imprint.

I did not know if that scrap could tell us anything, but I did not want to touch it any more than I had to. I had clean patches of linen in my pack that I used to oil my blades and armor, so I went up to my room to get one. I had no idea if the linen would contaminate the cloth, but I guessed it would be better than if I handled it, and I could think of nothing better at that moment.

I folded the scrap into the linen, told Karah she could clean the table now, and went back to mine. Ragnar bustled around settling his guests, refilling drinks, and replacing lost meals. I waited until things had calmed down and then went up to him.

"Ragnar, we need to talk."

"You'll be wantin' somewhere private-like?" His anger made him curt.

"Yes."

He made eye contact with Karah and then led me down a hall to a room with a table and a few chairs. We sat and he looked at me.

"First, I'm sorry. I saw them come in, and I knew something was wrong but—"

"Ach, be quietin'. I saw them too, and they were just to bein' too quick-like. The Man with the Tattered Smile knows they'd been plannin' and they were havin' that darkness magic."

"Yes, well, anyway." I paused and pulled out the scrap in its linen. "I found this at the table those guests were sitting at. You might be able to take this to a Reader and find something out about them. Assuming you didn't know them already, of course."

Ragnar sat back, thinking for a goodly time. Finally he spoke, still subdued for him.

"Well, as to them, no, I've not the knowin' of them before this afternoon when they were to be askin' for a room. As far as I was to be knowin', she was some falutin' noble. Not, to be sure, to be bein' of the nobilissimi as they would not be contemplatin' the likes of the Faerie. Still she's not the first, and I'm to be hopin' not the last of her kind to be stayin' here, so I wasn't to be givin' too much thought to her, in all truthfulness."

He leaned forward angrily. "Now I am to be bein' powerful curious as to who they were bein', given it was my taproom they were to be taken from."

He sat back. "The Sevens recognize gestriht…" He continued at my nod. "I was to be thinkin' so. Your kin and mine are not to be bein' all that much different." We both smiled briefly at that understatement. My own damsire was a Svellheimer who came to raid and stayed to herd those who herd sheep. "Those who stay under my roof are to be receivin' gestriht even if they're not to be knowin' what that means."

I nodded. I had known that without him telling me, but he had wanted to say it. Another few moments passed while we looked at each other.

"We're to be knowin' each other, and I'm to be thinkin' I can trust you. I don't know why yer here and not to be servin' with some lord, but I'm to be guessin' yer true to your oaths."

I thought of my father and Cynric and Penwulf and the battle that had been my doom. *Oaths are so easy to forsake*, I thought.

I started when I heard him say, "Edward." I wondered how many times he had said it.

"You've a tale to be tellin'," he said, sighing. "And I'm not to be pressin' you for it, but I am to be askin' you this…" I waited. "If I'm to be askin' for your oath, will you be givin' me that which you'd be swearin' to a lord?"

What could I tell him? The truth? That my father had sailed in a ship of flame? That I had been cast out because of two foresworn oaths taken at the knees of lords?

"Yes," I promised. I took a long breath. "But you should know I'm not here because I have kept all of my oaths."

He looked at me. "You'll tell me that tale someday, but I'm to be trustin' my eyes. You'll follow your word to me." I had no answer. "So, I'm to be thinkin'," he continued, "that you're to be bein' my best hope to be fulfillin' my promise of gestriht."

I raised an eyebrow at him. "Yes?"

"Yes." For once, his accent was virtually gone. "I am not the one to find who did this. Too many know me and won't tell me what I need to know. You've already shown me that you feel responsible, too. So, I ask you, Sevener, to be my man in this task. I will grant you a lord's bench-seat while you serve me. I wish those who broke my pledge to be brought before me. Will you swear to do all in your power to bring them to my hall?"

I could not answer him. For that matter I could barely breathe.

He waited.

I did not want to answer him. But I had come south to swear an oath. Why did I not fear to pledge my honor to an emperor, but the thought of pledging to this innkeeper terrified me?

"Yes," I finally whispered.

He looked at me until my eyes rose to his.

"Yes, I will swear to serve as I can," I said. "Though I don't know what I can do."

"Well, I'm to be thinkin' ya know more than yer to be thinkin'. You've done more than held your shield in the wall."

How did he know me so well? I had to know so I asked him. "How do you know me so well?"

He laughed. "Well, I could be tellin' ya that innkeepers learn to be readin' people, or I could be sayin' that I'm to be knowin' Seveners, but the truth is bein' that I'm an innkeeper because my... you'd be sayin' *liffrea*, was to be teachin' me some when there was snow to be standin' feet deep at home. Which was to be bein' more often than I was to be likin', which is why I was a'comin' with my sword to the south. Readin' people is useful in this business, and I am still recallin' some of what he was to be sayin'."

"I—" I paused. "I, too, knew a liffrea."

"You'll be doin' fine, then, for me. If anyone is to be findin' these pledgebreakers, it will need to be bein' someone like ya."

"I may not succeed."

"Success is sworn to no man, but you'll be givin' me the worth of yer word." He thought for a moment. "Yer to be lookin' like you'll be needin' some time. Stay here, an' I'll be sendin' Karah in so ya aren't to be gettin' dry. I'll be suggestin' that ya come to actually meet them that's here most nights in a bit, but yer to be doin' what you think is best." He paused again and looked at me. "I'm to be sure of this, even though yer to be bein' fearful now."

He left, and soon Karah came in, bearing a mug of ale and looking at me strangely. She started to speak but thought better of it.

I understood her. I wanted to look at me strangely, too.

Chapter 4
Evening, 5 Gersmoanne, 1712 MG

After Karah left, I decided wallowing in my memories would serve me no purpose. Bedarth trained me to reexamine the basics, especially the obvious things. "Darkness is the absence of sight," he had repeated to me many times. One of his many annoying sayings.

So I looked again at what I knew. The kidnappers clearly had not chosen their targets randomly. Therefore, finding out all I could about the victims was a place to start. Hopefully the scrap of cloth would help with that. Ragnar, Karah, and I needed to talk again in case they remembered something new. I needed to look at the rooms the guests stayed in. Also, they probably had horses.

I decided to start with their steeds, so I finished my mug and went in search of Eirik. I found him gathering dishes off of tables in the common room and put the question to him.

"Why, yes, milord, they were riding horses." A huge grin split his face as he remembered. "Fine ones, with long legs for their size, and they moved like the softest breeze. They were small, though, nowhere near the size of Deor."

"Are they still in the stables?"

"Why, I haven't checked…"

"Shall we—" I prompted, but he was already moving.

The horses remained where Eirik had stabled them, so they apparently held little value to the kidnappers. As organized as they had been, I had no doubt the kidnappers could have figured out a way to take the horses had they wanted.

I saw immediately why Eirik had been so happy to see them, as their light and glossy coats were smooth and unruffled even after their recent days of riding. I would apologize to Deor later for thinking of other horses, but they simply made riders want to try and fly. Money must not have been a primary object of the kidnapping because they were extremely valuable.

"Eirik, I don't know this breed."

"Well, they come from the south. They race them at the Hippodrome. As fast as there is."

"They're bred around the Great City?"

He paused. "Uh, I don't know where they're bred. But they're really, really fast. I've seen them raced a few times, and they're marvelous…" His voice trailed off in pleasant memories.

"So, they're fast, and you like fast horses."

He blushed and nodded.

"What kind of tack did they have?"

"Oh, it's right over here."

He went to a shelf and pulled their riding gear down. He spread it out over a long table in the back of the stables.

"Fine leather," I remarked mostly to myself. "In as good of shape as one could expect from road travel." Several pieces had been expertly repaired. Overall, the tack did not tell me much, as it seemed not very different from what I was used to. All Eirik could add, when prompted, was that it might be more of southern make than northern.

The black-and-white cat jumped on the table. I petted her absentmindedly.

"Akantha likes you," said Eirik. "She doesn't like many people."

"Mmmm," I said. "Did they leave anything else out here?"

"No, milord, that's it."

Akantha nipped my finger when I stopped petting her, and I shook the pain away as I went back into the taproom. There I found Ragnar regaling the crowd with one of his lengthy stories. I had no doubt nearly all had heard it before, but the retelling had returned his taproom to its normal rowdy level. Ebbing tide always flows again, and I could see that Ragnar was as strong as the tide, in his own way.

Karah brought me ale as I sat in what was becoming my accustomed spot, a table along the interior wall in the middle of the room, while I waited for Ragnar's tale to end. It took quite some time, of course, but I spent it placing the faces of the regulars in my mind. Marko still had the black eye. "Honk" was apparently short for "Honker Harald." He did have a truly magnificent nose. Flavian seemed an odd name to me, but I would always remember his weird, piercing laugh. Emilija laughed along with the rest, though she probably had other uncomplicated motives when she went to work later in the evening. A score of others laughed along. I figured I'd know them all soon enough.

Ragnar finished his tale and eventually came over to me.

"You'll be needin' one of us to be openin' some keystones, I'm to be thinkin', and we're lucky to be havin' those since Basil, not the Emperor a'course but bein' named for him to be sure, is bein' as fine a stonelord as there is, and he's to be havin' the good taste to be preferrin' my brew, so we've been comin' to a fair arrangement."

He motioned briefly at Karah and continued, "Let's be headin' up to those rooms, and I'll be lettin' you in and leavin' you be, so as you can be doin' what you're to be doin', and I'm to be doin' what One-Eye meant me to be doin'."

We went through the passage immediately left of the one that led to my room, up a flight of stairs, and down a long hallway. He opened two doors, one on either side of the hall, and went back downstairs trailing some story about the Thunder God hunting for his misplaced hammer.

The first room I entered was much more luxurious than the one I had been given. A headboard carved with a majestic griffon attached to a solid alder platform made a truly majestic bed with a mattress at least twice as thick as mine. A beautiful blue-and-white quilt highlighted with panels of griffons facing each other lay on the mattress. A shorter table with a matching chair, also of alder, with spiral motifs, sat below a shuttered window. A tapestry of griffons flying above a large palace, woven in brilliant colors, hung on the wall opposite the bed. A long alder table, its legs carved with precise spirals ran below the tapestry.

Any king in the Sevens would proudly claim this tavern room in Achrida as his bedchamber.

I turned my focus to the personal items. An opened pack stretched along the long table. It held women's clothes, richly adorned with gems and gold, but of no style that I recognized from either the Seven Kingdoms or Svellheim. I put them aside until I could ask Zoe for help.

Underneath the clothes lay a blue velvet pouch tied with a woven yellow thread. I lifted it out quickly.

Excellent. Surely, this will tell me something.

However, I could not unravel the knot. I twisted at it. Pried at it with my fingernail. Bit it with my teeth until my teeth hurt. I finally grabbed my saex hilt to tear into the bag, but the feel of my saex hilt calmed me. *I should ask Zoe for help before I do this.*

Nothing else in the traveling pack seemed useful, so I went across the hall to the other room. Though larger than mine, it differed little from my room. Ragnar clearly had many patrons with servants for whom he provided a convenient arrangement. Two beds, each with a pack set alongside it, ran parallel to each other. One pack held women's clothes of styles similar to those in the first pack, though with little adornment. The other had a man's tunics and trousers.

The velvet pouch looked too valuable to leave, even with the room's keystone lock, so I took it from the room with griffons. I did not want to advertise the fact that I had it, so I swiftly returned to my corridor, flitting through the taproom as quickly as I could without looking hasty. I put the pouch into my pack, buckled the straps, and set it on the far side of the bed.

I then returned to the common room. In between stories I arranged with Ragnar to have Zoe look at the clothes in the morning after she had put the bread into the ovens.

At this point, I sagged with fatigue more than I had any day during my climbs through the mountains. Since I could not think of anything else, sleeping seemed the most productive thing to do, so that's what I did.

Chapter 5
Late Night, 5-6 Gersmoanne, 1712 MG

My most frequent nightmare returned that night. I had gotten used to it, but for some reason it was more vivid than ever before.

The nightmare always plays in three acts, like the Old Imperial plays Bedarth forced me to read.

In the first act I feel my heart hammer on the inside of my skull. Each beat, I hope, is the last. Soon enough, I get past the pain and wonder why it hurts at all. Surely my head should not hurt this much in the Father of the Slain's golden hall, should it? With a spike of worry, I then wonder if maybe I have not earned my place at His table. I account for all of my faults and know that he could, in fact, judge me unworthy.

The first act concludes with my shame.

The second starts with me opening my eyes to see nothing but darkness, and not the golden brilliance I hoped for. I begin praying that some corners of Valhalla are black and cold. That prayer always takes me away for a limitless time. Someday, I will know if that prayer is answered.

The third act begins when I notice light entering my dream. At first it is but the small glow that heralds dawn. Soon, though, it shapes itself into a small candle that hurts my eyes more than the noon sun on a field of untouched snow. A soft voice wades through that ocean of light.

"Ah, you're awake."

I'm never quite sure how to respond to that and, anyway, all I can do is moan.

"Welcome to this hall," the voice adds. "Gestriht is granted. What is your name, then, guest?"

I can't really understand the question, though I somehow know it is important. I start to answer, "It is…," but I stop.

"Yes?"

I try again. "I… I am… I…"

It is then that I always begin to understand the question, and understanding brings terror because I do not know. There is an "I" here I think but I have lost who I am in a deep, cold, and black mind-sea.

The last thing I ever remember is falling back into that sea grasping for the remnants of my soul. I sink into the freezing, black death until the gray of dawn saves me.

But not this night.

The black sea's power, for the first time, brought life not death. I woke in the stillness of the night, shaking in my terror.

I am! I am someone!

For a few moments I felt the sweat on me, embracing the cold, clammy feel of the soaked bedding. Enjoying each and every one of the goose bumps as the cold told me I lived. Reveling in being. I caressed the hilt of my saex, which lay next to me as it had every night I could remember.

My mind began to think. Strange. No dawn awaited me, and stillness filled the Faerie.

I laid there, seeking any hint of Ragnar's laughter, or a restless guest, or even the horses nuzzling at hay below me.

Nothing.

I decided to walk around and swiftly put on my old, soft, quiet turnshoes and wrapped my belt with my saex around me. The wrongness of the moment prompted me to think about bringing my shield, but its bulk and size made me decide against it. I did, however, bring my sword. I made sure that my room door closed behind me and felt the keystone warm to my touch.

I had expected that once I was in the hallways there would be no light, but a soft glow allowed my eyes, once they had adjusted, to see well enough to move. Land magic from Ragnar's stonelord.

I moved slowly, staying along the wall and placing each step carefully. I made my way down the stairs to the common room, which the dull flickering of an untended fire lit with a soft redness. I stopped when I could see in, though I kept myself as much in the shadows of my wing's hallway as I could.

Harald and Flavian sprawled in their chairs. I was getting used to their mouths being open, but this time they lolled in sleep. Ragnar slept too, lounging on the stool next to his bar. Loud even in his sleep, his snores fairly rocked the common room. I inched my head towards the opening to see more of the room. Two more tables of regulars slept as if bored with each other's company. Karah, snoring lightly, lay curled up next to a tray of two mugs set calmly on the floor, snoring lightly. Melia sprawled on her back under a table, all four paws askew.

This time, the signs suggested Life magic. Karah had had time to set the tray down. Ragnar had seated himself. Someone had made all of us want to sleep. They had no way of knowing about my nightmares, my terror.

I was glad I had taken the blue velvet pouch with me earlier in the day.

I leaned out farther and slid just to my right, towards the wing where the kidnapped victims had stayed. I climbed the stairs one by one, willing each board not to creak, with some success. By the time I reached the upper floor, I could hear hints of people moving.

Finally, my luck ran out. As would be expected in a wooden building, a board finally spoke loudly when I shifted my weight on it. I had not hurried or gotten impatient and, really, had not gotten unlucky. It was just time.

Three figures appeared in response. I could see their outlines and a slight gleam from their knives in the dim light, but nothing else. Presumably they could not see any better than I.

In the moment before they charged, I slid my back to the wall and flipped my wrist so my sword pointed downward. When they charged, I twisted my wrist back up, swiveling my sword in front of me. I was hoping to block any thrusts, and that must have worked as I felt no stab. However, because I focused on having my sword occupy as much space in front of me as possible, I did not properly complete the rotation of my wrist and have the sword blade find the right-most figure's neck. Instead, I bounced my blade off of his chest; a painful blow but not deadly. The other two attackers ran past me as their companion grunted.

I took a step to the middle of the hallway to block my adversary. Despite his wound, he nimbly stepped past me. He cried in pain as I slashed towards his leg. I had connected, but again without real bite, and he followed his friends to the common room.

I pursued them, but not at a run. Too many places awaited where three people could trap me if I moved too quickly. Plus, I still had not actually checked the room. There were five people in the initial attack, and I did not know if the other two were behind me, so I made cautious progress.

If the open front door was any indication, by the time I reached the taproom they had gone. I closed the door, used the rarely employed latch, and went over to try and wake Ragnar. Ragnar attempted to give me a loving bear hug. As I did not want to make Zoe jealous, I put him back where he was for the moment. He returned to his snoring.

Still moving cautiously, I explored the rest of the lower rooms. I found Zoe, Eirik and Akantha sleeping soundly, but no attackers or anything out of place. All of the horses seemed to be where they were supposed to be, though they all appeared to be sleeping as well, probably dreaming of hills covered in long, green grass waving in a soft breeze.

I went back up to the two rooms but found no one there, either. It seemed there had only been three attackers this time, or, if there had been five, the other two had crept away silently.

There was no way, with the terror of my dream and the excitement of the fight, I could sleep immediately, so I went back to my room for my cleaning kit and returned to the common room. I lifted Karah softly into a chair, picked up her tray, and put it on my table. I sat there, drinking from the two mugs, and cleaned my sword and saex until Ragnar and his patrons started to wake about an hour or so later.

Once everyone shook off their fog of sleep, my exhaustion returned. I knew if I attempted to explain everything right then, it would be some time before Ragnar would let me sleep. Since I doubted the thieves would return, I went to bed and left him wondering about a strange evening.

Chapter 6
Morning, 6 Gersmoanne, 1712 MG

I put the velvet pouch into my larger, light-blue shoulder bag, made of heavy canvas, so I could keep it with me. I might not have known what exactly the pouch contained, but two attacks suggested it held something interesting.

Ragnar was puttering about, doing his morning chores when I came down. He motioned to the closest table and brought out two large bowls of gruel covered in honey. Over our breakfast I told him about the three burglars.

"Yer to be sayin' that they're to be bein' breakin' my pledge to them as to be stayin' here twice now?" He ate his porridge in quick, angry bites, grasping his long wooden spoon almost as he might a broadsword.

"Yes, that's exactly what I'm saying."

We finished our breakfasts silently. Afterwards, I followed Zoe back up to the rooms to look at the clothes. She unfolded and examined each piece with small, efficient movements, so different from Ragnar's wide, sprawling presence.

"This is a stola," she said, holding up a long, linen garment dyed to a glorious green with small citrine stones woven into a patterned collar. "It's not often worn these days. My only one was handed down to me by my dama. It might have been her dama's, as far as I know." She laughed. "Mostly, stolas are worn, if at all, on formal occasions."

She moved to the next item, a long-sleeved tunic that I recognized in form, embroidered and decorated beyond anything I had ever seen. I had seen silk once or twice before, but nothing as brilliant and smooth as this tunic. Zoe caressed it longingly for a moment.

"A simple tunica," she sighed, "though decorated in the Great City manner. See these?" She pointed at small iridescent circular beads sewn into the cuffs and neckline. "They're called pearls and come from shellfish. I've never seen so many at once, except in icons." She paused and murmured, "I've not seen this pattern in a while. I wonder if it's becoming fashionable again."

Next Zoe looked at two undertunics of plain, white linen and another undertunic of some soft fabric that neither she nor I had ever felt before. "It might be cotton. I've never felt cotton before, but it is a rare fabric that I think is grown somewhere far south of Basilopolis."

We shrugged and she looked at the last item in the pack, a shapeless garment of alternating green and blue gores, trimmed in red and yellow at the hems.

"Hmmm, this is interesting. It looks like a chasuble. Priests wear these. I didn't realize she might have been a priestess. She certainly didn't act like one."

"Do you know what sect this might belong to?"

"No, I don't. I've never really paid too much attention to any others besides Elena."

"No matter. I was planning on going to see the Readers anyway. I'll take it with me."

I started to fold it up, but she took one look at my folding skills and grabbed it from me with an exasperated sigh. Once she had condensed it into an impossibly small bundle she handed it to me.

I took it with a wry smile and then thought about all she had said.

"So, these things probably come from the Great City, or maybe even farther to the south. Their owner was certainly rich, perhaps out of touch with modern fashions, and possibly a priestess."

Zoe paused. "Yes."

"Anything else?"

She shook her head.

We looked through the clothes of the two servants, and the odd styles of the women's clothes matched those of the noblewoman. The man's clothes seemed normal and plain to both of us.

"Before you go," I asked her, "can you untie this knot? My fingers seem too big to get it open."

I pulled out the velvet pouch, and she spent some time fiddling with it, but she, too, could not unravel it. I thought about cutting it open, but that seemed a shame with something so lovely.

Zoe left me in the room to return to her cooking.

"Look and look again. And look yet once more," came Bedarth's voice in my mind.

"Yes, my master, I hear you," I sighed ruefully.

I looked at each of the things in the rooms once more, including the inn's furnishings. Nothing struck me, but I tried to mark everything in its place. After my examination, I took a tunic from each of the packs to add to what I could show a Reader.

I had more clothing than would fit in my walking bag, so I put the garments, the small scrap of cloth, and the velvet pouch into my larger traveling pack. Then I went down see if Eirik would have any more luck with the knot. Not surprisingly, he could not open it either. This was not a normal knot. I put it back in my pack. It seemed time to visit the Readers.

I went to find Ragnar. He stood in his brewery, carefully measuring out grains and putting them into a large pot under which he had lit a small fire.

"I need to talk to some people in the city."

"Not bein' surprised at that. A Reader I'm to be rememberin' for one. They'll be down past the Square o' Legends where Medusa Way is to be startin'. Once there, be goin' down Hydra Way towards the lake, but be cuttin' north on a small road about halfway to the water that's to be leadin' to their building on a small ridge overlookin' the lake."

He grinned. "They're to be enjoyin' their view of the lake, and I'm not to be blamin' them as she is bein' a beauty and cold and sweet. You should be drinkin' some fresh water from the springs on the mountain in that there cask that was to be bein' brought over this dawn from a boatman who sometimes is to be comin' in here when he can."

He paused to shake some grain back into its bag before continuing. "In truth, I'm to be thinkin' the water is bein' a part of why me ale is as good as there is, and you'll be walking the same route that cask will take when it's emptied, exceptin' turnin' at that road which is easy enough to see even though there's many a road down there."

"So you said something about a liffrea…"

"Hmmm, well, yes, they have a sort of them to be sure, and there's many of them, but they're not to be what you're thinking. Achrida is after bein' the most prayerful place you'll be seein'. There's to be bein' hundreds of small priestly places here, temples and chapels and shrines and such, and each of these godlings are to be helpin' with something particular from brewers to fishers to mothers, even to soldiers and horses."

He grinned at that. "Yet not a one a'them be a proper liffrea, and there's naught of signs bein' found of a true god like One-Eye or Trollsbane or even the damned Trickster. You can't find a Tree of Life or a Great Wyrm or anything that's to be bein' the truth of things. I'm still to be thinking it's strange, even as this has been to be becomin' my home."

"And all of these have priests whose prayers can shape magic?"

"Are you be askin' about the Five Streams?" He rattled off the singsong poem that I knew by heart:

> To change nature's guise
> One needs loves or lives
> Stone's laws or sharp lines
> Or lore of the wise

Bedarth had taught me that magic was a river fed by these five streams. The magic of symbols, or lines, formed the basis of all prayer. It was the most malleable of the streams, though, and each god or goddess was a symbol in his or her own right who shaped the methods and limits of their priests, unlike the other streams, whose constraints were much more predictable.

I thought about this as he nodded smugly.

"Aye, me boy, they're nearly all to be havin' some skilled with streams."

The arithmetic stunned me so much that I asked Ragnar to confirm his answer. He laughed, but complied.

I stood shocked. Not every priest could use magic, but a true god or godling had at least some amongst his or her worshippers who could. If people prayed to hundreds of gods here, and each had at least one with the talent, the likelihood was that probably over a thousand priests could shape the streams. And, then, there were all of the other kurioi in Achrida who were not priests, such as some of the Readers.

Bedarth had told me that roughly one person in ten possessed the talent to control the streams, but in the Seven Kingdoms there were so few teachers that far fewer had the skills to go with the talent. I had stayed in Brunanburh for some time after Bedarth's death, a city that had something like a hundred of thousand souls, about double what I'd been told Achrida held. Yet only a few hundred mages called Brunanburh home.

I shook myself as I realized that Ragnar had started talking again.

"I was to be sayin' that I'm thinkin' you might be wantin' to talk to Piri. There are bein' two great families here that I'm still not rightly to be understandin' that everythin's to be tied to, and only them as grew up here are to be truly knowin', as it's not anything easy like them as figurin' out who's plottin' what in the Seven Kingdoms or brothers that are to be jostlin' for their rights as to be bein' the case in my own Svellheim. In any case, Piri's a trustable one, as I'm thinkin' you've been findin' out, and she's to be bein' somethin' in one them families."

I looked at him and his grin, recognizing the look of arrogant experience. No one had ever called the politics of the Seven Kingdoms simple. By the bloody teeth of the Black Dog, what was this place?

Chapter 7
Late Morning, 6 Gersmoanne, 1712 MG

Ragnar's directions to find the Readers made me wonder. "Walk past the square and look for a certain road" seemed vague for a city of Achrida's size. However, I found the statue that marked Hydra Way easily enough, and the road that led from the way eventually angled to highlight a long, low building with many windows. It stood on its own ridge overlooking the lake, and it held some indefinable something that made it obvious it was the home of Achrida's Readers.

I walked into a large, open room lit by sunlight streaming through clear glass windows that were wonders in their own right. Long, tall tables filled the room, and open scrolls, codices, and papyri covered most of them. At least one person, dressed in the traditional Reader robes of plain gray, hunched happily over most of these tables.

One of them greeted me as I entered, motioning to an empty table. He was quite possibly the biggest man I had ever met, taller than any Svellheimer and broader than cattle in the lean years. His ponderous walk somehow avoided brushing any of the tables or other obstacles on his way over.

Sadly, under a spiky mop of unbrushed brown hair, his face held the normal Reader knowing smile. I have always found that smile truly annoying, especially since Readers do seem to know everything.

"I am Anastasius," he rumbled. "And you must be the Sevener who is staying at the Frank Faerie."

"Yes," I sighed.

"You must be here because of that excitement last night. And I'm guessing Ragnar asked you to come here because he's only got so many friends he trusts in the south, and most of those are in the Imperial Palace taking the Emperor's gold."

"Yes," I repeated.

"I believe you know our oaths and have questions we will not be foresworn to answer."

I nodded, reaching into my pack. "I have brought a number of items belonging to the travelers who were taken from the Faerie yesterday. Their kidnappers went after these specific travelers, focusing only on them, so something about them is important. Ragnar asked me to find those who did this deed, and lacking any hint of the actual doers, I thought I'd find out what I could about those who were taken."

First, I pulled out the velvet pouch. Interestingly, Anastasius held his hands back, refusing to touch it. "I would have thought you would have been sensitive to this," he murmured.

"I know that this is no normal knot." I frowned.

"It is a specific knot that only one person can untie easily."

"Lore magic?"

"That it is, but not ours. I have guesses, but cannot be specific as to its source."

"What is in here might tell me a great deal."

"An understandable expectation, but it will take much work to unravel it."

"I haven't wanted to cut it, but I will if I have to."

"Will you?" He smiled.

The more I thought about it, the more repugnant the idea became. That damned smile grew as he watched my struggle.

"Scholars know how to protect knowledge as well as dispense it." He bent over and studied the knot closely without touching it. "One need not be a master to know this technique, but no mere student would have created a knot so precisely."

"Can you open it?"

"I myself cannot, though undoubtedly my superiors could. However, we have a great respect for privacy despite our inquisitive nature. They may choose not to."

None but the Readers themselves truly understood their oaths. Perhaps I could make a case for the welfare of the owner, but that might not sway them, and in any case, arguing with Anastasius gained me nothing. I put the pouch from my mind for the moment.

"What else did you bring us?"

"I have clothes, here, of the victims. I would like to know what they can tell me.”

“Undoubtedly they do hold their wearers’ imprints, but reading that will take time. Will you be here in three days?”

“If that’s what it takes.”

He picked up the green-and-blue chasuble. “You have not shown this to any who were born in Achrida, have you?”

I shook my head. Ragnar and his family had moved here after Eirik was born.

“A local would tell you that this chasuble is decorated in a pattern that venerates one of its native sons, Naum. A priest of Naum would wear it in most of their ceremonies. His priests generally use Lore magic, so assuming both pouch and chasuble came from one of his priests would be reasonable, though of course not proven.”

“Of course.” I paused. “Ragnar says there are many temples, shrines, and chapels in Achrida.”

Anastasius nodded.

“Is Naum one of them?”

He nodded again.

“Is it small?”

He shook his head. “I can only think of one that is larger here. And before you ask, I cannot think of a reason a priest of Naum would not stay at their temple.”

“Perhaps I should ask them.”

“I think you should. Questions lead to learning.” Did they train Readers how to be pompous or merely accept only those who had the natural gift? Anastasius continued, “While you ask, my superiors will examine your items.”

And tell me only what they wish me to know, I thought but instead showed the next item. “I have this smaller scrap of fabric here, as well.” I explained where I had found it.

“I doubt the scrap will tell us more about its owner than his or her tunic, but it might tell us about the kidnapping, and we can always use the Principle of Relation to connect this scrap to the garment if it’s found.”

He gathered up the items carefully, took them through one of the many doors, and returned some time later with a scroll.

"I've taken the liberty of getting you a map of the entire city with many important locations marked on it."

He rolled it out and pointed at the Reader's Library of Achrida, the Faerie, Piri's barracks, and the temple to Naum. I took my leave as he smiled that obnoxious, knowing smile once more.

The sun had moved just past midday, so along my walk I stopped at a street vendor who offered skewers of some wonderful-smelling meat. I never did figure out what kind of meat, but it was as delicious as it smelled. I've eaten many worse things in my travels.

The temple to Naum sat on the southern edge of Achrida. The terrain rose in tall cliffs from the docks, and the temple was built into the cliffs themselves. There was a shining dome above the cliff face that, presumably, one reached from inside the temple. Two large columns carved in the shape of rolled codices flanked the entrance. Two immense, iron-bound wooden doors stood open to welcome worshippers, so I entered.

Inside, the coolness of the cavern provided a sudden relief from the subtle heat of the sun outside. I took a moment to enjoy a breath and look at the intricate mosaics of teachers passing knowledge to students, captioned with some script I had never seen before.

A young woman, pretty despite the serious cast of her eyes, approached. She wore a blue robe trimmed with letters of that odd script appliqued in green along the bottom and cuffs.

"Do you seek to teach or be taught?" She asked this question with startling precision.

"I'm not sure. Probably both."

She waited for me, somehow combining intensity and patience in the same look.

"I am guessing I probably need to speak to one of the superiors here."

She nodded without speaking further and went back into the temple. I spent the time waiting by examining the mosaics in greater detail. They included several depictions of green-and-blue chasubles.

"Naum was from here, but there were so many more he could teach in the Great City, so his greatest legacy remains there."

I turned at the voice to see a stately older woman also wearing blue trimmed with green.

"Did he succeed?"

"He would say that one can never fail when seeking wisdom."

I paused, sighing at yet another saying. "I am Edward. I am staying at the Frank Faerie."

"There was some incident there yesterday."

"Yes."

"How does that incident lead you to Naum?" She fairly quivered. Her normal state, I felt, was a calm strength, but right then she was tense and focused.

"Three travelers were kidnapped from the inn. Ragnar, the owner, asked me to look into who violated his trust. I took several items to the Readers to see what they could tell me about them. Included in the clothes were a chasuble in Naum's colors and a blue velvet pouch with a knot no one could unravel. The magic on the knot, he said, was Lore magic."

"Thus you were told to come here."

"Yes."

Something about her demeanor had changed. It was solid stone before and remained so, but perhaps there was some crack or flaw now? I could not tell how, only that it had changed.

"Do you have these items?"

"I left them with the Readers. I know nothing of your sect, and I know they can tell me much."

"If it is their will to teach it." Her frustration was almost palpable.

I shifted topics. "Are any of your priests missing?"

She thought for some time. "None."

"Have any of your chasubles been stolen?"

Again, she thought longer than the question required.

"No."

She clearly knew something more, but just as clearly she would not tell me anything else, at least at that moment. I tried asking in other ways, but she gave me no hint of another answer, so I said my farewells. She escorted me to the door and watched without moving as I went down the path.

The sun was now creeping down past the mountain, turning the lake black in its shadow. I figured I could speak to Piri after sparring with her tomorrow. I'd need my rest, I knew, so I returned to the Faerie, ate, and went to my room early. I sat in the chair, staring out the window at the stars over the fortress that loomed above me, until sleep beckoned.

Chapter 8
Morning, 7 Gersmoanne, 1712 MG

I armed and accoutered myself and set off for the barracks. Given the shabby quality of my strikes at the thieves, I clearly needed the practice.

Just after I left the Faerie I noticed a short man leave one of the neighboring doors. He followed me down the Fourth Serpent and Medusa Way. Although he carried an amphora, I had the strange feeling he was paying special attention to me. However, when we arrived at the square, he filled the amphora at the fountain like so many others. Being in full armor did attract attention, so I dismissed him from my mind.

Once I arrived at the Pathfinder barracks, it took a moment to clear my focus. At least this morning I was not angry, so I reached my balance sooner. I flowed through the drills smoothly and might have even earned a grunt of approval from Piri.

That thought relaxed me when we started sparring, and I handled Arkady with much greater ease than two days before. I simply dominated another Pathfinder, who I guessed was a new recruit who thought more of his skills than was warranted. Certainly, Piri had not matched us against each other to hone my skills, though she may have wanted me to remember how to teach.

Or perhaps she wanted me to become overconfident, as I suddenly realized that she had donned her own armor and stood before me as my next opponent.

We saluted each other and began. Our styles were vastly different. Mine relied on reach, both from my longer arms and the longer sword that I favored. I also used the greater width of my round shield, and its size helped compensate for Piri's greater skill.

Piri's shield was smaller and rectangular, and she danced behind it, her sword's point constantly jabbing at the scales of my armor. Time and again, one or another steel-shod corner of her shield slid smoothly into the path of my blade, deflecting the strike just enough to miss her.

After several passes I overcommitted slightly, bringing my shield around in anticipation of a thrust to my right side, only to feel the tip of her sword slide firmly into my left. She had repeated a sequence several times, and I fell into her trap. She had used the first two strikes in that sequence, and I assumed she was repeating the whole pattern. Instead, she started the next shot, hesitated, and then rotated her wrist to get the point of her sword past my shield, which I pulled too far trying to anticipate her strike.

I acknowledged the strike, and we stepped back to start again. And again.

Despite the fact that her smooth precise angles allowed her to defeat me five of our seven passes, the admiring glances from her watching Pathfinders made me feel better. I must not have shamed my father and Hlodowic, and their lessons, too much.

As we stepped back for a break, I thanked her for the truly enjoyable sparring.

"If you would use your mind, you might become a halfway decent swordsman," she replied bluntly. "Yes, you want to let your body move freely to do what it knows, but you don't watch and learn from what your foe does."

The point was just. My mind had wandered to the kidnapping and the attack the previous night. This seemed a good time to talk to her, though, for some reason, I thought I might want to keep that conversation private.

"I need to talk to you about what happened at the Faerie." I spoke quietly, pleased to note that her soldiers continued to give us space even though our sparring had ended.

She looked at me for a moment and then did something I never expected.

She laughed—not the slight chuckle of a blooded veteran or the guffaw of someone like Ragnar, but the light, tinkling laugh of a young girl, causing everyone on the training field to turn around in wonder. Somehow, at that moment, the powerful and stern hecatontarch seemed sweetly feminine, despite the fact she was standing in her armor, cleaning off her sword.

"Why, yes, Sevener." She grinned. "I would, indeed, enjoy having you buy me dinner. Your skill with words, I must say, had better be better than your skills with a blade, or you are doomed to a cold bed."

Nothing could have surprised me more, and I sincerely hoped that my mouth falling open looked, at least slightly, like that of an embarrassed suitor. After raising my jaw from the grassy field, the challenge of not laughing at the even more stunned looks of Piri's soldiers faced me. To them she was a force of nature, greater than any earthquake, as opposed to an actual woman.

But in that instant I saw what she had done. We could meet and talk softly and rather than being the meeting of two conspirators that it was, it appeared as though I was a man brave enough to chase the mighty Piri.

"Tonight, then, at the Faerie?"

"Aye, and tell Ragnar you want the second of his little private rooms."

Her lads and lasses snickered and hooted at the request, prompting her to glance at them, and they hastened off to do whatever it was they had been doing.

I sparred against two others, but I was still somewhat bemused and focused no better than I had the first day. Fortunately, neither of my opponents possessed anything like Piri's skill, and I did not make a fool of myself.

I left the field that day pleased with my returning skills, proud of the wondering comments by the Pathfinders of Achrida, and nervous about my upcoming evening with Piri.

Chapter 9
Morning, 7 Gersmoanne, 1712 MG

I went straight back to the Faerie and reserved the room Piri had insisted upon. Not surprisingly, Ragnar laughed at my expression when I told him with whom I would be dining.

"So you're to be flirtin' with Piri and that's to be a wonder, for sure, though you've as good of chances as any man to be havin', seein' as you're at least someone she might be respectin'…"

I ignored the rest of his speech, except to nod when he mentioned something about a hot bath, and perhaps even attention for my hair from Zoe. He called her out, and they took great pleasure in primping me for my "rendezvous." In truth, except for their gleeful smirking and snide comments about "not hurtin' the wee little lass or Zoe would be takin' it amiss," and how I didn't want to "have Zoe be protectin' her sweet, shy friend," I did not mind their ministrations. I doubted not that Piri would inspect my kit more than she did that of her Pathfinders prior to battle.

I was not sure how I felt about the idea that of a romantic evening with her, but I very much wanted to pass that inspection.

Thus, at dusk, still scaldingly hot from the bath and freshly shaven, I put on my best tunic, a newly cleaned and mended light-blue herringbone linen with two dragons elaborately embroidered on it. Their teeth snapped at my neckline and their tails wrapped around my arms to curl at my wrists. I wore this over an undertunic and my sea-green linen pants, both also freshly cleaned. Eirik had oiled and polished my riding boots so bright that Freya could have admired herself in their sheen. Zoe insisted I wear the jewelry she knew I had, an aesc-rune carved into a large piece of amber hung from a string of polished amethysts.

Ragnar insisted I wear all of my arm-rings, as well. "She'll be knowin' what they're to be meanin', though not many that's to be livin' here would be to understandin'."

I sighed and did as they bid me. I had to admit, as Zoe fussed over me in front of the large sheet of copper that they used as a mirror, that I looked as well as I could have hoped.

She finally pronounced me worthy. Ragnar bestowed his own long-winded praise. Karah even said nice things to me as I entered the common room.

The last bothered me. I began to wonder about my sanity. Melia's demands for petting helped, as at least one being in the Faerie was acting normally.

My wonder grew when Piri arrived. She would never be a beauty, but I could see her skills in the battlefields of love rivaled her skills in the battlefields of the Emperor. Her hair, normally so utilitarian, had somehow been arranged in an intricate twisting pattern. She wore a long, majestic dress of a shimmering gray silk. It was trimmed in the eastern style, with red and black alternating triangles along the cuffs, hem, neckline, upper arms, and just above her knees. Around her neck was a black, beaded choker holding a ruby pendant, and from her ears hung ruby earrings that danced in the light of the lanterns. The silk made her movements sensual, and the colors promised mystery, passion, and power.

The regulars of the Faerie stopped talking. I do not think it had ever been quieter than at that moment. Only a half-breathed "Is that..." interrupted the stillness. I had no doubts the conversations would resume more vociferously when we left the common room.

After giving Piri a chance to make her entrance, two of her troopers, in gleaming kits of their own, entered. One was Arkady. I would take great pleasure on the sparring field in wiping that huge smile off his face. It grew broader at my glare. The other Pathfinder was her senior decarch, Desimir, who usually had a smirk on his lean face. Tonight he replaced the smirk with a broad grin.

Meanwhile, Zoe came out from the kitchen and hugged Piri. Karah curtsied and hugged her as well. Eirik blushed and stammered. Ragnar beamed like a proud papa. A proud papa with an oiled and trusted broadsword at hand.

Truly, a memorable night. I sighed.

Ragnar led us to our room. He had laid a white cloth over a table and placed several decorations around a candle centerpiece that had a beautiful geode of amethyst in the center. A red ceramic bucket, designed with an intricate white Greek key, held a bottle of wine chilling in cool lakewater.

Fortunately, I had not forgotten the small bit of manners my proper ealdmodor had tried to teach me, and I helped Piri take her seat. Ragnar poured us the wine and then, somehow, quietly disappeared.

Once we settled in, Piri laughed at my expression.

"Well, Sevener, how are your word skills?"

"Undoubtedly insufficient to cross blades with you. You look worthy of the Emperor."

She accepted her due. "You look acceptable. Zoe must have helped you."

I laughed, nodding. "And Karah and Ragnar and Eirik. I've no doubt that they covered for each other this evening so they could."

"They're good folk."

"Indeed."

"So tell me what happened here. Ragnar told me the basics, but I want details."

I explained what I remembered. I added that I had discovered what seemed to be some connection to Naum and the city of Basil. I also told her about the second burglary attempt.

After I finished, she dissected my swordsmanship precisely, but without the scorn I felt I deserved from the fight in the dark hallway.

"You faced three with knives, and marked one twice without even a scratch in your linen. People have done worse. Undoubtedly, they were not new to knifework, either." She paused, thinking. "They were focused on one thing, which seems professional, as does the magic they had at hand. They had a way to create darkness and make everyone sleep, and a spell for dealing with Basil's keystones. They clearly have access to a wide variety of magic. Yes, definitely professionals. In fact, I wonder…"

I cocked my head at her, prompting, "Yes?"

She shifted topics. "You don't know enough, Sevener."

"I know they need something from the blue pouch."

"No, I mean something else. You don't know about Achrida and its place in the Empire."

"Ragnar suggested I talk to you about that."

The wine was a light, delicious vintage that kept our minds fresh, even though we were finishing our second glass each. Ragnar had surely known what we needed, just as he allowed us plenty of time to talk before bringing in the first course, which he did after knocking on the door.

He set before us a creamy soup of cheese and vegetables with a hint of chicken. He also served a salad of chopped cucumbers, which I had tried only the winter before, mixed with onions, the salty goat cheese, and an oily sauce. Piri commented that the salad, called shopska, was traditional in Achrida. Together its ingredients meshed perfectly and provided a light, cool complement to the soup.

We took time to enjoy the food before Piri started to talk again.

"You have to understand that the Empire exists as a collection of rivalries. The Emperor plays the larger temples against the smaller sects, the nobilissimi against the landed gentry, or maritime shippers against caravan leaders. If he can create a rivalry, he will. It has been the way every Emperor has ruled, no matter the dynasty. Without rivalries, I do not know if we would exist as an empire. Achrida is no different."

I lifted an eyebrow.

"Achrida is technically a part of the Empire, the capital of the province of Dassaretum. But that is only part of the truth, as the descendants of the Dassaretae compete with the descendants of the Enchelei to rule here. Their governors, called zupans, know that they are the true rulers here. The zupans squabble against each other. The Dassaretae are led by the Mrnjavcevic family, and our zupan is Vukasin. The Gropa family leads the Enchelei, and Pal is their zupan.

"I come from the Dassaretae, as do most of the Pathfinders. Sometimes, like the day you arrived, we are the guardians at the gates, taking tolls for the Empire, the city, and our tribe. Sometimes we stand there while Enchelei servants take the coins. Everything depends upon which zupan is currently governing. Even I do not really understand the negotiations involved in that dance."

"Wait. I'm already confused. The Dassaretae and the Enchelei are tribes? The Mrnjavcevic"—I stumbled over the odd name—"and the Gropa are families within those tribes?"

"Exactly, they are the premier families within the tribes." She smiled. "And what's worse is that while we usually mean the tribe Dassaretae or Enchelei when we say Mrnjavcevic or Gropa or even just say family, there are times when we mean the family itself instead of the tribe. For example, when I say I'm Mrnjavcevic, I actually mean I'm a niece of Vukasin Mrnjavcevic, the zupan of the Dassaretae."

That at least made sense to me. We'd often referred to all of Middlemarch as Cynric's when he was, in reality, only the lord of a small portion of the kingdom.

She paused to sip some wine and let me catch up before continuing. "Within each tribe and family are those who follow whatever godlings they will. They say there is someone to pray to in Achrida for each day of the year. These gods compete, as well, though less obviously. Some are local, tied to the tribes, and they ally themselves along family lines. Most, though, are from elsewhere and appeal to members of both families. They try to carve their own path. Sometimes this means Dassaretae and Enchelei allying against other Dassaretae and Enchelei who pray differently."

I poured her more wine.

"Then there are the other Imperials. The Lezhans, members of the province to our west, weave their own webs, and muddle our waters as we muddle theirs. Merchants from the western part of the Empire compete with eastern ones, and Achrida is in many ways the central point of transport. We sit on the caravan route to the north and west. The eastern traders can caravan to the Great City to the south, or take the direct route across the inland seas from Achrida if they wish to avoid the Emperor's tariffs. So, just about every merchant comes through here at one time or another, using their own alliances to make the trip as cheaply and safely as they can."

She laughed. "And, of course, I haven't yet touched on infighting within a particular group. The Dassaretae and the Enchelei have been splintered by brother fighting brother, as every tribe sometimes does.

Cobblers compete with other cobblers, and tailors compete with other tailors no matter the tribe. Yet cobblers will vehemently defend their competitors against tailors or any other guild, as will each guild. Priests fight over dogma as much here as anywhere. Worse yet, every Achridan thinks of themselves as a master of theology, and it, too, is a favorite topic of competition."

She smiled mischievously. "Do theological conversations end calmly in the Seven Kingdoms?"

I chuckled and shook my head. I had heard Honker and Flavian debate some obscure thing I had not understood my first night here. It had not been a quiet debate.

"And then there are Ragnar and folks such as yourself. People from outside the Empire or Achrida. In a sense you are ghosts. We know you will never truly understand the shifting alliances we find normal. You don't know enough to step into the dance, and we leave you on the side like poor foolish farmboys with two left feet."

She sipped as I sat for a moment, thinking about what she said.

"So that is why no member of the city came and investigated the kidnapping?"

"Yes, Ragnar is outside of any specific family protection and the Imperial quaesitors are mostly controlled by various members of both families. Neither family wants to see the other investigate a crime involving outsiders, for an investigation might make one or the other faction be seen as a patron of the outsiders. You are individually powerless here, but in the aggregate you might indeed matter in the great rivalry, and neither tribe wants to see outsiders affiliated with the other."

"So they prevent all investigations?"

"Mostly. Always when outsiders are the only ones involved. Fortunately, it is rare for outsiders to be attacked by one of the tribes. If one family were to attack Ragnar, the other would come to his defense, and, again, that might mean all of the outsiders joining a faction. Thus, outsiders are left alone by the tribes. Ragnar's only real threats, which are generally small in scale, come from other outsiders, and Ragnar is a… capable… man." I snorted. "The same is true for the sects, who equally ignore Ragnar's One-Eye and Thunder God. It's as if outsiders sail on the waters of the lake, but are ignored by the fish below."

"Yet sometimes a storm whips the waves."

"Yes. And when that happens, the outsiders are often the first to feel the lashing rain."

"So that is why we are having this dinner. We can talk without raising the hackles of the Enchelei."

She laughed. "Not at all. Their hackles are already raised. Some Enchelei are watching closely, making sure you don't fall under my spell. At this moment, Ragnar is selling ale and rakija and wine to some in the common room who will report to the Gropa as soon as they can. For that matter, there are some here who will speak to members of my family."

"Then why did you arrange all of this?"

She laughed again. "It gave me a chance to inspire Zoe."

Ragnar knocked on the door and brought in Zoe's inspiration, beef steak encrusted in a seared covering of oil and pepper, resting on a pile of some small grain, and covered in a mushroom gravy. He added a plate of buttered, grilled vegetable strips.

We both stopped talking to focus on our meal. Piri ate as daintily as any princess, manners I doubted she practiced in the Pathfinder barracks.

Ragnar returned at just the right moment to whisk our plates away and provide another bottle of that light wine. I wondered, later, about the delicate serving skills of this Svellheim berserker.

After he left, I said, "And I thought the shifting alliances of the Seven Kingdoms were confusing."

"We wouldn't know how to live without some sort of conspiracy," she admitted with a deep chuckle.

"So what are your personal allegiances?"

"Not much, really. I am a full member of the Mrnjavcevic family, so I support the Dassaretae. Most Pathfinders are the same. When the Gropa can, they give the better assignments to guard companies, like the Lakewardens, affiliated with the Enchelei, instead of us. I pray to Mithra, as do many guardsmen of both tribes. Some of the Enchelei soldiers are good friends that I drink with at festivals, but I've also brawled with them when times are livelier."

She paused for a moment and smiled slightly. "Occasionally, soldiers are contracted to escort caravans. Without worry, I've fought alongside Enchelei against bandits one day and the next shed their blood, deciding whether a boundary line follows one side of a stream or another. My ally today might be my sworn enemy tomorrow and yet be my ally again the day after."

She waved her wineglass slightly. "I also tend to keep track of outsiders for the family, mostly because I like Ragnar's ale and spend many nights here." She took a drink and added, "Have you met Svetislav yet?"

I shook my head.

"Drinks here often. Good man. Enchelei from a cadet branch of the Gropa. Tends to drop his shield when he gets overconfident. I marked his cheek once when I was very young. He carried me to one of the Helpers with his cheek bleeding because I'd extended too far to make that mark. I could have died there but for him. The Helpers healed the cut, but now I know when the weather is about to change. His scar is worse, but he thinks it makes him look rakish."

"Wait, he saved your life after you tried to kill each other?"

"It was only a minor dispute about which unit would get to escort a small caravan to the Great City and earn the fee."

"And you brawled in the streets?"

"No. That would irritate the city folk, upsetting the zupans, the sects, and the guild leaders. We're civilized Imperials, after all. We formalized our particular spats centuries ago." She grinned. "The mountain behind me is soaked with the blood of Achrida's guardsman, spilled on the castle training field deciding many a... 'legal dispute.' Mine included."

I poured more wine and thought about what she had said.

"So, would you tell me if the Mrnjavcevics took those people?"

It was her turn to sit back. "Probably, though I'd speak with the zupan first. I like Ragnar."

"And if Zupan Vukasin specifically forbade you to do so?"

"We'd have an interesting discussion. He'd have to work to convince me that not telling was justified."

"Could you disobey him?"

"We're all rivals, even within the families." She smiled. "I might lose my place in the family for a bit, but not for long."

I shook my head. "How do you keep it straight?"

"It seems normal to us." She chuckled. "The Great City is worse."

"So did the Dassaretae do this?"

"No. And I bet Svet will tell you the Enchelei did not either."

"Why do you say that?"

"As I said, we codified our rivalries long ago. If the Enchelei had done this here, at the place of an outsider, we would have to respond or see them able to threaten and control you outsiders. There are not so many outsiders, but as I said, if you all united, you would form a powerful piece on the board. Together, you could easily upset the balance we keep. The only reason the Enchelei would attack Ragnar would be if they were planning a major campaign to control all of you outsiders." She shook her head. "Such a campaign would be a major undertaking. I have heard no rumors of anything like that, and I think I would have."

"Could someone in one of the families have ordered this anyway?"

"Of course, but they then face the risk of a zupan's wrath, so the reward had better be worth it."

"What if I tried to go to the zupans and speak to them directly?"

"You'll do better with Svet and me, at least right now. The zupans probably wouldn't speak to you unless we supported it, given that he and I are the outsiders' channel to the family."

"And you won't support me speaking to Vukasin?"

"Right now? No. What would you ask him? Did you order this? It would just irritate him, unless you knew more or had some reason he would answer such questions. Pal would be the same. Right now, you are beneath their view. You give me a good reason, though, and I'll arrange it. For that matter, I'll even help you find a good reason. Until then, speaking to Vukasin will do you no good, and maybe great harm."

I nodded.

"You have a place to start, anyway, right? The Naumites?

"Yes, Piri, I do. The kidnapped girl had some Naumite garb, and I think the priestess I spoke to at the temple is hiding something. It would be a great coincidence if the tension I sensed in her had nothing to do with the events here."

She nodded. "Naum was an Enchelei prince. He could have been their zupan five centuries ago. I've never cared about the whole story, but he was known as a great diplomat. He was sent to various neighboring realms. On his most famous trip, he led an expedition to the east when the Berzeti came, probably at the behest of the Emperor at the time."

"The who?"

"The Berzeti. Easterners who married into the Enchelei."

"So, basically he assimilated them into the Enchelei, and they pray to him today?"

"That's somewhat simplistic, but yes. It was such a famous event then that he became a hero throughout the Empire. There are shrines to him in many places, and their prime chapel is in the Great City."

"Who is he a patron of?"

"He is supposed to have taught the Berzeti and other barbarians how to read Imperial, so he is a patron to teachers and the like."

"Teachers? Why would they be involved in a kidnapping?"

She shrugged and emptied her glass. I emptied mine and refilled both.

Ragnar returned with a small plate holding that flaky, honey-covered delicacy for us to share for dessert.

"Do they have baklava in the Seven Kingdoms?"

"Is that was this is called?" I asked between bites.

"Yes," she answered while licking honey off of her fingers.

I shook my head. "No, but I wish we did."

"I told you, Sevener, we're civilized."

We finished the baklava and sat back. Piri had that look in her eyes, the same one Bedarth had had so many times when he taught me.

"So, Sevener, what will you do now?"

"I can tell you expect me to know."

She sipped her wine daintily and then held it up, admiring the vintage in the light.

I sighed and thought through what she had said. The Naumites were not going to help me. I had nothing they wanted. Nothing to teach them that, in my naiveté, I had not already told them. They belonged to the Enchelei, meaning even if she wanted to, Piri could not help me.

But maybe...

"I should meet Svetislav."

"Mmmm." Like Bedarth, she had that irritating way of telling me I needed to think deeper and farther. Look and look again.

Ah, yes, they had rivals amongst the other sects.

"I should find their rivals." I sighed. "And possibly their allies."

"The Readers say Lake Achrida is one of the deepest lakes in the world," said Piri.

"My teacher told me to 'look and look again.'"

She nodded. Sipped some wine. Waited for my thoughts to catch up. Finally, she leaned forward.

"I lied before," she said. I looked at her. "We're not here merely because I wanted to see what Zoe would create. You interest me."

"I do?"

"Yes, Sevener, you do." She sipped more wine. "I have seen your skills with the sword. I have heard your word skills. It is time for you to show me what other skills you possess." She got up, took my hand, and led me to my room.

Apparently, I possessed skills enough to keep Piri's interest for the time we needed. However, when she did decide to leave, she somehow managed to still look immaculate.

"You'll do, Sevener, you'll do." She leaned over and kissed me. "But this doesn't mean anything on the practice field. In two days, Sevener, I expect you on the field, and this time your mind had better be focused."

At the door, she said, "Oh, and if you feel like you need assistance recovering from tonight, you might seek Achrida's native Helper." Her soft, relaxed laugh faded down the hallway.

Wheels within wheels, I thought as my body fell into a comfortable sleep.

Chapter 10
Morning, 8 Gersmoanne, 1712 MG

Zoe saw me first the next morning.

"How was the meal?" she asked slyly.

"It was one of the best I've ever had," I said truthfully.

"Of course." She sniffed and went into the kitchen to get my breakfast.

"So, how do you be feelin' this mornin' Sevener?" Ragnar bustled in as I was finishing my meal. "Piri was seemin' to have been enjoyin' her dinner somewhat, and it's a good thin' as if she hadn't Karah would be thinkin' to put some sort of spice not to your likin' in your eggs this mornin'."

Karah snorted in agreement from across the taproom.

"Now Zoe wouldn't be allowin' any such thing as she's to be bein' proud of her cookin', but I'm more feared of Zoe's quiet than Karah's tongue, if you see what I'm to be driftin' at." He laughed to shake the timbers. "But no, you've little to be fearin', especially since Piri cheerfully was to be pickin' apart the kit of Arkady and Desimir before havin' them escort her back to the barracks. Now everyone's to be thinkin' you're good enough to buy her dinner, but not enough to be keepin' her for the night. Ah, she's a sly one, she is, but all of them here are cunning from their cradles."

I ate some of the spiced sausage that Zoe had sent out with the eggs. Melia jumped up on the table to try for some of it, and I pushed her away. She settled for perching on the table, waiting for me to nudge a crumb in her direction. I sent some small bits of egg her way while I was thinking. I had nothing to say, really, though of course Ragnar did.

"Though I can't help but be notin' there was some time before she was to be leavin' after I was to be takin' the dishes from an empty room to Eirik to be washed." Ragnar punctuated his gossip by taking my empty plate and laughing like unsettled waves on a windy sea.

I was ready for him when he came back.

"I believe I need to meet Svetislav."

"So there were bein' useful things you were to be speakin' of while nibblin' on… the shopska and steak. And dessert of course." He grinned. "Well, I'm thinkin' he's not really a proper Gropa, but I'm not to be entirely sure, as their families are almost as confusin' as their feuds, and I'm thinkin' Piri told you somewhat about those. But to be sure, he's their kin and he's to be comin' in regular-like."

He paused in thought for a moment. "In fact, he was to be bein' here the day you arrived, though I'm to be thinkin' you'd gone to your bed before he was to be comin' in. I can make sure you're to be meetin' him the next time he's to be here, which is likely tonight or tomorrow, unless they're to be assigning his boat to a long cruise today, which I'm to be doubtin'."

"Thank you." I paused. "Also, she said something else. Who is Achrida's native Helper?"

"Native Helper? Ah, well, she's probably speakin' of Panteleimon who was to be bein' of the Fourteen Helpers, who all are to be havin' shrines here a' course, but he was bein' born up at the top of the hill where his shrine is. I'm not to be knowin' much about him, elsewise, but it's the really big buildin' that you can see from the square where Medusa starts her way up, just be lookin' for the shiny dome up high to the south."

"The Fourteen Helpers?"

"Ah, yeah, well I'm to be thinkin' they're to be bein' closest to your liffrea, but a'course they're not really bein' the same, and not pullin' from the Tree of Life as we're both to be knowin' is right and proper, but these from here, well they're to be goin' to these Helpers for when they're to be hurtin' and all, and while they aren't doin' things the way you and I are to be bein' used to, they're not bad—"

"Piri mentioned him," I cut in.

"Ah, to be sure, and I'm to be thinkin' she's mentioned him in the past and—"

"Thank you, Ragnar," I cut him off again. "I'll be visitin', errr…. visiting them today."

I escaped while I could and went back to my room. I got my walking bag because, while I was out, I wanted to pick up the turnshoes I had ordered. I also decided to swing by the Achridan Library again. Even though I doubted the Readers would tell me anything new about the items, they could tell me much about this Panteleimon before I went up to his chapel.

As I left the Faerie, I saw the man with the amphora who had come down the way the morning before. In only a few days, the neighborhood had begun to feel normal and routine.

At midmorn, after going to the Wall Road and getting my new shoes, I arrived at the Readers' hall. Anastasius came to me when I arrived.

"Edward. Welcome back."

"Thank you. Have you discovered anything about the things I left?"

"Not yet. Furthermore, while I originally suggested we'd know something tomorrow, I believe you will be sparring with the Pathfinders then, and more time might allow for more discoveries. Shall we say this time day after tomorrow?"

Pressing the Readers was unlikely to encourage them to provide more information, so I agreed. "I have other questions, though."

"How can I help?"

"Tell me about Panteleimon, please."

"Of course. He is one of the Fourteen Holy Helpers. About four hundred years ago, fourteen of the greatest healing gods in the Empire's pantheon were accorded the honor of this title. All of their devotees are trained in medicine, though each cult has its own specialties. Panteleimon's specialties are vision, childbirth, herbs, drugs, and medicines.

"He was a minor member of the Mrnjavcevic family, born here in Achrida about eight centuries ago. He became fascinated at a very young age with how people see. His work on the natural philosophy of human vision became well known even before the end of his second decade. Light is a fascinating thing, and nearly a millennium later, we have learned little more than he knew. He was skilled in Land magic, and he proved that one could sometimes use that magic to manipulate light, though no one is entirely sure how that works, even to this day. If I'm correct, you experienced something along those lines in the incident at the Faerie."

I nodded, remembering the flick of the wrist and the darkness.

"But he was less interested in how light works, in general, and more how light interacts with people. As I mentioned, he was primarily a Land magician, what we call a gekurios, but he was one of the rare magicians who could manipulate more than one stream of magic. In his case he could use Life magic as well. He is reputed to have cured blindness at least four times, something that is rarely successfully done. He had a way of following light through the eyes into the brain and reconnecting the two.

"He was also a capable herbalist and healer, he preferred medicine to magic. He had at least two children die in childbirth and dedicated many years searching for the reasons. Those deaths could not have been prevented, but he learned much from his studies. Many midwives are taught his methods, and as a result fewer children die in the Empire than elsewhere.

"People from all across the Empire, and even farther, traveled to Achrida to learn from him. When he got older, he decided to focus on that teaching, so he moved to the Great City and founded a school."

"He was part of the Dassaretae?"

"Yes." Anastasius smiled. "In fact, he's the greatest saint in Dassaretae history."

"And a teacher."

"Yes."

"So how would he and his followers get along with those of Naum?"

Anastasius chuckled. "You are learning at least some of the basics of this city. These two have competed for centuries. Who teaches the best lessons? Who has the greatest art celebrating their saint? Who does the most for the citizens of the Empire? And of Achrida? Who has the most followers? On any and everything they strive to show themselves greater than the other. Most of the time this is a good thing."

"But not always."

Anastasius nodded gravely.

"So if someone were to have taken something from the Naumites, the followers of Panteleimon would be natural suspects. And vice versa?"

"Possibly. At the very least, one shrine would not be displeased if something happened to the other."

I could hear Bedarth telling me to look and look again, but I could not think of anything else to ask at that moment. I left the library and headed up the hill to the southwest corner of the city, where Panteleimon's dome gleamed whenever the sun peeked through the clouds.

I found the same street vendor on the way and devoured the unknown meat-on-a-stick again. I climbed west from the Trade Road. The road switched back and forth up the steep hill to accommodate houses built alternately in the side of the hill or over the houses one street below. At the top I took a moment to catch my breath and look out over the lake, seeing the fishing boats sailing in and out of the dappling shadows of the sun and clouds.

It was well that I took the time to rest because my entry into the shrine to Panteleimon again took my breath away. As I entered, the sun forged a path through the clouds and joined me in Panteleimon's Hall. The sunlight flowed in patterns throughout the shrine. Stained-glass windows of impossible intricacy created images so perfect they seemed solid. Subtle mirrors and crystals caught the light and led visitors' eyes to various statues standing around the room. Panteleimon raising a child. Panteleimon at a workbench with a mortar and pestle. Panteleimon looking through a crystal that somehow created a rainbow in the middle of the shrine.

The artwork, especially the mosaics in the Temple of Naum, were more impressive than the artwork here, but in the sunlight Panteleimon's home carried my soul away.

After a few moments, I realized a short woman awaited my attention. She wore silk robes that seemed to shift colors in the light, and her bright, green eyes laughingly watched my reaction.

"I am Bisera, photodotis of Panteleimon. May I help you?" she asked after she was certain of my attention.

"Yes, may I speak with someone?"

"Do you require healing?"

"No, I need information."

"How may I help?"

"My name is Edward. I am a guest at the Frank Faerie and, as you may know, there was an incident there recently."

"That rumor flitted from ear to ear faster than the holy light in the city." She glanced at my clothing. "As did the rumor that Ragnar asked an outsider to help. You are he, I presume."

"Yes."

"Why come here? We are an order of healers and teachers. Assaulting guests of Ragnar is a deed foreign to us."

"The people who were taken included one who had a chasuble in the colors of Naum."

"And you wonder if our longstanding rivalry prompted us to do this deed."

"No matter how unlikely the idea, you do have that rivalry."

"Yes, and while we wish no harm to come to those people, I will admit we are certainly happier it happened to the followers of Naum than to ours." She looked me squarely in the eyes. "Nevertheless, Panteleimon, though from the tribe of the Dassaretae, was a healer first, and his followers would never attack anyone physically, even an Enchelei follower of Naum, no matter how strong the rivalry. Were I to come upon any Naumite who needed help, I would give it freely. We have served at the birth of many an Enchelei son and daughter, and ensured they were strong and healthy. We take our oaths to Panteleimon's memory seriously."

"Can you give me any hints or suggestions as to why anyone would kidnap them?"

"Hmmm. Perhaps I can, for a small favor at some future time."

"What favor?"

"We shall see, but I promise we will not ask anything that taxes your honor." She stepped back to one of the brighter spots in the shrine. "I swear this in the light of the sun."

I hesitated to make such a commitment, but from what Piri had told me, I had no reason to expect the information for free, so I agreed.

"Something catastrophic has happened to the Naumites. Yesterday they split into factions, a rival stepped up to contest their archimandrite, and cries of heresy rang out. This sort of thing happens to all faiths occasionally, of course, yet I doubt that it is merely a coincidence that their split happened yesterday, so soon after the assault in Ragnar's inn."

"And you will not help."

"What could we do? Both factions distrust us, as would we, were the situation switched. Our best option is to allow them to weaken their order from within, though I will not say we would not fan the flames, were a safe opportunity to present itself."

What a snake pit, I thought, shaking my head, though I knew my lords would have done worse.

"What caused it?"

"We do not know all of the details, though we know, as is so often the case when a sect fights amongst itself, that one side is calling for a return to Naum's basic principles and the other wishes to continue as things were going."

I nodded.

"The archimandrite in Basilopolis, Gregor, wishes to maintain the status quo. We are not entirely positive, but we think Kristijan, here in Achrida, has claimed the mantle of archimandrite with the hope of reforming the sect. He is certainly the most likely, as he is both the second-ranking priest in that order and the one who has most called for change."

"I was told that there is a saint to pray to for each day of the year here in Achrida."

"Even more than that."

"What do the other sects think?"

"As you can guess, if the sect has a history with the Dassaratae or Enchelei, they either think as we do or seek to quickly end any conflict. If not, they cluck sadly and are grateful that their sect is not subject to such a schism right now. The real person to watch, however, is Pal Gropa."

"The zupan of the Gropas and the head of the Enchelei tribe?"

"The very one."

"Ah, because the prestige of Naum directly influences the prestige of the Enchelei."

"Exactly. Right now Pal is trying to alleviate the conflict and ameliorate its effects upon the Enchelei as a whole."

"While Vukasin is trying to expand his influence."

"Yes, though he will do so softly and quietly."

I looked at her questioningly.

"Centuries ago, a conflict between the Enchelei and Dassaretae occurred. The zupans were not merely rivals, but each blamed the other for the death of the Emperor's daughter, whom both had loved. Both were looking for a fight, and when they had a pretext, the city exploded. The streets ran red, they say, and dozens of Helpers on both sides died from exhaustion trying to save those they could. The Emperor had to send in an army, carefully picked from the far ends of the Empire, with no affiliation to any of our rivalries, to quell the rioting and bloodshed. Our records indicate about one in four who lived here died and no one bothered to count the wounded. This was not Achrida's brightest time."

One in four? If Achrida was the same size then as now, that meant over ten thousand died. My shield-brothers had numbered thirty-two. If he had called all of his thegns, Cynric could only muster slightly over three thousand. He had only done so once, of course, because that would strip defenses in his entire realm. My mind boggled.

"The zupans ultimately died in the final battle, where Dassaretae fought Enchelei and Imperial soldiers and vice versa. Their heirs, whose hatred was stronger but not as fiery, met in the months afterwards and between them created a set of covenants for their rivalry. It was then that the Achrida you see today began to prosper."

"So, for example, if the warriors of the branches have a quarrel, they go to the training fields in the castle and fight there instead of in the streets?"

"Exactly."

"But the embers of that explosion still burn here?"

"Yes. While Vukasin and Pal will always strive to strengthen their positions, they are aware of certain lines that would, if crossed, prompt each to attack the other. They do not cross those lines for fear that the Sfagi might happen again. The Slaughter, you would say."

There did not seem to be much more to say, so I enjoyed the patterns of light once more and took my leave.

Chapter 11
Late Afternoon, 8 Gersmoanne, 1712 MG

I started walking back towards the Faerie, pondering all the things I had learned in the past couple of days. It never occurred to me that I needed to pay attention to the people around me as I strode in the street.

Suddenly I was on my back, looking up at the sunny sky of late afternoon.

I apparently had some logical reason to lie on the cobblestones of an unfamiliar street. It made perfect sense to remain there while four figures silhouetted in the sky kicked me. A fifth pulled my walking bag from my shoulder. My body trapped my saex underneath me. I could not draw it to defend myself, nor could they not take it from me, at least in the short time they apparently had. That was not a small favor.

Soon, an older gentleman bent over me and eventually I realized his mouth was moving.

"Alright then, laddie?"

A lady of a similar age, wearing an incredibly hideous shawl, tut-tutted the same question. I waved the questions off, and he helped me climb unsteadily to my feet.

"Did—," I caught my breath. "Did you see who it was?"

They both, along with the assembled crowd, shook their heads firmly in united ignorance. I could not blame them. I was not sure I wanted to get involved either. Sadly, I already was.

I looked around one last time, thanked my benefactors, complimented the woman on the ten or more colors in her shawl, and trundled away from the crowd. Mutely, they watched me totter down the hill.

Might as well head back to the Faerie, I thought.

I made my way, paying a great deal more attention to my surroundings. At least I had not pressed the Readers for the knotted pouch. I needed to make some alternate plans to store whatever the pouch held, should they be able to open it.

Ragnar took one look at me, gestured me over to my table, and brought me both a mug and a pitcher. It was still early for dinner, and I waved away a mention of food. Ale. All I wanted was ale and time to process what had happened.

I should not have been so naïve. I should have realized that, if someone was willing to kidnap people from a busy tavern, they would be willing to mug someone, even in daylight in the middle of a street. I had been surprised twice, and I needed to remember Achrida was not Middlemarch. I had more to worry about than my mother's kin raiding our side of the border for sheep.

I sat there, letting the alcohol soothe my bruises and counted my blessings. I had only lost my bag with the new turnshoes, some bronze and silver dinars, the older of my two carved-bone grooming kits, and my pride. I was only bruised, with no cuts or broken bones. Nevertheless, I pictured my father and Bedarth shaking their heads, agreeing that the bruises were less than I deserved. I had not looked once, much less looked again.

Some time later Ragnar brought me a plate of food—a sort of stew, reddish with the aggressive spice that he called by some weird southern name. The spice burned my tongue and brought me out of my reverie. Ragnar's brew and Zoe's food had restored my life, I supposed, but I did not look forward to tomorrow's sparring eagerly.

"Ah, so you've been enjoyin' the gulyas," came Ragnar's boom, "and to be sure Zoe is to be sayin' it is the recipe her mothers have been passin' down since they started usin' paprika, though that's to be bein' somethin' new to you and me. I was to be thinkin' I was dyin' the first time I was to be havin' that, what with my mouth screamin' like it was made for Surt himself." He grinned. "I'm to be thinkin' I've gotten to like it somewhat, but that's not really why I was to be comin' over, though I'm to be getting your dishes a'course. I'm to be thinkin' you're wantin' to talk to that yon fellow leanin' on the bar. His name's Svetislav, and I'm to be rememberin' that Piri was to be mentionin' him to you." He waved him over.

Svetislav was tall and very thin, but it was a wiry, strong kind of thin. He moved with quick, abrupt steps. I bet he had needed to shorten his stride to keep the right pace in a shield wall. Long bones and hollow, sharp cheeks formed an oddly shaped face. Piri's scar ran proudly along his left cheek.

He nodded at me and sat down. Ragnar brought over a fresh pitcher.

"Piri said I should speak to you."

Svetislav nodded.

"You're also a soldier?"

"Lakewarden." He nodded again.

"Is that a company affiliated with the Gropa like the Pathfinders are with the Mrnjavcevics?"

Another nod.

"How much do you know about what happened here?" I thought maybe if I asked an open-ended question, I'd get more than one word. I was wrong.

"Some."

"Was it done by the Gropa?"

He shook his head.

"You're sure?"

He nodded.

"How would you know?"

"I would be Pal's choice to do it."

By Woden, a full sentence! "You'd do that to Ragnar? You know it's a great insult to him, right?"

He nodded. "Not personal."

"But you know he'd take it personally?"

He nodded again. Melia jumped into his lap and reached out a paw until he started petting her.

"Are you this talkative all the time?"

This time, he smiled when he nodded.

"Well, in that case, can you shrug informatively about the Naumites?"

An actual chuckle and a shrug I took as a yes.

"So, the Panteleimonites say that the Naumites are having problems. Perhaps even a schism?"

He nodded.

"Do you know why?"

He shook his head. "I know Mithra."

"So, from a religious aspect, you really don't know much about Naum and his followers?"

He nodded.

"From a Gropa perspective?"

"Pal is unhappy."

"So if the kidnapping was done to start a schism, Pal would have prevented it?"

He nodded.

"And Pal is working to end the schism?"

He nodded again.

"Do you know of any Naumites who might be capable of the kidnapping?"

He shook his head.

"Of a mugging?"

Shook his head again.

"Of a burglary?"

Another shake.

"But the Enchelei have people who could do this?"

"As do Dassaretae."

"Pal did not assign a group of at least five to the Temple of Naum to serve as muscle?"

Again, a shake of the head.

I paused. "What were you doing today?"

He looked at me strangely. At least the look differed from a shake or a nod. I waved the question away and asked, "I may need to speak with your zupan about this. Would you be willing to pass him my request if I need?"

He nodded.

"Thank you."

We spent the rest of the evening chatting, sort of, about different fighting styles. He also invited me to join him on a lake patrol in the upcoming days.

I wished I knew what to do with this newly created line of

communication. At the moment, all I could do was go to bed and sleep the sleep of the heavily bruised.

Chapter 12
Morning, 9 Gersmoanne, 1712 MG

I dreaded the day's planned sparring when every kick from yesterday woke me in the morning. However, after our evening two nights before I knew Piri would not accept a little thing like a mugging as an excuse. So I armed myself and headed for the barracks, receiving bright and cheery encouragement from Ragnar along the way.

Careful, I thought, *keep that up and I take your beard for a trophy.*

My mood improved somewhat upon arrival at the barracks. All the Pathfinders, except one, looked at me nervously.

"Well, well," said the exception, "back to see if Piri will deign to take you on again?"

I grinned. "Yes, Desimir, after I show all of you how to use that puny thing you all wield."

"It's called a semi-spatha, barbarian, and I've two bronze dinars that says she'll take you five of seven again."

"I'll not take your money after taking your pride."

He laughed at my feeble excuse as we went into the sparring arena, bickering back and forth. Piri and others waited for us.

Piri kindly paired me with Edward, whom I had handily defeated the time before. Our bouts warmed up my bruised muscles. Piri stood ready after him.

I was not really trying to win our bouts, and it showed in some ways. Ostensibly, I worked on my footwork and interior sword angles at close range. I lost every bout, but the fighting challenged me at a distance I needed to improve upon.

In reality, though, I wanted to fight at close range so I could talk privately with Piri.

"I was attacked in the street yesterday," I puffed as we pushed at each other.

She grunted in response while trying to slide her blade past my shield.

"They didn't get anything I can't replace, but they're after something from the Faerie, I think."

She clearly did not need her full attention to defeat my defense. With a quick flick of her wrist she slashed her semi-spatha at my vambrace. We separated and restarted.

"Tomorrow I pick up what I had the Readers investigate."

"When?" she asked.

"Late morning."

"Might just have Desimir take his squad and patrol along that stretch."

"I wouldn't mind the support."

"How many were there?"

"Not sure. Maybe five, though this time I'll be paying attention."

She bashed me with her shield, creating space for her blade to thrust at my chest. We restarted again.

"Paying attention would be good. Might take your sword, too."

"With a peace-bond?"

She slashed across the lower drape of my scales. "I'm no longer worried about your skills with the sword."

I laughed at the truth of that and moved on to Dmitri, who allowed me to drink some water before sparring.

I returned to the Faerie with my muscles moving nicely. My bruises had been worked out, and my fighting wind seemed to be returning. At least I had energy for an afternoon ride. Deor and I had not exercised together for a while, and I wanted to get a better idea of the paths in and out of the city. I spread my armor on the table in my room to allow it to breathe, switched into my riding boots, and got Deor.

Lazy as he was, his tail swished in anticipation of a ride.

"I've walked him some in the yard," said Eirik as I saddled Deor.

"I'm sure, but he and I need some time."

Deor whinnied in agreement, though his meaningful look at the apple basket prompted Eirik to bring him encouragement. I packed several more of the apples, along with some waybread and a couple of waterskins, in his saddlebags.

"Where are you riding?"

"I was thinking just out of the city, maybe to the top of the mountain."

"Ohhh, you should take the Old Road. It's a path with four nuraghi that leads to a mountain meadow where you can stretch his legs out some. It then comes back to the road south of town."

"Nuraghi?"

"Oh, yes, milord, they're amazing."

"What are they?"

"Old buildings."

"How are they amazing?"

"Well, they've been there forever. Ma would know better, but I think they were here before there was a here."

"Who built them?"

"Nobody really knows, but some say the Giants did. There are always people studying them." He paused. "I don't know what they're finding, but I listen for everything I can about them. I wish I could come with you. It's been ages since Da and Ma took a day off and we went up there for a picnic."

He smiled in memory.

"Maybe I'll take you some other time." He positively beamed at that possibility. I switched topics. "So a caravan could avoid the city altogether by using the Old Road?"

"Well, not one with wagons, it's a bit tricky in parts for those. And if you're coming from the north, it's out of the way, up Crownstreet a bit and then looping around. Makes no sense."

I could think of a few reasons not to actually enter the city, but I merely listened to the landmarks he gave me and left. Deor and I retraced our entrance to the city and exited through the Upper Gate. The Pathfinders at the gate waved me through, past the caravans they were inspecting.

About a mile along Crownstreet up the mountain sat a tall pile of masonry that seemed so feeble, I expected the wind to strew the granite about for miles. Eirik had told me this was the first of the nuraghi and that it marked the Old Road.

The initial part of the path was terraced almost into stair steps. This was clearly one of the tricky wagon sections Eirik had mentioned, but Deor fairly ran up the path in his enjoyment. I mostly let him set the pace, though I did rein him in periodically.

At one point I had a nice view of the entire northwest corner of the city. The walls did not completely enclose all of the dwellings. I could see many buildings in the valley carved out of the mountain by a stream that flowed down to the lake through the city. Above the buildings the mountain rose forbiddingly, and, with the wall to the east, I wondered if they got any sunlight at all.

I approached another nuraghi on the uphill side. The first had seemed to be merely a piled-stone tower, but this one had a gatehouse and two wings, each with smaller towers. Something about the proportions or angles seemed off. I wondered if Eirik's enthusiasm had been for this particular nuraghi, as I felt uneasy under its gaze, almost as if it had judged me unworthy to stand in its presence.

It also reminded me of something. I stood there trying to remember what that something was, but the nuraghi simply stared back at me, taunting me with a smug superiority. Even Deor felt something, but he glared in equine fury and trembled to bring it down with his hooves. He let me lead him away, snorting in pride.

Soon after, I let him prove his worth in the meadow that Eirik had told me we would find. We raced back and forth, laughing in the bright sun, sneezing at the pollen his hooves raised.

After we tired, I led him to a mountain stream and let him drink his fill. I sat on a few stones, basking in sunlight and nibbling on the waybread I had brought. Deor took a few steps into the meadow and ate the fine tall grass. Eventually he tired of the grass and nuzzled me until I got the apples I had brought from the stable. We munched happily, enjoying the pleasant day.

Finally, I remounted and we raced once more to the far end of the meadow. From that point we climbed to the highest point on the path, navigating carefully a tricky bit that fell off dramatically to our left. This part of the path included a small plateau hundreds of feet above Achrida. We looked over Panteleimon's Hall to the far docks. We also saw a brilliant expanse of open limestone I guessed to be the amphitheater that the regulars had discussed. I could even make out figures on the training field of the castle.

I opened up the map Anastasius had given me. I traced the major roads, getting a much clearer picture of the arrangement of the city. I followed the Trade Road from the Upper to the Lower Gate, going through the Square of Legends, Heartsquare, and several other, smaller squares. The blue of the lake framed the gilded dome of the Shrine of Naum, a combination of brilliance I would never forget. The castle obscured the Faerie, of course, but I could see the Serpents leading off Medusa Way. I followed the roads to Piri's barracks, though the three- and four-story houses in the neighborhood around it obscured its low-lying, spread-out structure.

Truly a beautiful city.

We pressed on to another plateau. Though the view was similar to the previous one, a nuraghi was this plateau's main attraction. It was a long, rambling pile of stones that almost seemed like a wall or, better yet, a tower stretched on its side.

The last nuraghi stood just before the final turn that led to the Trade Road. Its almost pristine marble contrasted with open windows and ruined metal gates wounded by centuries of onslaughts. It did not impart any sort of feeling to us, though the perfection of the marble seemed odd.

Sitting on the marble was a tall, well-built man with a precisely trimmed beard. His eyes were set close together and looked as though they could not quite focus on what sat before them. Ink stained his hands, suggesting his eyes had been pulled by constant reading. Something about his manner, however, made both of us uncomfortable. Deor snorted his anger.

"Greetings, Edward," he said. "And you as well, Deor."

We gritted our teeth. "Do we know you?"

He shook his head. "No, not yet, but you will, and you'll want to learn everything you can about me."

"What is your name?"

"Davorin, Davorin Gropa."

"So you're a member of the Gropa family?"

"Not simply a member of the family but also of its council."

"Its council?"

"Yes, Pal is our zupan, but that is not an easy position, especially in times of stress."

"And with the schism, this is a time of stress."

He chuckled and clambered off the wall. "Yes, Sevener, it is. We would be lucky to have Pal during this time…"

"But?"

"But he has more than merely the schism to challenge his skills."

"Did the Gropas kidnap someone from the Faerie?"

He laughed. "We certainly didn't make any such plans in a council meeting."

I looked at him. Nothing about him felt… right. Not even the truth, and I somehow felt that this statement was true. Mostly.

"You aren't telling me the complete truth."

"Welcome to Achrida." He laughed and started walking down to the Trade Road alongside us.

"Why are you speaking to me?"

"Let's just say I like to take my measure of the important people in Achrida."

"I'm not important. I'm an outsider. I'm merely a friend of Ragnar."

"Do you not think that a kidnapping at a local inn that prompted a schism in one of the larger religions in the city is important?" He paused and looked up at me. "By the simple virtue of your involvement in that event, you are important. Furthermore…"

I looked at him.

"Well, we shall see what we shall see," he continued.

"One thing you shall see is the redemption of Ragnar's honor."

"Having met you, I have no doubt you will make the effort. But you will underestimate what it takes to achieve that redemption because you are not of this place." I could not deny that after yesterday's mugging. "Don't worry, though, there are people out there who will help you. Me for one."

"Why would you help me?"

"If the Gropa family gets richer, I get richer. I have many… expenses."

"How will I help the Gropas get richer?"

"I'm sure you're smart enough to figure that out. Nevertheless, smart as you are, there may be times when you do need some help."

I looked down at him, and Deor stopped with a glare of his own.

"Ruzica, the little rose. She is the only one I trust to make a cotton tunic. I know you have several linen tunics that are being cleaned and mended. Nevertheless, I think you're a man who likes good clothes. Remember her if you feel… underdressed." With that he walked back up the Old Road, making us feeling cleaner simply by leaving our sight.

Within a few minutes we regained the mood we had achieved in the meadow. Deor twisted his head southward, away from Achrida, and I let him gallop down the Trade Road for a few hundred yards. Then, laughing, we wheeled and charged back towards the city.

We entered through the South Gate and took the Trade Road to the Square of Legends. As the sun started to set, we rode happily up to the Faerie. I slid off Deor, suddenly feeling all of the day's efforts, and made no protest when Eirik came out to unsaddle him. A sniff at an outstretched apple showed that Deor was as tired as I was, and I patted him before laying his saddle blanket over the stable wall and brushing it off.

"I'll be taking care of that, now. You go have one of Da's ales. Ma's been marinating a pig all evening, and you'll be wanting to have changed and be ready for that. I'll bring up some hot water for you to wash off after I brush the big lad down."

I patted Deor once more. He nuzzled me, and we both happily settled into the care of Ragnar and his family.

After dinner, I tried to plan for tomorrow, but I could not. Even the odd conversation with Davorin did not prevent me from falling into an exhausted, dreamless sleep.

Chapter 13
Morning, 10 Gersmoanne, 1712 MG

I looked at my armor in the morning, after breakfast, and rejected the idea of wearing it to visit the Readers. Piri would ensure that Desimir's squad would protect me, and I did not want to appear too obviously on guard. As Piri had suggested, wearing my sword only seemed prudent. I also took the bigger pack I had taken the first time, anticipating getting all of the clothes back.

I adjusted everything until I could easily draw my sword or shift the pack quickly enough to work as a sort of shield. Ragnar watched me from the door, all the way down to Medusa's Way.

At the corner, coincidentally, two Pathfinders casually examined the wares of some street vendors. They studiously ignored me, though the man with the amphora turned his head when he recognized me.

I had to appreciate, in general, the artistry of Desimir's plan. He had spread his troops out along the way. At least two of them could always see me, though none of them obviously looked my way.

Desimir stood next to the fountain in the Square of Legends. I greeted him publicly, since anyone who had been following me knew I had been sparring with the Pathfinders. They would have been suspicious if I had ignored him. So I didn't.

"When are you going to spar with me," I said loudly.

He laughed. "Tomorrow, then."

"You think you can take Piri's place?"

"To deal with an arrogant Sevener? Absolutely."

We clasped hands and laughed, and I said quietly, "This is brilliantly arranged. Well done." He grinned, and I moved on.

Anastasius waited for me at the Readers' Library, calmly standing by a table. He had my items spread before him.

"First, the chasuble is indeed one that has been used, recently, for religious ceremonies devoted to Naum. As we suspected, all of the other richly adorned items belonged to a woman from the Great City."

"Do you know who the woman is?"

"We cannot confirm who she was within an acceptable degree of certainty."

In other words, they knew, but telling me broke their vow of neutrality.

He continued. "The other clothes you brought also show traces of the Great City. The plain dress does have another interesting trace. It was in the Kingdom of Matara, far to the south, less than six months ago."

"Matara?" I had heard of it but knew little more.

"Yes, it's a small, but wealthy, kingdom to the south. It's one of the Empire's important trading partners. It does, in fact, produce linen, though it's more famous for cotton. Mostly they trade raw materials, but they have some artisans as well. About a quarter of their textile trade includes finished clothes."

"Cotton," I said. *Did this have any connection to Davorin's Ruzica?*

"The dress was fairly new, but we have no idea whether the woman who owned it purchased it in Basilopolis or Matara. I can also tell you that the Enchelei and their allies control most of the trade route from Matara to Achrida."

I supposed that suggested some sort of connection to Ruzica and, thus, to Davorin, but only a weak one. Other than that, these facts seemed worthless.

"What about the scrap?" I asked.

"The scrap of cloth hinted at recent time in the Great City. However, we cannot discover much from such a small sample. The person who wore that shirt might have been the same person who wore these tunics, but might have been someone else. However, should you find the man or his shirt we could match it."

"So, you could prove a particular person or shirt was there if I found them first?"

"Exactly. And we could match the other pieces to specific people, as well."

"Thank you."

"However, you're here for the contents of the pouch, I suspect."

"Yes."

Anastasius laid out the empty pouch, two small books, and a small expensive writing kit.

"The pouch was skillfully protected. It took much of our power to open it. I fear, however, that what was in it will not seem as valuable to you as the protection might have indicated."

I looked at him questioningly.

"First, there is this writing kit. It includes real paper made in Markanda, which is far to the east of us. There are no quills, but there are five reservoir pens. The ink is atramentum librarium from the inkmakers of the Emperor. There are eight vials plus one that is about two-thirds empty. As you may guess, the kit is extremely valuable, but not extraordinary."

I nodded.

"I also fear the two books will disappoint you." He pointed to the one that had an intricate blue key pattern that wove around Naum's odd, green script on the cover. "This is a Pismenech, the holy book of Naum. An exquisite version, as you can see, but nothing different from many others. It tells the story of Naum creating the Glagolitsa, his particular script, and then teaching the Berzeti how to read using it. The second part enumerates the curriculum that Naum expects his priests to be able to teach, including literature, rhetoric, philosophy, astronomy, geometry, mathematics, and many other subjects. They add to this list as their knowledge expands. Again, extremely valuable but not extraordinary."

"And the other book?"

"Now, it does have some information that you might find pertinent. It is a journal that describes the projects and research of the author."

I opened it, but it was written in the odd Naumite script. Anastasius smiled at my expression.

"Yes, she used the Glagolitsa, and very few outside of Naum's order know it today. She mentions that she is coming through Achrida on her way to pursue a specific avenue of research but is vague about the details of that avenue and her ultimate goal. More interesting to you, I suspect, is the surprise in her writing when she was ordered to come north. She had apparently asked repeatedly to be allowed to make this trip, but it was only recently she was given the support of the order allowing her do so."

"That is interesting. I wonder why."

"That we do not know."

"What else can you tell me?"

"I doubt there is anything more in here to help you. You will not be interested in her research. Much of the rest of the journal is personal, and we do not feel comfortable sharing it with you. However, we swear upon our oath that we are not holding back anything we feel would help you find her and save her from this kidnapping."

I thought for a few moments. If they were willing to swear that oath, then whether or not it was true I would get nothing more from them. I started pondering what to do with the pouch. It held nothing I needed to keep with me. However, it might still be useful to again entice the kidnappers. They had, after all, returned for something, and while it might not have been in the pouch, they might not know that.

"What I would like to do is leave the journal here until it can be returned to its rightful owner." I did not add, "Or her heir."

"But you wish to keep the pouch, the Pismenech, and the writing kit?"

"Yes."

Anastasius slowly nodded. "The pouch no longer has any protection on it."

I nodded in return, gathering the items together and putting them in my pack.

I left the Readers' Library and quickly picked up two of the Pathfinders. I now hoped people would see the protection afforded me by the Pathfinders, as that protection might advertise that I had something valuable. However, I knew I must do so subtly or my foes might wonder and hence suspect a trap. The trip back might have only been a metaphorical passage between Scylla and Charybdis, but by the time I reached the Faerie I was exhausted.

Whether or not someone watched me leave the Readers, as far as I could tell nothing happened as I made my way back to the Faerie. I would ask Piri or Desimir when I could if they had noticed anyone paying too much attention to me.

I found the Faerie more fully occupied than usual. I was looking for a place to sit when I heard Flavian punctuate a command with his piercing laugh.

"Move your arses from the lad's table," he bellowed.

I saw with amusement, and some guilty hubris, that three burly drinkers got up from my table. They yelled back various versions of "Fuck off, old man" good-naturedly to Flavian as they passed his table. Then Flavian, followed by Honker, Marko, and all the rest rose and grandly bowed as I passed by. I could not help but laugh. I also noticed that there were many cudgels and belaying pins and other things to hit people with conveniently lying about the room. Piri, Desimir, or Ragnar had apparently spread the word.

"Put out a few extra pitchers, Ragnar." I smiled as I handed him a bit of hacksilver.

"No, be puttin' away your silver—"

"You gave me bencriht," I cut him off, "and I am grateful, but if I am to thank them properly then I must be the giver."

"Ah, you've got the right of it. I'm to be apologizin' for not thinkin'. The lads'll be enjoyin' the full worth of this, and you'll be hearin' them drink late because of it, not that I'm to be mindin', of course. Strange how they all decided to show up today, isn't it?" He grinned and moved on.

I spent the afternoon and dinner planning. First, something was out there that, at least at the time they mugged me, the attackers still wanted. I now knew whatever that thing was probably was not in the blue pouch. I had no idea how to find the item or items, but I did have some ideas about how to find the attackers. I could use myself as bait. I decided to routinely wear my sword from now on, and to offer my opponents some more opportunities to attack me. I would be paying attention, though.

Second, I needed to stir things up with the Naumites. Maybe I could go to the Temple of Naum and offer to sell the contents of the pouch. I might do better if I could offer the pouch to someone in each faction, but that meant identifying who belonged to which faction. Maybe Svetislav could help, especially if I could figure out a way to get him to convince

Pal to help. The next time I saw him, I would ask him if I could meet with Pal.

Surely some contacts amongst the Mrnjavcevics could help, but I suspected that Vukasin would prefer me to focus on the Enchelei side. The Enchelei kettle simmered, and both he and I needed to carefully spice that pot with Mrnjavcevic, with Piri being the obvious exception. It would take something extraordinary to get Vukasin to actively aid me. I did not have anything extraordinary, yet. No, I only had straws to clutch.

Dinner time arrived while I pondered. Zoe served us a sort of red sauce that was pungent with the aroma of garlic over some irritating long strips of something bread-like that kept sliding off of my spoon. It tasted fantastic, but I never quite got the hang of eating it. The regulars managed without a problem. I was just glad I was not wearing one of my better tunics.

As I mopped up the last of the sauce with bread soaked in butter and garlic, both Piri and Svetislav joined me. Piri placed a pitcher of ale in the middle of the table.

"Am I going to have to break up a fight between you two?"

"I told you Sevener, we're civilized," said Piri. "Svet and I have spent many a night together waiting to slaughter the bull at the rise of the sun. When I want to mark his other cheek, we'll head up to the castle, as I told you."

Svetislav nodded with a slight smile and leaned back with his ale.

"I believe Ragnar owes you some thanks for the business today," I said.

"Actually, that was Svet's idea. I was too busy with other things."

"Desimir ran things well."

"He's a good lad. He'll do just fine when I decide to retire to a life of relaxation."

I snorted at that. Svetislav smiled. "Did any of your troops see anyone follow me?"

"No, but I wouldn't pay too much attention to that. If they were smart and were following you they would probably have set up relays like Desimir did. No way to spot them."

I thought about that and decided she was probably right. I refilled all of our mugs.

"So, if you're not here to ask me to moderate your family disputes, why are you?"

"Nothing in particular, but we're both here, and if one of us is going to chat with you, the other would be expected to listen in."

I shook my head. "Probably just as well, I need some help. Svet, can you arrange a meeting with Pal? I have a request, and I don't want to step on his toes."

Svetislav shrugged.

"Tell him I don't think I can make things worse, but I might be able to help with the schism."

He thought for a moment, nodded, rose, and walked over to another Lakewarden drinking in the Faerie. He spoke to him and returned as the Lakewarden left.

I turned to Piri. "I do not, however, want to talk with Vukasin right now. As you said, I have nothing to give him, and until I do, I want him out of the cauldron."

Both Piri and Svetislav nodded at that last bit.

I looked at Piri. "I'm going to do some risky things. It might be bad if I am constantly rescued by Pathfinders in uniform. I will be walking some fine lines to avoid causing a spark."

She looked at me and nodded slowly. Something was going on behind her eyes.

We chatted about fighting techniques and enjoyed another pitcher of ale until the Lakewarden returned. With a nod to Svetislav, he spoke formally to me.

"The Zupan requests the honor of your presence for dinner tomorrow evening."

I lifted an eyebrow to Svetislav and then replied, equally formally, to the Lakewarden, "Please pass on my acceptance of his gracious request." The Lakewarden bowed precisely, turned around and left the Faerie again.

"A formal fellow," I said.

Svetislav nodded. "Since a child."

"Thank you."

He nodded again.

"You'll report this to Vukasin," I said to Piri.

"Probably not."

I looked at her.

"I'd be surprised if he doesn't already know."

"Yes?" I said quizzically.

"Civilized, me boy, civilized. Pal undoubtedly passed the information on to Vukasin at the same time he sent Ilija back here."

"How many unwritten rules are there in this town?"

"More than you can count, Sevener, more than you can count." She finished her ale and happily refilled it.

A thought crossed my mind. "So, if Pal positively did not supply the kidnappers, and if Vukasin would be crazy to do so, who did? They're not the sort of men the sects would have access to, right?"

They shook their heads.

"Do the caravans coming through Achrida have enough thugs? Could they have supplied the kidnappers? The way you talk, most of their guards come from Achridan companies."

Piri and Svetislav leaned back and looked at each other. "The caravans could supply the kidnappers. Enough caravan owners prefer their own guards to us," responded Piri. "But it seems unlikely that the timing would work out, especially since most guards are outsiders picked up here and there. We can check if any caravans came through at the right time."

Svetislav agreed with his own nod.

"So," I mused, "if not the zupans, the sects, or the caravans, who else would be capable of providing a group of five professional thugs for this job?"

They grimly looked at each other. Piri said to Svetislav, "Katarina?"

"Or Gibroz."

"Mmmm." She nodded. I waited, impatiently, for an explanation. "It seems awfully political for them," Piri added.

Svetislav shrugged.

"Yeah, I suppose with the right amount of money…," Piri trailed off. He shrugged again.

"Or something else. They're both devious as hell," she mused.

Devious as hell? From someone who grew up thinking in terms of half a dozen different factional disputes? I did not like the sound of this.

Another shrug from Svetislav.

"Alright, who are these people?" I burst out.

"The current kraljevics. You might say that they are the zupans for crime in Achrida."

"Are they affiliated with the Enchelei and Dassaretae?"

Both shook their heads.

"No, they're completely different," Piri muttered. "It doesn't matter to them what your tribal background might be, only if you can fill their coffers stealing or fighting or screwing."

"And they're organized."

"Oh my, yes, more so than the two families."

By the Hanged God, another level of strife in this damned city.

"Do they resolve their conflicts in as civilized a manner as you do? Bouts in the castle?"

"Not hardly." Piri grinned. "There's always a body or two appearing here or there that we find out gambled too much or liked to beat whores or whatever. Fortunately, dealing with those is the job of the quaesitors, not us."

"And you would say that it would take a large amount of money for one of the kraljevics to actually commit this crime?"

"The kraljevics don't want to get the zupans too upset at them. If both zupans agree the krals are overly involved, they might join forces and purge them completely. It's happened before. Of course, the krals spring right back up after being knocked down. A new kraljevic steps up and takes the reins afterwards. Nothing really changes, so it's usually a waste of time, blood, and money, and the zupans really don't want to face the cost. But it has happened, and each time the kraljevics are all killed. Their own lives are held in surety to keep them from overstepping too much."

Another fine line to walk. What a strange place.

"How would I find out if the attackers are kral?" They looked at each other. "Do they wear an identifying symbol?"

Svetislav shook his head emphatically.

"They try to stay hidden," added Piri.

"Do they meet in particular neighborhoods or taverns?"

They looked at each other uneasily.

"Yesss..." Piri paused before admitting, "The neighborhoods outside the wall are rife with them."

"And the Stracara," added Svetislav.

"But really, they're everywhere. Frankly, there's nothing preventing either of us having some loyalty to the kraljevics."

Svetislav grunted in agreement.

"So they could be anyone?" They nodded. "How would I meet this Katarina or Gibroz?"

They were both taken aback at that. I do not think I ever saw Piri more uneasy than at that moment.

"Sevener..." She paused again. "One just doesn't visit them. They don't host high teas."

I accepted that, but my mind was trying to work through the knot. However, I needed to sleep, and I could not think clearly enough to make any more headway.

I wished them all a good evening and went upstairs, hoping for nightmares, nice straightforward nightmares, to take me from this strange place.

Chapter 14
Morning, 11 Gersmoanne, 1712 MG

I had enjoyed the rhythm of practicing every other day at the barracks, but two things prevented me on that day. First, if Zupan Pal wanted to speak to me, I wanted to be properly prepared. That included both dressing properly and scouting out the lay of the land. Piri and Svetislav could both assure me that, as an outlander, the rivals would ignore me, but who knew what could change?

Ragnar brought me breakfast and some news.

"Well, you'll be wantin' to know that the maelstrom is startin' for those of Naum. Two of them are supposed to have the killin' of each other in one of the south quarters."

The news had somewhat calmed his normally cheerful mania.

"You wouldn't be thinkin' they were all that much with blades, and I'm supposin' that's to be proved, but slashin' and slashin' can be effective. 'Specially if one be ignorin' the slashin' of the other fella. I'm to be thinkin' this can't be endin' well." He sighed.

Melia cared not as we both petted her fat belly, but for me this promised to be a tense, busy day. Before any of my other errands, I wanted to take a look at the place where the two Naumites had killed each other. Also, the theft of my new turnshoes irritated me. I decided to order a second pair while I walked around the city.

I put on the freshly cleaned, white-trimmed green herringbone tunic and blue pants. My adornments included my sword, of course, but also my rings and pendant. I looked sharp. Melia meowed her approval as I left. Karah was less impressed.

I headed south from the Square of Legends, following Ragnar's directions. The street where the two priests killed each other sat just west of their temple. Under the temple dome's morning shadow, the street sat eerily quiet. Most of the vendors here sold foodstuffs. Permanent shops in the buildings alternated with street vendors who sold perishable items like meat and vegetables. I guessed most of the temple's food was purchased here.

No one purchased food at that moment, though. The murders had clearly upset the normal pace. The street kiosks remained, but their vendors huddled within doorways, talking quietly. Few potential customers could be seen.

I made my way down the street, asking what had happened. At first no one would speak to me of anything other than food. Then I changed my approach and began the conversations differently.

"I am from the Seven Kingdoms. I don't understand what happened here, can you tell me?"

Eventually, by emphasizing my outsider background, I convinced a one-eyed seller of garlic and spices to actually talk to me. He had an accent roughened by years of bad weather.

"Well, now, it was somethin', I'll tell you," he rasped. "I lost my eye as a Lakewarden, you see, and there weren't my first time seein' the blades flashin', you know? So, it was funny, you see, the way they had no clue what they were doin'. But still, usin' the pointy end on the other guy ain't that hard to figure out, you know?"

I did know.

"And they were after screamin' about somethin' to do with letters while they were stickin' knives in each other." He laughed heartily.

Now that the ice had been broken, the other man in that doorway decided to speak. "I watched them both come down the road. The Naumites buy most of the rye that I sell, so I was calculating what I would charge. They saw each other in the road and immediately got to arguing. Then one said something and the other went crazy. I didn't even know they carried knives, really."

"Could you hear what they were saying?"

"Not really, just some arguing about where something was or how something was. The Naumites have always been confusing."

"And they were just looking for a spark?"

"Pretty much."

"What happened then?"

"Not much for a bit, but soon two separate groups of Naumites came down from their temple. Although, they were careful to be nice in what they were saying to each other, they glared at each other while picking up the bodies.

"Aye, it was to be touch and go, you know," rasped the ex-sailor. "I was planning to head in here with Mikjal and bar the door."

"Did you recognize any of the priests?"

They shook their heads.

"But they went back without fighting again?"

"Taking two roads." Mikjal laughed.

"And, you see, they'll both be buying separate." The one-eyed man chuckled smugly. "Yeah, they'll be buying less each, but, you know, they'll buy more total."

I hacked off a small bit of silver to give them. They looked at each other and immediately shook their heads.

"Too much, my lord," said Mikjal.

I held it out again. They sighed and gestured that I should wait.

The one-eyed merchant gave me a long string of garlic buds, and Mikjal came back from his shop and handed me a small wrapped, ceramic jug.

"Ajvar," he said. "Something I'll bet they don't have in the Seven Kingdoms."

They cut the small strip of silver in half and happily nodded their thanks.

I decided the garlic would help me with Zoe more than with Pal, so I went straight back to the Faerie. She gladly took the garlic and promised I would get to try the ajvar.

I then returned to the cobbler and asked for another pair of turnshoes. He initially looked at me strangely, but soon sympathetically, when he heard what had happened.

"I'll be charging you a mite less, good sir," he said. "Ain't right, especially since you're a visitor here."

I thanked and paid him. He still had my pattern, so I was able to leave quickly.

Then I walked along the Wall Road that looped around the north side of the city, ending at a cliff overlooking the lake. Here, a smaller gate led to the High Road. It separated the shopkeepers and artisans that worked along the wall from the rich lakeside neighborhoods where the gentry lived.

The Gropa manor house sat at the peak of the northern hill on High Road, overlooking the lake. I went through the neighborhood and found the house described to me by Svetislav. The size and opulence of the Gropa mansion and the neighboring houses put Cynric's meadhall to shame. They were all walled and fenced, but not necessarily fortresses. Not necessarily.

I followed the road down the hill. The houses got smaller and less spectacular as I got closer to the docks. The noise, however, got progressively louder.

Ragnar had told me the slums near the docks were called the Stracara and were rowdy and violent, especially at night. This afternoon dozens of boats jockeyed for the best docking spots. Cheerful, and not-so-cheerful insults, threats, and comments about parentage filled the air. Dockmasters yelled instructions above the din that some people occasionally heeded. Fish spilled from nets to crates. Porters and cranes lifted a seemingly infinite variety of boxes off of ship after ship.

I enjoyed the profane yet surprisingly delicate dance as the sun stepped across the sky.

Chapter 15
Late Afternoon, 11 Gersmoanne, 1712 MG

Soon the time came to head back up the hill to visit Pal. When I approached the gate to the Gropa manor a small woman with black hair, solid black eyes, and a plain brown tunic slid out of a hidden niche. I could only see two knives, but the way she moved hinted at a murderous hidden variety of others.

"Zupan Pal invited me to dinner."

She looked at me quietly. "Yes?"

"My name is Edward. Svetislav arranged the invitation."

She murmured something quietly and made a small, swift gesture. She looked at me for a long, intense moment, and I could almost feel her picking through my mind, looking for untruth.

Apparently satisfied, she turned and led me through the niche and the small entry gate. As we entered the manor grounds, a man of sharp precision greeted me. The slight breeze off the lake barely ruffled his perfectly kept, dark brown hair. He wore an immaculate short black tunic and gray pants. He bowed to me with what was undoubtedly the exact angle befitting my station.

"Good sir, may I escort you to the zupan?"

I followed him into the house. The marble in the entryway was a type I had never seen before, a swirling combination of mesmerizing green and white. Two ornately-carved, slender columns flanked the center walkway before leading to a surprisingly plain door. I suspected its exterior hid a virtually impregnable core.

Light filled the large room we entered. Ahead, a series of tall and amazingly clear glass windows funneled the blue reflection of the lake. Behind me, smaller windows set high in the wall let the setting sun grant the remnants of her golden wealth for that day. I had thought the windows in the Readers' Library were amazing, but these held barely any shimmer of imperfection.

A walkway circled the central area, which sat two steps below. Doors led to my right and left from this walkway, and on each side servants waited patiently. Reclining couches and chairs filled the lower area, arranged primarily to show off the lake vista. Towards the end, closest to the window, a group of people rose as my escort led me to them.

Average is not normally described as striking, but no better description fitted Pal Gropa. Not tall. Not short. Streaks of gray emphasized the plain brown of his average-length hair and beard. He wore a long, saffron-dyed tunic of a common style, unobtrusively adorned with two vertical stripes of blue-and-white trim. His eyes, however, made him striking. They held the calm understanding of his power, reach, and responsibility. He clearly knew he did not need to look extraordinary in this, his realm.

At his side stood one of the most beautiful women I would see in my entire life. She gracefully introduced herself as Vesela. Her features were so similar to the zupan's that she had no need to tell me she was Pal's daughter. Her features held all of the vibrancy that might have once existed in Pal's face, as if he had intentionally bequeathed it to her. The hair was the same color, but on her it glowed softly. Her face showed the soft welcome of a warm harbor, while her father's face displayed the rough experience of the black hills I had grown up roaming. She, too, wore a long tunic, hers a warm red embellished with pearls and extensive embroidery. The power in her eyes tugged at my heart and soul.

Next to her another woman rose who in many ways was the polar opposite of Vesela. Jeremena Gropa reminded me of an ealdmodor before her hearth. She had tried to pull her gray hair back in a neat bun, but strands escaped in several directions. Her plain clothing had been skillfully patched in several places. I almost expected her to bring out something baked, smelling of apples and nutmeg, until I saw her eyes. They looked at me, calculating my worth to the nearest penny.

A large bear of a man stood in the middle. His beard and hair might have been white, but he still moved with a ponderous power that bespoke years in armor. At some point someone had broken his nose and, at another, had given him a long scar that ran up the back of his right wrist and into his sleeve. He clearly preferred coats of scaled steel to tunics of linen. His left hand rested on a long, curved dagger that hung across his body. He may not have grown up with the dagger as I had with my saex, but I recognized his need to have steel about him. He glared at me suspiciously as Pal introduced him as Andrija. I suspected he looked at everyone suspiciously. He reminded me of Einarr, who had served my father loyally for longer than I had been alive.

Another bear of a man lounged next to Andrija, but where Andrija was the bear of fury and rage, this man was the seated bear with a fish in his mouth and a honeycomb in each paw. He was the kind of bear that would only attack if he had eaten old apples that fermented in his stomach. Otherwise, he would merely look for tastier and easier prey. He casually introduced himself as Zacharia. His tunic was barely tinted yellow, as though the dyer had introduced it to saffron but separated them before they could get to know each other well. It was not linen, wool, or silk, so I guessed it was cotton, but I did not care enough to investigate more thoroughly. There was an aura of danger about him that led me to think he sought out those fermented apples whenever he could.

Near to him sat a slim young lady. I would have said girl, since she probably had the same number of years as Eirik, but she held herself with a stern propriety that suggested she had never really had a childhood. She softly introduced herself as Agata Kyranna. While she was the quietest of the group, she watched everything carefully. She desperately wanted to appear shy, but even in her youth she had the strength of will to hold my eyes. I wondered if the rest of the family feared her.

Finally, there was Davorin. I understood, almost immediately, two things about him. One, he wished to keep our previous meeting secret, so he greeted me with no recognition in his eyes. Two, everyone else shared my impression of him. They each felt the same wrongness about him that I did. They had showed their feelings by moving his chair slightly away from the rest of the council. Fortunately, their feelings meant they all expected me to stumble in my greeting, so they took no notice when I did so as I met him. I later realized he used his isolation from the other adults on the council to his benefit. Because they wanted to ignore him, many of his actions went unobserved, even in Achrida. He smugly counted that isolation amongst his assets.

When the introductions were completed Pal gestured at a cushioned chair and said, "Welcome to the house of Gropa. Please take your ease. Svet says you enjoy Ragnar's ale—would you like that or wine or something lighter?"

"I've heard of the wines of the south but haven't sampled them much. Wine would be wonderful."

"Excellent. Sanjin, please bring us all some of that protropos that we've been contemplating."

My escort bowed and left. We sat down.

"Svet has said you wished to meet us. I realize you asked only to speak to me, but if you can help with the schism, I thought it important that all of the Gropa Council hear your words."

I nodded as Sanjin returned with our wineglasses. I took a sip. It was sweeter than I expected, and the taste filled my mouth with an almost pleasant burn. After the first sip, the flavor expanded to fill the rest of my senses.

"Exactly what we hoped for," sighed Pal happily. "Don't you think, my dear?"

Vesela nodded demurely. None of the others seemed to care much except Davorin, who smirked when his appreciation twisted both Pal's and Vesela's mouths ever so slightly.

"So what did you wish to speak of?" Pal added after a moment.

"As I'm sure you know, there was a kidnapping at the Frank Faerie several days ago." They nodded. "Ragnar has asked me to look into it. Where we come from, the host is honor-bound to care for the well-being of his guests, and he has asked me to reclaim that honor."

They looked at each other, and the low level of tension I sensed when I first bowed to them spiked.

"We did not realize his honor was involved," said Pal. "I would like to personally assure you, and him, that the Enchelei and this council never requested, authorized, paid for, or in any way was involved in that kidnapping."

I glanced at Davorin. "Neither Ragnar nor I believe that you were."

They inclined their heads again, and the tension eased somewhat.

"However, a connection to the Enchelei definitely exists. The clothing of the targets suggests at least one was a priest of Naum, and it is beyond belief that the schism that started in that church the day after the kidnapping was unrelated. I know that Naum was Enchelei and that this schism is something that is hurting you."

"And you think if you find out who ordered the kidnapping you might be able to help us?"

"Yes. I don't know the philosophical reasons why the Naumites are at each other's throats, but knowing who did what and why might alleviate the schism. Given that they have already taken each other's lives, it cannot get much worse."

Pal sighed. "Yes, you are correct."

"Hecatontarch Piriska of the Pathfinders has assured me that the Vukasin did not order this kidnapping."

"No, neither of us would strike at the other in that way," said Pal.

"We are too afraid of the potential consequences," added Vesela primly.

"We can plan for those consequences," rumbled Andrija.

"We have been rivals for centuries because we are so closely matched," Pal added with a look at Vesela and Andrija. "That balance has been our curse and our blessing. Vukasin and I or our heirs could kill each other, but Enchelei and Dassaretae would remain. Yet could either family pay the cost?"

Vesela had been staring out the window again but turned back. Andrija snorted and emptied his wine glass. One of the servants brought him rakija.

"No, Vukasin did not order this, though he is seeking any opportunity that this creates," she snapped.

Jeremena spoke up. "Piri, for example, knows that if we use our companies to keep the violence from spreading, her Pathfinders and the other Dassaretae companies will gain a greater hold on the caravan trade. We will not be able to prevent this, and it is but one opportunity they would exploit. Whoever has done this has indeed harmed our family and we shall not forget." From the looks on their faces, everyone agreed.

"So, we want the same thing," I said.

"To a point," replied Pal.

"Then, to that point, we could help each other."

They all leaned back and sipped their wine. Sanjin, with Ragnar's sense of timing, arrived to refill our glasses.

"How can a Northern barbarian help us?" rumbled the angry old bear.

"Perhaps if we listen we'll find out, old man." The fat young bear smirked.

Pal glared at both for a moment before turning back to me. "Excuse them—though the question itself is pertinent."

"I am struggling to understand the exact reasons behind the kidnapping. I think they wanted to take something, some treasure, from the woman who led the missing people. I don't think the kidnappers found it, though, because they came that night to search again. Then, later, they attacked me in the street and stole my walking bag. If they sought the woman herself, why continue to attack after taking her? However, nothing that the woman had seems valuable enough. I thought there would be something in a warded pouch she had, but all that was in it was the Naumite holy book, her own journal, and a writing kit. The only other items I found were her clothing, the clothing of her servants, and their tack."

Andrija blinked at me and hissed. "You have nothing else?"

"No."

They sighed. Andrija and Jeremena clearly didn't believe me. I never did figure out what Agata was thinking.

"We had hoped you would come here with it," Vesela added.

"With what?"

"You were right," said Pal, "there is something else she should have had. Naum, before teaching the Berzeti, was the leader of an expedition to the Kreisens. The Empire was expanding, and he was an ambassador. One of the kreisarchs imprisoned him. He spent his time in a cell writing and forming his philosophies. This text became the basis for the Pismenech." He looked at me questioningly.

"The Readers told me that it is the holy text of the Naumites."

"Yes, and that text, now called *The Notes of Naum in His Captivity*, was later edited and adapted into the Pismenech. You can see why the Naumites hold it dear. The young priestess, Marija, was headed to that kreisen to recreate that moment. She was a powerful zokurios who had some talent with Lore magic as well. She hoped that by being in that spot with that item she could capture tendrils of Naum's thoughts."

"Ambitious."

"Yes," he confirmed

"But if it is so dear, why did they send it with a young priestess and no escort?"

"It was decided by the archimandrite that it would be wiser to keep the mission quiet."

"Gregor?"

"Yes. Kristijan had not claimed that title yet. One of the reasons he cites for his claim is the lack of respect shown by Gregor to perhaps their greatest relic."

"Which do you support?"

"Gregor, I suppose. He is the established archimandrite"—he smiled—"and as an established leader in my own right, I think it unwise to encourage such revolts. But I find Kristijan's preference for tradition soothing. In any case, it has always been the policy of zupans to avoid taking sides in religious disputes. Both factions are favored by some of my people, and I do not wish to alienate anyone."

"So you are powerless?"

"No, not powerless, but a mediator."

Vesela stared out the window. Mediation did not seem her preference.

"So where is this text?"

They all sighed.

"Gregor is convinced Kristijan stole it to give his archimandracy legitimacy. Kristijan is convinced that Gregor is hiding it for the same reason," said Vesela.

"Those who doubt both stories think you have it," added Pal. "Many have been pushing for harsher means to take it from you. There are some in this house who would have me take you now and use whatever means I need to force the location out of you."

Andrija's glare clearly suggested that was his preference.

"But now that you see I'm such a charming soul, you can't bear the thought anymore?"

"You jest, but I can see the truth in your eyes. Besides, I invited you to dinner, and our honor demands your safe passage. Those who suggested taking you deem you a Northern barbarian bereft of true honor and thus unworthy of that respect. Neither Vesela nor I agrees with that."

"Indeed, Father, and I do find him charming." Vesela's sudden smile beamed like a sunny day on the river.

Pal sighed.

"Could Kristijan have ordered this?" I asked.

Pal sighed again. "I would not think he could have ordered a kidnapping, though of course, he was quick to make his claim after it happened."

"So how do we find this text?" I asked.

"We believe the text did make it to Achrida. I have assigned some of my more talented servants to determine this for a fact. However, even mages need time, and whoever is behind this has mages of their own hindering the process."

"The ones who have attacked the Faerie were skilled and experienced."

He nodded.

"Who could that be? You've already excluded the Dassaretae. The Panteleimonites have told me they're watching with some enjoyment, but no involvement. Who else is there?"

"A good question."

"The kraljevics?"

There was a pause as all of the Gropas sat back for a moment. Except Agata, who had a curious look in her eyes.

"It is out of character for them to engage in open warfare with koryfoi," said Pal finally. "They'll take our money and laugh at our needs, but they know we could destroy them."

"Koryfoi?"

"Yes, their word for those who are not kral."

"Could they have been hired to do so?"

Zacharia spoke up, "They might for money."

"You should ask them."

They looked at each other and shared a smile. Davorin laughed too loudly and too much.

"No, Sevener," Vesela said, "you should. They might actually tell you something. Of course, they might just decide to kill you instead, but dealing with the kraljevics has always been risky."

"Nothing too hazardous for you, I'm sure," added Zacharia slyly.

I looked at their smirks. "How do I reach them?"

Jeremena said, "Gibroz is usually at one of his gambling dens, primarily his main one in the Stracara."

Zacharia added, "Katarina is hard to find. She's probably more often at Tresinova's Treasures, a large brothel outside the walls." He paused. "But she likes to roam, and she's really good at disguising herself." He giggled. "She could be here, in this room, for all I know."

They all looked at Zacharia a bit strangely but turned quickly back to me.

"You should tell Gibroz that I would think it a small favor if he would talk to you," said Pal. "We understand favors, and he and I have a bit of history."

I nodded.

Sanjin reappeared. "Dinner is ready, milord."

"Excellent. Shall we?"

Vesela offered me her hand and let me lead her into a sparkling room paneled in sheets of malachite trimmed with citrine. A green-and-gold woven table runner covered with steaming dishes ran along a stunningly beautiful table. Different woods laid in a key pattern and polished to a mirror sheen formed a work of art around which we gathered.

"Trout from the lake is quite a delicacy, and our cook has grown up preparing it," she said pressing her body closely next to mine as we walked. "We also have a wine that we have developed expressly to pair with the trout. Dinner should be exquisite."

Dinner was, indeed, wonderful, but also odd. The Gropa Council clearly knew too much about each other. Davorin especially took great pleasure in subtle comments that meant nothing to me, but elicited, at best, a halting laugh, and more often a flash of temper from his target.

Only two of the Gropas seemed to view me in any straightforward way. Andrija gauged my fighting skills, preparing to kill me should he get the chance. Vesela spent the meal flirting with me. I was not sure who was more dangerous.

Vesela's advances prompted nothing but an indulgent lack of concern from Pal, some flashing, steel-tipped looks from Zacharia, and hints of past improprieties from Davorin. Jeremena and Agata remained quiet throughout the meal, though they seemed to be calculating angles.

Afterwards, we all carried the required glass of rakija while we socialized in groups of two and three. I noted that each of the family members managed to separate me for a private conversation at least at once during the evening.

Andrija seemed to want me to know my place, which he did by grasping my shoulder firmly and painfully as he pontificated about axe-fighting techniques. Agata simply talked to me with a lack of agenda that was chilling in its absence. Pal appeared almost complacent, which seemed odd, given everything that had happened.

But each included me in their plotting, spreading their wings and hovering like falcons looking at a recently fed mouse. My only hope was that each would guard against the others swooping in for a meal and, in their distraction, I could slide out of reach of their claws.

Vesela continued her campaign, drawing me near the windows, and let the romance of gleaming stars on the lake give her a reason to insinuate herself along my body. Fortunately, I had no desire to actually breathe.

Davorin eventually saved me with his pointed humor. "Are you going to undress him here, cousin? Or will you at least wait until later? Are we going to have to replace some of these couches as when the new cotton factor was here?"

Unperturbed, she turned to him. "He's too uptight for couches. I was going to bring him back to my bed. Which I may yet do." I nearly melted into the floor after the look she gave me.

"Better lock your door, though. Not all of your cousins restrict their love to the kind proper for families." Zacharia's glower lightened as she walked away, chuckling.

Davorin took his turn. "My sweet, innocent cousin. Smart enough in her own way, I suppose…"

I simply stared at him.

"You'll be off to Gibroz's den, I presume."

"Yes."

"In that case, don't forget to visit Katarina as well. She'll be insulted if you don't, I've no doubt." He laughed as Zacharia approached and then whispered, "Mention Pal's name to Gibroz. Pal will back any favor you promise if it ends the childish spat of stupid priests. And if that's your best tunic, you should really visit Ruzica first."

Zacharia brought with him a bottle of rakija, insisted I toast with all of them, and refilled my glass after we were done. Apparently, this was some sort of ceremony that concluded all Achridan dinners, since I was the only one to blink at rakija's harsh burn. Even Agata smiled slightly at my coughing.

Once the toast had ended, Zacharia turned to me. "My zupan seeks an end to this conflict. I am his eyes and ears. He paused for effect. "I know nearly everything that goes on in this city." He flicked his eyes at Vesela. "I might be very useful to you in your investigation," he added meaningfully.

Finally, Jeremena's turn arrived. "You've sworn an oath to Ragnar?"

I nodded.

"I admire a man who can keep his oaths. I especially admire a man who can keep his oaths without hindering the affairs of others." Her implacable lack of humanity intimidated me too much for me to actually ask about her affairs.

Once each of the family had had their chance to speak with me, they allowed me to make my escape. Sanjin stood by the door and bowed politely as I left.

Chapter 16
Late Evening, 11 Gersmoanne, 1712 MG

Though the sun had set, the night remained fairly young, so I decided to swing by Gibroz's gaming parlor on the way home. The rakija toast and the wine with the meal combined to make my head swirl a bit. I strolled slowly down the hill, letting the cold lake air clear my head.

Pal had given me directions to follow. I turned left at the main avenue and walked east to the square by the fish market; up Samiel's Way and followed Metodi Mean until it ended at three large houses. The house on the left, the one with no lights, was Gibroz's. I knocked on the door with the hard-soft-soft-hard-hard pattern Jeremena had emphasized would be in my best interests to perform correctly.

A tall man with a face ravaged by fire or disease opened the door and looked down at me. He stepped back and allowed me into the foyer, a tiny oppressive room with the same feeling and function as a castle gatehouse. I looked up, but it did not seem like there were any murder holes in the ceiling. At least, none that I could see.

"Sir?" he said in a harsh voice.

"I'm here to see Gibroz. My name is Edward. Zupan Pal said he would count it a small favor if Gibroz would take the time to speak with me."

He responded by opening the inner door and leading me into a sitting room. He gestured at chairs scattered around the room. I sat and waited until he returned.

"Come."

I followed him up two flights of stairs to another large room at the end of which was a door he opened.

He gestured me in. "Edward, zur."

Gibroz sat in a fairly plain room. A triptych I did not recognize hung on one wall. It served as the only decoration.

Three large men and an equally large woman sat at a table, playing some sort of game while drinking rakija. Each had a weapon easily accessible. My sword and saex did not seem to daunt them. One of them stared at me like he owed me something bloody and painful, though I had never seen him before.

A large desk dominated the far end of the room. Leaning on the desk was a slim woman with very short black hair. I could not determine what kind of magic she knew, but clearly she had some talent.

The man behind the desk controlled the energy of the room. He had a face shaped by the same gods that had carved Achrida's mountains. The forest of his eyebrows and beard were a rich deep brown and obscured his thoughts.

He rumbled, "So Pal is willing to owe me a favor to speak with you. He is not fuckin' known for giving favors to me. Why the fuck would he?"

"I am in a position to help him."

"A little shit like you?"

"Ragnar of the Frank Faerie has asked me to discover who dishonored him by taking his guests. Pal and I both feel that this kidnapping is connected to the Naumite schism. If we can find out who was behind the kidnapping, he is hoping we can alleviate the schism."

"And you fuckin' accuse me."

"I think it possible. I do not think that either Dassaretae or Panteleimonites did this. They are the two most obvious culprits. It hurts the Enchelei, so I can't see any reason why Pal would do this. I think Kristijan could have ordered it, but the people who did the kidnapping were professionals. I doubt the Naumites have easy access to professional thugs, but I think he might have contracted with you to provide them. You could also see profit in the kidnapping that I cannot. So yes, I do think that you might be involved."

He rose and looked out the window to the lake that carried the reflection of the moon like an arrow's flight. "And why the fuck should I speak if I was? If I can get blades like you fuckin' think I can, why wouldn't I just have you fuckin' aced? You're just an outsider."

"Well, if you kill me, Ragnar will feel obligated to do something. So you'll have to kill him, and probably his family. Yeah, we're outsiders, but I know both Enchelei and Dassaretae like his ale. They might not be pleased. I know you don't want too much attention from the zupans, even if Pal now owes you this small favor. So, unless I really aggravate you, you get nothing by killing me. You might not tell me anything, but you won't put a blade in me. At least not now."

He turned around with a stony smile. "Don't shit yourself that I won't the moment I make a fuckin' profit."

I felt a sudden, hot rush of anger. Good thing I wasn't one of Ragnar's berserker kin. My left hand caressed the hilt of my saex nonetheless.

He continued. "I don't often make a fuckin' profit talking, either. Whatever the fuck I may or may not be involved in. Why should I fuckin' talk to you?"

"There will likely be more profit talking to me than not. I'm not stopping until I get to the bottom of this. Pal says you understand favors. I owe Ragnar."

I figured saying that was easier than explaining what *comitatus* really meant.

"Also, Pal sent me here to learn what I could. I'm sure you can get some value from him. You'll have to kill me to stop me. Yeah, I know you can do that, but as I said, I'll be expensive. How much are you willing to spend?"

Nearly two feet of water steel that had shaped my hand since it had been placed there by my father when I was a bairn was singing to me from the sheath at my back. I consciously pulled my left hand away and crossed my arms over my chest.

He looked at me.

"I can spend enough, if it comes to that." He paused. "But I got no fuckin' reason to fuckin' talk or to fuckin' kill you. You don't fuckin' matter. Fuck off."

I looked at him. There was nothing more to gain, so I fucked off.

Chapter 17
Midnight, 11 Gersmoanne, 1712 MG

My anger at Gibroz and the mugging enhanced my senses as I walked home in the dark. The occasional flicker of a fire or candle from inside a building provided the only light. The moon had already set. No shadows moved in the darkness, but as I started up Medusa's Way I knew something stirred out there.

My anger disappeared the moment I sensed something wrong.

I had never felt comfortable walking in the middle of the road in Achrida, and as things got more confusing in this strange place I tended to stay to the left side of the road. When I felt that something, that something in the night, I slid even farther to the left. I did not really change my stride, nor did I put my hand on my sword and saex, but I poised myself to draw them.

My hands held my weapons almost before I realized I had seen the movement of three shadows slightly darker than the night.

One came from behind me. I felt him more than saw him. I jumped backwards, slashing where I hoped his knife arm would be. I felt my sword connect, heard a grunt of pain and the clatter of metal on cobblestones. I took two more steps past his shadow, pivoting around my sword hand. A second thrust and the tug of suction as I pulled my blade back told me I had, at the very least, taken the fight out of him.

I took another step back to put his body between me and the other two. I also took the time to sheathe my saex, slip out of my cloak, grab the cloak pin in my left hand, and flip it around my left arm to give me a sort of shield. In the darkness, having that slight protection seemed wiser than another blind attack.

I was again lucky when one of my opponents stumbled over the body. I guessed it was the left attacker, so I took several quick steps that way, slashing down as I thought I strode by him. I felt an impact, but not a solid one. I heard a number of small items clattering to the cobblestones.

Now I thought I had a clear path to the Faerie, so I took off at a run.

While I had put one of them down and maybe hurt another, at least one attacker remained, and we still fought at the place of their choosing. My success so far had been as much from Frey's fortune as Woden's skill, so at the very least I wanted to shift the field.

I charged up Medusa's Way until I got to the Fourth Serpent and immediately fell to my knees around the corner. My boots were designed to control a horse and to protect my feet and shins. They did not help me run swiftly, and I doubted I could outrun them all the way.

I stopped none too soon as two figures charged past me in the night. They realized I had stopped just as, sword swinging, I reached one of them. This time I felt a solid thunk and heard a fading grunt. I used the force of my springing assault to pull my blade out of the falling body.

I charged directly into the third one, leading with my covered left arm. I aimed mostly to knock him down, but it turned out I was already too close. Nevertheless, my cloak blocked most of his knife strike and I ignored the scraping along my elbow and upper arm. I punched my hilt into what I hoped was his face. A sharp yell answered me and the pressure along my left arm disappeared. I stabbed blindly and felt my sword slide into flesh, though I knew not if the blow was deadly or not.

If there had only been three attackers, I had defeated them all. However, I had no way to know how many had attacked me, and my heart raced too much for me to listen clearly for footsteps. I reached down and grabbed what I could, finding one of their daggers in the dark. I slid it into my wrapped cloak and started up the Serpent at what eventually became a dead run.

Breathlessly I burst into the Faerie and locked the latch immediately. A quick glance at my left arm showed a great deal of blood soaking into my cloak and dripping on the floor.

Ragnar jumped behind the bar, reaching for his broadsword. Only three regulars were drinking at this late hour, none of whom I remembered well. Nevertheless, they each stood, grabbing whatever weapon they could reach.

Several eternal moments later, after nothing happened other than my blood dripping on the floor, I looked at Ragnar.

"So, how about a pint, then?"

Ragnar laughed a great, comforting laugh. "Aye, that would do us all." He pointed at one of the others. "Cvetijin, pour us some pints."

He strode off into the kitchen and returned a few minutes later with Zoe and Karah in tow, each tugging overdresses into place.

He started one of his running commentaries, but in the aftermath of battle I did not hear anything he said. Zoe clucked at the sight of me and went behind the bar for a leather bag, from which she pulled bandages and poultices that had been prepared earlier. Clearly, mine was not the first blood shed here.

That my blood was not the first did not ease Karah a bit. She sharply told me to sit and stop tracking blood around as she grabbed a bucket and rag from the end of the bar.

"It's never your lot that cleans it up," she sniffed, roughly unwrapping my cloak from my arm and dropping the knife to the floor. Squeamish she was not, squeezing her hand along my wool cloak, pushing most of my blood into the bucket. The blood would stain the wool, but long years of use had stained it already. Then Karah efficiently mopped up my blood.

I felt softer fingers and light wool start cleaning my arm. I had a cut reaching from my elbow up to my shoulder, but fortunately the knife had not gone in too deeply. Nevertheless, as I calmed down my arm started to hurt. I greedily drank the pint Ragnar had shoved into my right hand after I set my sword on the table. He finished a pint of his own and grabbed us each another. Cvetijin had actually lined up several pints on the bar, anticipating our needs.

The other two regulars stood by the door, each with a cudgel in one hand and a mug in the other.

Eirik entered then, saying he had locked the stables. He then grabbed a short sword from behind the bar. I noticed that Eirik was more familiar with that sword than his father's deprecating humor had suggested a few days before. He moved to the back side of the door.

A sharp tug at my arm made me bark in pain, and I looked over to see Zoe already stitching up the wound. She had scattered some sort of powder into the wound, and I watched her efficiently sewing up the cut. I supposed any woman married to someone like Ragnar would have had to deal with cuts before. A few moments later, she held a light cloth poultice to my arm as she wrapped linen around the wound.

Just like my ealdmodor, she chastised me with a raised eyebrow but without saying a word. How did they do that?

I shook my head and realized that Ragnar's monologue had ebbed. Soon he asked me what had happened. I skipped past most of the events of the day, though I did explain the fight. Even Karah approved of my survival, though she snapped harshly at me a few times to make sure I knew she cared.

"This will be what was to be givin' you that nice pretty scar you'll be havin' on your arm?" Ragnar asked picking up the dagger that had fallen to the floor. He did not wait for my nod.

"Well, it won't be tellin' much of a story. She's not bein' a cheap blade, but nothin' like the steel o' your knife. It's to be havin' a leather-bound hilt with a wee bit of a crossguard, and there are to be bein' hundreds and more of the like here."

"No use taking it to the Readers, you think?"

He shook his head. "I'm to be thinkin' you should be keepin' it as a man never was hurtin' because he had more blades bein' around him, and I'm thinkin' Eirik might be havin' a nice scrap of leather and a bit of wood hidden in his stable and be wantin' to make you a proper sheath for her."

Eirik nodded happily as Ragnar handed me the dagger, so I pushed it towards him.

"Now with that bein' taken care of, why don't we be sendin' these lads home and I'll be lockin' up properly? They'll be makin' sure all of me neighbors be knowin' what's to be happenin', and none of them will be bein' too pleased at someone as tryin' to be killin' another around here, even though they be knowin' there's a chance their own zupan or some such be wantin' this to be happenin'."

As he was saying his piece, one of the three regulars peeked out of the door and they slid out quickly.

"And I'll be havin' some words with Basil about strengthenin' these doorwards, but I'm thinkin' that tonight we can be doin' just a bit for that. There be bein' the latch and then the true keystone that I've not been busy mentionin' to many, and we have ourselves these here heavy alder tables that aren't to be likin' to move after we've stuck one of them in front of the door." He had matched deed to words. I had no doubt that he would sleep here in the common room, so I sent Eirik up to my room for my spear and shield.

Zoe began to object, but instead paused at my look and said to Eirik, "Grab one of his tunics as well." She turned to me. "I'll get some bedding for the bench over there."

When Eirik returned, I switched tunics. Zoe sniffed and took my green-and-white one to clean and mend. Thus, with my weapons as bedmates, I slept as best I could in the common room, despite the pain in my arm and Ragnar's bellowing snores.

Chapter 18
Morning, 12 Gersmoanne, 1712 MG

Bright sunlight shining into my eyes woke me up the next morning. The fight and sleeping on the bench combined to make my body ache. I had gotten too used to the luxury of a pallet bed. My arm hurt worse, but a quick peek under the bandage showed that the stitches had not broken. I yawned and creaked upward, feeling older than my da—and he rested in a barrow with golden rings.

Karah angrily swept around the fireplace. Her broom rasped along the stone. She sniffed at me. I did not blame her.

At the bar Ragnar spoke to a man and a woman, both dressed so plainly they almost faded into the woodwork. He saw me sit up and, with an odd grin on his face, waved me over.

As I approached, some of the sleep left my eyes. I took a moment to more closely examine them. Tall and thin, the woman owned a face only a geometer could love. I would learn that she thought with those same exact angles.

The man almost looked like an intricately carved statue, with a still face adorned by a sharply trimmed beard. His movements were just as carven, with never a bit of wasted effort. Faceted blue eyes effortlessly looked through the crevices of my mind with the magic of experience and cynicism.

"I was to be wakin' you soon, Sevener, for we are to be bein' honored with mighty guests. I'll be makin' you known to Tagmatarch Kapric and Kentarch Zvono, who'll be bein' tasked by the city to clean up after crimes." He was almost curt in his dislike for the pair. From their scowls, I saw no reason to doubt Ragnar's opinion.

"So what can you tell me about three bloodstains on Medusa Way?" The woman awaited my answer with a wax tablet and a stylus.

"Who are you?"

"We're quaesitors. We're who the city sends out when murders are committed. What can you tell me about three body-sized bloodstains on Medusa Way?"

Zvono was implacable in her questions. I waited to see if the man would move at all.

"Self-defense is still not bein' murder in the fine city of Achrida, right, Tagmatarch?"

Finally the man moved, swiveling his head slowly to Ragnar, saying, "Correct."

"Well, you've never been lyin' to me, I'll grant you that, Tagmatarch. I'll at least be grantin' you that. You don't be comin' to look into things when I'm to be needin' you, but you've never been lyin' to me. That I've seen yet, at least."

Kapric stared at Ragnar for a long moment before returning his eyes back to me. Zvono asked again, "So what can you tell me about three bloodstains on Medusa Way?"

I took a breath and told Zvono what had happened on the way. I saw no reason to lie, so I did not, but I also saw no need to tell everything that had happened.

"So you were coming up Medusa's Way late and three people attacked you?"

I nodded.

"And you don't know why they attacked you?"

I nodded again.

"But you had your sword with you?"

I nodded again. I had a good rhythm going.

"And you don't think it has anything to do with the three people who accosted you several days ago, in broad daylight, near the Temple of Naum?"

It seemed a shame to break up the rhythm, but I said, "No."

"Where were you coming from?"

"Zupan Pal's."

If that affected her, I didn't see it.

"You weren't coming from Gibroz's?"

"Yes, I stopped there briefly since it was on the way, but I didn't understand any of the games, so I came back to the Faerie."

Zvono repeated all of the questions in a few different ways. I gave the same answers each time. Zoe and Eirik came in and out, completing various tasks. Karah finished sweeping. Ragnar puttered around, straightening things behind the bar, but he always remained within hearing. Kapric never moved, though his eyes caught everything.

Kapric finally concluded the conversation. "You're not planning on leaving the city anytime soon?"

"No, I'll be here for a while. Ragnar has been generous enough to give me a place to stay."

"You'll be telling me anything else you happen to remember?"

I nodded. It had worked before. He responded with his own short, sharp nod and they left. Even the sun and moon would have appreciated how smoothly they moved in tandem.

Ragnar let out a deep breath after they left.

"You don't seem to like them very much."

He sighed. "No, I'm not to be likin' them much. And I might even be admittin' that I'm not to be bein' fair to them. Those two are not to be bein' liars or dishonest or anythin' along them lines, but they're but creatures of the city, and that's not to be bein' somethin' I'm to be approvin' of."

"Creatures of the city?"

"Well, the Emperors have the insistin' of an Imperial government in every city, and that means there's to be bein' one here, but it's a collection of them that are beholdin' to one zupan or another, generally speakin', and that's to be meanin' them who are to be workin' with the city be doin' whatever the zupans are to be wantin'." He snorted. "And that's to be assumin' that they're to be bein' honestly workin' for a zupan."

He wiped the already clean bar a little more and shrugged. "None a' them seem to be wantin' to care about helpin' out with inns that be bein' run by Svellheimer. So whatever justice might be sittin' in Kapric and Zvono's souls is likely bein' trapped by someone who's to be pushin' them into somethin' that's not be bein' right."

"Piri told me the quaesitors are often limited by their superiors from helping outsiders."

Zoe came out of the kitchen with a small woman in a perfectly fitted plain brown wool dress that, despite its fit, needed hemming.

"Mistress Branimira also wishes to speak to you," said Zoe.

"I am Edward." I bowed to her, despite my soreness. "Would you like breakfast? I know I'm hungry."

She shyly looked at me and shook her head. "No, gospodar, I cannot stay long. I must get back to our work. We're of them that helps Mistress Zoe with her linens. I'm a weaver and me husband's a tailor, and we've a shop there on the Medusa, see?" I did. "We were openin' up today and settin' out me man's measurin' table on account the sunlight is better on the road than in the shop, and we noticed some strangers about. They had a great, large horse and wagon. We start movin' out with first light, gospodar," she added, "as do our neighbors. But it's nearly always just us shopkeepers. We never see a big wagon."

I nodded when she paused.

"There were three of them, gospodar, though we weren't really lookin' at them. My Gordan and I were hurryin', as the sooner we're set up the sooner we can start workin' on the orders from the day before, until the new customers arrive usually midmorn, see? But they started throwin' canvas over the back of the wagon as soon as we all started comin' out. And then like a flash they led the wagon down the Medusa. At first, we weren't really to be thinkin' much of it. But when we was settin' up a rack to show my work, we noticed a long red line and stain."

I remembered Kapric and Zvono had referred to bloodstains, not bodies. Someone had removed them before the quaesitors could come.

"And then I saw these, gospodar." She held two coins I did not recognize in her hand. "We were going to be keepin' them"—she paused—"but by then Cvetijin was comin' by with a tale from the night. And he said you'd be right grateful to have the coins and know about the wagon."

I was grateful. I was grateful enough that I gave her three silver dinars to offset the worth of the coins and her time. The shining thanks in her eyes confirmed my guess that this would be an appropriate reward.

"Did you, by chance, mention this to those who were here a few minutes ago?"

She shook her head swiftly and looked down.

"Thank you for telling me. Don't worry, if they need to know, I'll pass it on." I paused for a moment. "And, I think I might need at least one more tunic." Davorin had been right in that at least. "I'll come and talk with your husband when I can."

She bowed and left quickly.

"That was to be well done, Sevener, and they'll be doin' you well on the tunic. Zoe's been bein' pleased with the work they've been doin' for us. Now I'll be gettin' that breakfast for you, and we'll be lookin' at what they were to be givin' you…" his words faded when the kitchen door closed behind him.

I sat down and looked at the coins. I assumed that these had caused the jingling sound I heard after I slashed by one of the attackers. At first glance, I thought one was a simple Achridan dinar, but I quickly noticed some slight differences. The other coin showed the vigor of recent minting, but I did not recognize its source. A script I did not recognize circled crossed spears on one side and a ship on the other.

Ragnar arrived with breakfast for five, as Zoe, Karah, and Eirik joined us. We ate eggs scrambled with onions and bits of Zoe's sausage while Ragnar talked.

He quickly dismissed my curiosity about the first coin. "This is just be bein' minted in some other of the Emperor's mints. I'm not to be rememberin' which, now, but I am to be knowin' it's somethin' we're to be acceptin' easy enough."

He had more interesting things to say about the other coin. "Now you're to be seein' that this coin here is one of the ones that is to be comin' from a tradin' kingdom far to the south, past the great deserts to the southern ocean, whatever it is that they're to be callin' it. They sometimes be bringin' strange spices and art and other bits from the East, around the caravans directlike to the Great City, and they're to be doin' that despite pirates and strange winds on account a' there bein' no taxes on the sea, if you're to be bein' able to make it. And that's not always the case as the bones of a couple of me cousins that are to be lyin' in the sea are to be tellin'." He added, piously, "They were to be tradin' a'course."

"Of course," I said as Zoe rolled her eyes. "So this coin comes from Matara?"

"I'm to be thinkin' so, though I wasn't to be recallin' its name at the first, but yeah that's the kingdom I was to be thinkin' of. Whatever its name, its coins ain't to be bein' seen all that often around here, and this coin is to be lookin' new, so I'm to be thinkin' it's not too long since it was to be bein' brought here, though of course there's no real way to be knowin' exactly when it came even if we was to be bein' Readers."

He shoved some eggs into his mouth. "And I'm to be thinkin' that we can be sure that them as cleaning up weren't from either of the zupans, bein' as they wouldn't be runnin' off as soon as there be bein' people around. Given that more of them along the Medusa and the Serpents are Mrnjavcevic, you can be sure it wasn't to be bein' them, but even so Vukasin wouldn't be likely to be stoppin' Pal from cleanin' up if it's to be needed."

"They do dance around each other, don't they?" I mused. "So we're back to the krals. Last night I was coming back from Gibroz's, and he made it clear that he would be willing to kill me."

"I'm not really to be knowin' him, but neither he nor Katarina are known for not killin', if you're to be takin' my meanin'. There are them as to be sayin' that Katarina likes killin' somewhat for the killin' itself, though I've not met her that I'm knowin', though she's supposed to go around in costume a goodly bit, and never to be recognized unless she's to be wishin'."

"I think I will look her up. Zacharia Gropa mentioned she's often at one of her brothels in particular."

"Yes, but you'll do it later," interjected Zoe.

"I will?"

"Yes, you need to practice. Piri is expecting you."

"She is?"

"Yes. She and I do talk, you know."

I hadn't, but the fact did not surprise me.

"You'll be wantin' to do as she is to be sayin', me boy, for I'm not wantin' to be hearin' about it if you weren't to be doin' what me love is to be tellin' and..." Ragnar rambled on while he gathered the dishes and cleaned the table. Karah returned to her work cleaning the taproom.

Zoe bade me stay while she checked last night's cut. She rebandaged the wound, this time wrapping it tighter so I could practice. A light touch and a smile let me know when she finished, and I went to my room and armed myself. She came out of the kitchen and waved goodbye. I smiled back and wondered if Ragnar had stopped talking during the time I prepared to leave.

As I walked down Medusa Way, I took closer note of the various vendors. I stopped briefly to thank Gordan and Branimira again, which they accepted as shyly as before. I also noticed that many of their neighbors now nodded at me with their own shy smiles. *Three of the best dinars I ever spent,* I thought.

I remained alert, despite wearing my full armor. I doubted anyone would attack me in the streets while I was dressed in steel, but I had made too many assumptions already. Whoever had ordered last night's festivities was likely to continue inviting me to those kinds of parties.

I got to the barracks and received the chaffing I was getting used to. I went to the pell and started my routines. By the time I had completed the first set, my left arm moved without too much pain. By the time I had finished all of the drills, Piri and Desimir had arrived. Desimir had a broad smile on his face.

"Getting better, Sevener," said Piri. "Now take off the armor." The strength of her command voice had me unbuckling straps even before I began to wonder why. Piri continued, "You made it through last night well enough. Three in the dark with blades? There's always going to be a cut. But I told you, Sevener, we're civilized. You can't always use your steel." She turned briefly. "You know Desimir is my senior decarch."

I nodded.

"What you don't know is that he's our best wrestler. Except for me, of course."

I looked at him. He was a couple of inches shorter than I, and he had a lean build much slimmer than mine. He seemed not to care.

"You're going to start practicing with him every day, for the time

132

being. At least until Zoe says you can stop."

"And you're going to tell her how I'm doing?"

"No, Desimir is gonna stay at the Faerie for a while, and each morning you'll work in the back stables where they keep the hay. She'll know when it's time."

"The hay'll be useful," Desimir added happily.

"And, he'll be walking around with you."

"I don't need a bodyguard."

"Hell you don't. Besides, you argue with Zoe. I won't."

Desimir raised his eyebrows, waiting for me to answer Piri. I sighed. Zoe and I would, indeed, have to talk.

After a moment, Piri snorted. "I thought not. Now, let's see how good your wrestling skills are."

We spent the rest of the morning with Desimir throwing me around the training grounds. I had wrestled all my life, and I had thought I was pretty good. At least I had won my share of bouts with my brothers and shield-kin.

Desimir was better. He had a way of taking control of my balance or putting my limbs in awkward and painful positions. He seemed to enjoy pinning my left arm. He never pinned it enough to spring any of the stitches—*and annoy Zoe*—but always enough to remind me that it already hurt.

We fought the first set at full speed so he could convince me that he owned enough skill to teach me. He succeeded.

Next, we stood in a variety of positions and moved from one stance to another. We worked on memorizing which stances nullified other stances, and how to shift. He had as organized a system as I had ever seen.

When we were done, he changed out of his Pathfinder tunic and got his already readied pack as I was putting my armor back on.

We walked back to the Faerie and when we arrived he nodded to Ragnar and went directly up to a room. Ragnar clearly expected his arrival. We cleaned up and met back in the common room for lunch.

Before lunch, though, I spoke with Zoe. At least I tried to. I insisted

I did not need a bodyguard. I know she heard me say the words, but she showed no reaction.

"Might as well just be acceptin' it, laddie. She's got the hardest mind I'm ever to be knowin'. She was to be provin' that when we were to be meetin', as I'd been plannin' to stay in the Emperor's service all of me days, but somehow I'm to be findin' myself here in Achrida bringin' the likes a' you beer, and that's still to be surprisin' to me."

Zoe continued to primly prepare dinner. Ragnar did not obviously gloat when I finally gave up. Not obviously.

Over lunch I discovered the source of Desimir's wrestling skills. He pulled out a book detailing the positions we had worked on in the morning. More interesting were the theories and philosophies underlying the wrestling moves. The diagrams and body positions reminded me of some of the texts Bedarth had shown me. The book fascinated me so much I did not even notice what Zoe served for lunch.

"Piri said you could keep this for a bit," he chuckled.

I nodded my thanks and continued flipping through the book. Desimir leaned back for a while but finally stopped me.

"So what's the plan, besides having a few more pints?"

"I'm under the impression you're not here to drink."

"A man can do more than one thing."

"I need to visit Katarina."

"Yeah, Piri thought you might. We'll have time for a nap then," he said happily and waved his mug at Ragnar for a refill.

"We should go later?"

"Yeah, she keeps track of her ladies, so they say, and the brothels are busier at night. She's supposed to be mostly at her largest one. I figure we'll just go check out what she's offering."

"You do realize I'll be there for information, not a good time."

"Yes. I also realize I'm not going to be sleeping with Piri anytime soon."

I had no answer to Desimir's smirk, so I resumed reading the book. As I read, I asked a few questions while Desimir drank two more pints. Finally, he decided to take a nap. I read for a bit more, but soon recognized Desimir's veteran wisdom. Never pass up an opportunity to sleep before going into a battle. So I went upstairs and napped until early evening.

Chapter 19
Early Evening, 12 Gersmoanne, 1712 MG

When I rolled over the pain from my wound woke me, but it was time to rise anyway. I dressed for the impending trip to Katarina's. I wore a comfortable tunic, dyed with madder and embroidered with a simple yellow line around the collar, cuffs, and hem. Nice enough, but nothing suggesting great wealth. Since I had not yet gotten the new turnshoes, I decided to wear the boots again.

I went down to the taproom to find Desimir already eating at my table.

"Wondered if you'd decided to stay in that bed instead of finding a warmer one."

I let that pass and concentrated on the bowl of stew and plate of cheese bread Karah brought out. A moment later she placed a mug of ale in front of me as she moved around the taproom. It was a busy night. Most of the regulars were there, and Ragnar stood majestically amongst his people.

"So what's your plan at Katarina's?"

"So far, I haven't really made any plans. I was going to do the same with Katarina. I was just going to go ask questions and see what happens."

"How's that working for you?"

"It's gotten me beat up in the street, knifed at night, mocked by Readers, and threatened by kraljevics, so probably not all that well."

"And Katarina is supposed to be the craziest of them all. Thought of any better plans yet?"

"Only other one I've thought of is to eat Zoe's food and drink Ragnar's ale until he denounces me as lazy and dishonorable and kicks me out."

"So we go ask questions."

"And you tag along so neither of us irritates Zoe by dying."

"Definitely that."

Before we finished dinner Eirik bustled in, bursting with pride. He had with him the dagger and its new sheath, along with a small strap to secure the sheath to my leg. The sheathed dagger fit inside my right boot, and I practiced sliding my hand down and drawing it. I found the process trickier than I expected. Desimir's mocking laughter told me I would need to practice.

We finished dinner and prepared ourselves to leave. I had my sword, my saex, and the new knife. Desimir decided to leave his semi-spatha behind.

"The only ones who carry those are in one company or another. You're going to have enough problems getting Katarina to talk to you without her thinking some koryfoi soldier is involved. I'll be fine without it." He grinned.

We wove our way to the largest brothel in Achrida, cutting back and forth under the western walls, through gates, doors, and several closed-air markets where memory cut through the air like a rusty blade. We walked along a street up to a garishly painted building whose large balconies hung over the road, like the breasts of the whores showing their wares over the railings. Well, at least some of them. Others were rail-thin and gaunt, as if each transaction traded life for cash, and all they could lean over the railing was their despair.

"Zoe was right," I murmured to Desimir.

"Yeah, and it's a good thing I'm braver than Alcaeus or I'd be pissed she told me to follow you."

We each took a breath and went inside. Girls sprawled on ugly couches lining the walls of the garish entry room. Though bright red dominated, it seemed like every color of the Rainbow Bridge battled for attention with spears of shafted light, shedding drops of reflected blood soaking into the floor.

A stunning, dark-haired woman greeted us. Lush where needed and slim everywhere else. A perfectly fitting silk dress, saffron-dyed and adorned with small blue crystals, accentuated her body. Her face was perfectly made up to emphasize skin as soft as a mother's love, but her eyes shined as hard as midwinter ice. She frightened even the part of my mind that normally would have hungered for her.

"Good sirs, welcome to Tresinova's Treasures. How may we delight you?"

"We'd like to speak to Katarina."

"We don't have a Katarina working here. What kind of lady would you prefer? We can also provide a girl or boy."

"Zupan Pal told me that this brothel was run by Katarina and that this was the most likely place to find her."

"Zupan Pal did?" I turned to face the speaker, one of a number of slim and fairly short people lounging in comfortable-looking tunics around the room. This one looked at me with wide-set, open eyes which proclaimed honesty. I noticed everyone else had all tensed in preparation to strike.

"Well, actually Zacharia Gropa did," I answered, "but I was told that Pal would count it as a small favor if she would grant us a few moments of her time."

"What care would she have for the favors of a koryfoi?"

"I don't know that she would, but I do know this. If I ruled a domain, I wouldn't let a guard, no matter how skilled with whatever weapons you have, make decisions about whether I got favors or not."

He grinned, stretching his sharp eyes wider. "That may be true, but if you ruled a domain, you'd not want me to just let anyone in, would you?"

I smiled. "So do we pass?"

"I'll let her decide. You may want to see your blood spilled, but I don't." He giggled. "She does like her blood."

He ascended the broad staircase that led up from the large sitting room. You could almost see the fin of a shark in silk clothing cutting the sea as the hostess waited for actual customers. Those in comfortable tunics watched us. I felt safer with the shark.

After a time that seemed longer than it probably was, the guard came back to the top of the stairs and beckoned us up.

"She'll actually see you."

We followed as he led us to the fourth floor. He opened the door to an empty sitting room. Softer, more welcoming colors, mostly deep maroon, adorned this room. Chairs and chaises formed a large circle around a low table. The table held six crystal glasses and a decanter that appeared to have rakija in it

"Wait here. She'll come when she wishes. She said you may help yourself." He pointed at the rakija. "Don't leave the room. I may be headed back downstairs, but there are guards deadlier than I in this house."

We watched him close the door.

"Well, I'll test the rakija," volunteered Desimir. He matched word to deed and sprawled on a chaise.

"I'm not particularly thirsty."

"Too bad, it's delicious. This one's quince."

"Quince?"

"Yeah, rakija's made from a bunch of fruits. I don't know how they do it exactly, I simply try them all."

"What the hell's quince?" I was too tense to be polite.

"It's a bitter fruit, sort of like an apple and a pear, but much tarter than either of them. My dama made the best quince jam." He smiled at the happily remembered flavors.

He was too happy for me, so we waited in silence for a tedious time until a slim woman with wide-set eyes and long blond hair opened the door. She wore a rich garment of pure white with green-and-gold trim around the edges. It looked like the stola Zoe and I had found in the kidnapped woman's bag. She walked in and seated herself on one of the chaises, opposite Desimir.

"Please sit," she commanded.

I did. I looked at her. I paused. Looked again.

"Did it take you that long to change clothes?" I asked.

"Oh, delightful," she giggled. "I love it when they notice." Her giggle seemed all the more frightening because it reminded me of a sweet teenaged sister.

Desimir looked up, confused.

"It's your eyes, Katarina, they are distinctive. Especially when you smile."

"Oh, they are indeed, but nobody ever looks."

Desimir finally caught on and laughed. "Well done, Sevener, I had no idea."

"So now you know one of my secrets. That makes you dangerous." She giggled. "I like danger. Do you?"

My left hand twitched towards my saex. I caught it immediately, but long after she saw the motion and laughed.

"Don't mind danger if you have your steel, eh, boy?" This time her voice sounded caustic and ancient.

"I've had my saex since I was a boy. It helps me hold on to that which is me."

"And you think I want that which is you? You think it's worth anything to me?" A new voice, that of a haggling merchant.

"No, but it's worth something to me."

Another giggle. "And yet you come here knowing I take at least a little from everyone who enters. What will I take from you, I wonder?"

"And what will I get in trade?"

The merchant returned. "What are you asking for? What do you have to offer?"

"What I want is to know if you were involved in the kidnapping at the Frank Faerie last week. And if you were, why?"

The giggling lass returned. "Oh, you're so serious. A mere kidnapping. Not even a murder? So sweet you are. And if I had answers to give, what would I get?"

Before answering, I leaned back and thought for a bit. I somehow knew the answer. I had not minded death since it had eluded me three years ago. I sensed she demanded that as the least of the stakes in her game. But it was risky…

"I was told to tell you that Pal would consider this a small favor, something valuable in this town, but you didn't care about that when you were a mere guard and you don't care about it now that you're a queen on her throne. But, I can give you something you do care about."

Giggle. "Oh, I do so love surprises. What do you have that I could possibly care about?"

"I have nothing myself, but I can still give you that which you crave.

I can give you the anger of the koryfoi. I can give you the risk that they'll deem it in their interests to put the krals down. More importantly, the chance they'll kill the kraljevics and let the krals start over. I can give you both the danger you wish and the danger Gibroz wishes not. Death is your friend, not his."

That might have been the only time Desimir ever looked at me without even a hint of a smile on his face. I would have enjoyed the shocked look, if I had not needed to stare into Katarina's wide eyes of pristine, crystalline, nothingness.

This time she answered with a deep, long, full-throated laugh. A new voice, that of a calm, self-possessed woman. "My, you are the bargainer aren't you?"

"All you need give me are the arrows to the bows that will be aimed at your heart."

I leaned back and waited.

"Gibroz," she said scornfully, caustic again. "People think he's a gambler because he owns gambling parlors. But he rigs his games. He risks nothing. I let him have the gamblers, for I care not. I run the whores because sex is the greatest gamble, the risk of putting your innermost soul out there for someone to mock, because you only get the perfect release if you make that gamble."

She laughed bitterly. "Sex is ugly, in itself, but orgasms are the pearls plucked out of that ugliness. The uglier you allow yourself to be, the brighter the orgasm. Yet to enjoy the brightest orgasms, you must expose your ugliness to all. That is risk. That is gambling. I give people the chance to be as ugly as they want and they love me for it. Gibroz? He gives them nothing but dice that roll certain ways and cards that have certain marks. He's ugly in every way, but terrified to show it and gain his freedom."

Another long laugh. "You have me, Sevener. I will trade some of what I know for the risk you bring to Gibroz and me. But I will still have my little games."

I cocked my eyebrows. That earned another giggle.

"I will ask you a question, Sevener. Do you think you can answer it?"

"I doubt it, but I'll play your game."

Giggle. "Oh, what sport." She clapped her hands gleefully. "So, who was it that was kidnapped at the Frank Faerie on that night?"

I sat there, stunned. The answer bloomed like a spring meadow after a cool sweet rain. "You kidnapped or killed her on the road. She never made it to Achrida. It was you in one of your precious disguises, and two of your employees at the Faerie. They didn't take you, they simply walked in, and you all walked out. No wonder the kidnapping went so smoothly."

Giggle.

"You have the book the Naumites seek."

"No." She laughed at my expression. "Oh, I had it, but what use would I have for it? If I knew someone who would use it in ways that are exquisitely enjoyable to watch, why would I not pass it on?"

"And you sit back and enjoy the schism."

"Isn't it deliciously ugly?" Another giggle. "My, my. Priests and daggers and blood shed on a peaceful daytime street. So horrible to contemplate."

At first I had no answer to that, though as I thought further…

"I think that you still owe me something. Perhaps not right now, but, yes, you are in my debt."

"And what, Sevener, gives you the right to think that?" came the haggler's voice.

"I promised danger to you and Gibroz. That I will give you. But I am also giving you a play, a tragedy to most, but a comedy to you. I am the protagonist, but you can watch from the chorus and add a line here or there. Without me, you don't get the play and you don't get the lines."

"Oh my, where have you been all my life, laddie?" asked the haggler. "You are right. I will help you open the next act."

I waited.

"You are like so many who have traveled through Achrida. You come selling your sword to the Emperor, or if he will not have you, to those who will pay the most." She paused and looked at me closely, eyes picking through my thoughts. I did not think she used magic to look into my mind, yet I knew she prowled effortlessly through them. "But, in your quest to run to a place you can claim as your own, you run from a place that you think will no longer have you."

I glared at her. "How do you know this of me? I have spoken of this to none in years."

She laughed. "I'm not without skills, me boy, not at all. So glare all you will, I still have your measure."

"Apparently." I sighed. "In any case, I already know why I'm here. Tell me what I seek."

"So hasty. You have the rudiments of cunning, but you need patience."

I wondered if she knew I was cursing her soul to the Greediest One while I waited.

She laughed at the look on my face. "Oh, Sevener, I am so glad you have come to my city." She paused thoughtfully. "You came here because you have nowhere else to go. Had things not been so, you would have stayed, comfortable and lazy in your spot, like a dog curled up in front of a fire at the feet of his master."

"Yes, that's probably true."

"But no one in this city feels their spot is warm enough, or their scraps sufficient to remain curled up and rested."

"So?"

"So? When you can ask the right questions, I will throw you some scraps. Ponder this, though. What would you be able to do with the *Notes of Naum*?

I looked at her. The longer I looked, the more she laughed.

"And I will have one more small favor before you leave."

"What?" I asked warily.

The ancient crone spoke. "Let me see the blade that lets you hold on to yourself. Let me see your steel, boy."

Almost mesmerized, I stood up and approached her. I drew my saex and held it mere inches from her graceful neck. She reached up and ran her fingers along the water pattern, not touching the blade physically, but caressing it with her mind. I thought pleasantly about the possibility that this blade might spill her lifeblood. She shuddered in orgasm. I sheathed my blade.

"Oh, yes, Sevener, I hope you learn the right questions, for I burst with the desire to answer them."

Chapter 20
Late Evening, 12 Gersmoanne, 1712 MG

Desimir and I made our way back from Katarina's without incident. It was just as well, after our experience at Tresinova's Treasures. The Faerie beckoned a bright welcome and, despite the late hour, I asked Eirik if bathwater remained.

"Oh, aye, I still have some. We only put out the fire after we wash all of me ma's dishes. It's not been very long since."

Desimir and I gratefully scrubbed Katarina's memory off our limbs. We changed into fresh clothes, and Desimir took what we had worn for Zoe to clean. I grabbed my oil and patches and met Desimir at our table. We spent the rest of the evening mixing our thoughts with Ragnar's ale while cleaning and oiling our blades, their sheaths, their belts and straps, and our boots. Melia helped, despite not liking the smell of my oil very much. Fortunately, she had shed most of the fur she would shed in the spring season, and we could keep her hair off of our blades.

We still felt dirty afterwards, but at least we had sharp steel at hand. Desimir had five blades that he pulled out, cleaned, and then returned to various convenient places.

The Faerie held a crowd, even at that hour, with quite a few faces I had never seen before. I wondered how many of them were spying for a zupans, a kral, or a sect. Many were probably spying for rivals I had no clue existed. At least the ale was cold, and tonight's scop was impressive. She was tall, slim, and beautiful, with wide, cheerful eyes and blond hair that spilled down her back. Her voice soared high and strong across the busy taproom. Her song hammered at my guilt.

"The measure of a man
Stands or falls with what he leaves behind
Gather on the sand
Let your voices carry to the sky
Rise in light
Let the gods look down on this and wonder"

The gods were not the only ones looking and wondering. I liked not what I knew of the measure of myself. What would I leave behind? Would I forever remain only a kinslayer? An oathbreaker? Could I still rise above my past failures?

While I sat listening and wondering, Ragnar came over and joined us. I welcomed the opportunity to tell him what we had discovered.

"So, the lassies and lad were not bein' actually the right ones? Katarina simply was usin' the Faerie to be creatin' havoc for herself?"

"I don't think she was creating havoc just for herself. I think someone asked her to do this, though I think she only accepted because of the chaos and havoc. I don't think she cares that much about money."

"And you're to be thinkin' that whoever fits the answers to them right questions she was to be suggestin' will be the ones who were to be offerin' her the deal? I can't be arguin' that, but how are you goin' to be discoverin' these questions?"

"I have to answer many of the questions floating in my head, Ragnar. Who planned the kidnapping in the first place? Kristijan? Gregor? Who helped them if it was one of them? I doubt Gibroz would risk something like this without being paid. Who else would care about the *Notes*? Who told Katarina about the book, allowing her to steal it before anyone else? Why would she then fake a kidnapping? Who did Katarina give it to? I'd also like to know how many people think I have the book and will come after me to get it."

Desimir nodded as we pondered the questions.

"I think I need to talk to Kristijan directly. I'll play on Pal's favor if I have to, but I bet he knows something." I thought some more. "In fact, I think the entire Gropa family is hiding something. I met Pal, his daughter, and five others. But, I don't know enough about them. I should start with Svet. I think tomorrow I'm going to visit him as well."

I paused and finished my ale. "I also think that, somewhere on the road to the Great City, scavengers have picked apart the bones of the real travelers."

Ragnar nodded, got me another pint, and returned to his other customers.

Desimir toasted me. "I have to say this won't be the most boring assignment the hecatontarch has ever given me."

"I seem to recall hating boredom until we were actually standing shield to shield, looking across a field," I said, looking at him through the memory of a foggy morning pierced by insubstantial steel spearheads.

"Spearpoints across the field do remind us why we like to be bored, don't they?"

We both chuckled ruefully and took a drink.

"Worth the trip, at least," said Desimir, switching back to Katarina.

"Yeah, it was. Most worthwhile thing I've done so far, I think."

"Wanna do it again?" he asked slyly.

"I'd rather have Woden replace his eye with mine."

"So after we practice in the morning, we go visit Svetislav and Kristijan?"

"Yeah."

"No plans after that, unless something changes, right?"

"Nope."

"So we don't have to start early. Wonderful. I feel like this is a night for good ale and bad song."

I laughed. "And worse stories. No better way to forget Katarina."

We clanked our mugs and emptied them.

"Ragnar!" shouted Desimir. "Another pitcher!"

We drank that pitcher. We irritated the scop until we bought her some rakija and she joined in. I seem to recall singing about seas and spears and joyful death. I also seem to recall Eirik staring wide-eyed until Zoe, shaking her head, sent him to bed.

Desimir, between flirtations with the scop, sang songs of the heroism of somebody named Milos, songs that all who stayed late knew and sang with him.

Ragnar added the tale of the Thunder God in an apron dress. I had heard it before, and so might they, but how can you not laugh at that?

I know we went to our beds at some point because I woke up in mine, but I could not tell you when that happened.

Chapter 21
Morning, 13 Gersmoanne, 1712 MG

Neither Desimir nor I awakened early the next morning. Even Ragnar moved slowly. He tried to curse us as we entered the taproom, but we laughed at his feeble wrath.

Of course, we laughed quietly. Very quietly.

Zoe, on the other hand, was extraordinarily cheerful and talkative. Why is it that people who do not drink enjoy mornings so much? Karah, at least, snapped with her normal curt voice. Eirik got a promise from his da that if he asked one more question, Eirik would not go to bed so early next time.

"It's to bein' far past time for you to be learnin' how to drink anyway, me boy," he bellowed softly.

Zoe raised her eyebrows and went merrily back into the kitchen.

Desimir took me to the back of the stables, where we proceeded to beat the previous night's beer out of each other. At least, Desimir did that for me. I can only presume the strain of throwing me across the hayroom helped him too. I certainly could not stop him.

I began to see bits and pieces of the process and theory in his wrestling style. Twice, I think I actually switched to the right stance at the right time. Of course, that made Desimir work harder, meaning I bounced higher in the end.

With our souls and bodies brighter and happier after the practice, we returned to the taproom. Ragnar glared at us while leaning on his bar, drinking a pint.

We headed to the bathhouse and washed. Afterwards, we dressed appropriately to meet an archimandrite, even if he was only a claimant to the title. I wore my freshly repaired and cleaned white-and-green herringbone tunic and dark blue pants.

I strapped the dagger sheath to my bare calf and wrapped the brown winingas with the red thread around it. By making my pants baggier over the top of the winingas, I hid the hilt of the dagger to all but the most observant. I wore the old turnshoes. I could pick up the new ones on the way and just change into them. They would be much harder to steal that way.

I entered the taproom feeling fit and looking good. Melia meowed her appreciation—unless, of course, she just wanted me to pet her. I stroked her back, making her lift her tail, while I waited for Desimir.

The bustle of early lunch was beginning at the Faerie, and Ragnar had regained his presence. Karah was too busy being rude to other customers to be rude to me. Zoe, however, did take the time to wink at me as Desimir came in. I winked back and we left.

We first went to the cobbler's so I could finally get my new turnshoes. I switched them with the ones that had carried me from the Sevens, across the north, and down to this strange city.

The cobbler took a look at my old ones and immediately grabbed them. "Oh, gospodar, these still be havin' some life in them. I'll be fixin' them right up for you."

I let him take them, though I wondered what he could do to fix two years' worth of dirt, mud, blood, shit, and the splinters of a longboat. I worried only a little, though, as the normal pinching and irritation of new shoes bothered me less than sliding on cobblestones with worn leather.

The sun honed its light every day I stayed in Achrida, turning its beams into spearpoints that jabbed at my tunics. I had already been warmer than I wished for a couple of weeks, and spring was merely halfway through. It did not take long for my sweat to soak my undertunic, but, of course, that was one of the reasons for wearing an undertunic in the first place. When we arrived, Desimir and I welcomed the cool of the cavern that formed the entrance to Naum's temple.

The same young woman, in what appeared to be the same script-lined robe, welcomed us, and this time she knew me. She nodded a small greeting, left, and returned with the same superior from my previous visit. Stately, the superior bustled in, covering her agitation with years of proper behavior.

"You have returned, Goodman Edward. We are thankful, for the archimandrite has expressed an interest in speaking with you," she said.

"The archimandrite?" I raised an eyebrow. I could almost feel

Desimir grinning at my back. I thought about asking which archimandrite, but I merely smiled at the thought instead. "I'd be honored," I said.

She led me through several caverns and up a curving stairway cut out of the stone. The stairs opened into a long room, finished with shelves top to bottom. A row of desks on either side of the walkway faced each other. At each desk a scribe or scholar read or scribed whatever weighty matter they studied. They barely gave me a look as we passed through. A low conversation between two men debating some point on a scroll provided the only noise other than the scrape of quill on parchment or paper. In this room, the schism did not seem to exist.

Eventually she led me to a chamber that was both cavern and room. Mosaics decorated the cavern stone. The finished walls held shelves and drawers. To the left, behind a sheer curtain, a slightly raised floor held a large, comfortable-looking bed and a table set with six plates. A large desk and table sat to the right. They were stacked with parchments, papers, codices, and other detritus of knowledge. Bedarth would have died to rummage through their archives. Too bad he already had.

At the far end, an opening overlooked the lake out of the cliff face. A slim figure stood before the opening, silhouetted in the light of the day. He turned as we entered, and gestured to some chairs near the opening.

"I am Archimandrite Kristijan. Welcome to Achrida's Temple of Naum. Would you like something to drink? We have lakewater flavored with pomegranate or some light wines. If you have not had the lakewater yet, I would suggest it, as I find it delicious and cooling on a day such as this."

Desimir and I agreed to the flavored lakewater, and the archimandrite went to his personal area and brought back a large ewer with three mugs. I looked at Desimir, and we both wondered at the lack of a servant, though the archimandrite seemed not to notice or care that he served himself.

I examined him. His long beard had turned gray. Neither slim nor large, he moved with a steady strong step more reminiscent of a smith than a scholar. Ink stains covered his blunt hands. He sat, looking at us with strong eyes that betrayed his weariness and sadness. Bedarth would have loved loudly and contentiously arguing with Kristijan late into the night.

Once we settled, he said, "It seems like we both have things to talk about."

"Yes, it does."

"You came here eight days ago seeking information about an incident that happened at the Frank Faerie. At that time, you asked Cassandra several questions. She was not entirely truthful in her responses. Do not blame her. She obfuscated at my request. At the time, things were so chaotic and confused it seemed prudent to keep some things to ourselves. I have since regretted that decision, and I resolved to rectify that mistake at my first opportunity. Thank you for providing me with that opportunity."

"You're welcome." I continued, "What should she have told me?"

"You asked if there were any priests of Naum whose whereabouts were unknown. She responded in the negative. I have been informed that you were told two days ago by Zupan Pal that a priestess by the name of Marija was missing. He also told you of our missing relic, *The Notes of Naum in His Captivity*. I can confirm the loss of both. Pal has also informed me that you have pledged to Ragnar Longtongue that you would discover who dishonored him. Hence, it seems that our desires have, for the moment at least, merged, and that we might, perhaps, benefit each other."

"Eight days ago I was just some outsider."

"Yes." Nothing in his demeanor held an apology, simply recognition of a mistake.

I thought for a bit. "You do not have the *Notes?*"

"No, we do not."

"And you are also sure that Gregor does not?"

He sipped the cold water before answering. "Not entirely. I would have accepted his word two months ago, but… things have changed. Nevertheless, if he does have it, his ability to feign anxiety is impressive."

"How do you know? I was told it takes three weeks to travel to the Great City, and it has been less than half of that time."

"What do you know of Naum?"

"I know that he was a teacher, a scholar, and a mage. He brought a tribe into the city as a new ally for the Enchelei. Pal told me he was also an ambassador for the Empire to the northern kreisen. That's about it."

"It is enough that you are aware that he was a scholar and a mage. You would say that he was an expert in the magic of lines, the magic of symbols."

"We call them 'leorners' in the Seven Kingdoms.

"Not simply a symkurios, he also could perform Land magic. He developed a technique that allows all of the temples of Naum to share symbols across long distances using the energy inherent in all of the earth. Few know that we do this, and fewer still know how. Gregor and I 'speak' every day."

"Despite the schism?"

"The schism has made the conversations more strident, not less frequent."

"What is the basis of the schism? Is it the loss of the *Notes*?"

"The loss of the *Notes* precipitated the schism, but did not cause it. Gregor and I have philosophical differences in the way we believe Naum should be glorified. These differences have existed for centuries, and periodically the debates become more heated."

"Pal would like you two to resolve your differences."

"We would like to as well. The debates are ongoing and becoming more bitter with each day. Neither of us wishes to see a repeat of the violence that has already happened. Nevertheless, we are both convinced that we are seeking that which Naum would wish. Until we can either convince or force one to accept the other's point of view, the schism will continue. I fear the loss of the *Notes*, while, not a root cause, has exacerbated our displeasure with each other, and our conversations will likely not be productive until the fate of the *Notes* is determined. This is why I hoped to speak with you. I wish to know what you have discovered."

"I have discovered that Marija was sent with the *Notes* to the Kreisens to research Naum's actual writing process. Her original plan was to come through Achrida as secretly as possible. She intended to tell no one, including Ragnar, that she was a priestess of Naum. He thought she was a noblewoman from the Great City."

"Not at all. She's the daughter of a baker who was too poor to care for another child. Yet she is talented."

I sighed. "I think she *was* talented."

"You feel she is deceased?"

Desimir and I looked at each other and nodded. I guessed Kristijan would know soon anyway. "I don't believe she actually made it to Achrida. I believe she was waylaid on the road here and that her body lies somewhere along the way."

"How can that be? She was kidnapped at the Frank Faerie."

"No, she wasn't. It the kraljevic Katarina who was 'kidnapped' in the Faerie."

He sighed, and it was as though his beard got whiter in that instant. His blunt fingers tightened around his mug.

"I had feared that her captors would harm her, of course, but I hoped they would know we would value her life even above the relic, and ransom her. If she was attacked on the way..."

"It would be less likely for her attackers to keep her," I finished.

We sat for a few moments and looked eastward over the lake.

"So someone else knew."

"That she had the *Notes*? Yes. As did you."

He rotated the mug in his hand several times before draining it. "Yes. And before you accuse me, I will plead guilty to arranging for the *Notes* to be recovered and brought back to me where they could be guarded properly."

"You didn't feel they were secure enough?"

"A young priestess with one acolyte and one guard? For our greatest treasure?"

"Why did you not invite her to the temple and offer protection for it?"

"Gregor had commanded her to remain hidden, and she would not have broken her word to him. For good or ill, at the time he was her sworn archimandrite. She would not have willingly given me the *Notes*, nor would she have waited for me to arrange a strong enough escort."

"So you ordered her kidnapped?"

"No. I ordered the book be regained. She was not to be harmed."

"By making everyone sleep."

"Yes. They were supposed to put you to sleep, find the *Notes*, and return with no one getting harmed."

"Except Ragnar's honor. And Marija's panic."

"It is rare for us to truthfully claim ignorance, but we did not realize that Ragnar's honor was at stake. We have since researched gestriht, and now know we owe Ragnar a debt. As for Marija, she would have been distraught, of course, but she would have come here first, and we would have assuaged her despondency. However, you say she was waylaid and, presumably, murdered before she arrived here."

"Yes, before she came anywhere close to Achrida."

"How do you know this?"

"Katarina told me she did it."

"The kraljevic?"

"Yes."

"Why would she be involved? How did she know?"

"She would not tell me. In fact, she didn't really tell me precisely what happened, but she did say she disguised herself as Marija afterwards. I believe she killed Marija and her companions, took her place, and followed her planned route. Then she faked Marija's kidnapping before your people could get there."

"My people," he said distastefully, "were not aware of the kidnapping until after returning."

"Did they all survive?"

"Yes, despite two sword wounds to one."

Desimir smirked.

"He's lucky I was out of practice," I said.

Kristijan looked at me sadly. "Yes, I suppose that is true."

"Something's been bothering me, though…"

He looked at me. "Yes?"

"You're an order of teachers, scribes, and scholars, right?"

He nodded.

"Your order is very skilled at using a small knife to sharpen a quill pen."

"Yes, we are."

"But I bet there aren't many of you skilled with knives in dark corridors. Probably aren't skilled at walking quietly in those dark corridors in the first place."

"No." He could see the path, but he needed to make me ask the question.

"So where did you get 'your people?'"

With deliberate motions, he poured himself more water.

He drank some.

He looked out over the lake.

He drank again.

"You know we are affiliated with the Enchelei."

"Yes."

"When we have need for skills that we do not possess, we go to Pal."

"Pal insists he was not involved."

Kristijan sighed. "In this, he, himself, was not as far as I know. The threat of a schism would have convinced him to prevent this deed. Now I wish I had let him."

"So...?"

"So, we eliminated a step. The Gropas have, in the past, contracted with Gibroz for many tasks. I chose to send someone directly to Gibroz."

"In Pal's name," I guessed.

Kristijan smiled ruefully. "Yes, it seemed easier."

"And you knew the regular courier, and you convinced him or her to perform this task."

"I will say no more of the matter. I must admit my failures, but I will not incriminate others."

"It wouldn't have been any Dassaretae," I mused. "It had to be somebody amongst the Enchelei, someone that Gibroz was used to dealing with."

"Speculate as you see fit. In any case, it's irrelevant. What is relevant is discovering how Katarina found out about Marija and was able to ambush her."

"How did you find out she was coming?"

"Some at the temple in the Great City were as worried as I was. All knew of her hope to investigate Naum's Captivity. We also knew that Gregor had, generally, resisted the idea. Before you ask, I do not know why he changed his mind."

"So Katarina could have found out from the same informant."

He sighed. "It cannot be ruled out, but I despair that any of our order would communicate with her for any reason. She is… anathematic to our principles."

One could certainly describe her in that manner. I would have chosen "*completely fucking insane,*" but that seemed too crude to actually say out loud.

"So, to be clear, Marija and the *Notes of Naum* were supposed to secretly leave the Great City. In reality, everyone except Ragnar and me knew she was leaving. Katarina killed her. She took the *Notes* and gave them to someone. She faked the kidnapping. Your people, not knowing the book was already gone, tried to steal it again by putting everyone in the Faerie asleep. Not finding the *Notes* at the Faerie, you then thought I had them so your people attacked me in the street and stole my bag. Since the book wasn't in my bag, they tried to kill me on the road coming back from Gibroz's gambling parlor, and I killed or seriously wounded each of them."

Kristijan had nodded his way through the entire litany until the last item, to which he shook his head vigorously.

"No. I mean, yes, 'my people' accosted you, though not at my behest. Gibroz was livid that he had not recovered the *Notes* and hence not earned the agreed-upon fee, so he sent them after you with the thought that you might have it with you."

"You weren't involved in the attempt to kill me?"

"No." Either he could act better than I thought or he was telling the truth.

"Could Gibroz have done so?"

He sighed. "Yes, I suppose so. After they attacked you in the street, we spread the word not to harm anyone, but kraljevics are not known for their pacifism."

"For now, then, we'll assume we're correct on all the rest. I'll go back to Gibroz and get him to tell me."

Kristijan looked at me for a moment. "If you think that is wise, Edward."

I shrugged. "It's a place to go. I'm floundering in a place even the Trickster would find strange. I have no better plan than to keep poking around."

He nodded.

"But you need to do something for me," I said.

Kristijan looked at me.

"You need to find out who told what to whom and when in the Great City."

"That will be difficult," he said. "Our philosophical differences occupy most of our conversations."

"I suggest you convince Gregor to set those differences aside for the moment. We need to find out how Katarina knew about Marija's errand in time to attack her."

He sighed and nodded. We sat and finished the cool, sweet water while we contemplated the depths of the dark blue lake. Then Desimir and I left.

On our way back, we walked down the street where I had been beaten. I recognized the old lady. She wore a different shawl that was even uglier and more colorful than the one I remembered. I braved her chromatic chaos to press two bronze dinars into her hand.

Then we went towards the docks to find Svetislav.

Chapter 22
Midday, 13 Gersmoanne, 1712 MG

At least, we tried to find Svetislav. As we walked into the Heartsquare, Kapric and Zvono joined us, as if they had been waiting for us.

"Quaesitors, what a welcome surprise. Were you waiting for us?"

"Yes."

"How did you know where we went?"

Kapric ignored the question. "Since you're so close, why don't you come to our office?" He pointed at a large stone building that rose on the northeast corner of Heartsquare. A long set of wide, shallow stairs led up to doors shadowed by a carven overhang, supported by columns headed with roaring marble lions.

"Nice of you to phrase that as a question."

"It was, wasn't it?" he replied with a twitch that might have been a smile.

Getting into a scuffle with city officials seemed unlikely to help Ragnar, so we followed Kapric up the stairs and through the building, which smelled of ink and rakija and sweat and fatigue. It looked worse than it smelled. Nooks and niches, each occupied by a desk and a chair, littered its labyrinthine arrangement. Parchments, quills, and mugs covered most of the desks. The people who occupied the chairs glared at anyone who disturbed their important work, though I noticed that few of them glared too long at Kapric.

Finally, we reached a long room in one of the lower basements. The room reminded me of the scribal room in the Temple of Naum, with desks along both long sides, facing each other across an aisle. All of the desks were covered in the same detritus we had seen elsewhere in the building. Most of the chairs were empty, except for two on the left whose occupants were arguing over horses and chariot racers.

Kapric paused for a half-moment, and suddenly the pair started debating evidence in a recent horse theft.

He led us down the aisle into one of two smaller rooms at the far end. He sat behind a large desk, also covered in parchments, and waved us to chairs where we sat. Zvono leaned on Kapric's desk.

For a long moment they simply stared at us, and I got angry.

"So what does a tagmatarch do besides annoy outsiders whenever he deigns to notice one?"

"I haven't annoyed you yet. But I can," rumbled Kapric.

"You're off to a good start. We had plans for lunch and a pint." No need to mention Svetislav.

"Keep pushing and we'll feed you. Won't be as good as you get from the Svellheimer and his wife, but we'll feed you as long as we want."

"Whatever. Hurry up and finish intimidating me so we can be on our way."

We glared at each other. Zvono sighed. Desimir chuckled.

"We'll continue this whenever the herd bulls get done butting heads to establish dominance," Zvono said.

"Gonna be awhile," I growled.

"That'll help us find out who tried to kill you," said Kapric.

"Tagmatarch, I didn't know you cared."

"I wouldn't, if it had been your body."

Zvono laughed. "Bullshit."

Kapric paused and gave a half-smile. "Yeah, you're right."

That broke our stares.

"Neither the tagmatarch nor I likes dead bodies. All of the people in this room are quaesitors. It's our job to investigate crimes. He and I focus on the dead bodies, and since each one makes more work for us, we'd rather not see any."

"Sorry to add to your workload."

Kapric bristled at my sarcasm, but Zvono cut us both off. "Shut up and listen, Sevener."

She was right. I took a deep breath and nodded an apology to both of them. She pulled out a large wax tablet. I saw no reason for her to hold it, since she never looked at it, but she carried it like a scop's lyre.

"The three who are dead were two brothers and a cousin. Last name of Blazevic. We've seen them before. They intimidate store owners. They make sure a fisherman sells his catch to a particular warehouse or taverns buy what they're told. They're muscle for turf disputes in the Stracara. Mostly they just do thug work, though they might have left a few bodies here and there. We've never been able to prove enough to allow us to get past their protectors."

"Their protectors?"

"Yeah, every time we've tried to get rid of them, one or another of our superiors has suggested we let them be."

"How do you know it was these three? I thought someone cleaned up the street."

"Yeah, someone did," responded Kapric, "but a guy owes me a favor, and he knows I like to hear about any random corpses. He found them while doing something I didn't ask about and led us to their bodies."

"We can't prove it's the three you killed, but there *are* three of them and their wounds match the strikes you told us you did to them." Zvono paused. "And a street attack is the kind of thing they would be asked to do."

"So who were their protectors?"

Kapric looked at me. "I've dealt with a few Northmen and Seveners before. You all have these oaths you swear."

I nodded.

"I have sworn oaths too"—he waved his hand—"not the same, not the same at all. But we are a part of the city. You would do as your lords would instruct. We do as those who rank higher than us instruct."

"Questions are not always encouraged," said Zvono.

"Does this have to do with the tribal rivalries?"

"She is Dassaretae and I come from an Enchelei branch," said Kapric. "But here, we find killers and take care of them, Enchelei, Dassaretae, kral, or whomever."

"Unless your bosses tell you to ignore them," I said.

"Unless that."

"Except," said Zvono, "when we can get enough information to get other bosses to support us."

"And you don't have enough information yet to figure out who their protectors are."

Kapric got up and stared at something on the back wall only he could see. Without turning, he spoke. "Not really. We know who have protected the Blazevics before. But, it's not necessarily that simple."

"The problem is that these three," said Zvono, "have been protected by members of the Enchelei, both of the kraljevics, and a number of sects."

"They're hirelings."

"Yes."

"Could be hired by anyone."

"Yes."

"And you'll only have an idea who sent them if someone tells you to stop looking into their deaths, because then you'll know who their protector owes."

"Yes."

"Which probably won't happen this time," said Kapric. "The person who told me where they were only told me. I told Zvono. We've told you."

"And they're already dead," said Zvono.

"So, nobody knows they're involved, and even if they did they're not in need of protection anymore."

They nodded.

"That's why you so generously invited us here. You wanted a secure place to tell us."

Nodded again.

"So what do you want from us?"

"Despite Kapric's need to be the stud bull," said Zvono, grinning, "neither of us is all that unhappy you put these three into the ground. We can fill out the parchments, write 'self-defense,' and file them away as the Emperor desires quite easily."

"But, you're going to push this," Kapric added.

"Yes, I am. I have sworn an oath to Ragnar."

"You've proven you know how to use a sword, and I would be shocked if you didn't also know what to do with that shorter blade. Piri has this animal walking around with you, and I can't even take his deadliest weapons away from him. And there's something deeper here," said Zvono.

"You're going to bring us more corpses," Kapric concluded.

"It wouldn't surprise me."

"But you have a problem."

I sighed. "Two actually. One, if I keep killing people, then sooner or later I'll kill the wrong someone and force a zupan or a kraljevic or you to respond."

Zvono agreed. "We don't like extra work, and we'll lock you away. The others might be more direct."

"It's a good thing I don't really enjoy killing."

"Everyone is a lot less excited if you just leave people bloody," said Kapric.

Kapric and I stared at each other. This time I looked away. "I'll do what I can, and whatever you might think about him, Desimir is helping me learn some things that might mean I don't have to kill anyone."

"He's broken a few bones in his time. Those are fine too."

"But there's my second problem," I added. "Someone's already trying to kill me."

"We noticed that too," said Kapric drily.

"Don't get us wrong, Sevener," Zvono added. "We'd rather not have to look at your corpse, either, and if it's a choice between those three dead or you dead, I'll pick them. But the moment you kill someone who doesn't need killing…"

"Then you'll be there."

They nodded. Kapric reached into his desk for a bottle of rakija and four small cups. He filled them and passed them around. We emptied the cups. Kapric replaced the cork in the bottle, fastidiously wiped out the cups, and placed everything back whence it came.

Once we had returned to the portico, Zvono looked at me.

"Don't forget, Sevener, someone does want you dead."

Chapter 23
Early Afternoon, 13 Gersmoanne, 1712 MG

We managed to arrive at the Lakewarden base without anyone else waylaying us. The base sat in caves dug into the cliffs underneath the row of mansions that included Pal's manor. I wondered if some route from the mansion led down through the hill.

The pathway along the shore led to a series of piers. A variety of vessels were moored at the piers. The largest, an ancient dromon, looked as if its last refit had occurred when my damsire was young. Had it been kept up, I wondered if any other ship on the lake could have challenged it, but that mattered not at the moment.

A dozen other ships and boats bobbed on the light waves. All the other craft showed signs of regular maintenance. All had their gunwales painted the blue of the Pathfinder tabards, and matching yellow towers peeked up from the hulls as the lake lifted them out of the water.

Two Lakewardens stood at a gateway built of stone arching out from the hill. They glared at us, especially after they recognized Desimir.

"I am Edward, and I am looking for Svetislav."

"What business would the Dassaretae have with him?"

"I am not Dassaretae. As for Desimir, Piri told him to guard my back. Neither of us is capable of successfully arguing with her. Are you?"

With bitter smiles, they shook their heads.

"So, you are going to have to accept Desimir for the moment." I waited while they acknowledged, ever so slightly, my argument. "So I ask again, is Svetislav here?"

"I'll get the protokarabos," one said, shrugging. "He'd want to know anyway."

Soon Svetislav joined us. He looked agitated, almost as if he wanted to talk. We walked away from the gate to the middle of the path.

"I need information from you that you might not wish to tell me."

He chuckled sarcastically, but kept looking at me.

"I have to know more about the Gropas. I am convinced that something is roiling under the surface, and I don't know enough about

163

the members of the council. I think that this something has to do with the schism, which you know Pal wants to end. I need you to tell me what you can."

He shifted his gaze to look over the lake.

I waited.

I continued to wait as his agitation flowed and, ultimately, ebbed.

He walked back to the gate. I followed.

"Elatos," he said quietly.

"Yes, sir?" said one of the guards.

"Prepare the skiff."

The guard ran off and, presently, returned. "Skiff readied, protokarabos."

"Thank you, elatos. Now, care for the Dassaretae. Properly. You know where I keep my rakija."

"Aye, sir," he said with a hint of confusion.

He gestured at me. "Promised him a lake cruise. Today's nice."

Despite its warmth, Svetislav had accurately described the day and he led me to a small boat. Svetislav got into the bow, by the oars, and watched as I entered the stern. Though I had not boarded such a small boat in years, I managed without too much embarrassment.

He nodded at the rope anchoring us to the pier. I uncoiled it from the mooring, curled it up, and laid it down in the hull. I sat on the bench and watched as he smoothly pushed the skiff from the pier and rowed us out onto the lake.

After some time, he stopped rowing. He pulled a large, cheap, ceramic mug from the floorboards, dipped it into the lake, and drank his fill. He then cooled himself by pouring the remainder over his head. He filled the mug again and handed it to me. I followed his example. The water tasted cold and delicious, and after I had poured some over my head, I realized how much relief the water gave from the hot sun. Svetislav took the mug back and continued rowing.

Soon he turned the skiff so that I could have a good look at the city rising from the lake and let the boat drift. From here, the fortress loomed impossibly mountainous. We could see the Stracara with its bustling commerce and crime. I noted two larger vessels with blue gunwales sitting calmly out from the docks. We drank more of the lake, and since the sun had quickly dried the water from our first dousing, we poured more water on our heads.

The Lakewarden clearly needed to tell me something, but just as clearly did not want to actually say anything. I forced myself to be patient while he made up his mind.

Svetislav started rowing again, this time towards the north shore, into a small channel that cut through a landing where the mountain had met the lake. Several houses sat here, each with their own dock. He rowed up the channel a hundred paces and again pulled out the mug.

"Biljana's Springs," he said, after drinking the water.

I looked at him and tried the water. Surely, they always drank ale or mead in Valhalla, but, if they chose to drink something else, it would be this water. I could see the bottom of the channel. Glittering rocks and vivid green plants competed for attention on the streambed.

"Biljana's Springs?"

He pointed to where water flowed from under the mountain, over a long low fall, to carve this channel to the lake. He filled his mug again, drank, handed me the rest, and rowed us back towards the piers. There, under the shade of the cliffs and the great manors of Achrida, he stopped and let the skiff drift.

"What would you ask?"

I paused. "I know nothing about the members of the council. I have met them, but I know very little about them. I need to know how they interact."

Svetislav sighed and gathered his thoughts. "Pal has ruled for two decades. In this time, Enchelei have faded."

"His fault?"

Svetislav shook his head. "He's smart. Wise. Capable. But fortune ebbs and flows. And Vukasin is also… capable."

"Do all Enchelei feel as you do?"

Svetislav snorted and shook his head.

"So, not all Enchelei are pleased with Pal's reign. I'm guessing some think they could have done better."

He shrugged.

"Vesela?"

"Smart. Beautiful."

"But?"

"But she's been heir for years."

"And she knows she's smart, and she might feel herself ready to assume the title?"

"Perhaps, though our tradition expects zupans to retire."

"So, she doesn't necessarily have to wait until Pal dies?"

"No. And her power is already great." He took a drink from the mug. "Different than Pal, though."

"You're saying she has a different style than Pal?"

He nodded.

"I'm guessing she wants to be more aggressive?"

He nodded again.

I thought.

"Can Jeremena make delicious pies?"

He chuckled. "Handles the caravan trade. No clue about her pies"

"She handles all your trading? Including that done over the lake?"

He hesitated. "All of the regular Enchelei trade, lake or land."

"So, that means many of those over there"—I waved at the docks—"are following her plan."

He nodded. "Greedy. Exacting."

"In other words, a skillful merchant?"

He nodded again.

"Does she also wonder how things might be if she were in charge?"

"Knows she can do it. Was deputy for Pal's father, and he was sickly."

"So, at times, she had to take charge."

He nodded. "Pal was young. His father was old when he sired him. She was his sister. Was to be zupan of Enchelei until Pal's birth."

"Does she resent Pal?"

He shrugged.

"Does Pal resent her?"

"Was Pal's deputy too, until Vesela came of age."

I looked at him.

"I was young too." He smiled.

"Is Zacharia as lazy as he looks?"

He nodded. "Pal's cousin."

"What does he do for the family?"

"He collects secrets."

"Is he the type to use secrets to harm others?"

Svetislav sighed and nodded.

"But his job is to gather information to inform Pal and the others?"

He nodded again.

"Does he care about anyone else in the family?"

He paused. "Yes. Not Pal, though."

"Who then?"

"Vesela, in a way. Also, his daughter."

"But if he thought he would benefit, he'd take over?"

"Probably knows he'd be worse than Pal. Doesn't care."

"Completely corrupt?"

"Almost. Everything and everyone but Agata."

"Agata Kyranna?"

He nodded.

"She's his daughter?"

He smiled. "Surprising, no?"

"Indeed. She seems so tight and precise, and he's this great, sprawling corruption."

"He let her mother raise her. He knows who and what he is. Mostly doesn't care. Does for her."

"Tell me of her."

"Smart. Will be the flow to our current ebb, I think."

"I think you might be right." I paused. "What does everyone else think?"

"They all wonder what she will become. Vesela fears her. Pal recognizes her potential. Zacharia shelters her. Andrija isn't sure what she is. Jeremena doesn't care because she knows she'll be dead soon enough. Davorin lusts after her."

"Tell me of Davorin."

"Another cousin. Also corrupt."

"In what way?"

"Every way. He takes all he can."

"Money?"

He nodded.

"Rakija?"

"And strange herbs, medicines. Also people."

"He takes people? Sexually?"

He nodded. "Male or female makes no difference. Flowers, whips, blood, whatever."

"The rest of the council sat apart from him when I met them."

"He almost smells wrong."

"So he'd take power if he could."

"To feed his lusts." He grimaced.

"But not to sate them?"

"That is impossible."

"Would you follow his orders?"

Svetislav looked over the lake, not answering.

"Why do they keep him?"

"Capable. Inventive. No one else thinks like him."

"So he expands the family's power while tainting it?"

He nodded. "And wealth. New trade."

"New trade routes?"

He nodded again.

"Probably from faraway places. Like maybe Matara?"

Another nod.

I thought a moment. "Andrija?"

"The Old Bear."

"I also thought of a bear when I met him." I smiled.

"Even now, he would crush you."

"He might at that. How does he view Pal?"

"Andrija was his trainer."

"He trained Pal in weaponwork?"

Svetislav nodded.

"And he loves the boy he trained?"

He nodded again.

"So, of them all, he would be the only one who doesn't think about being zupan?"

"Probably not Agata."

"No?"

"Too smart."

"She's too smart to wonder about becoming zupan?"

He smiled. "She is right now."

"But she's smart enough to gather power as she ages?"

"Yes."

"How good is Pal?"

"He knows all this and more."

"So he plays the game and knows what each piece can and will do?"

He shrugged. "Achrida."

"He's asking all the same questions," I stated. "But he doesn't entirely know what's going on. I need to speak to him again."

He considered that, but did not answer.

"Are the zupans ever overthrown?" I said, after a moment.

"Rarely. But, this is Achrida."

"So. Few have done so, but everyone is jostling with each other, and zupans have lost bits and pieces of their power here and there at times?"

Svetislav lifted the oars and started rowing back to the pier. "This is Achrida."

"Wait." He stopped, looked at me. "You haven't told me everything."

We stared at each other for a while. A seagull cried raucously over us.

He opened a pouch and handed me a scrap of parchment. It read, "low high low skip high."

"What is this?"

"I think it is someone messing with fish prices."

"What do you mean?"

"Several larger fishing boats have demanded odd prices."

"Recently, you mean?"

He nodded.

"And their odd prices matched this pattern?"

He nodded again.

"You said Jeremena controls the Enchelei trade. Could this be her doing?"

"No."

"Because she already sets most of the prices?"

He nodded.

"Were the boats fixing prices owned by Dassaretae trying to push Enchelei out of the trade?"

He sighed. "No. All Enchelei."

"So, all of these are Enchelei boat captains messing with Jeremena's plan?"

He nodded yet again.

"She didn't strike me as someone who would take this news well."

Svetislav laughed at that. "No, Sevener, she does not."

"Why would they risk her wrath?"

"Was planning to ask day after tomorrow."

"May I join you?"

He shrugged.

"Desimir will feel he has to be with me."

He shook his head. "I will answer to Piri for you."

I laughed. "You get to explain that to Desimir, then."

"Two days, late morning."

Chapter 24
Early Evening, 13 Gersmoanne, 1712 MG

We returned to the Faerie in time for an early dinner. Zoe started us off with melted cheese on bread. Later, Ragnar slid us plates with grilled chicken and onion with a hint of pepper. Bedarth had given me pepper once before and I had liked it, though it was fantastically expensive here and ten times more in the Seven Kingdoms.

Desimir remained unhappy that I had gone off with Svetislav without him. He got his revenge by focusing on the conversation with Kapric and Zvono.

"Must be kinda thrilling to know someone wants to kill you." He grinned.

I looked at him.

"Welcome to Achrida, where special people get targeted for death."

"Shut up."

"Not sure if I've ever known anyone who someone personally wants to kill."

"It's your job to prevent it."

"Yup. Still kinda fun, don't you think?"

"Does Piri know how strange you are?"

"Piri knows everything," he said happily. We finished our dinner and waved to Karah for refills. "So, hunted man, what's the plan for the rest of the night?"

My glare washed off of him like a light rain in the summer.

"When do you think is the best time to go back to Gibroz's?"

"As I recall, the last time you went to his place someone tried to kill you, right?"

"Yes."

"Sooner the better then. This is fun as hell."

Annoying as Desimir was, he was right. I really could not think of a better time than the present. So we went.

The ravaged man met us in the gateroom. He shuffled off when I asked for Gibroz. He returned and waved us in, leading us to the same room. Same table. Same four thugs. Same lovely assistant. Same desk. Same bearded criminal patriarch.

"What the fuck do you want?"

Same triptych.

"Well, I remembered you had this incredible triptych on the wall, and I wanted to see it again."

He looked at me for a long while. "I got enough fuckin' idiots around without your shit."

"You probably need my shit, but I'm here to ask you why you tried to kill me."

"I didn't fuckin' try to kill you, but I'm sure as shit thinkin' 'bout it now."

"Gibroz, after all we've meant to each other?"

"We ain't meant shit."

"Ah, but we have. I've meant profit for you. Why, I do believe no less of an important figure as Archimandrite Kristijan had you do something for him."

"Where the fuck did you hear that?"

"Kristijan and I are old friends. We go back to at least this morning."

"So he told you what the fuck he had me do. And that's what I fuckin' did. I do what I fuckin' say. And you weren't ever fuckin' involved, 'til you put your fuckin' nose where it ain't supposed to be. You ain't one of Andreyev's fuckin' favorites, neither."

I looked at the table. The man who had stared at me on my previous visit nonchalantly cleaned his fingernails with a knife. It appeared to be a well-worn knife, comfortable in the hands of a man who loved knives and caressed them every day. Probably named them all something like Juraj.

"Tell Andreyev not to come into the Faerie to steal something. With or without help."

"Andreyev says to tell you to pay better fuckin' attention walkin' down the fuckin' road," said Gibroz, and all four sitting at the table guffawed. The lovely assistant cracked a small smile.

"I hope the shoes fit someone."

"Fit fuckin' perfectly." One of the others at the table leaned back, showing them off.

I turned back to Gibroz, "I want my bag back."

He sat back for a moment. "You're shittin' me. You know I can fuckin' kill you and you're here askin' for a fuckin' bag?"

"I like that bag."

"Well, you ain't fuckin' boring, I'll fuckin' give you that."

"So, why did you send the Blazevics to kill me?"

He laughed. "If I sent them to fuckin' ace you, how come you're still fuckin' alive?"

"Because I killed them instead."

He laughed. "Did you now?"

"Seen them around?"

"I don't fuckin' look for 'em. But, say you fuckin' did. I didn't fuckin' send them. If I was fuckin' serious about your body in the fuckin' sewer, I'd have fuckin' made sure of it. Yet, here you are, fuckin' annoyin' me."

"I really liked that bag."

"Fuck! I'll see if the fuckin' bag is still around. That way, when I do have you fuckin' aced, it'll have your fuckin' blood on it too."

"That would make it extra special."

"Fuckin' would at that."

He drank some rakija. I took a breath. "So, Kristijan asked you to do something, but he would never actually come here. Who was it that actually told you to send Andreyev to try and steal from someone at the Faerie?"

"Why the fuck do you want to fuckin' know?"

"Did you get paid?"

"No, I fuckin' didn't get paid. We didn't get the fuckin' papers, whatever the fuck they are."

"Why didn't you get the fuckin' papers?"

"Because they were fuckin' already gone."

"So, who took them before you could? Who knew they were there before you?"

"I don't fuckin' know, but I'm willing to have Andreyev stomp that fee out of their fuckin' skulls."

"So, the person who told you about the papers is at least one person who knew before you."

"Yeah, that's fuckin' true." He thought for a moment. "Fine, I got no profit not fuckin' tellin' you, now. You already fuckin' know who wanted the fuckin' contract."

"Yep."

"So, it was the normal fuckin' guy from the fuckin' Gropas. What's his fuckin' name, Gabrijela?"

"Frano, Gibroz," said the assistant.

"Yeah, his fuckin' name's Frano, he's been walkin' between us and the fuckin' Gropas for fuckin' years. He came and fuckin' told me what they fuckin' wanted, and we fuckin' agreed on a fuckin' price. He said it was for the fuckin' Naumite, whatever his fuckin' title is now, and that made fuckin' sense on account they're all fuckin' Enchelei. Not that we really fuckin' care about no koryfoi, but it's fuckin' business and it ought to make fuckin' sense. And a fuckin' profit."

"So, presumably, Frano and maybe a bunch of other Gropas knew about the attack."

"Yeah, that's what I fuckin' said."

"And you didn't send the Blazevics after me?"

"To fuckin' kill you? Naw, Andreyev is fuckin' lookin' forward to that. He'd be fuckin' pissed if I asked someone else. I fuckin' take care of my fuckin' people. And my fuckin' business. Speakin' of which, I think our business is fuckin' done."

"Just one more thing, besides my bag."

"By the fuckin' balls of the White Bull, what is it with this fuckin' bag? Fine, Gabrijela will fuckin' check on that. Fuckin' brave or fuckin' stupid, I haven't fuckin' decided yet. What's the other fuckin' thing?"

"Can you say a full sentence without fuckin' saying fuckin'?"

"Now, I fuckin' know. It's fuckin' stupid. Get the fuck out of here."

We did, with Desimir grinning the whole time.

"That was fuckin' fun as hell."

"Shut up."

Not surprisingly, he chattered stupid things the whole way back to the Faerie. I began to understand Gibroz's attitude towards me.

Chapter 25
Evening, 13 Gersmoanne, 1712 MG

We returned to the Faerie early enough that Desimir could regale most of the regulars with the story of our conversation with Gibroz. "Fuckin'" this and "fuckin'" that all around the taproom. Karah sniffed in disapproval. Zoe took Eirik with her to finish cleaning up from dinner. Ragnar mostly stayed quiet while he rubbed Melia's belly. Well, quiet except for his roaring laughter.

I sat there and responded whenever I had to, but, mostly, I was thinking. Somewhere, something did not add up. Svetislav had told me the Gropas had not ordered the kidnapping. Pal had told me the Gropas had not ordered the kidnapping. Vesela had told me the Gropas had not ordered the kidnapping. Katarina told me she had done it herself.

But Kristijan had told me he asked Gibroz to help him, and now I knew that Frano had been sent by some Gropa to get Gibroz to steal the *Notes*. Svetislav, Pal, and Vesela all claimed they were not that person. Of course, Vesela, Pal, Kristijan, or, for that matter, Svetislav, might have lied to me. But if I believed them, that left Jeremena, Zacharia, and Davorin as obvious suspects.

Maybe Andrija liked Kristijan's desire to return the Church of Naum to its roots. He had struck me as a person who would generally want things that way. So, I could not exclude him. Nor did the plotter have to be one of the Gropa Council. Clearly, the possibility existed that someone lower in the Gropa ranks might seek to force their way into the council.

Plus, Svetislav had told me about fixing the fish prices. How did that fit in? Was someone challenging Jeremena?

I had no doubts that Pal and Vesela would lie or conceal whatever they wanted from me. They had no real reason to tell me anything unless I could help them in some way. They had to know I would keep asking around and that, sooner or later, I would find out that Kristijan tried to steal the *Notes*. But if they knew, why did they not tell me the first time we talked? Telling me would have made it more likely that I would find the relic more quickly, meaning the schism would be more likely to end, and ending the schism helped all of the Enchelei. Or at least so I hoped.

I realized I did not even know if I was asking sensible questions, but everything appeared to hinge on the Gropas. I knew much more than I had when I awoke with a hangover that morning, but now I might have too many pieces and parts. My thoughts roamed around my mind like foxes playing in the fields.

"I think I need to meet Frano," I said. "Preferably quietly."

"How are you going to do that?" asked Desimir, turning back to me.

"If I was in charge of a family, and I competed constantly with important rivals, I would keep track of as many of their movements as I could. I'll bet Zacharia does that for the Enchelei."

"Yes-s-s-s," Desimir said thoughtfully.

"So, who amongst the Dassaretae would Vukasin have asked to keep tabs on the Enchelei?"

"Personally, I just tell everything to the hecatontarch. I don't really know…"

"Aren't you due to report back to her?"

"What?"

"Piri wants you to report back whenever you can do so without leaving me alone on the streets, right?"

"Well, yes."

"I'm going to stay here, either in the taproom or my bedroom, for what's left of the night."

"Yes, that would mean I could report."

"So, why don't you? Might want to mention in your report that I'm interested in learning everything I can about Frano. You might even mention that it would be helpful to talk over lunch tomorrow."

"Right now?" he said, as his hands caressed his mug.

"Yes." I grinned.

Desimir sighed, finished his beer, and left. I nursed my ale, but the normal camaraderie of the taproom grated on my restless nerves. I needed a break from sorting the pieces in my brain, so I went to the stables.

"Can I help you?" Eirik came out and asked.

"No, Eirik, I've just come to brush Deor."

"I've already done that. And cleaned his hooves, and fed and watered him."

I laughed. "I have no doubt. You've done a fine job. I just want something to do, and I've barely seen him since we rode around the city."

He nodded, somewhat doubtfully, but handed me a brush. Deor nickered when he saw me. I grabbed an apple. He nuzzled me for a moment before taking the apple.

"I've missed you too. I'll take you riding again, soon." I began brushing him, which was, indeed, a fairly pointless exercise given Eirik's diligence.

Akantha took the time to stretch while balancing on the stall wall. She yawned a loud "Meow" at me and went back to sleep. Clearly, I ranked amongst her favorites.

The mindless communion with my old friend did not provide me with any insights, but did occupy some time. Anyway, I had missed him.

"It ain't, I mean isn't, right for you to be doing that," said Eirik.

"I won't tell, if you won't," I said, smiling.

He smiled slightly, but he could not relax until I had finished and returned to the taproom.

When I entered, the regulars greeted me with cheers and shouts, including a variety of ways to say "fuckin' well done." The absence of both Desimir and me had not stopped the conversation. Flavian's weird laugh pierced the noise, adding a strange counterpoint to the profanity.

I waved cheerfully to all of the comments, though I actually heard few of them, and sat down. Karah sloshed a mug in front me as she swiftly made her rounds, giving me no chance to thank her. The strong laughter and fellowship in the Faerie that evening reminded me of days with my kin, when the sun burned brightly through our sweat-stained tunics at harvest time.

Desimir had not returned by the time I went to bed. Knowing Piri, I had Ragnar walk me to my room so that, upon his return, Desimir would not feel obligated to wake me to confirm that I had not left the Faerie without him.

I reclined on my bed, still thinking.

Sleep arrived before any answers did.

Chapter 26
Morning, 14 Gersmoanne, 1712 MG

Desimir pounded on my door to wake me up.

"Bring the book. I know damn well you haven't looked at it since I gave it to you."

I sighed because he was absolutely correct, and I hated to admit it to him. I tried to ignore the issue as we studied the various stances over breakfast, but that merely made his smirk broader. Desimir spent most of the time emphasizing the versatility and importance of the Long Guard. He generally started each bout in that position, though he would often shift immediately to one of the others.

"You've not the time to be learning the whens and wheres for starting with something like the Front Guard or Boar's Tooth. Let's just be focusing on the Long Guard to begin with. You'll use the other guards, of course, but for someone who is new, starting at the same place every time can help you move with the flow of the battle."

He ate some of his eggs. "Few of your opponents will have as much training as you have, even though we've barely scratched the surface. That means, though there are ways to counter the Long Guard immediately, you'll not need them much." He paused and his grin came back. "Unless, of course, you've the chance to fight me or someone as can fight as well as me."

"So, the Long Guard is good for blocking longer attacks, right? Especially if I need time to figure out what they're doing."

"Correct."

We continued breaking down the advantages, disadvantages, and shifts of the stances until the moves that he used to beat me started to make a little more sense. We then went to the hayroom to practice. For the first time Desimir kept the pace slow throughout, forcing me to check the stances in the book and compare them with the flow and balance of our actual bodies.

By halting midmovement, he forced me to stay balanced throughout the motion. However, the slower pace exhausted me more than his tossing me around and gloating.

Afterwards, we cleaned up. When I entered the taproom I found Desimir focusing on a bowl of beef soup and a platter of cheese bread. Next to him sat a short, voluptuous woman with extraordinarily long, lustrous, black hair. She punctuated her loud speech with wild, gesticulating hands.

She barely paused for breath as she harangued Desimir. She ranted about how long it had been since he had showed her any attention. She emphasized how he was not worthy to speak to her father, though her father had introduced them to each other in the first place. She complained how he was a bad example to their two boys, even though, she would admit, he was a good provider. Desimir had clearly met his match, and, to the rest of us, it appeared to be a match made in Olympus.

I sat down next to Desimir. Ragnar, smiling as widely as I had ever seen, brought me a plate. The woman did not seem to notice me, Ragnar, or Karah. Karah struggled to glower like normal, but she was laughing along with the rest of us.

Desimir offered the requisite nods, noises, and even occasional mumbles that confirmed he heard her words. When she had finished both her ranting and her breakfast, she rose, kissed him thoroughly, and left with a cheery "I love you" that everyone in the taproom studiously avoided noticing.

"My future wife," he said.

"Mmmm," I said. It was all I could say without laughing at my friend… my friend who was teaching me wrestling.

"Sometime I'll have to thank Piri for that," he sighed.

"She arranged your future marriage?"

"No, she sent Andrijana to tell me about Frano. That rant was her saying everything she couldn't say to me over the past month."

"Did I hear her say you had two kids?"

He smiled proudly. "Yeah, yeah I do, and both of 'em could already throw you."

"How old are they?"

"Six and four, I think. Sometimes I forget."

"You've been with Andrijana for seven years?"

"More like nine."

"So this marriage idea is more along the lines of a possibility than a specific plan," I teased.

"May the Rich One take your tears," he laughed. "Someday I'll leave the Pathfinders, or get promoted. Then her dad will actually let me marry her." He paused. "Maybe marriage will calm her down some."

"Mmmm," I repeated for exactly the same reason I had said that moments before. I waited a bit. "So, what did she tell you about Frano?"

"He works in the Stracara, at one of the warehouses. Part of the reason he's the messenger between the Gropas and Gibroz is that he likes his gambling. Mostly dice. Pretty good at it, but no one ever wins at Gibroz's. Frano lives in one of the many rooms available in the Stracara because the woman he keeps time with runs it. He helps keep the building up some, too, when they're not yelling at each other."

I thought about this. "I know you won't lie to Piri and let me talk to Frano alone, but, I think it'll be important for me to talk to him by myself. You're Dassaretae, and I bet he's more likely to talk to me if you're not around. So, I want you to follow me at a distance. Any distance is fine as long as Frano doesn't notice."

Desimir scowled. "If I'm that far behind you could lose me."

"Yes." I nodded. "But, as I'm in no mood to get Piri angry at me either, I promise I won't try to do so."

"That's good." He thought about it. "I'll hold back as best I can, but Piri will have my ass if I let something happen to you."

"Well, I'd rather stay alive, myself."

Desimir laughed. I thought through the plan a bit more. "Actually, here's what I would like to do. Why don't you and I walk around the Stracara this afternoon? You can show me Frano's warehouse, his boarding house, and Gibroz's. I'm thinking I want to follow Frano as he walks from work to home and get him to talk to me on the way."

"How are you going to get him to talk to you?"

"Appeal to his better nature?"

"Better nature? Of an Enchelei?"

"More likely than appealing to the better nature of some uppity Dassaretae."

Desimir snorted and finished his mug. "Well, we're both done with lunch. The Stracara isn't small, so we might as well get started. But we should dress the part."

We went back upstairs to change. I muddied my riding boots before putting them on and covering them with my brown linen pants. He loaned me a tunic cut in the local style.

I decided to leave my sword, as it would be easily recognizable even if I covered the fittings. Swords were not that common. Long knives like the saex, on the other hand, were everywhere. I wrapped leather around the hilt and stuck it into my belt. I strapped the smaller knife onto my left arm, above the elbow, where I could easily grab it with my right hand.

Desimir took a moment to look me over. "Yeah, you'll do."

Desimir and I spent the next three hours exploring while clouds periodically obscured the sun. When shaded the Stracara looked sullen, sad, and pitiless. In the sunlight it shone with corruption and filth.

We passed the fish market, where a fleet of boat captains sold their catches in a triangular courtyard in front of the market. The captains and the wholesalers battled with numbers, fish names, and flowing vulgarities for profits; crossing verbal swords with the skill of long and bloody practice.

We continued along the docks, past the piers where the fishing boats disgorged their smelly wares, to other piers where more esoteric foodstuffs arrived. The next set of piers accepted common trading items. Stevedores unloaded planks of grained wood, varieties of stone, copper pots and implements, woven rugs, bolts of fabric, sleek furs, and even the occasional horse. The farthest piers hosted small, swift vessels. The tiny chests unloaded from these ships suggested perfumes and silks and jewels.

At the end of the docks, our route ran along curving roads that generally paralleled the coastline. Samiel's Way roamed two streets up from the lake. It was covered by overhanging extensions of the houses that loomed above, creaking alarmingly in the wind. No houses fell on us while we strolled.

We saw boarding houses, temples, shrines, bordellos, inns, taverns with musicians, taverns without musicians, shops selling gear for sailing, shops selling goods from sailing, shops selling food and clothes and anything else needed to live. People milled, pickpockets lifted, thugs strutted, whores leered, vendors shouted, dogs sniffed, cats perched. Fish and crap were the dominant smells, though periodically another smell such as urine or beer clamored for attention.

The heart of the Stracara pulsed with life and death. Desimir's presence comforted me.

Frano lived in a boarding house set slightly back from the Kosta Abras. The warehouse in which he worked sat across the road, next to the docks. We decided to watch the shorter of the two routes Frano was likely to take from work to home.

"It's some time before he'll be heading home. We should leave the Stracara, make sure there's none to be following us, and then come back."

I nodded my agreement, so we strolled for a bit around parts of Achrida that I had not seen, choosing random turns. Eventually we turned back towards the Stracara. Along the way, Desimir disappeared.

I returned to Frano's boarding house and wandered slowly from there towards his warehouse. I stopped at various vendors and even drank some wretched ale. Twice. Each time cursing Bedarth for teaching me to actually taste. If I could not convince Frano to talk to me with sweet reason, I could always threaten him with the beer.

I stayed constantly alert. I watched for Frano, pickpockets, and anyone trying to mug me. The skills of the pickpockets and muggers made this challenging. I resisted the blandishments of whores. The skills of the whores made this easy.

I had strolled all of the way to Frano's warehouse and was dallying when I saw him exit the building. He walked with a friend, each exhibiting the constant wariness that the Stracara encouraged.

They were not wary enough.

Ready to pounce and tense to separate him from the herd, I stood even more vigilant than earlier in the day.

I was not vigilant enough.

I had started to approach Frano when four men dressed in shabby browns and tans attacked. They had dirty faces and short, tangled hair, but they moved quickly with a definite plan. Brusquely, they pushed Frano's friend into a street kiosk of fish. The kiosk fell over, the fish slithered, and confusion exploded.

I jumped forward, but by the time I could cover the fifteen yards between us, each of the four attackers had stabbed him at least twice and fled in different directions. Frano was dead when I reached him. I briefly thought of giving chase, but I doubted I could catch any of them. Worse yet, I might.

I looked for Frano's friend, but he had run away with the rest of the crowd.

I could not see Desimir, but I knew he watched as I stood looking at the body of a man who had wanted to live his life. Not a great rich life of poetry, song, and fine foods, but a steady life of dirt, sweat, and cheap beer. A life he clearly enjoyed, despite often losing at dice and arguing with his woman. A life in which he had learned something I needed to know, but now could not tell me.

I turned away and walked directly back to the Faerie. I passed a Pathfinder at the Square of Legends. I told her to deliver a message to Kapric. When I returned to the Faerie, I realized I owed her an apology as I had not even asked her name, merely ordered her to carry a message. I wondered if she had sent the message—I would not have blamed her had she not.

I took off my boots before entering the Faerie, set them by my table, and went to my room to change. The mere act of returning my saex to its proper position helped my attitude. I grabbed my cleaning supplies and sword and went back down to the tavern.

I returned to my table to find a pitcher of cool ale waiting. A purring cat beckoned me with curled paw, and Desimir leaned back, sporting one of his rare scowls.

"Did you tell anyone our plan?" I asked.

"No."

"Did it seem like someone knew we wanted to talk to Frano and

185

prevented us?"

"It could have been a coincidence."

I cocked an eye at Desimir. Melia chirped and lightly ran a claw down my hand because I had stopped rubbing her belly.

"Well, it could have," he said with a grimace.

"Was anyone following us?"

"I didn't see anyone. And I was keeping an eye out."

"So was I." We thought more. "Chances are that anyone following me would have been fairly obvious to you," I added. At his nod, I continued. "Either they were really good at following us, or they had already planned to go after Frano."

"Yes."

"So, who knew we were interested in him?"

He took a drink. "You. Me. Andrijana. Piri. Anyone we told."

"I didn't tell anyone. You didn't tell anyone. Piri, sure as the Feeder of the Wolf, wouldn't have told anyone other than those she had to. I'm guessing Andrijana wouldn't want have told anyone?"

"No, not about something like this."

"That means if it's a leak on our end it's someone higher than Piri."

"Yeah."

"Tell me, Dassaretae, how likely is that?"

"We've had leaks in the past."

"When was the last one?"

He thought. "I can't think of it, exactly."

I nodded. "Gibroz could have told someone."

"Yeah." He drank some beer. "But why? Gibroz doesn't care about the koryfoi, except for the money he can get from us. And, who could he tell who would care enough to kill Frano?"

"Maybe it's one of Gibroz's people?"

"I suppose."

Look and look again.

"Let's start over. We think he was killed by someone who feared what he knew."

"Yes."

"But, we could be wrong. What other reasons can we think of for someone to kill him?"

"Someone wanted something from him?"

"No one tried to rob him. They just killed him. If they wanted something, it was something he didn't carry."

"Did he have anything worth inheriting?"

"Your report didn't suggest great wealth."

"Had gambling money."

"But gambled it away."

"Could he have been killed because of debts to Gibroz?"

I sat back. "I suppose. Though, why not simply hurt him? Now he can't possibly repay any debts."

"How about jealousy over his woman?"

"Hmmm. I suppose that's possible, too. But four assassins because someone's jealous?"

"He had two jobs. Could someone have wanted one of them?"

"Four assassins for a warehouse job?"

"Yeah, that's less likely than jealously." He poured another beer. "It could be someone who wants a different courier between the Gropas and Gibroz."

"That might be. We'll have to see who takes over.

"Yeah."

We looked at each other.

"Or, he died because he knew something," Desimir concluded.

"So, the most likely reason we can think of is that he learned something as a courier that someone wanted erased."

"He was killed for something he knew." He drank. "We talked for an entire pitcher of ale and only came up with the same answer we already had?"

"Yeah, Desimir, we did. Well, basically. We postulated some other possibilities, doubtful though they may be."

"*Postulated*." He snorted. "Are all Seveners as strange as you?"

"Some are worse."

"Glad I'm in a sane place."

"Where dockworkers are assassinated."

Desimir waved that off as he got up to get another pitcher. I began cleaning things, starting with the Stracara-stained boots.

Chapter 27
Afternoon, 14 Gersmoanne, 1712 MG

The Faerie's afternoon regulars relaxed while we cleaned things, but at one point I noticed an indrawn silence and looked up.

I murmured to Desimir, "Who was the Pathfinder I spoke to on the way here? I owe her an apology."

"Tanja. Why do you owe her an apology?"

I ignored him and waited until Kapric and Zvono arrived at our table.

"I see you got my message. Please sit." I waved at Karah for two more mugs.

They sat. "How many bodies are we going to find around you Sevener?" asked Kapric.

"I don't know," I sighed.

"We know what happened," said Zvono. "It was so public that even the Stracarans spoke to us. You're going to tell us why?"

"I would, if I could."

"You know more than we do."

"Here's what we know." I recounted the conversation Desimir and I had finished minutes before.

"So, you think he was killed to prevent him talking to you."

"Or anyone."

"What do you think about the timing?"

"I don't like it."

"When did you first think about talking to Frano?"

I paused for a bit, rotating my mug, on its edge, in a circle.

"Sevener," said Kapric, "I'm not going to drop this."

I sighed. "Last night. Gibroz told me Frano was the regular courier from the Gropas."

"So, if someone wanted him dead before he talked to you, they must have almost immediately made arrangements to kill him."

"Yes. And the setup was smooth. They attacked Frano outside his work, where they knew he'd be. They even planned escape routes. From a military perspective, the plan was brilliant. Simple, fast, deadly."

"I'm not a soldier. Fuck brilliant," said Kapric.

Desimir snickered. I looked at him. "Hey, I'm just here to make sure you don't get killed," he laughed. "So far, so good for me."

That response earned glares from all three of us.

Kapric turned back to me. "So what are you planning, Sevener? What other bodies can we expect?"

"I don't know. I think there's something funny going on with the Gropas. Given the kind of snakepit this city is, how often does someone try to become zupan? I've been wondering if someone is after Pal and Vesela."

Kapric sat back. Zvono answered.

"Completely overthrowing a zupan? It's happened a few times. Last time I can recall was about 150 years ago. Andrejan of the Gropas had the misfortune of having twin boys."

"So, someone could be seeking to take over?"

"It could be, but what do you have for evidence?"

"Not much. Someone gave Gibroz orders from the Gropas. These orders risked the *Notes of Naum*. Someone told Katarina ahead of time so she could kill Marija, fake her kidnapping, and steal the *Notes*. The loss of the *Notes* turned the arguments amongst the followers of Naum into an outright schism. That schism is hurting the Gropas. There might only be two people who knew who prompted Gibroz to start this maelstrom, Frano and whichever Gropa sent him to Gibroz. Now Frano's dead and the only logical reason seems to be that he knew something. The only thing he knew that could have been dangerous was the name of the Gropa who sent him."

"All that proves is that something's happening within the Gropas. Something is always happening there," said Kapric.

"What did you ask his widow?" asked Zvono.

"His widow?"

"Yes, did you go ask his widow if she knew anything?"

I grimaced. "No, I wasn't smart enough to think of it."

Zvono sighed. "You should have thought of that immediately. We did."

"What did she tell you?"

"Nothing you haven't already told us, but we weren't thinking in terms of Gropa internal politics. We didn't ask the right questions."

"It's still light enough...," said Kapric.

Desimir stood up. "Let's go. You won't be happy until you talk to his lover."

"Do you want to come along?" I asked, looking at the quaesitors.

"No, actually," said Kapric. "You have a better chance of getting answers if we're not there. She didn't like us earlier, and she won't like us now."

"She won't like you, either, but it's possible you can be persuasive," added Zvono

"Money will help," I chuckled.

Kapric and Zvono nodded. "Send us a report," he added.

I nodded. We left them with their mugs filled, retraced our steps down to Frano's boarding house in the Stracara, and went up to his room.

"Yeah, who's there?" came the response to our knock. I have had more joyous welcomes.

"My name's Edward."

"Don't know no Edward, go the fuck away."

"I'm looking into the killing of Frano."

There was a pause, a latch slid, and the door opened slightly. All I could see through the opening was dark clothing and a red-rimmed eye.

"Fucker got hisself killed. Happens in the Stracara. Why the fuck do you care?"

"I wanted to ask him some questions."

"I guess you'll have to visit the Wealthtaker's Palace."

"I was hoping you might be able to answer them."

"Why would I fuckin' do that?"

"Two silver dinars?"

"Three."

"Three."

"Show me."

I held them in my palm.

191

"Gimme."

I closed my palm. "Let us in."

The red-rimmed eye flicked nervously from Desimir to me. The door closed, and other latches slid back. She opened the door just enough to let her use it as a shield. I dropped the dinars into her hand as we entered.

"So what do you want to know?"

"Frano walked between the Gropas and Gibroz, right?"

"Yeah. Idiot was goin' to Gibroz's most nights anyway, might as well get some money for doin' what he'd be doin'. A'course he lost all of that, and more, with the damned dice."

"How often did he deliver messages?"

"How should I know? I just know when he'd come home from Gibroz's."

"Do you know who told him what to tell Gibroz?"

"Nope."

"Can you tell me anything about those that did?"

She sighed. "It was some Gropa woman he usually talked to. He kept calling her bakica, when he wasn't calling her kuja."

I looked questioningly at Desimir.

"She said he called her either grandmother or bitch."

"So she was older?"

"Yeah, I guess."

"Did he ever mention Jeremena?"

She shook her head.

"And which of Gibroz's people did he talk to?"

"There's that tall, ugly fucker at the door. I think he talked to him afore throwin' our money away."

I asked several of other questions, but aside from expanding my vocabulary of Achridan swearwords I learned nothing.

We returned to the Faerie where, apparently, Kapric and Zvono had not moved.

"Discover anything?"

"That the word *kuja* means 'bitch.'"

They snorted.

"She did give me an idea of which Gropa typically gave Frano the messages for Gibroz."

"Who?" asked Kapric.

"She said Frano called her bakica or kuja."

"Hmmm, probably means Jeremena."

"That was my guess too."

"Doesn't mean she gave these orders."

"No, it doesn't."

"Maybe I'll find out more. Tomorrow, Svetislav and I are investigating something that may also be affecting her prerogatives and place in the Gropa family."

"Yes?" asked Zvono.

"We'll see. It could be nothing. I'll let you know if it means something."

"Try to not let anyone around you die tomorrow."

"Can't promise anything."

Chapter 28
Late Morning, 15 Gersmoanne, 1712 MG

The previous evening, I had told Desimir I would walk around with Svetislav, and without him, the next morning. This irritated Desimir, and that irritation apparently festered all night. He then spent the night cursing me instead of sleeping.

Unfortunately for me, wrestling gave him the perfect opportunity to relieve his anger. As I rose from the ground for the fifth time, he growled that the Gropas could not be trusted.

I painfully nodded my agreement.

For the sixth time, he returned to the Long Guard and struck.

This time, I just stared up at him. "I know they're not to be trusted. But, there's no other way to find the answers. If you hammer me much more, I won't be able to defend myself, should I need."

He stomped off to the jug of lakewater Ragnar provided us each morning. I got up and dusted myself off.

"I know you don't want to fail Piri. Given that your failure means my death, I don't want you to fail her either. But, I have to investigate, and as far as I can determine, the path leads back to the Gropas." I paused. "Besides, wouldn't Piri trust Svet?"

He said nothing, but he did spend the rest of our session teaching me instead of beating me. After cleaning up, we ate breakfast in silence.

When Svetislav arrived, Desimir glared at him instead of properly greeting him. Svetislav ignored Desimir, and we quickly left.

We went down the hill towards the Square of Legends. Walking past us, carrying his amphora of water, was the man I had seen twice before. He still made me wonder, but again, I put his presence down to coincidence.

"Where are we going?"

"Tavern."

"Where the fishing captains relax?"

Svetislav nodded and led me through a warren to an ugly building that smelled of old fish. We entered a dark room with oppressively low ceilings. Both of us ducked as we passed under tar-filled crossbeams. At each table small lamps burning fish oil shaped the faces of those there into murderous scowls, all of which were aimed at Svetislav and me.

He motioned me to a large table, and then stalked around the room, tapping several shoulders and pointing to my table. Finally, he went to the bar and snapped for something to be brought to the table where we gathered.

Up close, the five men and one woman sent to the table looked crueler and smelled worse. Each had a prominent scar or a finger missing. Or both. One stomped up with a footlong piece of tar-stained oak attached to his knee.

Were she clean, the woman might have been mildly attractive in a lean, hard way, except for the slash that started at her left eye, passed through the remains of her nose, and clipped the right side of her mouth. Despite the scar, her face appealed to me more than the water-ravaged beards of the men. Interesting drinking buddies, especially given that none wanted to be there.

Svetislav sat down, and a pitcher of mediocre ale, with a few extra mugs, showed up a moment later. I filled mugs for Svetislav and me. The ale tasted better than that from the Stracaran street vendors, but I had not known until then that beer could pick up a fishy aftertaste.

While I studied the ale, Svetislav stared at the captains.

"Tell me," he said.

All but one burst out in denial and questions. The exception smelled more than the rest and possessed the longest beard. He cackled out, "Go fondle the Horse-Tamer's Trident."

Svetislav cocked his head at him and, again, glared at them all.

"Tell me," he said in the same tone. This time, they all stayed silent. Svetislav calmly waited, staring at each, in turn, with a blank face.

"Jeremena didn't send you, boy," cackled the one.

Svetislav looked at him.

"Why wouldn't she send him to you?" I interjected. With that question, I became more than merely Svetislav's subordinate. They quickly turned their anger at me. They appeared cruel, but I had already faced worse in this city.

"Yeah, if everyone helps you, we'll probably die, but if you attack us, I promise that you six will die before either Svetislav or me." After all, the light made me look cruel, too, and this seemed like a fantastic place to get rid of my frustration at Frano's death. Svetislav chuckled and nodded.

"So I ask again, why wouldn't she send him to you?"

The woman answered. "Yon lad's a Lakewarden. Upright. Come at you all straight-like. Not like Jeremena, as trusty as a spring afternoon on the lake."

"Why would Jeremena send anyone, then?" I asked.

All of them, except the cackler, looked away from us.

"Bitch don't like it when people don't do what she say," he cackled louder, raising a stump of a finger. "I'd know best of all of these other undrowned."

"And you didn't do what she told you to do?"

He laughed loudly. "Sure as hell didn't."

The others glared, trying to shut him up, but Svetislav stopped them with a tap of his knuckles on the table.

"Took money, too, be stupid not ta, but Earthshaker knows that's not why. And so does the bitch."

"You messed with the fish pricing."

"Surely did. And someone made a heaping pile of coins for whats we'd been doin'. Weren't Jeremena, though." He cackled again.

"Who told you to do it?"

"Tartarus knows. I didn't give a fuck. All I needed to hear was they were fuckin' with the bitch. Greedier than the Child-Eater, that one."

I looked at the rest. "So, who was it?"

They shrugged.

"We weren't really paying much attention. She'd messed with prices to get her gold for years," said the woman. "We wanted a bit of that ourselves."

Svetislav snorted.

"Was it a Dassaretae?" I asked.

They looked angry as hell. "Not stinkin' likely," snorted one.

"How would you know?" I wondered.

Svetislav chuckled. "Knew the words, did he?"

They looked anywhere but at us. I glanced at Svetislav, who still chuckled. I turned back to the captains.

"You're telling us that an Enchelei you don't know suggested you mess with Jeremena, a boss not known for patience and kindness, and you did it?"

"Made sense then," cackled the one.

"Well, can you describe him?"

They all paused and shook their heads.

"Well, he was sort of tall…"

"But not really…"

"Black hair."

Everyone in Achrida other than me had black hair, it seemed. At least no one could accuse me of helping fix the fish prices. Given what I had already discovered, that seemed like major progress to me.

"Beard?"

"Yes…" and "No…"

"You don't remember?"

Various forms of "not really" came from the captains.

I sighed. "Did he have any scars?"

"Nooooo…"

"Did he have eyes?"

They answered, "Of course."

"What color?"

They all shrugged.

"What was he wearing?"

They shrugged again. Pants. Tunic. In brown. Or light red. Or dark green.

"I hope you have better stories for Jeremena when she shows up. She will, you know."

Four men and one woman looked scared. The other cackled. Svetislav dismissed them, and we left.

Chapter 29
Afternoon, 15 Gersmoanne, 1712 MG

As we left the tavern, Svetislav's face held a rare hint of a smile.

"Why are you smiling?"

His smile grew broader.

"You know something."

He nodded happily.

"You knew that something for a while."

"Beard."

"Fenris stalk you! You knew something when they couldn't tell me about the beard?"

He chuckled.

"And you let me keep going?"

"Going good." He grinned as he led me around the Stracara and up the southern hill.

"My questioning was going too good for you to stop me?"

He felt so smug, he actually said, "Yep," instead of just nodding.

"There's a limb on the World Tree waiting for you," I grumpily chuckled.

"Probably."

"So what did you learn?"

"Know a Berzeti, has this way."

"You know a member of the Berzeti, a family that is sept to the Gropas, who has a way of not being remembered. Or of disguising himself?"

He nodded, though he quickly became serious.

"What?" I asked.

"Makes no sense."

"Something about him makes no sense?"

He nodded.

"It doesn't make sense that he would co-ordinate the price fixing by the captains?"

"Does not."

"Why?"

He shrugged. "Jeremena's."

"He's one of Jeremena's? Isn't the price-fixing messing with Jeremena's plan?"

He smiled.

I answered my own question. "Maybe not. Maybe she's got another iron in the fire."

He nodded.

We went through a number of small squares under the ridge. Each small square held a small fountain, small stores, small kiosks, and small people. Eventually we returned to the larger streets and followed one until we stood over a wide-open place shining in the sun.

"Amphitheater."

"The amphitheater of Achrida?" I asked.

He nodded and walked around to the southern side, where several smaller buildings were attached to the back of the theater. We entered a small door wedged into a corner. Once my eyes adjusted to the darkness I saw a room filled with a strange collection of objects. In one corner a pile of busts, chipped and worn by hard use, leered in every direction. In another swords, helms, shields, and bits of armor mustered in a chaotic pile. Flat structures of heavy fabric nailed to light planks leaned against the far wall. Through a door I could see piles of clothes.

Svetislav led me through another door, and we passed shelves filled with more things. Random things. Mugs and jewelry and hammers and plates and shoes and quills and clocks and tongs and bowls and so much more.

In the next room, a young woman ignored our entry. She kept her focus on the tunic she was repairing. When she did look up, I saw pretty eyes cursed to blindness from long toil in dim light.

Svetislav politely, though as curtly as ever, asked, "Kemal?"

She shook her head. "Haven't seen him today. Tried the 'Side?"

"The Hillside?"

She nodded.

"Not yet. Where's his home?"

"I'm not sure, though it's not for lack of his trying to get me there."
She giggled. "I think it's close to the 'Side, as he's always saying it'd just
take a moment to get to his bed." She giggled again.

Svetislav nodded, and I thanked her as we left.

The Hillside proved to be a small, odd, square building built directly
into the limestone. Inside, dripping cave rock formed the back wall. The
room held rickety tables, tired benches, and fresh people. Strata of
memory covered the masonry walls. Nailed-up tunics competed for space
with interesting paintings and illuminated manuscripts. Someone had
arranged shelves adorned with sculptures and oddities around the room.

I liked the place immediately.

At one table four creatures played a serious game. They wore
formless and stained smocks, three stained from paint and one from clay.
At another table a tawny-haired woman with ink-stained hands looked up
from a deep discussion she was having with a nattily dressed man who
had accentuated his intelligent eyes with slight makeup. Two people sat on
either side of a third table sitting next to the back wall. Each wore
comfortable but colorful clothes. Their calm demeanor suggested that
their young faces lied about their age.

The woman at the back table nodded to Svetislav. "Protokarabos,
what brings you here?"

Her companion quickly dismissed Svetislav but covetously eyed me
as he added, "And who is this fine, young lad?" He kept playing with a
small knife, tossing it into the air. Each time he either caught it by the hilt
without looking or let it stick vertically in the table. Hundreds of small
knife marks formed a two-inch circle on the table.

Svetislav ignored him. "Kemal?"

"Really, protokarabos, have you not yet learned to make whole
sentences?" She laughed.

He shook his head.

"You're hopeless," she added. "As for Kemal, he's not been in for a
couple of days. He's probably chasing some girl who's far too young for
him who prefers a different drinking place."

"He's not worth it," snorted the man with laughing eyes, "but this one might be. He looks like he knows how to use his sword."

I smiled modestly.

He laughed and said to the woman, "Ah, but he's for you dearie, not poor old Darijo. Keep an eye out though, laddie, I might convince you one of these days."

Flip, flip, flip went the knife.

I laughed. "Probably not but if you do, you'll be the first to know."

Svetislav smiled, but turned back to the woman and said, "Home?"

"Got one," she shot back with a smirk.

"Kemal's."

"He's got one, too."

He stared at her for a moment and then sighed. "Proreus Amalija, would you please tell me where Kemal lives?"

I looked at Svetislav in amazement while Amalija laughed at my dropped jaw. "Fifteen years I was a Lakewarden and that's probably the most words he's ever spoken to me." She chuckled at him. "See, that wasn't so hard. He lives three buildings to the right, on the third floor, third door down. I think he likes threes."

Svetislav nodded his thanks. She raised her hand.

He sighed, "Thank you, proreus."

"You're welcome, protokarabos."

Darijo laughed as we turned to leave.

"Come back soon, Svetislav," Amalija said warmly.

"Especially if you bring your friend," added Darijo.

Svetislav paused and looked at Darijo. "Need a new table, decarch."

"I'll just turn it to a different corner," he laughed, and flipped his knife almost to the ceiling. It landed straight up in the middle of the circle.

As we left, I could not help chuckling.

"Old friends," muttered Svetislav.

"You know, I do believe I noticed that. Why, I do believe I noticed that very early in the conversation, but you were going so good…" I laughed.

"World Tree," he growled.

As we opened the door leading to the rooms above, I laughed even harder. "I've known there's a limb on the World Tree waiting for me as well for a long time."

We left our laughter outside and began climbing the gloomy stairs. These steps had clearly never met a broom. They creaked with years of drunken stomps. Svetislav knocked on the third door down the hall. We heard some quiet sounds and then a loud thump. A smaller thump followed. We looked at each other and slowly slid our swords out of their sheaths.

Svetislav knocked again. With no answer, he tried to open the door. A latch kept it closed, so he took a half-step back, twisted his body, and kicked the door in.

The loud thump we had heard had probably been the fall of a body off of a small platform covered with sheepskins. Wet crimson streaks now dyed the skins. The body stretched his hand to us in hope, but the deep slash across his belly ended his hope as it ended his life. Blood pumped from the stumps of the fingers with which he had attempted to shield himself.

A shutter moved in the wind, creating the softer thump. Svetislav went to the window and looked out over the street. I went to the dying man.

He looked sightlessly at me.

"Had to."

"You had to do what?"

He didn't answer, just kept repeating, "Damn him," in time with the ever-slowing puddling of his blood on the floor.

Finally, he died. Later I would try to remember his face, but even death could not make it memorable. All I could remember were his fingertips scattered on the floor.

I looked at Svetislav, who shook his head with a shrug to the window.

"Kapric and Zvono aren't going to be happy," I said. We stared at the body. "But there's no help for it," I continued. "I'm going to go get them."

He nodded. We sheathed our swords. As I left he started searching the room.

Chapter 30
Afternoon, 15 Gersmoanne, 1712 MG

I went to Heartsquare and entered the big, looming beast of limestone. Eventually, I wound my way to the quaesitor room. Zvono needed only a quick look at my face.

"Well, Sevener, you didn't promise, I'll give you that."

"Might as well follow me and I'll explain on the way. Do we need to stop for Kapric?"

She shook her head as she put her wax tablet in her pouch and rose. "He's in a meeting, but we do need two others."

I followed her around the labyrinth to a dark room filled with drawers and niches, each filled with small boxes. Zvono motioned to two men who were puttering around. One studied a walnut-dyed shirt. The other stared at a sheet of parchment. They were so focused that Zvono had to clear her throat twice before they noticed her.

"Another body, lads, come on."

They put down their immediate projects, and followed us out. As we walked back to Kemal's apartment I told Zvono what I knew. By the time we returned, Svetislav had thoroughly searched the room, much to the displeasure of Zvono and her followers. Nevertheless, she waved at the room and they got to work.

We watched as they searched the room. Periodically they stopped and stared at something for a long while. Zvono noticed my curious look.

"Magicians. One is trying to pick up traces of emotion and help us place the murderer. The other is looking for traces of living creatures left behind, subtle traces that only magic can find."

A grim look appeared her face as she realized her magicians were shaking their heads in frustration. She turned to Svetislav.

"Protokarabos, you know I don't like you muddling in my work. It messes with their magic."

He shrugged. "Enchelei problem."

"I don't care whose problem it is, it's our job to solve this."

He shrugged again and held out two items. First, he showed us a small scrap of parchment that read "Low skip low low high."

"It's a new pattern," I said.

He nodded and pointed to five more scraps he'd uncovered. They all said the same thing.

"They were going to do it again."

"Do what?" asked Zvono.

I explained our thoughts about the price-fixing. Then Svetislav produced the second item, which prompted Zvono to explode.

"May Kerberus eat his fill... slowly," she growled.

Svetislav nodded, and I saw that he held a small bronze rose, about the size of a dinar, intricately cast, with the barest hints of thorns on its coiled stem.

"What is that?"

Svetislav looked out the window.

Zvono snapped, "It's a pass, a token of entry."

"To where?"

"Bronze Rose," rumbled Svetislav.

"I can see that it's a bronze rose, where does it let you pass?" Now I was getting irritated.

"It lets you get into the Bronze Rose," said Zvono after a moment. "It's an establishment for"—she paused—"a variety of interests."

"Interests?"

"We're a pretty flexible people, Sevener. Some families still encourage their sons to find an honorable 'uncle,' as has been done for many centuries. No one minds this. There's a big market for things that supposedly augment the fun. We don't mind those either. People can pretty much do what they want with whom they want. We'll shrug and move on. But there are a few things we won't accept."

"So, this is a place that caters to things people won't accept?"

She nodded.

"Is this one of Katarina's places?"

She nodded again.

"What is it that happens there?"

"Children," snapped Svetislav.

"It's a place for people to have sex with children?"

"Five, six years old, something like that," grated Zvono.

"Where is it?"

"I wish I knew," she snapped. We'd stop it. But it moves often…" she trailed off.

"So this allows someone to enter the Bronze Rose so they can have sex with young children. I suppose gender is irrelevant?"

"Both are there."

I turned to Svetislav. "Kemal had one of these tokens?"

He nodded.

"Do you know if it was his, and not one he'd taken from someone else?"

Zvono shook her head. "Doubtful. They're rare, and nobody wants to be caught with one."

Svetislav shook his head as well. He went to a shelf and pointed behind it. There, cut smoothly into the wall, a small opening large enough for the rose. A clever little door obscured the opening.

"He had a hiding place for it, one that took some time to make."

Svetislav nodded.

"So it wasn't hastily built and that means he was a patron of the Rose."

"Yes," hissed Zvono as she was scribbling in her tablet.

"You told me he was a Berzeti who mostly worked for Jeremena," I said, turning back to Svetislav.

He nodded again.

"Did Jeremena know about this?"

"Doubtful."

"Would she care?"

"Bad for business."

"She'd care because, if he was her factor and he was caught with the Rose, the connection to her would hurt her ability to control the Enchelei trade?" I guessed.

Yet another nod.

"And Kemal would know that?"

"Probably."

"Then I think Kemal had a problem. He kept repeating, 'Damn him,' as he was dying. At first, I thought he was cursing the person who actually stuck the blade into him, but now I'm not so sure. You said it didn't make sense for him to fix the fish prices because it didn't seem to help Jeremena."

Svetislav shrugged.

"So, I don't think he was working for her. I think someone knew about his rose and made him fix the prices even though it would hurt his patron. Someone—" I paused. "Some man was after Jeremena and used Kemal as a tool."

"And now he's dead and you can't ask him," said Zvono.

"Exactly."

"This makes two people, in two days, who were killed to keep them from talking to you."

I sighed. "Yes."

"Good thing I don't really want to talk to you."

Chapter 31
Late Afternoon, 15 Gersmoanne, 1712 MG

We left Kemal's apartment and headed towards the Faerie. Svetislav walked beside me, babbling in his normal manner. His silence allowed me to contemplate the events of the day as we walked in a bubble of silence amidst the crowd filling the Trade Road.

Before we reached the Heartsquare I noticed someone coming towards us. I immediately entered the nearest shop, a small shop specializing in fabrics and clothes for moderately wealthy women. I hid behind a stand displaying a number of small pieces of brightly colored silk and looked down the road. I saw no signs the man had noticed me.

Svetislav's eyes asked why we were in here.

"See the man in the walnut-dyed tunic, just walking underneath the sign with coins painted on it?"

He glanced quickly and nodded.

"I've seen him a number of times while I was leaving the Faerie. Each time he happened to be carrying an amphora down Medusa's Way and would follow me at least to the Square of Legends. In fact, he passed us when we left today." I paused. "I don't know. I guess he's always seemed somewhat interested in me. Do you recognize him?"

Svetislav glanced again and shrugged.

"Not Enchelei?"

"He might be. Looks familiar."

"I'd like to follow him," I said.

I had never followed anyone before, at least not without intending to meet them openly. Svetislav, on the other hand, had some experience and led the way. I spent as much time watching him as I did our quarry.

I discovered that the large number of people on the road both helped and hurt. It was much easier for us to remain hidden from him, but it also made it easier for him to hide from us. Several times I thought we might have lost him, but Svetislav never faltered. He also made sure we dawdled when we needed to and sped up when we had to. No doubt every child in this city learned by their fifth winter how to follow someone unobtrusively.

We halted at a kiosk where we ostensibly stared at the wares. The man left Trade Road and ascended the hill into what appeared to be a fairly nice neighborhood. I fretted that we would lose track of him if we did not hurry.

Svetislav smiled softly. "Wait."

He was right. In a few moments the man returned to the Trade Road, glanced both ways, and moved on. Svetislav's caution seemed to have kept us far enough away that he did not see us.

"What happened there?" I asked, as we continued to follow.

"Always wait. Can be a trick."

"Wait at turns, you're saying, because it could be a trick to catch anyone following?"

He nodded.

"What if he turns immediately after the first turn?"

He shrugged.

"You lose him?"

He nodded.

"So, you lose track of some this way?"

He nodded again as he slyly led the way through a caravan of smelly camels and smellier drovers.

"Always lose some," he added.

Fortunately, we did not lose this one. Unfortunately, somewhere along the way he noticed us.

At a corner leading to a shabby neighborhood whose major adornments were chipped limestone bricks on the houses and smashed ceramic roof tiles on the road, we turned the corner and came face-to-face with him and three of his buddies. His larger buddies. Not Anastasius-sized of course, but large enough. Each had a cudgel, and the sincere desire to use it.

I stepped up. "I just want to talk."

The friends growled and stepped forward. Svetislav advanced and glared back.

"I just want to know why you follow me," I said, speaking to the man.

"I didn't follow you here," he sneered.

"Amazingly, I realized that without you telling me. But, you have followed me up and down Medusa's Way for several days."

"Whatever. I do what I want to," came the snarl.

Suddenly, I'd had enough. "By Wolfsbane, you'd better want to stop following me," I shouted. "I just had a man die in my arms. Yesterday I watched another die right in front of me. Three days ago I killed three men who attacked me in Medusa's Way. I'm tired of dealing with irritated quaesitors, and they're damn well tired of picking up bodies behind me. I'm not in a good mood, and One-Eye take me if I'm not willing to add you to the fucking list."

Somewhere throughout this rant I completely lost focus, stomped up to him and berated him nose to nose. Well, my nose to his chin, given that he stood a couple of inches taller than me. The rash stupidity of my action shocked everyone, including me once I realized what I had done.

One of the man's big friends gave a booming laugh. "Better watch out Sebastijan, this sheep's dick wants to fuck you."

Now everyone laughed, including me. Even Svetislav smiled.

"Alright, Sevener, I won't follow you again," Sebastijan chuckled.

"Who told you to follow me before?"

He looked affronted. "Please, I stay bought."

"Better leave him be, boy. He's not much, but he does keep his word," rumbled the big friend.

"Fair enough." An idea struck swiftly. "Where can I find you if I want to buy you?"

He looked at me strangely. "I'm not sure I want to tell you right now, Sevener. But I know where to find you, if I change my mind."

"Fair enough," I repeated.

"So what did that tell us?" I asked Svetislav after we left Sebastijan and walked north, up the Trade Road.

Svetislav shrugged.

I nodded. "I don't know either. I'll have to think about it."

And that is what I did as we walked back.

Chapter 32
Late Afternoon, 15 Gersmoanne, 1712 MG

When we arrived at the Faerie, it was bustling more than usual. I could barely hear the scop, who gamely kept performing. We had returned in time for dinner. As we entered, I saw Flavian, Cvetijin, and others curled around platters holding grilled slivers of lake trout atop a bed of the small grains. Their plan looked excellent, and hoped to implement the same one myself.

Sadly, two things distracted me from that idea. The first was Desimir, who stomped up.

"Where the hell have you been?"

"Looking around. I'll tell you everything if you let me eat dinner."

Karah handed me a mug as I tried to sit down while dodging Desimir's rantings, chairs, and Melia's twining herself in my feet. Svetislav joined us as Desimir described in detail my lineage, sexual preferences, and general worthlessness. I never realized I wanted to do that one thing with a goat, but Desimir assured me I did. He started to do the same with Svetislav, but Ragnar swooped in with plates for all of us. He also handed me the second distraction, which had the effect of stopping Desimir mid-rant.

The distraction was a message written on a small scrap of parchment that had obviously been scratched and erased many times. It read, "Meet me at Milos's Mare midday tomorrow." There was no signature. The only thing that might have identified the sender was a fleeting hint of cinnamon.

"It's a trap," growled Desimir.

Svetislav nodded.

I thought about it for a while. I even ate some of the steaming trout in front of me. Zoe's trout was so good that I guessed many of the extra guests that evening came in just to taste it.

"So it's a trap," I said eventually. "I think I want to go anyway."

Desimir started ranting again, but before he could name more than two new flaws in my parentage, I stopped him.

"We'll prepare for a trap. We'll look for an ambush. We're not going to be easy to kill. But I want to know who sent this. Can you tell me?"

Desimir shook his head.

"Even with the hint of cinnamon?"

He shook his head again.

"I didn't think so. So let's figure out how to walk out of the trap."

Desimir scowled but relaxed a little when he described Milos's Mare. "It's a small taberna overlooking the lake. From our perspective it's a good spot, fairly open and upscale. It's not a good place for an ambush."

"What about the roads leading there?"

"In this city?" snorted Desimir. "That's a problem. There are many places attackers can hide."

"Svet, do you know if any of the Gropa leaders frequent the Mare?"

He shook his head.

I tapped the parchment on the table and thought. "I wonder..."

The next time Ragnar passed I flagged him down and asked, "When did the note arrive?"

"Well, I'm to be thinkin' it's not been bein' all that long ago. Now let me be seein' what was I doin' whilst the messenger was to be comin' in through the door?" He thought for a moment. "Right, I was to be servin' Cvetijin and Flavian and Honker rakija, because Honk was to be leavin' on account a' his wife was to be havin' somethin' special with her folks, and they were all to be drinkin' a bit to make the night to be goin' better for him, as he's to be thinkin' her ma's not so bad, but her da's somethin' to do with the cult of Aglais, and isn't she to be bein' a strange godling who's to be tellin' her folk that they aren't to be doin' much of anythin', but especially that wine and ale and rakija are to be bein' bad things, and a'course Honker's not one to be passin' on my ales, so he's never been bein' lookin' forward to seein'—"

"The message, Ragnar."

"Oh, aye, I was to be gettin' to that. That was to be bein' right before me Zoe was to be tellin' me to start bringin' out some of the dinners, so I'm to be thinkin' no more than an hour or so."

I let Ragnar get back to work, and looked at Svetislav. "After we found Kemal."

"Yes," mumbled Svetislav around a mouthful of trout.

"What do you mean, 'found Kemal?'" demanded Desimir. "And who's Kemal anyway?"

So in between bites of dinner, with the help of Svetislav's shrugs and nods, I explained the events of the day.

"You forgot your stances when you stepped up to Sebastijan?" snapped Desimir, and he started another rant that lasted long enough for me to finish the trout. Once he had quieted down, he promised to drill the Long Guard into me until I instinctively took that stance.

I turned back to Svetislav. "Do you think the timing of the message is a coincidence? It's about the right time for someone to find out we almost got to talk to Kemal and decide to ambush us, or at least to find out if he had, in fact, talked to us."

Svetislav shrugged.

"Doesn't matter," spat Desimir. "We assume it's not."

"Right, we assume it's not a coincidence and prepare for that possibility. I'm not sure what that means, though," I admitted.

"Afterwards," muttered Svetislav.

I looked at him.

Desimir added, "He means he thinks the trap will spring after the meeting. That whoever this is wants to speak to you and will then signal whether or not to attack."

I thought for a moment. "Svetislav, do you want to be there?"

"Patrol." He shook his head. "But tell me later."

Desimir shrugged. "No matter, Piri will let me use my squad."

I thought for a while. "I want to make sure we deal with someone, whether it's because they're attacking me or because we're talking," I mused.

"So, you don't want the entire squad there until after you've had the meeting?"

"Yeah, I doubt anyone will attack if we have an entire squad of Pathfinders with us. But I'm not sure they'd talk to me, either."

Svetislav chucked.

"So, you and I leave from here, and the Pathfinders leave from their barracks. We time it so that they are behind us by a few minutes. Then they wait and escort us back."

Desimir nodded. "That'd work, but the timing is tricky."

"I thought of that. You should go to Piri and report."

Desimir said "No" at the same time Svetislav shook his head.

"That might warn whoever wants to talk to you to stay away from the meeting. Someone here is spying for them, I guarantee you," declared Desimir.

"My job," added Svetislav.

I looked back and forth at the two of them and finally sighed. "I guess you know what you're doing."

They nodded, and Desimir said, "More than you fools from the Seven Kingdoms."

Svetislav and Desimir laughed together. I sighed and leaned back to enjoy the rest of the evening, but Desimir had other ideas.

"Get up before you're too drunk."

"Why?" I asked warily.

"We have something to do."

I looked at Svetislav. He shrugged. I shrugged. I got up.

"I told you, Sevener, you were going to get extra drill for fucking up on the field..."

And he proceeded to drill dinner right out of me.

Chapter 33
Late Morning, 16 Gersmoanne, 1712 MG

If I had any hopes that Desimir would count last night's drilling as replacement for practice the next morning, he dashed them when he woke me up early in the morning. Now I sat in the Faerie, petting Melia and waiting for him after a morning of throws and bounces. A bath, and breakfast of leftover slices of grilled vegetables chopped up in scrambled eggs, refreshed me.

I even had time to ask Karah the name of the strange vegetable, but her answer proved less helpful than anticipated. What kind of word is *zucchini* anyway?

Desimir finally sauntered down, but not before giving me enough time to have second thoughts about the plan.

"How do we know your squad will get the message?"

"Svetislav said he would take care of it. You heard him, yourself."

"Yeah, but how?"

Desimir shrugged.

"But you trust him?"

He nodded.

"Even though he's Enchelei?"

He nodded, again.

"By the Great Wyrm, now you're acting like him. Quit nodding and say something before I have to clean my saex."

He nodded… and then laughed. "I think he and Piri have something worked out between them."

"They do?"

"Yeah, they always seem to be on the same page with each other."

"Ever since I came?"

He laughed. "Ever since she became hecatontarch. It was the same with the one before her."

"You're saying the leaders of the Pathfinders and the Lakewardens have some way of communicating with each other?"

He nodded. "And the Akritoi, the Feroun, the Altmezzers, and even

215

the damned, arrogant Pronoiars. I think whoever, in each company, holds Piri's position talks to the others in that same position."

"A total of six companies?"

"Yeah, plus some Imperial companies from across the Empire."

"Are all six Enchelei or Dassaretae?"

"Yeah. The Akritoi are Enchelei, like the Lakewardens. The Pronoiars are mostly Berzeti, because the Pronoiars are cavalry and the Berzeti are still skilled horsemen. The Feroun and Altmezzers are affiliated with the Dassaretae. The Altmezzers, though, are a little odd, as there are more foreigners in their ranks than any other company, mostly from the Kreisens. They're also known for carrying some evil-looking knives."

"In any case, you think Svetislav went back to the Lakewardens, and sent a message to Piri, using this method?"

"That'd be my guess. And, I think they usually communicate every day to each of them, so no one should find anything unusual."

"Convenient."

"It's Achrida. There are a lot of 'convenient' traditions here." He smirked.

"I noticed."

"I'm willing to trust that Svetislav and Piri fixed things. You?"

"And if I say no, you'll mention that to the two of them and they'll pound on me while we train?"

His only answer was a self-satisfied smirk.

"Then I think I trust them, too." I grinned and got up. "So let's get moving, you laggard."

Melia clawed at my hand in frustration when I stopped petting her, but I expected it so I avoided her claws. However, I could not avoid her plaintive mewling when I left her alone, bereft of attention, loving, and food for at least two seconds. She retaliated by jumping to the next table, where four large, harsh-faced, and cheerfully loud women of the neighborhood cooed over her.

Both of us expected trouble. I had sword, saex, and knife. Desimir had his five knives, and he wore his semi-spatha openly. We decided against armor, though. We arrived at the Mare without incident and found Zacharia sitting with a bottle of wine chilling in lakewater and an empty stemmed glass. He delicately drank from another glass. He motioned for me to sit, and looked up at Desimir.

"Dassaretae, I've a table for you right there."

He pointed to another table, where a bottle of rakija and a glass waited.

"As you surely can see, it overlooks both this table and the entrance. I have no interest in harming your ward, nor do I want Hecatontarch Piriska to be any more displeased with me than she already is. You can do your duty sitting there, but not hear to what I wish to say to our outlander friend."

Desimir grumbled but sat at the other table.

"Milos's Mare is actually a pun. Did Desimir tell you that?" Zacharia asked after he poured me wine.

"No, he didn't."

"Milos is one of the heroes our epic poets write about. He's supposed to be a son of a dragon. Stronger than any man. Swifter than any horse. Wiser than any wizard. You know the type."

"Yes, I do. I've spent many a night listening to a scop recount the deeds of such men."

"His last name, Obilic, means 'mare.' Don't ask me how he got the name, but it explains why this lovely little spot is named as it is."

We sat at a table, shielded by a sunfly of canvas, at the side of the cliff overlooking the lake. A slight breeze flowed from the lake up the cliff, enough to riffle our hair a bit, but not much more. A small pot of purple flowers added a pleasant scent.

"What do you think of our fair little town?" asked Zacharia, waving at the view. "Is she not glorious?" He laughed. "Of course, from what I've heard, you've had a tough time appreciating all that this city has to offer."

"Murder, kidnapping, and theft can, indeed, distract. I wonder how much of that is your fault?"

He raised his hand in mock horror. "Surely, you don't presume to suggest that I have raised a dagger or sword against you?"

"Of course not. But I do presume to suggest that you might have sent someone else to raise dagger or sword against me."

"Well, you might be right, at that." He smiled.

I tired of the verbal testing of the waters. "You asked to meet me?"

"Yes, I wanted a chance to chat with you outside of, shall we say, the family influence."

"About what?"

"About how you can help me help the Gropas."

"I would guess you care more about helping yourself."

"Of course, but I also recognize that I am tied to the fortunes of the Gropas."

"So, what do you think I can do?"

"I have a problem. In fact, I have a problem that, I think, you know something about."

I looked at him, questioningly.

"I have had an agent doing some work for me. Unfortunately, he had the bad luck to discover what knives do to the inside of a man." He chuckled at his wit.

"Kemal."

"Why, yes, I do believe that was his name."

"You are telling me that you sent Kemal to several Enchelei fishing boat captains with the goal of fixing prices so that you could hinder Jeremena's strategy?"

"You are quick, aren't you? Yes, I did that."

"You didn't kill him?"

"Not at all. I hear he bled quite a bit. Blood distresses me."

He did not look particularly distressed.

"In that case, did you have him killed by someone else?"

"That would be what I would do."

"That didn't answer my question."

"No it didn't, and while I'm enjoying playing with you, I will relent and tell you, truthfully, that I did not want him dead, either by my hand or by my bidding."

I had to ask those questions. That didn't mean I trusted the answers. "If you didn't kill him, why did you have him convince the captains to fix the fish prices?"

"As you can undoubtedly guess, one reason was to make a number of extra dinars appear in my coffers."

"Wouldn't those dinars have eventually ended up in Gropa coffers?"

"Probably." He waved that away. "But now I have them. Do you not think that's a good thing?"

I looked at him. "Not really."

"I am greatly saddened to hear that." He smirked as he drank a sip of the wine. "However, I am truthfully saddened that Kemal is no longer here to deliver my messages to my captains."

"That, I might believe."

He chuckled. "And now we get to the point of inviting you."

I looked at him.

"When I heard Kemal was murdered, I immediately thought of his family."

"Did he have a family?"

"Surely he had some sort of family. I have no doubt they're distressed. I truly feel their pain."

"Mmmm," I muttered.

"But, of course, after feeling their pain, I felt my pain, at least the pain his death would cause me."

"Because, suddenly, you needed someone to deliver those messages to your captains."

"Indeed. And when I heard you found him with our mighty Svetislav, I had an epiphany."

"Yes?"

"Well, you are clearly a capable fellow, what with all of the deeds you have performed in your short time in our fair city. I think you might be just the man to take over Kemal's responsibilities."

"You're asking me to become your messenger?"

"You have, indeed, grasped my meaning. And I pay very well, even to someone who is not Gropa."

I looked at him for a bit, hoping I appeared to be considering his offer. Eventually, I shook my head.

"I don't believe I'm at liberty to accept your offer," I said, slowly.

"What do you mean?"

"First, I have an obligation to Ragnar to find the ones behind the kidnapping at the Faerie."

"Oh, I think you already know that Katarina arranged that."

"Yes, she actually faked the kidnapping."

"So, you can tell Ragnar, and he can restore his honor."

I shook my head. "Katarina did it, at least partially, at the behest of someone else. I need to find that someone else before Ragnar can restore his honor."

"Ah, well, the things you learn." He did not look particularly enlightened as he continued. "I said I would pay well, and I can pay not only in gold but in information, as well. I can help you discover who involved Katarina."

"That would be useful," I agreed. "But, that is only the first reason. While I have sworn no specific oath to Pal, I do not feel it would be honorable to sabotage his family."

"I said, before, I did this not only to fill my coffers, but for the benefit of the family."

"I do not see how."

"I am not surprised. Now, I am guessing that Svetislav has told you the basics of our family hierarchy."

"We've talked some."

He continued with another smirk, "It is so peaceful on the lake, isn't it?"

I sighed. "Yes, it is."

"So, you know that Jeremena has coordinated the Gropa trade for decades. Well, at least all of the regular trade, not including that which Davorin created."

"I had heard that."

"Truthfully, she has been quite successful. Until the past few years."

"And you think she's no longer capable?"

"Not at all, she's still as capable as ever."

"Then, what?"

"Capability does not guarantee success."

I waited for him to continue. He did.

"She's used the same strategy for decades. The Mrnjavcevics are not stupid. They know her pattern, and now they are undercutting us."

"So, tell her to change the pattern."

"Shockingly, she doesn't believe me. Even with the numbers staring her in the face."

"Amazing. So, why don't you convince Pal to force her?"

"Don't think I haven't suggested it to him. And to Vesela. She and I have, quite often, talked about this and many other things."

"And…"

"Pal wants more evidence, and so does she." Zacharia shrugged and took a sip of wine. "Truthfully, I cannot entirely blame them. Jeremena has brought many a dinar to the Gropas and the Enchelei. However, the numbers do not lie."

"And, you want to provide more evidence."

"You are swift. Yes, I do. I want to try different patterns and compare my numbers with hers."

"You think you'll be able to prove that your plan is better for the Gropas."

"Yes, I do."

"With the added advantage that you'll make lots of money in the process."

He smirked, and finished the bottle of wine. He motioned for another. I thought some more.

"There's another advantage for you, isn't there?"

"What do you mean?"

"If you manage to prove that Jeremena's strategy is flawed, and that your strategy is better, then you take a step up in the family power structure."

"I fear, outlander, that your time in our fair city has made you suspicious."

"That doesn't mean I'm wrong."

"No," he chuckled. "You are correct, and I wonder if you'd have noticed that two weeks ago before you came here."

"Whether or not I would have is irrelevant. I have noticed it, but I'm not sure your ascension would be beneficial to Pal or Vesela."

"I can't deny that I am ambitious. But so is Jeremena. She looks like such a sweet grandmother, but the truth is that she is very dangerous. After all, someone killed Kemal."

I nodded. "I believe she is dangerous. I don't know, though, if I believe she killed him."

"See, not everything I have said to you tonight is a lie."

"But some of it is."

"Just because you don't believe everything I've said doesn't mean that I have not been truthful to you." He paused and spoke in a tone not natural for him. "But believe this too, my friend: I will do whatever it takes to strengthen the Enchelei."

I thought for a moment. "Because of Agata."

"Yes." He smiled proudly. "Because of her."

I thought some more. "I will think about your offer. I can't deny your ability to give me fair value, but I am an honorable man, and I must weigh my debts."

He looked at me with a sly smile. "I have no doubts about your honor..."

"But?"

"But for my plan to succeed, I must have a courier delivering my messages to the captains soon, or the plan cannot succeed."

I nodded and switched topics. "What makes you think I won't go to Jeremena and warn her?"

"You said it yourself. You're an honorable man. I think you will at least talk to me again before telling her, and if I'm wrong..."

"Yes?"

"If I'm wrong, I still come out ahead. One, I will know how much I can trust you, and since information is my true business, that is something important to know. Two, I'm sure she already knows I'm behind the price-fixing, so nothing you tell her is truly secret. Three, if you tell her, she might actually change her plans of her own accord."

"So, while you might not get all of the money, you might still attain your overall goal."

"You are a quick study, my friend." He paused as a waiter arrived to open a new bottle. "So, my friend, think about what I have offered. I will expect you here tomorrow evening to tell me either way. If I don't receive an answer, I'll simply have to hire someone else to do this task."

I got up and nodded.

"Oh," he added, "I'm afraid you have unnecessarily disturbed those Pathfinders in the street. Nevertheless, I commend you on your prudence." He smiled smugly and twitched his wine glass in farewell.

Desimir joined me at the entrance. Once outside, his squad formed around us. Their presence reassured me, even though I believed Zacharia's parting words.

Chapter 34
Afternoon, 16 Gersmoanne, 1712 MG

"So?" asked Desimir, once we sat at our table in the Faerie with ales before us.

I looked at him.

"So," he demanded again, "what did Zacharia want?"

"Well, for one thing, he wanted to tell me that he didn't kill Kemal."

"Of course, he wants you to think that," he snorted.

"He might not have been lying."

"He's always lying."

"Not always."

Desimir shook his head and grumbled, "You are such an innocent fool."

"That may be." I grinned. "But I do believe that he wants to make Agata the next zupan of a strong and powerful Enchelei tribe."

"I don't know anything about that."

"Trust me, that part makes sense. I don't, however, believe all of the other things he told me."

"Like?"

"Like whether he killed Kemal. His story's solid and consistent, but I have no doubt he's a good enough liar that any lie he tells would be solid and consistent."

"What was his lie?"

"His story was that he planned the price-fixing to pull Jeremena out of her rut, a rut that the Dassaretae are taking advantage of."

"The death of Kemal ends that."

"Don't be too sure about that."

"What in the waters of the Anvil Sea do you mean by that?"

"I mean, all he has to do is find someone else to pass on the messages…"

"And you're the someone else!?!"

"He offered. I said I'd think about it."

Desimir got up and stomped about the Faerie. We watched him with amusement. The scop played something fast on his lute, in time with Desimir's stomping. Melia meowed curiously every time he passed the table she sat on.

Honker leaned over and snorted, "What did you say to the lad?"

"Nothing much, really. I just said I was thinking, and you know his opinion about thinking."

We all laughed and waited. Eventually, after many invectives, Desimir calmed down enough to return to his seat.

Ragnar came over, grinning. "Don't you be frettin' me boy, I'm to be sayin' Zoe'll be givin' all of us somethin' tasty you'll be bein' able to get around, and that'll even make whatever this loon has been sayin' sound a might more reasonable, even if it's to be bein' as stupid as you obviously are to be thinkin' right now. Here now, be takin' a mite of my rakija with me as we're to be waitin' for this fool to stop grinnin'."

I grinned back. "It's going to be a while. I know tomorrow he's going to get his revenge by throwing me across your hayroom, so I might as well laugh at him while I can."

"By Zeus's cock, you'll fly," he growled.

Honker, Flavian, Cvetijin and the rest asked for rakija as well, and together they toasted to the "stupidity of all Seveners." I saluted that toast with my ale. Then I turned back to Desimir.

"Of course I told him I'd think about it. How else was I going to keep him talking?" I paused. "And some information I want to know might be in the messages he's sending to the captains. I would have expected Svetislav to be more upset than you. I am, after all, tearing the Enchelei system apart, not the Dassaretae one."

He sighed. "I just hate the thought of you working with the Enchelei."

"Svetislav and I worked together for hours, yesterday."

"I didn't like that, either, and I respect him."

"Remember why I'm here, Desimir."

"I know, I know," he sighed, "you're here to help Ragnar. You're not Dassaretae. You're an outsider."

"Yes, and if I have to hurt the Dassaretae to fulfill my oath and restore Ragnar's honor, I will. You know that. Piri has always known that."

"I'm just…"

"Frustrated, I know." I took a drink. "Trust me, Desimir, I have no desire to harm the Dassaretae. I admire you, Piri, and the Pathfinders very much. And I appreciate your teaching me wrestling."

We drank our ale quietly until Ragnar brought us dinner. Desimir and I shared a whole chicken accompanied by spiced honey turnips. I hate turnips. I have always hated turnips. Until I ate Zoe's.

While we ate, I thought about my next step. I murmured, "I think I need to talk to Vukasin, Desimir."

"After telling me that you'd hurt the Dassaretae if it helped you fulfill your oath?"

"In fact, I think I need to talk to him before I answer Zacharia, and that means we need to go after we finish dinner."

He was shaking his head. "It doesn't work that way."

"It does if you don't want to see the Dassaretae harmed."

"What do you mean?"

"I need to figure out what's going on in the Gropas, and to do that I need to tramp around in their garden, so to speak."

"What does that have to do with Vukasin?"

"Think, my friend. If I tramp on the wrong path, I will upset this balance that Pal and Vukasin have worked to maintain. I've talked to Pal and I have some idea what he wants. I have no idea about Vukasin. And if I do accept Zacharia's offer, then I will surely be tilting that balance at least somewhat." Another thought crossed my mind. "If Vukasin is taking advantage of Jeremena's predictability, then by helping Zacharia I might very well cost Vukasin and the Dassaretae a great deal of money. If I talk with him he is at least warned."

"Won't Zacharia be upset?"

"Well, he won't be happy, but one of his goals is to prevent the Dassaretae from taking money out of the Gropa coffers. If Vukasin stops, even temporarily, to wait and see what happens with me, then we have at least allowed Jeremena to continue without loss."

"I actually follow that."

"Of course you do, you're from this crazy city."

I figured that would be the most approval I could get from Desimir at that moment, so I simply got up and walked out the door, ignoring his demands to wait.

Chapter 35
Evening, 16 Gersmoanne, 1712 MG

Desimir chased me and only caught me once I turned onto Medusa's Way.

"Vukasin's not going to like this," he yelled.

"Oh, I don't know. All of this craziness has surely helped him, but he's a noble. Back in the Seven Kingdoms, craziness always makes nobles nervous, and I can't imagine they're any different here."

I paused once we reached the Square of Legends. "So, Dez, which way do we go?"

He sighed, pointed towards Heartsquare. "That way, then up the hill. And, don't call me Dez."

"Thanks, Dez."

He glared at me for a second, giving me another chance to speed away. Spitting out a variety of strange words I was glad I did not know, he ran after me. I followed his increasingly irritable lead to a long, rambling building embedded into the hillside. Though built like many other houses in Achrida, with limestone and a red tile roof, it stretched longer, with fewer levels than any other I had seen thus far. Primarily a single floor with a few portions that rose to a second.

Where the Gropas had chosen an ornate, well-defended, obvious gate for their mansion, the Mrnjavcevics had opted for a small, inconspicuous entrance. Nor could I see any doorwardens, given that we simply walked through the entrance.

Couches packed the entry room. A small sideboard holding a gleaming selection of rakijas stood along one wall. A single doorway led inward. The lack of armed guards, coupled with the welcoming opening room, spoke softly of a veiled fist, relaxed in its confident power.

An extraordinarily short woman, whose presence filled the room, greeted us.

"Edward wishes to speak with Vukasin, Baka," Desimir said meekly.

"Indeed?"

She followed the comment with a long, deliberate examination of our

228

worthiness to enter. She clearly approved of Zoe's skill at bandaging my arm. She just as clearly disapproved of everything else. Nevertheless, she decided to grant us entrance.

"Come with me."

We followed her through a maze of rooms and doors. We passed a large scriptorium burrowed deep into the hill. Another room, painted in a pleasant green, held six people basking in sunlight streaming through a skylight. They watched us closely as we walked past. We went through another hallway of doors. One archway opened into a large area with several skylights and a splashing fountain.

As we went further, the furniture and fittings became increasingly luxurious, though they never reached the opulence of the Gropas. Even Vukasin required no great opulence in his sitting room.

He reminded me of Piri. Short, fairly broad, relaxed, and confident. Lush beard with trimmed hair. Basalt eyes. He felt connected to the bones of the earth, so much so I wondered if he was a stonelord.

He turned to Desimir, saying, "Might as well go with Baka. I do believe that she would like to chat with you." He had a deep voice like large rocks and slow ice. Desimir shrugged and went with her, leaving me alone with the zupan.

"Welcome, Edward. It is a pleasure to finally meet you." He handed me a glass of rakija, and gestured to a seat. I bowed, and we sat. "You are here to ask if I am guilty of attacking the Gropas."

"Yes, Zupan, among other things."

"I am not." So might a boulder, sitting alone on a peat moor, rumble.

"I am not surprised. Can you tell me what you think is happening?"

He shrugged. "I admit I am somewhat puzzled as well."

"Had you heard any hints of this tension before it happened?"

"Not really." He paused. "My people told me the Naumites were primed for a schism. Some advisors suggested ways I could initiate it." He leaned back. "A kidnapping was not one of those ways," he added with a slight smile. "In any case, I chose not to try because the reward was not worth the risk."

"What kind of rewards would have been worth the risk?"

"The Naumites bolster the Gropas, to be sure, but none of the sects that are affiliated with either the Enchelei or Dassaretae cause any harm to the other tribe. A sect's strength may add power and prestige to a tribe, but willingly serves the other when needed."

"Yet your advisors tell you about opportunities."

"They tell me what I *can* do."

"Would you go after the Naumites as part of a larger campaign against the Gropas?"

"I might, and it appears someone else might have done so."

"That was my thought, as well."

"None of these actions are beyond my capabilities, but I did not initiate this assault. The Mrnjavcevics are ascendant of late, and I have no great desire to change the status quo."

"You don't want to kick the Gropas when they're down?"

"Not really. I desire what existed only a month ago, a calm and stable Achrida, with the Dassaretae slightly superior. We gained wealth with very little risk."

"And now, would you help Pal?"

He thought for a moment. "Actually, I might. If I thought this was an assault on the city of Achrida, I would definitely help him. And if outsiders did attack the Enchelei, he might welcome the help. Might even request it. As I might."

"So, you don't think this comes from the outside?"

"No. A month ago we were filling the Emperor's coffers with our taxes while giving him no reason to think of us, so he had no reason to intrude. He is our most constant outside threat."

"The Emperor?" I interjected.

"Yes."

"Why?"

"The Emperor is probably the single most powerful individual you could think of. For some reason, though, no emperor in memory is ever satisfied. Also, they always seem to think they know best. Few are correct in this belief, but no one ever tells the Emperor he is wrong."

"Could he, or any of his advisors, have prompted this?"

"Doubtful. They usually feel no need to be this subtle."

"What other outside threats are there?"

"The Lezhans compete for our trading routes."

"Trade does not seem to be at the heart of this conflict."

"I agree."

"Anyone else?"

"For millennia people have migrated through this valley. This valley is also a prime invasion route for someone at war with the Empire."

"That doesn't seem relevant either." At his nod, I continued, "What about Gregor? Could he have started this as a plan to eliminate his rival?"

Vukasin laughed. "You are certainly learning to think in Achridan ways. But no, I don't think so. The schism hasn't been good for him, and won't be, even if he can eliminate Kristijan. Historians will question him for centuries, and the Naumites care about that. No, he wanted to prevent the schism from ever happening."

"So, we're back to someone playing internal Achrida politics."

"Yes," he rumbled.

"It's not you, you say, but are there mavericks in the Dassaretae who might do this?"

He leaned back and paused. "Yes." He thought for another moment. "Though I don't see them doing this. Most of my mavericks are merchants and tradesmen."

"Even Piri?"

He laughed. "She's definitely a maverick, but she is loyal to me, for which I am profoundly grateful. She is more cunning and capable than I. Yet, she is also honorable and honest, traits unusual in Achrida."

"I'm beginning to see that." I paused. "Speaking of capable, what do you think of Agata?"

Vukasin chuckled. "My heirs will have their hands full."

"You don't seem worried. My impression of her is that in a few years she'll be eroding the ascendancy you spoke of. That seems like a good reason for you to attack the Enchelei, now, before she comes into her full power."

"You are correct." He smiled.

"So, you might be lying when you said you aren't attacking them right now."

He laughed. "In a sense, I was. I'm always looking for corners to nibble away. However, I have no desire to escalate the rivalry past where it currently stands."

"And Agata?"

"She will undoubtedly have her successes. In fact, I expect she'll erase our current advantage, and may elevate the Enchelei to the same ascendancy we now possess."

"So…"

"So, she is also incredibly sane. I have to look out for the interests of all the Dassaretae, not simply the ones whose coffers I can fatten. I, and my heirs, will defend, as best as we can, the prerogatives we have gained these past years. Success or failure will happen as they do. However, with Agata I have no worries that she will lead us to another Sfagi. My people may be poorer, but they will be safe and alive, and that is my first responsibility."

"Did your advisors suggest a preemptive strike?"

"Of course they did."

He leaned back, incredibly relaxed. I could see his point, though I did not necessarily trust him. I shifted topics.

"You are looking for ways to nibble, though?"

"Yes."

"Would one of those ways happen to be taking advantage of the price of fish?"

He grinned. "That is especially satisfying. Jeremena has managed that market for decades and earned many thousands of dinars for the Enchelei during that time."

"And now?"

"Now the prices are fluctuating for reasons outside of her control," he said smugly.

"So, the recent price-fixing hasn't bothered you?"

"Oh, there's no doubt I would like to keep skimming profits from the Gropa coffers. However, I think chaos in the fish market is a good thing. I'm not sure who is mucking with her prices, though my guess would be Zacharia, but we're losing no more than we used to, and she has a fight on her hands."

"You get all the advantages without the risk."

"Now you are seeing a glimmer of why I don't want to attack the Gropas right now any more than I need. Pal is a good man, and he is capable. However, the Enchelei leadership as a whole is not as skilled. Vesela is too aggressive. Jeremena is too predictable. Any Dassaretae could run rings around Andrija, though I admire and respect him greatly. Agata is too young, though she will be a foe worthy of respect. Zacharia is too selfish. Davorin is too corrupt. Pal needs help, as do I, but at the moment his council is weaker than at any time I can recall."

"You are taking advantage of that weakness."

"I am."

"What if I told you I might help the Enchelei and it might cost your tribe?"

"You are welcome to do whatever you wish. I know that Zacharia offered you some sort of job. I am not positive what that job might be, though my guess would be to become his courier since the messenger he was using was murdered yesterday."

"Did you kill Kemal?"

"The messenger? No, of course not. The secondary price-fixing cut us out of the profits but, again, harmed Jeremena. As I said, that's beneficial to us, in a larger sense."

I paused, again, before saying, "We agree the schism is probably part of a larger campaign aimed, in some sense, at the Gropas."

He nodded.

"You've said that it is not your campaign. There's no evidence the campaign is being orchestrated by Gregor or any outsider."

He nodded again.

"So who do you think might have a reason and the opportunity to lead it? Could it be one of the kraljevics?"

"Gibroz is fairly straightforward. He is, within his sphere, powerful and forceful. He is one of the few people in Achrida who doesn't depend on subtlety. Can he be subtle? Absolutely, and he has a few plots of his own, here and there, that are devious. But, I don't think he cares about the Gropas enough to attack them. Also, I have heard they have several mutually beneficial agreements in place that would be at risk if he attacked Pal."

"And Katarina?"

"She is an interesting character. No one truly understands her. If she thought it might be fun, she'd attack the Gropas in a bloody heartbeat. She's obviously involved to some extent, arranging the murder and kidnapping of the Naumite priestess and the theft of the *Notes*. However, would she lead a large-scale campaign against the Gropas? I don't think so. I think she'd get bored too quickly. I think she'll poke her nose in when and where it helps stir the pot."

"Is there any other Enchelei who is not part of the council who might lead the campaign in order to gain admittance?"

"Absolutely."

"Who?"

"Well, Cemil, the strategos of the Pronoiars, thinks very highly of himself." Laughing oddly, Vukasin shook his head in bemusement. "All the Pronoiars do, in fact. No one else would use *strategos* as the name of a company commander."

I questioned him with my eyes.

"*Strategos* is the term for a general or a governor of a region, not a company of cavalry."

I nodded as if I really understood. "Who else?"

"Well, Neven is the unofficial leader of the fishing boat captains. He's been upset at Jeremena's control of the fish market for some time, and now he's upset about the secondary price-fixing. Primarily, he'd like to be on the council to protect himself, though he'd help the other captains, too. He's not likely to get onto the council, though, as both Jeremena and Zacharia oppose him and he has no patron voting for him."

"The fish market seems to be full of turmoil. I've watched them working and didn't see all of this tension."

"They must hide it well, because it's there."

"Who else?"

"I might once have suggested Kristijan, but he is too focused on his religion. Outside of the temple, he seems too innocent to have planned this campaign."

"Anyone else?"

"One more, Radmila." He paused. "She's the leader of a coalition of Enchelei tradesmen. They're members of a number of guilds: tailors, cobblers, jewelers, smiths, and the like. Usually, they work within their respective guilds, but they have interests greater than their trade skill, and, for some time now, she's been pushing for more representation in the Gropa family's long-term planning. Interestingly, I'm told that Davorin, of all people, is the one most pushing for Pal and Vesela to help her."

"Davorin?"

"Yes. I find that odd, too. I wouldn't think Davorin would interest himself in mere tradesmen. Nor is there any hint of a personal connection between him and Radmila, and that, too, is surprising. Davorin is a deeply corrupt man, though, and I can see him helping her if she was bribing him in some way."

"What else is Davorin interested in right now?"

"He is, at least, paying attention to the fish market. He's made a couple of comments that lead us to think he might be behind the price-fixing, though the preponderance of evidence leads us to think it was Zacharia. Still, it might be Davorin, or Zacharia at the prodding of Davorin."

"What else?"

"You know the majority of trade with Matara is shipped in Enchelei caravans and ships?"

I nodded.

"Well, Davorin dramatically increased that trade and locked it into the Gropa sphere of influence. He did that when he was very young and has treated it as his personal fiefdom ever since. He's also looking at other exotic, far-flung trading possibilities. He's got several factors in the very far east trying to get greater control of spices and jade, for example." He sighed. "There are also rumors of slaves, even though that trade is prohibited in the Empire, except in certain very specific instances. He is flighty, evil, and corrupt, but he does have an ability to create new ideas and possibilities."

"Could he be angling to be zupan?"

"It's certainly possible, but I would suspect, if he's behind this, he's angling to use Pal as a puppet rather than take the title himself. He knows everyone instinctively recognizes his corruption. He's also smart enough to know if he can get a figurehead he can control, especially if it's Pal, he'll have that much more power."

"What about Zacharia?"

"Ah, now there's someone who bears watching. He is absolutely convinced that he's the most capable Gropa, at least for now."

"Because Agata will be the greatest Gropa ever?"

"Precisely. I don't think he would ever want to hurt the fortunes of the Enchelei, but I do think he would prefer to be in Pal's shoes, where he could run the family and tribe more profitably than Pal is doing. Then, when the time comes, he could hand the reins of a strong and mighty Enchelei tribe to his daughter and she could, possibly, take it to heights never before seen."

"Is he capable enough to orchestrate this larger campaign?"

"Absolutely."

I nodded. "Jeremena?"

He leaned back. "I wouldn't have thought Jeremena would have actively attacked Pal. But she is older, and she might have ambitions she worries she can't fulfill in the time she has left. Also, she might have been angered more than we know about the challenge to her control of the fish market."

He chuckled. "I said before that she's too predictable, and she is, once she's made her mind up what to do. But she's been playing politics in Achrida since before the rest of us were born, and one is never quite sure which path she'll take. Once she chooses, she'll follow it, but with her it's best to wait and see."

"Would the issues of the fish market take too much of her focus? Is she capable of dealing with that while also attacking Pal?"

"Oh, my, yes. I have my successes with her because I've watched her succeed all of my life. Do not doubt her. Or trust her."

"What is Vesela's role in the family?"

"She's the heir, as I'm sure you know. What you may not realize is that Pal essentially lets her run the family with his guiding hand to restrain her."

"What does she think of those restraints?"

"They chafe. She is an angry horse held by ropes, tugging and pulling to be allowed to run free."

"And, what happens when she gets free?"

"I don't know." Vukasin shook his head. "I worry about her. She's capable, though not as capable as she thinks she is. Nowhere near as capable as Agata. Unfortunately, she's angry enough to lead us down roads that might hurt all who live in Achrida, not simply Dassaretae."

"So, she could be attacking her father as a means of escaping those bonds?"

"I suppose, but…" He leaned back and thought for a while.

"But?" I finally asked.

"I doubt it will surprise you to hear that Pal and I talk periodically."

I nodded.

"He has told me something in confidence. I am debating telling you. It might be to his advantage for you to know."

While he thought, he got up and refilled my rakija, then paced around the room while I sipped it.

He finally returned to his chair and said, "I think it is to his advantage for you to know, but I am not so sure that I will tell you right now. I will urge him to tell you, or at the very least to allow me to tell you. Enemy or not, I have achieved my success, in part, because I am known for keeping my word. You can't trust everything I say"—he smiled—"but if I say I'll do something, I will."

I nodded. "Does this thing make you think it more or less likely that Vesela is behind the threat to Pal?"

"Less."

"What about Agata, could she be more precocious than we already think?"

"She could be, but I doubt she's behind this."

"Why?"

"The more precocious she is, the more likely she knows when to make her move. This is not the optimum time. So, if she is behind this, then she is not as dangerous as I believe her to be."

"There's only one left."

"Andrija."

"Yes."

"He is a throwback to a more innocent time. There are not many who can face him with steel. Fewer still can match his will."

"But…"

"But he's honorable and honest. I happen to know that he swore personal fealty to Pal when Pal was about the age of Agata. I have been surprised and outmaneuvered many times as zupan. It would be the greatest surprise of my life were the campaign led by Andrija."

I sighed. "Well, at least we can exclude one person in this city. Two, if you count me."

"Not me?" teased Vukasin. "Not Piri?"

"Piri, maybe," I smiled. We chuckled. "I assume Desimir will meet me as I leave?"

"He's undoubtedly guzzling my rakija in the foyer right now."

I bid him farewell and left with a smile of thanks. Desimir and I walked back to the Faerie, where I left him to drink his frustrations away, while I went to bed early.

Chapter 36
Morning, 17 Gersmoanne, 1712 MG

I slept poorly that night. I kept dreaming of flashing knives plunging into bloody backs. These dreams woke me, sweating and tense, with my saex in my hand. After each awakening I lay there, thinking through possible scenarios until I managed to sleep again.

And dream again.

And awaken again.

Desimir felt just as tired as I did in the morning. He had stayed up drinking with Cvetijin until Cvetijin staggered home and Ragnar poured him into bed. Hence, wrestling practice started slowly, until I made the mistake of throwing Desimir. I had shifted from the Boar's Tooth into the Iron Gate quicker than either of us expected. Then, without thinking, I guided his lunge into the Fourth Play and took his chin into my hand, which allowed me to flip him over my hip.

Suddenly Desimir was awake and alert and angry. He made me pay for my success, though I accepted the price as the cost for a major victory. I chose not, however, to be smug at breakfast, at least on the outside. Especially since...

"You're not going to be too happy with me today."

"That's already true," grunted Desimir.

"I'll bet you'll be less happy when I tell you my plan."

He glared at me.

"I need to track down both Davorin and Jeremena. The best idea I have to find them is to see if Svetislav is available to help. I doubt you'll be able to come along. Also, I need to go back to the Mare to meet with Zacharia. I'd like your squad there again, in case of an ambush."

"You're right. I'm not happy with you," he growled.

I ate some of my breakfast.

"Damn all Enchelei, anyway," he added.

I ate more. Eggs mixed with cheese and onions.

"They'll all lie to you. You'll be back where you are now, as clueless as the foolish son of the Piercer."

"I'm learning. Slowly, I'll admit. This town is filled with blind alleys, but I'm learning nonetheless."

"What have you learned, then?"

"I've learned the Gropa Council is a snakepit."

He snorted, "I could have told you that."

"Ah, but could you have told me specifically how it's a snakepit?"

He shrugged.

"Now I have to see if I can manipulate any of them into telling me more. The only way I'll be able to do that is to talk to them directly, nudge them, push them, see how they react."

He sighed. "I guess."

"I know you're worried about having to look at my dead body. I am, too. But, anything that would kill both Svetislav and me would also kill both you and me."

"That's probably true."

"You'll escort me to the Lakewarden dock, and we'll decide our plans from there?"

He nodded, grumpily, and we finished our breakfast.

We went to the base. Today's guards were Ilija and a Lakewarden I had never met. Ilija greeted us.

"Milord, as neither of you are Lakewardens, we are not permitted to allow you to pass. May we inform one of our superiors that you wish to speak with them?"

I let his natural formality shape my polite response. "Yes, Lakewarden, would you please inform Protokarabos Svetislav that I wish to speak with him?"

He nodded and left, returning with Svetislav a few moments later.

"Svetislav, I need your help again."

He looked at me.

"I need to find Davorin, if possible, then Jeremena. Other than starting at the Gropa manor, I have only vague ideas where to begin. However, I don't want to speak to Pal or Vesela just yet."

He thought for a while, and nodded. He gave Ilija a series of orders I could not hear. He then turned to me, and we strolled away from the gate.

"I don't really know how to find either of them. I have heard that a seamstress named Ruzica might know where Davorin is, and since I do need a new tunic, I thought to start with her. Do you know where her shop is?"

He nodded.

"However, Svet, I have no idea how to find Jeremena. Any thoughts?"

He nodded, again.

"So, you'll lead me to Ruzica and then to Jeremena?"

Svetislav nodded yet again, this time looking meaningfully at Desimir. Desimir understood the look immediately and glared at both of us.

"Oh, for fuck's sake, may the Sun-High One burn both of you." He stomped up the trail, leaving Svetislav and me behind.

"Don't forget my meeting at the Mare," I yelled at his back. I guessed that his rude gesture meant he had not forgotten.

Svet and I took the road along the docks and the Stracara. He led me into a neighborhood in the southern hills to a small shop hidden behind some larger buildings. A row of fabric bolts, each dyed a slightly different color, leaned against one wall. Across from them a slight woman puttered behind a long table. Initially she ignored us while she delicately sheared triangular portions of fabric. Her method, at first, seemed odd, until I realized she was not actually looking at the fabric. Instead, she held her head back, almost raising it to the sky, while her nimble fingers felt and cut the material.

Eventually, she turned to us.

"Svetislav, it has been too long." She came over and hugged him tightly. "I've missed you."

She turned to me. Delicate features and luscious, dark swirling hair made her stunning. She looked at me with piercing, intelligent, milky-white, unseeing eyes that held the memories of a well-lived life. "Now, who is this? No, Svet, let me guess. You don't actually want to talk to me, anyway."

She paused and then reached out to me with her fingers. She lightly touched my clothes, belt, and sword. "He's not as tall as you, but he moves well. His sword handle is smoothed and worn by long use." She thought some more, and again brushed my tunic. "Linen, not of a southern weave. Dyed with madder." She paused once more. "So, you're the Edward I've heard so much about."

I nodded, then stopped, and she laughed.

"No, I can't see it when you nod, but I know you did."

I laughed. "I'll try to say things out loud, but how do you deal with Svetislav?"

She giggled. "I learned how to listen to his silence when we weren't old enough to realize that there were places on each other we shouldn't touch."

Svetislav blushed. "Kids," he muttered.

"Well, Svetislav, as you grew up, you should have kept in touch, so to speak. Your playmate is now a lovely woman," I teased him.

She giggled and raised her eyebrows at me. "I tried, believe me, but he's such a fool, worried about his duty and everything."

Svetislav's frown at me made her laugh even more. "I bet he's glaring at you, because he knows I can't actually see it."

I laughed because she had described Svetislav's expression perfectly.

She continued, "You're here for one of two reasons. One, you need a new cotton tunic. Two, you need to get a hold of Davorin."

"There's a third possibility," I said.

"Both." She giggled. "Hold on, then."

She went into the back room. I heard some conversation and a door open and close. Soon she returned with a long strip of waxed cloth that she used to measure me, all the while muttering to herself.

After a few moments of measuring me, she stepped back. She hung the tape around her neck and fluttered her fingers lightly over me and my tunic.

"I can have a tunic for you in a week. What color is your hair?"

"Sort of a light sandy brown."

"Excellent, I have a maroon you will look nice in."

"Maroon?"

"Yes."

"You're blind, how do you know that maroon will look nice on me?"

She sighed. "We live in an age of magic, and you wonder if I can tell whether or not a color will look good on you?"

Svetislav was shaking his head at me while I laughed.

"You're already wearing something dyed in madder, meaning you like reddish tones," she added.

"I'm sorry I doubted you."

She sniffed. "I forgive you." She turned to Svetislav. "But, I don't forgive you." She marched up and to him, nose to chest. "Where have you been? And, don't give me that silliness about always being on the lake, serving the city." The flickering fingers that had measured me were now poking into Svetislav's chest.

"I know where you live, and if you can walk up to that northerner's tavern twice a week, you can occasionally stop by here. By the Lady of Cythera, I wouldn't even mind if you occasionally stumbled over after a few pints, just to touch some of those places that we now know what to do with." She sniffed. "At least I know what to do with them—you might have forgotten."

I rarely saw Svetislav shocked, but this small woman, who saw everything in his heart, clearly had.

I tried not to laugh, though not successfully, and he glared at me.

"Better watch out. Just because I can't see doesn't mean I can't tell that I'd have a fine time letting this one into my bed." Now it was my turn to blush.

After a thoughtful pause, she mused, "You know, we have some time before the mighty Davorin makes his appearance. Interested, Sevener?"

"Very much so," I said, laughing, "but I'd rather not give Svetislav a reason to kill me."

She giggled. "So, Svetislav, which will it be? Some nights visiting me, or shall I have to settle with this innocent outsider?"

Svetislav glared at both of us.

"He's glaring at both of us, isn't he?" she slyly whispered to me.

"Yes, yes he is."

"He does that. I'd relax that glare if he'd let— Oh, look at who's here." Davorin walked into the shop. "You need your privacy. I'll take care of this one." She grabbed Svetislav and dragged him into the back room.

I looked at Davorin. "An interesting woman."

He smiled. "My niece."

"I didn't realize you cared."

"I don't, not about blood at least. But she is one of the few people I've never lied to."

I looked at him. "I'm not sure I believe that."

"Nobody really believes anything I say. Probably wise of them." He paused. "I'm a disgusting man. I'm not sure why, but everyone thinks so. Ruzica is the only one who doesn't care. At least, if she does, she's the only one who hides it so deeply that I can't see her hesitate around me."

"Even Deor, my horse, felt your corruption."

"It's always been so, and I've come to expect it."

"Still, it is nice to be accepted by at least one person."

He nodded. "Yes, that is why I care about her. Even I, who cannot truly love anything, come closer to loving her than anyone else. But you did not come here to find out about Ruzica," he added. "You came to see if I'd tell you the things I promised I would on the Old Road."

"Yes."

"What would you ask?"

"Did you give Kristijan's message asking Gibroz to steal the *Notes of Naum* to Frano?"

"No, I did not."

"Can I believe that?"

"Of course not." He grinned. "I can think of many reasons why I'd have made sure that message reached its destination, many more than you can."

I sighed. "You said, when we first met, Pal ruled in a time of stress. The schism is not the only stress that challenges him, is it? What are some of the others?"

He laughed. "Me. Most of the other Enchelei. Zacharia is probably the worst of us all."

"Not Vukasin?"

"No, not him. He's too honorable." Davorin smirked.

"The sworn enemy of the Enchelei is not someone the leader of the Enchelei should fear?"

"Of course not," he laughed. "I'm sure you know why."

"Vukasin only wants some of Pal's money."

"See, I told you I'd help."

"Why?"

"Because it helps me achieve what I want."

"And what do you want?"

"Quite a few things. "

"Such as?"

"The occasional trinket. This and that. Maybe a perk or two."

"Going to tell me anything specific?"

"Not at all."

I wondered what to ask next. I remembered Kemal. "Do you go to the Bronze Rose?"

"Now, that's a personal question."

"Yes, it is. What's the answer?"

He laughed. "Of course I do. Everyone feels this corruption about me, so I might as well be corrupt."

"Did you know that Kemal visited the Bronze Rose, too?"

"Did I know that the servant of Jeremena worked for Zacharia behind her back so he could afford to pay for three girls no older than seven? Yes, I did." His supreme self-satisfaction showed in his smile. "I was actually a little jealous about one of the girls."

"So, you could have blackmailed him into doing whatever you wanted?"

"Making love to six-year-old girls is worthy of blackmail? I didn't know that." His smirk deepened.

I sighed. "You could easily have blackmailed him, but you won't tell me if you did."

"That's what I said."

"Did you help Zacharia fix the fish prices?"

"Fish? Fish!?! I care not a damn bit about fish. Speak to me of cotton, and we'll talk. You know of goods to trade that come only from the Seven Kingdoms or Svellheim? We can talk about them, too. I'll even promise to never sell you into slavery. But fish? Jeremena can have the fish."

"And Zacharia?"

He dismissed the idea with a wave of his hand. "If he wants to play with Jeremena, he's welcome to."

"You don't care about them?"

"No. There are four people in the council who have any thought for tomorrow. Only three of us matter, right now: me, Vesela, and Pal."

"Because Agata is too young to really matter right now?"

He sighed lustily. "Yes. It's so sad. I have so much to teach her, but Zacharia doesn't trust me for some reason."

I shuddered. "I'm not sure you've told me anything I didn't already know."

"No?"

"I knew your soul was damned and the council distrusted you," I added. "I knew Jeremena and Zacharia were fighting over fish prices. I guessed, though I did not know, you frequented the Bronze Rose. "

I paused. "Tell me why you support Radmila."

He smiled. "What good would that do?"

"At least I'd know. What about Radmila is interesting enough for you to support her? No one knows of a personal connection. I think she's too old to interest you sexually. Are the tradespeople she represents so important to you?"

"Actually," he chuckled, "they are." He waved his hand around Ruzica's shop. "There's my niece, of course, but I also think what Radmila wants will benefit the Enchelei."

I looked at him, disbelievingly.

"Tell me you won't run straight to Vukasin," he demanded.

"No, but since I always seem to be the last to know, I don't know as it will matter."

He laughed. "I wouldn't be surprised if he told you I supported

Radmila." He paused. "But the why matters more than the what."

"So tell me why."

He paused again, thoughtfully. "It probably won't be a secret for much longer, anyway. Radmila is planning to present aspects of the plan to her people next week." He looked back at me. "You know that I'm the one who expanded the cotton route here?"

I nodded.

"There are many more wonderful things in the world besides cotton. Materials, jewels, animals, you name it. I want to import these goods here and have Enchelei artisans make wonderfully new and expensive things with them. Ruzica matters to me not simply because of our personal relationship, but she is truly a wizard with cotton. I would have all the crafters of these new items be Enchelei."

I looked at him with a raised eyebrow.

"You doubt me?" He laughed. "You're not the only one, but you're smart enough to think things through, though. Remember this, I am Gropa. I am smart enough to know that no other family will have me."

"You're going to make sure your family is well run."

He looked at me. I had no idea what his look meant, and before I could ask him, he walked out.

Chapter 37
Afternoon, 17 Gersmoanne, 1712 MG

After Davorin left I called out for Ruzica and Svetislav. After a few indefinable noises, a scuffle or two, they returned. Ruzica looked smug. Svetislav looked bewildered.

"My goodness, Sevener, I must say I'm glad you need a bodyguard. I don't know what else would have brought Svet here. I might have succeeded in persuading him to come back in the future on his own, though." She giggled.

"I'm sorry to have to take him away at what seems to be… a delicate point in your negotiations."

"Oh, I planned for that. Did you get Uncle Dav to answer the questions you wanted?"

"I'm not sure. Then again, I'm not sure I understand anything in this city."

She laughed. "Achrida is an interesting place."

"Speaking of challenges, how can I convince this confused ox to lead me to Jeremena's? Any suggestions?" She laughed again as Svetislav glared at me and started walking away. "Thanks for your help, milady," I said as I followed.

"Goodbye to both of you," came the laugh from behind us.

I did my best not to chuckle at Svetislav's muddled state, but I found it impossible to completely hide my humor. Nevertheless, with a few glares, he led me to a small limestone building we had passed on the way to Ruzica's. Its only windows were high in the wall, and rust streaked down from them, as though the limestone wept blood. A heavy, iron-bound door provided the only entrance. A covered slot in the door allowed those inside to look out.

We knocked on the door. The slot's cover slid open.

"Yeah?"

"Sevener to speak to Jeremena."

The man closing the slot cover grunted, providing what seemed our only answer. After a moment, though, I heard several latches release and the door opened.

We entered a well-lit room filled with tables covered in scrolls and notes. Four men hunched over one table, rapidly clicking their abaci. Jeremena, sporting a scowl no grandmother would appreciate, sat behind another table, fingering her own abacus.

"I told you to stay out of my business."

"I told you that Ragnar's honor is at stake."

"What do you want?"

"I hear you're having trouble."

"Not at all. What makes you think that?"

"You're squeezed between the Dassaretae on one side and someone trying to fix your fish prices on the other."

"What do you know of that?" she demanded.

"I have been listening to things ever since I got to Achrida."

"That problem has been dealt with, at least for the time being."

"Because you murdered Kemal?" I laughed. "Do you really think that will stop the price-fixing in the long run?"

"No," she snapped, "but I don't think I'll have to worry about the long term."

"Why do you say that?"

She paused and glared at me. "Because I've been playing this game since your father was a boy."

"Not because you're organizing the Enchelei so you can overthrow Pal?"

Another pause. "Get out. Get out of my office, you worthless worm. May Aita carry you away with his spear up your ass."

"One more question. Who amongst the Gropas was authorized to have Frano deliver messages to Gibroz?"

"How does that matter? He's dead. And I'll see your blood in the streets, too," she snarled.

I had nothing to say to her threat, so I left. We had a little time before meeting Zacharia at the Mare, and threats to my life always made me hungry. Svetislav and I hunted for the mystery meat vendor and eventually found him along the edge of the Stracara. Svet could not identify the meat either, but it still tasted delicious.

At the Mare, I relaxed when I saw Desimir and his squad obviously awaiting us. Zacharia had known they had escorted me last time, so their presence would not frighten him off. Still, I wondered if there was some trap.

Zacharia sat at the same table, sipping the same vintage. For all I could tell, he might not have moved since I had seen him last. He nodded to Svetislav and pointed to the table Desimir had occupied the day before.

"What do you say to my offer?"

"I appreciate it, and I would love the information you have, but I don't feel it is the right thing for me to do at this time."

"I'm shocked to hear that, Sevener. I'll just have to find another courier. Might be difficult, what with the frequency that couriers are, of late, coming to harm."

He did not seem overly worried.

"Speaking of which, who told Frano what Kristijan wanted Gibroz to do?"

"That's a question, isn't it? The kind of question someone in my employ might actually get an answer to."

"Who else knew that Marija was coming from the Great City to Achrida?"

"Another excellent question. You may assume I was one of those people. You may also assume I know of others who knew she was coming."

"When did you know? When did the others know?"

"I don't know, exactly, when the others knew."

"Not going to answer anything for me, are you?"

"I might, if I saw some value in it. For example, I tell you, truthfully, that I want what's best for the Gropas." He smiled broadly. "Though it's fairly clear that we have different viewpoints as to what exactly that means."

"I think that's true."

"I will also tell you this. Something has to change. Pal is not strong enough to deal with both the Dassaretae and a council that is filled with the vipers that we are."

"You're the agent of change?"

"I'm one agent of change." He paused. "I will also tell you that you should be prepared for whatever Jeremena threatened you with."

"How do you know she threatened me?"

"Please. You talked to her. I know her."

I nodded. I rose to leave.

"Oh, one other thing, Sevener."

I looked back.

"I know you think you are honor-bound to discover who is behind the kidnapping and murder." He paused. "But you are mucking about in our family. Sooner or later, you'll do something you shouldn't and Jeremena will no longer be your greatest threat."

"For example, if I interfered with Agata in any way?"

His eyes became the color of the lake's deepest point. "Exactly."

"Or, perhaps, even if I indulged Vesela's curiosity?"

Now his eyes were the like the Fire of Heaven. He tried to speak but could not, at first.

"Sevener," he rasped, "do not doubt that this lake could be your eternal home."

A second threat to my life in but two hours. Zoe's dinner called to me.

Chapter 38
Evening, 17 Gersmoanne, 1712 MG

Zoe served a plain stew that tasted of leftovers from previous days. Nevertheless, she had woven the various threads of flavors into a tapestry of tastes.

Since Desimir sat sullenly instead of snapping in livid wrath, I was able to enjoy my meal. He ate his stew, jabbing sharply at the bowl with his spoon, while I ate and thought. Stuff was happening in the Faerie, but none of it intruded into our consciousnesses.

After dinner we stretched out to relax. Desimir finally relented and asked me what I had learned.

"I'm not entirely sure. I know that everyone on the Gropa Council has their own agenda, and that they're working against each other. I know that Pal has his hands full. If Vukasin were only reasonably intelligent, you Dassaretae would be making inroads on the Enchelei simply because of their infighting. Of course, Vukasin's extremely sharp, and he's making major progress."

I drank some ale. "But I don't see how any of this tells us who got Gibroz and Katarina to attack Ragnar's guests." I took another sip.

"Fill me in on the details, and maybe something will come to us," came Piri's voice as she sat at our table.

"I think there are seven people playing in this game, plus two others who are on the side of the chessboard. The two on the side are Agata and Andrija. They're more interested in seeing the family survive these times than using it to advance themselves. The rest of the Enchelei council are five of the main players. They are fighting amongst each other. Katarina and Gibroz are playing whatever game they see fit, which seems to include creating as much chaos as possible. The only thing I know for sure about those two is that whatever they're doing is good for them and no one else."

"No other players?"

"I don't think so. At least, none that I've found. Vukasin told me about several people who want to gain entry into the Gropa Council, but I don't think they have the skills or power to do so right now. If the Pronoiars really are as arrogant as Vukasin says, I doubt that Cemil has a strong enough power base. Neven has to go through Jeremena and she seems immovable. He said Kristijan wanted to step up, but he's fighting for his place as archimandrite. Radmila is the one person who might be able and capable. However, she already has Davorin fighting for her and, while I'm sure he'll fight for her against the rest of the Gropa, I don't think he's pushing for her to be on the council."

"Anyone else?"

"Not in the Enchelei that I know of. Maybe there's someone in the krals, but for some reason that doesn't seem likely."

"No, probably not, the kraljevics have always zealously protected their privileges. They know they gained their place by killing the previous kraljevic, and they know the same will happen to them. They're not interested in a council or in sharing power."

I nodded to Piri. "I got that impression myself."

Piri asked again. "Anyone else?"

I thought for a moment. "I don't think so. Vukasin told me why he doesn't think whoever's behind this is from Achrida. Whatever is happening, it's not focused on trade outside of the city. He thinks it's too subtle for the Emperor." I paused. "And I don't know of any Dassaretae who appear to be involved. If it's you, Vukasin, Desimir, or any other of the Pathfinders, you have completely confused me."

She laughed. "I'm sure we could have easily confused you when you first got here, but you're learning. There's no doubt about it. For what it's worth, I agree with you in all you've said, but it bears reviewing, especially since you're not sure."

"That leaves us with the five active members of the Gropa Council and the kraljevics."

"Let's look at them one by one."

"I'll start with Pal."

"Reasons why he might have done this?"

I thought for a while.

"I really don't see much of a motive. It's clear that the schism is affecting the stability of the Enchelei, and that means it makes his job harder."

"You're such an innocent." Piri laughed. I looked at her. "Could he be creating all of this in order to rid himself of meddlesome relatives?"

I thought for a while. "I suppose. But he's already the zupan, and he seems able to get the council to mostly do his bidding."

"Mostly."

"Yes. They are a difficult group to control in normal times, but I think the schism is distracting him from keeping the others in line."

"Could he have arranged the kidnapping?"

"Yes. Frano would pass on whatever message to Gibroz that Pal told him. I don't know if he communicates with Katarina, but there's no doubt he could figure out a way to do so if he wanted. He's smart enough to plot all of this. It's also likely he knew Marija was coming to Achrida, and that she had virtually no escort."

"But…"

"But he has reasons to maintain to the status quo. He is losing ground, but it's a slow and safe process, right now. He has to know that, in the long run, Agata is likely to redress the imbalance if he can merely hold things together. Vukasin, and for that matter Zacharia, made it clear that they see him thinking long term. Also, Kristijan thinks he would have prevented the attempted theft of the *Notes*, had he known, so whichever Gropa Kristijan went to had to have been someone else. However, as you keep reminding me, this is Achrida and logic doesn't mean anything."

"Pal absolutely has the ability to run this scheme, but it doesn't seem to make much sense for him to."

"It does seem like an awful lot of work for minimal gain."

"Next?"

"Vesela is not at all happy with things as they are. She wants to act decisively and aggressively. She thinks Pal is letting Vukasin walk all over the Enchelei, and I think she's worried about the status of the Enchelei when she finally inherits. I'm sure she knows how to contact both Kristijan and Katarina. She's the unofficial leader of the Enchelei, so Frano would have taken her instructions without question." I paused.

"This plot seems awfully oblique for her. She seems to prefer a more direct approach. She has the skills to plan this, but everything going on seems directed at the zupan. If she hurts the prestige of the zupan, she hurts the prestige of the position she will likely inherit."

Piri and I sipped our ales.

"Jeremena is full of anger and frustration at what's going on. She doesn't think in the long term right now. She's thinking that a strong zupan would have prevented Zacharia's attack on her. She's thinking that a strong zupan would have prevented Davorin's entry onto the council in the first place and denied him the influence he has. She resents Vesela using her sexuality on Zacharia and me, among others. She was Frano's boss, so he'd have done whatever she asked."

"Any reasons why she isn't behind this?"

"I don't think she and Katarina would get along. Jeremena would have had to deal with Katarina enough to plot the kidnapping and murder of Marija. While there's no doubt she could have found out about Marija's trip, she seems to be more interested in trade and less in religion. She'd have had to step outside her usual focus and use unusual resources to get the most crucial information. However, she's been doing this sort of thing forever, so there's no doubt she's likely to have the broadest set of contacts."

Piri nodded and waited for me to continue.

I drank, again, before doing so. "Zacharia wants to see change so when Agata takes over, the Enchelei will be in the best possible position. I believe he is convinced the old guard of Jeremena, Pal, and Andrija are part of the problem not the solution. He's a collector of information, so I believe he knows the details of Marija's excursion. He would likely have had the opportunity to take advantage of the situation."

"But…"

"But, at least to some extent, he's working within the system. The price-fixing scheme attacks Jeremena, not Pal. He wants the power of the zupan to remain intact, but increase the power of the Enchelei. While he surely had a way to send messages to Katarina, would Frano have taken instructions from him?

"And Davorin?"

"He's the hardest one to figure out. I think it's possible he's the most straightforward of the Gropas, except for Andrija. I think many people don't believe him because of his wrongness, so he tells the truth often and allows people to make mistakes based on their assumptions."

I thought for a bit longer. "In some ways, I don't think he cares who is zupan, but I do think he wants the Gropas to be stronger and more successful. He has a place in the family, where he might not have a place anywhere else. However, he'll need to make sure the Gropas are successful enough to allow him to afford his habits. He doesn't care who makes that happen, only that it happens."

"What does that mean?"

"If he thought it would benefit the family he'd try to be zupan. Or make Pal his puppet. Or manipulate anyone else who took charge. He's certainly got a connection with Katarina, probably stronger than we want to know. I don't know that Frano would take instructions from Davorin without concern, but I wouldn't be surprised if Frano did what he asked rather than spend time questioning him and dealing with his wrongness."

"So, why not him?"

"Too much turmoil. He's smart, possibly the smartest in the family, including Agata. He's got to know if there's a protracted fight over who controls the Enchelei his position can only suffer."

I poured myself more ale before admitting, "I'm not sure what to do."

"Tonight, you should relax and take a break. Maybe have some rakija with the ale. I think you might be thinking too hard and missing things that are right in front of you."

I nodded.

"Tomorrow," she continued, "after Desimir is done with you, come over to the barracks in armor. See if things look different after sparring with all of your weapons."

Piri's plan sounded far better than any plan I had, so I dutifully executed it. I asked Zoe to bring the ajvar the merchant had given me. It paired well with some flatbread Zoe made. It also went well with rakija.

Maybe too well.

Chapter 39
Afternoon, 18 Gersmoanne, 1712 MG

Piri's plan succeeded partially. Relaxing the previous evening, wrestling with Desimir in the morning and sparring with Piri and the other Pathfinders at midday had, indeed, helped clear my head. Nevertheless, I still had no real idea what to do. I took slight solace in the fact that my lack of ideas proved Piri was mortal.

Still, that left me at the Faerie, idly spinning an ale mug in my hands, after finishing lunch. Svetislav would join me for dinner, but that left the afternoon free.

I thought about returning to the Readers and inquiring about each of the council members, but they most likely would not answer my questions. They would tell me the exact price of fish on any given day so I could track fluctuations, but they would not tell me how family politics influenced those fluctuations. In fact, they could probably answer every question I had, but their oaths prevented them from doing so. Visiting them would only frustrate me.

I decided to visit Kapric and Zvono.

"Who died this time?" asked Kapric when I arrived.

"No one, actually."

"Congratulations, Sevener, does that make a whole day without your involvement in a murder?"

"Two."

"By the Luckbringer, I'm impressed."

"Look, Kapric," I snapped. "You know I didn't want anyone dead. Let it go or I'll take another hand for the Wolf."

Kapric started to snap back, but Zvono cut him off with "Herd bulls," and a sly smile at Desimir.

We glared at each other for a moment, but both backed down.

"I came to see if you'd found out anything about Frano and Kemal," I said.

Kapric nodded at Zvono, who flipped open her wax tablet.

"There's a good chance some of the other Blazevics or their friends were the ones who killed Frano. They've been spending more than usual of late. However, that doesn't really tell us much. They don't talk to us, and I doubt they'd talk to you. They'd have to actually tell us who hired them. They'll do whatever someone pays them for. And many people have."

I thought for a moment. "It may not tell me much, but it does tell me something. It tells me that whoever is behind this routinely hires the Blazevics. Who has hired them in the past?"

"Name a Gropa, any Gropa. Not just the council. There's Gibroz. And his lieutenants. Fishing captains have hired them to muscle in on competitors. First mates have hired them to kill their captains so they can step in. Members of guilds. Leaders of guilds…"

"I get the picture. Any Dassaretae?"

"Yeah, though none of the more important ones. They're not used for official Dassaretae family business like the Enchelei use them."

"I guess that's another confirmation that we're looking for a Gropa. How about the person who killed Kemal?"

"That's a bit more challenging. I don't think it's a Blazevic, though. Whoever killed Kemal was far less direct than the Blazevics are. And none of them are really the type to escape through a second-story window, across a series of rooftops."

"Is that how Kemal's murderer got away?"

"Yes."

"Anything else?"

"People knew Kemal could disguise himself to quietly pass messages. He was also known for keeping quiet about who he was working for."

"So, whoever killed him or ordered him killed probably found out about the messages from someone other than him."

Zvono nodded. "It's not much."

"It's all tied to the Gropa Council, though."

"So it seems," she agreed.

"On a different note, I recently ran into a fellow named Sebastijan. What can you tell me about him?"

Kapric let out a harsh laugh.

Zvono smiled. "Quite a bit, actually, he's Kapric's brother."

I looked at Kapric.

He shrugged. "We all have family."

"Who is he?"

"In a sense, he's like the Blazevics," answered Zvono. "He'll pretty much do anything he's paid to do, but, as far as we know, he's never taken a job specifically to murder someone." She looked slyly at Kapric, who assuredly noticed but never reacted.

She continued, "He's a capable man who can be trusted. In Achrida, his talents are always in demand. He's widely respected here. There are probably dozens of things we quaesitors should arrest him for, but he always seems to avoid trouble."

"Because of patrons limiting what you can do?"

"No, because he's careful."

"Is he honorable?"

"Yes," rumbled Kapric. "He'll do what he says. I don't like him. He's caused our mother all kinds of irritation, both when we were growing up and now, but none of us have doubted his honor—only his choices."

"What about his friends?"

"You met the pack of thugs he sometimes works with?" asked Zvono.

I nodded.

"They'll do what he says."

"Who hires him?"

"Anyone and everyone."

"Gropa? Mrnjavcevic? Kraljevic?" Zvono nodded as I named them.

"He'll work for anyone," she said, "as long as the job falls within his limits."

"He was following me. I asked him not to. He said he wouldn't anymore. I just wanted to know if he'd keep his word."

"He stopped because you asked him?"

"Yes."

"That's surprising," said Kapric.

"I wasn't in a good mood. I think that affected his decision."

We talked for a while longer but said nothing that mattered.

Chapter 40
Late Afternoon, 18 Gersmoanne, 1712 MG

Noise filled the Faerie when we arrived, as though everyone had already been drinking heavily. A scop played loud drinking songs everyone knew and bellowed more or less in time with him.

Piri relaxed at my table. She had mugs and a pitcher waiting for us.

After we filled our mugs, I looked at her and asked, "What is going on?"

She smiled. "See that wee lad over there?"

Standing next to Honker was a hulking young man, swaying with drink. He had clearly inherited his nose from Harald.

I turned back to the grinning Piri.

"It seems someone challenged him to a wrestling match. Didn't know that Honker used to win quite a few matches when he was a pup. Apparently, Honk taught his boy a thing or two. They're drinking off the money he won in time-honored fashion."

I laughed. "Karah has probably hurt her nose sniffing her disapproval at all of us."

Both Piri and Desimir laughed.

"Piri, did you send a message to Svetislav?" I asked.

"Yes, though I am only assuming he received it."

"I hope he did. I need to see the Gropa Council so I can see them interact as a group again."

Piri nodded. Suddenly, the din faded and the question of whether Svetislav would join us became moot. Vesela stood at the door, surrounded by the kind of entourage a princess deserved.

She wore a dress that captured the blue hidden in the lake's depths. Almost black. It shimmered across her body, catching briefly at her interesting points and making everyone aware of the curves underneath. The surprisingly short sleeves allowed her graceful arms and hands to flow, letting her communicate whatever she wished merely simple gestures. Her glistening hair haloed around her head in piles of artfully woven braids placed ever so precisely. They exposed a graceful neck, adorned with gold and dark garnet, and framed her lustrous, ebony eyes.

Her entourage positioned themselves throughout the room as befitted their station. Two guards with gleaming armor and glowering eyes took up station by the door. One servant approached Ragnar and offered to help. Two more servants sat at a table across from us so they could fulfill any wish of Vesela's.

Vesela wished, at that moment, to have dinner in a private room. Ragnar nodded and began to make preparations.

"Sevener, you shall join me."

Her peremptory command normally would have annoyed me. But my desire to speak with her prompted me to nod and rise from my seat. Ragnar led us to a room smaller than the one Piri and I had dined in. Instead of cozier, the smaller size made the room cramped.

Before we could talk, Ragnar brought in a white wine about which he and Vesela debated the merits until she deigned to take a sip. She accepted it, and Ragnar filled our glasses.

"I had hoped to speak to you again. I have more questions." I was proud of myself for not stuttering.

"Do we need to speak of them tonight?"

"What would you like to speak of?"

"I would like to speak of you. You're quite the mysterious man here in Achrida."

"There's very little to tell."

"Oh, I doubt that Sevener. You've been here such a short time, yet you've become someone people in this city talk about. You couldn't do that if you had no story to tell."

"Yet, it is true."

"I believe men who are shy are very sexy."

I took a deep breath, and Ragnar saved me from trying to answer by bringing us our salads. I focused on the cucumbers, onions, and salty goat cheese.

"You like our shopska salads?" she laughed.

"Yes, I do."

She took a small bite. I worked diligently at mine. She casually stretched out a leg and placed it next to mine. The room became even more cramped.

"You seem to enjoy many of our foods."

"I've been blessed with excellent cooks. The trout you provided was prepared as well as any fish I've ever had. And Zoe never disappoints."

"I've heard good things about her cooking. I hear she is not limited to the plain fare she normally serves here."

"No, she is not."

"You like good food. I can tell."

"I had a teacher who taught me to appreciate everything that my senses could tell me, especially things that are beautiful, or in this case, delicious."

"A wise teacher. When did he teach you?"

I sipped some wine. "When I lived in the hall of my father's lord."

"Tell me about your father."

I finished my wine and poured more. "He is dead. He died well."

"That is all?"

"What else is recorded in the Halls of the Dead?"

"More than that, Sevener, more than that." She took a sip of wine. "How did he die?"

I stared above her head for a measureless time. "Oaths were sworn. Oaths were kept. All but two."

Time passed, again.

"I would rather speak of the Gropa, your father, its council, and what you know."

"Pal knows he has a smart, tough, beautiful daughter. He knows I am a capable heir to a large and powerful realm. He knows we have sworn enemies that we should someday destroy. He knows how to wait, looking for the best time to strike. He knows that the Gropa family is well-respected throughout the Empire."

Her eyes gleamed like a mountain meadow stream in early winter as she recited her list—a smooth stream with a strong current running underneath the top layer of ice.

"Why haven't you destroyed the Mrnjavcevics?"

"Because the time hasn't been right," she snorted bitterly.

"When will the time be right?"

She shook her head. Before she could answer, Ragnar arrived with the main course, chicken with rosemary alongside a grain I did not recognize. I focused on the food, but when I glanced up, the look in her eyes had become predatory. Her leg started moving up mine.

"Tell me, Sevener, what do your eyes sense about me? Am I beautiful? Am I worth appreciating?"

She smiled and demurely placed her hands in her lap. Her foot sliding along my calf gave the lie to pose.

"You are, indeed, beautiful and I have admired you since I first visited your manor."

"You could have stayed that night."

"You made that clear."

"You could have me stay tonight."

Although I had never been to a desert, the dryness in my mouth gave me an idea what life there might be like.

"I am getting that impression." I was wondering how long her legs really were.

"But you won't."

I could not immediately answer, but after a moment finally shook my head.

"Why not? I can feel your desire." She cocked her head, not moving her foot a whit. She seemed curious, not angry.

"Many reasons."

"I have time." She grinned and lifted her foot ever so slightly.

"I swore an oath to Ragnar to discover who kidnapped his guests, and I don't think sleeping with you will help me find that answer."

"I hear you have already discovered who did this deed."

"No, I have found the actor, not the author."

"I also hear you have spent an evening with a certain hecatontarch." She smiled sweetly. "Why her and not me?"

"She's not involved."

"You think I am?"

"I know at least one person in the Gropas is involved. You are at least as likely as any on the council to have arranged for Katarina to murder Marija."

"What if I were to tell you that I was not involved? That allowing me to please you would not lessen your chance of finding your author? On my word as a Gropa."

I paused. I decided to answer honestly. "I don't trust you."

"Oh, my, Sevener." She arched her back and lifted her foot even higher. "You could not have said a more erotic thing to me if you had tried."

At least, I think that is what she said. I was too busy trying to find something to breathe in that airless room. Ragnar saved me by entering and retrieving our dinner dishes. He then brought in sliced apples covered with honey. I could not concentrate on the food, but I would be able to tell Bedarth when I saw him next that I never stopped paying attention to my senses.

We ate our desserts in silence, though she slowly moved her foot between my thighs, never letting me forget her sexuality.

"This has been quite the delicious meal, don't you think?" she asked with malicious humor.

"Indeed," I muttered.

"I don't think I'll forget it anytime soon." She sipped the last of the wine.

I replied honestly that I would not either.

"In fact, Sevener, I've rather enjoyed both of the meals we have shared. I would like to share another. Tomorrow evening at our manor. You may ask my father and me the questions that burn in you."

I nodded jerkily. "And the council?"

"Oh, them too. We can have so much fun with Zacharia." How could she grin so shyly, slyly, and sexily at once? "Maybe I can convince you that I am no threat to your oath, though I might threaten your pride." She laughed, loudly and fully, at the look on my face. "Tomorrow, though, leave the Dassaretae behind. I will send guards to escort you and ensure your safety."

I looked at her. "Desimir comes and goes at his pleasure. I have less control over him than I do over you."

"Well, he will not be allowed entrance. The Mrnjavcevics would not allow a Lakewarden in their manor, either. He will understand." She moved her foot sensually down my leg and rose from her chair. "No, Sevener, stay here. I have many escorts. You should remain and"—she smiled sweetly—"let your dinner settle."

She left with a last caress of my cheek.

I let my dinner settle. But I never got comfortable.

Chapter 41
Evening, 18 Gersmoanne, 1712 MG

Svetislav had joined Piri and Desimir by the time I returned from my dinner. After catching my breath, I informed them of the following night's dinner plans. Desimir, not surprisingly, used his skilled and diverse vocabulary to express his displeasure. Even Svetislav chuckled at some of his descriptions of the Enchelei.

Piri finally had enough. "Hush, lad," she commanded.

He grumbled to a halt and I spoke. "I have to go. My answers are hidden in how they interact with each other. I have to see that again."

"It's too dangerous."

"Svet." I looked at him. "Will the guards that Vesela sends be capable of guarding me as well as Desimir?"

He nodded.

"Anything they can't stop would be more powerful than anything Desimir could protect me from?"

He nodded again.

"How many will Vesela send?"

"Probably four."

I looked at Desimir. "Well?"

"It's still stupid," he said stubbornly. Then he snarled, "Get up." He stomped off to the hay room.

I looked at Piri.

"He'll feel better after throwing you around for a while."

"What about me?" I smiled.

"He won't hurt you too much." She grinned. "Come, Svet, let's fill our mugs and enjoy the show."

The show left me bruised at my table, contemplating turning in for the evening. Piri and Svetislav enjoyed it too much for my liking.

At least Desimir felt better and merely sat in quiet frustration until I went to bed.

The next morning he focused on ensuring I would react into my stances by keeping our drills slow. We also practiced shifting out of wrestling stances into some of my usual sword stances, both with my shield and without. He had clearly added these new drills because he worried that something would happen that evening.

We spent the rest of the afternoon cleaning our gear. Desimir made sure I had perfectly cleaned, honed, and oiled all of my blades and that they moved smoothly in their scabbards.

Even though we had finished the day's drills, he made me practice drawing the dagger out of Eirik's ankle sheath. I could not draw the knife as instinctively as I could my sword or saex, but, by the end, I could get it quickly and smoothly.

The afternoon passed quietly, with many things left unsaid.

Chapter 42
Early Evening, 19 Gersmoanne, 1712 MG

Cleaned and dressed in the embroidered, madder-dyed tunic that Zoe had repaired, I sat alone in the Faerie, waiting for my escort. Desimir had made Ragnar promise that he would not allow me to leave until the Gropa guards arrived. Then he had gone back to his barracks.

Soon enough, four guards in the livery of the Gropas appeared. They bore teardrop-shaped shields adorned with the blue and yellow wavy lines of Achrida under a black chief with three of the yellow Eastern crosses. The guards bore semi-spathas on their belts and long spears, without peace-bonds, in their right hands. I saw no body armor, but they wore pointed conical spangenhelms. Their steel gleamed with the faint rainbow sheen of oil.

The four guards surrounded me when we left. Most in our path moved out of the way without prompting. Those who moved too slowly were pushed out of the way by my escort's shields. I felt uncomfortable walking so openly in the middle of the street, but the guards arrogantly claimed the middle as their due.

Our route passed through the Square of Legends and veered off slightly to the left. The street ran along the Stracara, which, in the early evening, quivered in anticipatory silence. It almost seemed a normal neighborhood. The people in the slum slyly watched us and left us alone.

An open gate flanked by guards with spears awaited my return to the Gropa manor. The guards moved less than the caryatids supporting the great temples of Basil's City.

Sanjin met us at the door, and led me back to the same room as before. Pal, Vesela, and the council rose to meet me.

Pal spoke. "I've taken the liberty of opening a vranec, an excellent local grape that begins with extraordinary sharpness before mellowing into a wine with a myriad of complementary flavors. It is Vesela's favorite, and Seveners appreciate the hints of oak at the end, I'm told."

He handed me a glass filled with a ruby-colored wine whose flavor I would remember to describe to Bedarth when I next saw him.

"Delicious," I murmured as I picked through the medley of tastes.

We made ourselves comfortable.

"My daughter tells us you have more questions."

"Yes, lord, I do."

"Please, call me Pal."

I inclined my head. "I fear you may not be so agreeable once I ask my questions."

He cocked his head at me. "Yes?" The rest of the council also shifted in response.

"I don't believe you have told me all you know about the attack." I looked around. "In fact, I don't believe any of you have told me all you know about the events at the Frank Faerie."

Andrija and Jeremena snorted. Pal responded, "No? Probably wise of you. I rarely tell anyone all I know about anything. Except for Vesela, of course."

"Of course." I paused. "And the others?"

"I cannot say what they have done or what they have told you."

I nodded. "So tell me what you yourself haven't told me."

He stared back, anger flickering below his benevolent expression.

"You dare badger the zupan in his own house?" rumbled Andrija as he started to stand, his dagger half-drawn.

I looked at him. "I'll dare anything to clear the stain on Ragnar's honor." I stayed still as he started to loom.

Vesela motioned Andrija down. Andrija hesitated.

"Obey my daughter, Old Bear."

Andrija glared at Pal for a moment and sat down, slamming his dagger back into its sheath as he did. Davorin chuckled his sly, annoying laugh.

"Let Andrija kill him," snapped Jeremena, "He's done nothing but meddle in Enchelei business since he came to Achrida."

"No," said Pal. "Vesela invited him to dinner. If we decide to kill him, we'll do it when it's appropriate, not when he is our invited guest."

They looked at me like an aerie of hawks gauging which would get to eat the mouse.

"Vesela, Davorin, and Agata are the only three here who have not threatened my life. I think I know how Vesela would kill me."

She laughed.

I looked at Davorin and Agata. "How about you two?"

Davorin chuckled. "Oh, I would make sure it was painful, and I'd get people to pay me to watch you die." Chilling as Davorin's response was, Agata's calm quirk of her head and calculating eyes were worse.

"But that doesn't help any of us," I responded, turning back to the others. "The schism with the Naumites is hurting all of you, yet I think I'm the only one who actually cares what caused it. Vesela is too busy lusting after me. Davorin is lusting after Agata and others younger than her. Jeremena and Zacharia are squabbling over fish prices. Zacharia's also jealous over his cousin's attention to me. Andrija's being noble and frightening. Agata here is simply watching how not to run a family."

I paused in my rant to glare at everyone. "That leaves Pal. Your squabbles make it difficult for him to keep Vukasin from taking advantage of the turmoil. Don't forget Katarina is doing whatever she can to get you to kill each other, or me, or anyone just so she can laugh at our corpses."

Agata gave me a short, sharp nod, and Davorin leered as the rest of the family burst out in protest. I simply waited. Finally they settled down.

I took a deep breath. "Let's start again, please." I turned to Pal, "When we last spoke, you told me you were trying to find the *Notes of Naum*."

He shrugged in frustration. "Yes. Unfortunately, we have not been able to pinpoint their exact location."

Zacharia spoke up. "The mages still think the *Notes* are somewhere in or near Achrida, though."

"Why do they think that?"

"As I understand it, the magic obscuring their divinations is focused on Achrida and its environs. They've not sensed the *Notes* outside the city walls, and they feel they would, if they were outside the perimeter of that magic."

"That makes sense."

I changed topics. "You also said that you were not in any way involved in the kidnapping."

"We were not."

"I'm not so sure of that."

The council exploded again.

"Nephew," growled Jeremena. Pal made a calming gesture.

"Just as you have the right to expect safety when we have granted hospitality, we have the right to expect you to be polite."

I took a moment to rephrase my thoughts. "You misunderstand me. I don't believe that any of you, personally, were involved, but someone in the Gropa family did arrange for all of this. I know this because of the attempted theft later that evening after the kidnapping. Kristijan told me that he sent a message to Gibroz asking for help stealing the *Notes of Naum*. Kristijan felt they would help him in his conflict with Gregor. Gibroz confirmed that Frano brought him a message asking him to steal them, so someone in the family had to approve the theft by sending Frano to Gibroz. It's not something that Frano would do on his own."

"Kristijan did this?"

"Yes. Which means at least one member of your family knew of Kristijan's plan and his reasons why. I believe Frano's usual contact was Jeremena, though I am not sure. I also have no idea if she was the only one in your family who spoke to Frano. You would know better than I. Whoever sent Frano could see the *Notes* were vulnerable and felt there was an opportunity."

"An opportunity?" Pal demanded.

"If Kristijan had the *Notes*, you'd probably still have to deal with a schism in the temple, but you could probably control the conflict. However, if neither of the archimandrites had the *Notes*, and no one knew where they were, you'd have to deal with the schism while everyone suspected the worst of their competitors both inside the temple and out. None of this would be good for the Gropas, and your own position would be weakened." I looked around the council. "You would all wonder who did what, which is exactly what is happening right now."

Everyone sat completely still. The members of the council avoided looking at each other.

"Vukasin tells me he feels the Dassaretae are ascendant at the moment. This means the Enchelei are at a low point, and you are currently facing a series of threats. I now wonder whether, in this situation, some in your council might feel it is time for you to give up some of your power. Maybe even replacing you or turning you into their puppet."

"Preposterous."

"Not at all. Think about it. Everyone in this city plots. You compete over everything. Why would your position be inviolate? Now remember Katarina. Why is she involved? Someone had to promise her both money and chaos for her to agree to take the *Notes* from Marija. Also, why would Frano be assassinated if not to prevent him from naming who sent him to Gibroz?"

Pal was fuming.

"Someone has attacked your family, used both kraljevics to do so, and killed at least five people affiliated with the Enchelei. It has to be someone within the family, most likely someone in this room. The only reason I can think of for someone to do this is to weaken your position, and the only reason I can think of to weaken your position is to strengthen their own. Who would gain the most? Who thinks they could replace you? You know your people best, who should I look at?"

"Jebi se! Fuck off!" He rattled off a long string of profanity I could not quite keep up with. Interesting. I would not have expected Pal to have that much of a temper.

"Father…"

He simply motioned at Vesela and the council, stood up, and stomped to the window. He stood staring at the surface of the lake, which hid its many predators and the chase for life and death. I could feel him shedding the rage.

We waited.

Suddenly, he picked up one of the heavy chairs that faced the window and tossed it across the room. The chair bounced off the marble wall, and two legs sheared off with a wrenching scream. Sanjin appeared at the door, watching impassively.

Pal continued stomping, though he did not throw anything else.

We continued to watch and wait. I started to speak. Pal stopped me.

"Shut up, Sevener. You've had your say. I've even heard it, and if you're not lying about Gibroz, Kristijan, and Katarina, then you're right to ask those questions. By my half-eaten liver, I did not know that the Gropas had personally attacked Ragnar. We owe him a debt, and I swear to his one-eyed godling that I'll pay it. But I'll clean my own bedamned house first."

I looked at him. "Clean as you will, but I owe Ragnar a debt, too, and I will not leave this alone. I will keep pressing Gropas, or for that matter Mrnjavcevics or kraljevics or anyone else in this crazy place, to fulfill my oath."

We glared at each other until Sanjin came in and removed the chair and its broken legs.

"Who talks to Frano? Who threatens your reign? Can you trust Davorin? Zacharia? Jeremena? Or even Vesela or Andrija? When will Agata become zupan?"

He glared at me. At least he was only one of seven angry faces now.

Vesela finally spoke. "We should use him father."

He finally decided. "No, my daughter, we must see to our own."

"As you wish, father."

"Sevener," he said, "you should leave."

Vesela was startled, "But our duty as hosts—"

"I know our duties," he cut her off. "And I will make my amends to him before he leaves Achrida. But tonight, daughter, we have work to do."

I was already rising. "So do I."

"Sanjin," he bellowed, "have his escort readied." He ignored me from then on, staring out the window.

Vesela came to me just before I left. "I apologize."

"No need. I knew I was pressing you."

"I had hoped for a better, shall we say, climax to the evening." She smiled, her smile grew wider as we felt Zacharia's jealousy from across the room.

"I know."

She stepped close and ran her finger along my chest. "But, I must admit that the hunt has been quite enjoyable."

"Aside from the murders, theft, and schism."

"We'll fix that." She definitely had her father's steel.

"If I don't first."

She sighed. "I will try to change his mind, but he is right, it is our responsibility. Please, let us be."

"You know I cannot."

Sanjin showed me out. Vesela watched me thoughtfully until I was out of the room.

Chapter 43
Evening, 19 Gersmoanne, 1712 MG

The four guards lined up around me as they had before. Undoubtedly, they had expected me to stay much longer, but the change in plans showed in neither their kit nor their faces. Sanjin led us to the street and silently bowed an apology.

We returned the way we had come. More people were moving around the Stracara, but I had not been at the Gropa manor for long and most watched us pass with lazy calculation. I did not realize I was tense until we started up the angled road towards the Square of Legends after passing the Stracara. I felt myself relax as we now walked through a normal neighborhood.

So, when things happened, I was surprised.

I flinched when, out of the corner of my eye, I saw something flying towards me. It went over my shoulder and thumped behind me. I paid no more attention to whatever that had been because a spear tip slid across my right shoulder, ripped through the linen of my tunic, and veered away as the guard behind me twisted.

I never heard Desimir shout, but I guessed he had. What I did know was that he suddenly appeared in the midst of my escort with knives in both hands. The other three guards were raising their shields and aiming their spears at him.

Before they could attack him, though, others descended upon my escort and me from a shop to our right.

I had little idea what was happening, but I knew someone with a spear stood at my back. I leapt forward, splitting my escort's two lead men, who had reacted slightly slower than me. Of course, a spear tip had not flown by their ears to motivate them.

As I leapt, I drew my sword and turned to face the cluster of guards and attackers. Desimir had jumped at the guard at my back. That guard was dropping his spear, which still had a scrap of my madder-colored tunic stuck on the point, and was blocking Desimir's knives with his shield while pulling out his semi-spatha.

Before I could move to help Desimir, two of the people from the building charged at me. Fortunately, they wielded short blades no longer than my saex. I took advantage of their momentum and my reach by stepping forward with my left leg and thrusting at the face of the one on the left. He paused to deflect my blow. It was a feint, though, and the moment he paused, I took a full stride farther to the left, putting him between me and the other knife-man. By flipping my wrist over and raising it slightly, I eluded his block and my blade smashed into his face. The blow held just the power of my arm and wrist torque without any power from my hip, but it only takes a little force to hurt someone's unprotected face, and he fell.

As he fell I spun on my right leg, striking over his head with the easy following shot of flipping my wrist back over. The second attacker stood at the edge of my range, but I brought my left leg forward and my right hip back, and cut deep into the back of his skull. He, too, went down.

I was moving easily, and the recent training and pell work was paying dividends. It also helped that the day still held the light of early dusk.

I slashed at a right arm that was thrusting at one of the guards and clipped it slightly. It gave the guard the moment he needed, and a quick punch from his shield knocked the attacker down. He stabbed the man casually as he stepped over him and hit the right flank of some others.

I followed at his left quarter, taking advantage of the cover provided by his shield. Now that I stood in a shieldwall, I knew what to do. I flicked thrusts out past the angle of the teardrop shield, and if those missed, I rolled my wrist over and leaned to my left, bringing my edge down on their hamstrings. Meanwhile, the Gropa guard was battering with his shield and stabbing low. We killed three or four quickly this way, but there were so many.

They had enough attackers that even though we had blunted the initial assault and inflicted some casualties, they could still encircle us. Their movement forced me to stop attacking the flanked line and tuck myself into the Gropa guard's back quarter.

Now four stood in a line before us. They were taking turns jabbing their swords at me, preventing me from finding an attack. I drew my saex to provide a little more defense and spent the next eternity trying to keep both of us alive.

The guard knew I was holding off a small line, and he had the skill to help. When he could he popped the tip of his shield out at the knee of one of the attackers. This gave me the time to roll my wrist over into a solid thrust at the one next to him. That attacker fell as I pulled my blade out of his chest. The attacker on the end tried to respond with a slash at my left side, but I twisted and blocked it with my saex. The Gropa guard's presence allowed me to make the strike without exposing myself completely, and I was able to recover before the response came.

Now only three faced me. Not good, but certainly better. If I had been alongside my kin, I would have known how to break the stalemate, especially since they were watching for the shield tip trick. However, I had no idea what commands to shout. If I shouted the wrong command, as was likely, we would be separated and die.

But we had to do something.

A quick glance showed me the two of us were now facing a half-circle of five, and sooner or later they *would* kill us. Worse yet, I had no idea what was happening to my back. I had no idea where Desimir was. Nor did I know where the other guards were, which bothered me especially since at least one of them had attacked me.

It was my life-steel. My father had given it to me on my nameday. It had rested in my crib until I was a toddler. He and his friends had tied the blade into its scabbard and drunk long into the night on the day I finally became old enough to untie the complicated knots. They had laughed at me when I cut myself with it the following day. I could not remember a day as a child that they had not taught me how to use it. In all that time, however, we never practiced how to throw saexes. You simply did not part with them. They proclaimed our freedom.

Nevertheless, I slung it sideways across the line in front of me, aiming at the middle of the five. The crazy throw made the middle three attackers flinch. I heard an impact, though I ignored the sound and used the momentum of the throw to help me spin completely around.

If something is stupid but works, it is not stupid. Even Piri would agree with that sentiment. And it worked. As I finished the turn, I came down, striking the end attacker's head with my hilt. I hoped that stunned him for a moment, but I had no time to check as I followed that strike with a slash at the next attacker's face. It connected solidly, and he went down.

I stepped over things on the ground. I trusted the Victory Father to guide my steps because I knew I could not stop. I was relying on speed and shock, and I could not let the attackers recover their balance.

I jumped at one with a brutish downward chop. He blocked it, but I had put all my momentum behind that clumsy blow and it knocked into the man next to him. That gave the Gropa guard time to focus on the right-hand attacker, and I heard a thunk and a yell as shield and sword hit him.

But the second attacker had gathered himself more quickly than either the guard or I expected, and he slashed past my guard's shield into his ribs. My guard collapsed with a sigh like wheat waving in the summer breeze.

I never knew his name, but I would never forget his shield.

Using a simple step and wrist rotation, I thrust at the attacker in front of me. He almost blocked the blow but moved too far to one side, and my sword sliced along his arm. His sword fell to the ground.

He was not completely out of the fight, but I kept moving. With the full power of a flipped wrist, a completely turned body, and anger at the death of a comrade, I struck at the next attacker in line.

Piri would have shaken her head at that blow. Though technically correct, I struck much harder than I needed to. My sword went deeply into the attacker's skull and lodged itself there. He twisted as he fell and yanked my sword out of my hand.

I had not seen my saex since I had thrown it, and the hilt of my sword had fallen out of reach.

Now time was another enemy. I doubted I had time to get my sword. I reached for the first steel I could think of, the short dagger from the earlier scuffle on Medusa Way.

I was right. I discovered, however, despite all of Desimir's training, I did not even have the time to pull the dagger out. I probably would not have had enough time even if I had not been so stupid as to lose my sword. I would never know.

What I did know is that suddenly I heard a shout and movement at my back.

I turned to see another attacker. He should have killed me. He stood with his sword aimed directly at my back, and only Desimir's chest had prevented his sword from sliding through my ribs.

Desimir's chest protecting my back surprised the attacker.

Desimir's chest protecting my back surprised me.

Desimir expected and accepted the blow, and saved my life.

I exploded in rage and leapt over Desimir with no finesse or skill. I drove the attacker to the ground, thrusting my dagger into him repeatedly, cursing his arms and his legs and his heart and his liver and his brain to Fenris's loving care.

I spun around. Bodies lay about, but none stood. Blood flowed as the fight ebbed.

I fell to my knees and cradled Desimir's head.

"Sevener?" he hissed.

"Yes?"

"Told you bad idea. Shoulda listened." Foam came from his mouth.

"Yes."

He coughed. More foam.

"You get to explain this to Piri and Zoe."

I nodded.

"Wish I could watch."

I wished that, too, as the foam finally stopped and he died smiling cheerfully.

Chapter 44

Evening, 19 Gersmoanne, 1712 MG

Piri would have at least two reasons to be angry with me. My stupidity had killed her friend and comrade. Then, in that moment, I compounded that stupidity by losing track of everything around me. A lake trout had time to crawl up from the depths of the lake and cut my throat with a fin for all I would have noticed.

Others close to me had died in battle. Lives will be stolen when one plays with life-steel.

My father had shed his battle-dew on the day of my shame. My lord and all of my shield-kin had died on that day as well. Of my lord's thegns, only I had survived.

At least my father had died without seeing me foresworn. I knew he had, because I broke my oath when a sword took his life. It was the same sword that sat in a skull not ten feet from me, and it had been my hand that wielded it.

I had not cradled his head. Nor had I the chance to cradle my shield-kin.

Desimir had died solely to protect me.

I had thought my shame and guilt could be no greater than breaking my oath to my lord. But in some small sense, I had been Desimir's lord. He had died proudly. Now I could only live shamefully.

A tap at my shoulder halted my wallowing.

I looked up to see Kapric holding my saex. He gave it to me, and since it had shed no blood, I slid it into its sheath.

I supposed that made me a freeman again. One without honor, but a freeman nonetheless.

Piri and several squads of Pathfinders soon arrived. She saw Desimir's body and spoke some words to two Pathfinders, and they trotted off. She ordered the rest to form a perimeter.

Zvono was moving around the battle scene, occasionally noting things in her tablet.

Kapric squatted by me and finally spoke. "What happened?"

I shrugged. "I was coming back from meeting with the Gropa Council, and then Desimir was coughing on his blood."

"Step by step, Sevener."

I paused and thought. "We had come past the Stracara. For some reason the Stracara bothered me today. But we came past it. We were past the danger." I looked up at Kapric with tears in my eyes. "We were past the danger."

"Then what?"

"Something. Something flying. Flying past my head."

I looked at the right shoulder of my tunic. Both the over- and undertunics were ripped, and I realized I had a long slice on my shoulder. I looked at the head I cradled.

"It was one of Desimir's knives."

"Yes?"

I could only lift my wounded shoulder at Kapric.

"That's from a spear tip."

"The attackers only brought swords."

"No, from a Gropa."

"A guard?"

The events became clearer.

"Yes. One of the guards behind me was about to stab me in the back."

"And Desimir threw his knife."

"Yes. I didn't realize it until now."

Kapric waited for me to continue.

"I flinched."

"From a knife thrown at your head?"

"Yes."

"And the guard missed thrusting you."

"I think he flinched, too."

"Then what?"

The flow of events became more coherent, more real, helped no doubt by the fact that at this point I had started fighting instead of merely reacting. I traced out the rest as I remembered it.

"We'll have you go over this again when Zvono can take notes."

I nodded.

"Your sword is over there. Still in his skull."

I nodded again.

"I'm going to keep it for now. I'll return it to you tomorrow morning."

I did not respond.

"Piri will have some Pathfinders take you back. I don't think they'll attack you again tonight, but no need to risk it."

Yet another nod. Then I realized fatigue owned every part of me. Piri came over.

I looked up. "Desimir saved me."

She nodded. "Let's go back to the Faerie and you can tell me about it."

"I killed him."

"If that's true, then you'll owe a debt to the Pathfinders."

"Yes." I noticed little else until we arrived at the Faerie. Zoe met me with tears. Arkady had already come with the news.

They removed my belt and tunics outside. The tunics they burned.

They unwrapped my winingas, including the ankle sheath with the dagger. I wondered when I had resheathed it. I sighed when I realized I had not cleaned it before doing so, and blood was drying on the blade and inside the sheath.

Zoe clucked at the leg wraps but kept them. Eirik spent the night cleaning my leather and steel.

I was wearing only pants as they led me through the Faerie's taproom. People might have spoken to me, but I did not notice. Piri bathed me. Zoe stitched up my shoulder and brought fresh clothes. They dressed me and led me to my table.

They laid out food. I ate it. Ragnar brought beer and rakija. Piri made me drink a hefty slug of the liquor.

"Tell me," said Piri.

"I killed him."

"How?"

"He told me not to go. I went anyway."

"Why?"

"I needed to talk to the Gropa Council. Something is very wrong."

She sipped her beer. "How did he die?"

"He wasn't even supposed to be there. He promised me he'd stay here."

"And you expected him to stay?"

"I told him to."

She smiled slightly. "Both Zoe and I told him to stay with you. Who would you ignore?"

"I still told him to stay."

"So what did he do?"

I described the battle.

"Would you have been able to turn around quickly enough if you hadn't lost your sword?"

"Yes! It would have been close, but yes."

"Are you sure?"

"Yes."

"Did you see all that happened?"

"No, my back was turned. That's why Desimir had to save me."

"So, you don't actually know what happened."

I paused. "What?"

"You don't actually know how fast everything behind you happened. The only two who do are dead. You definitely killed one of them, and it wasn't Desimir."

"But…"

"We'll break it down tomorrow. Eat some more."

She poured out another slug of rakija.

They took me to bed at some point. I have no idea when.

Chapter 45
Morning, 20 Gersmoanne, 1712 MG

If Piri had not awoken me, I might not have risen the next morning. I had not slept well, tossing from one wounded shoulder to another. My muscles ached from the battle. And the rakija they had made me drink pounded the inside of my brain.

If ever there was a day…

But Piri did come. She bullied me into dressing. Then she took me to the hayroom and showed me that she had taught Desimir to wrestle. After bouncing me off a wooden wall, a stack of hay, and the stone back wall, she relented and let me get cleaned up.

I do not recall that we said a single word.

I dressed in my green herringbone tunic and brown pants. Eirik, presumably, had put my belt, turnshoes, saex and knife into my room while I practiced. I put on each of these things carefully.

I realized this had been the first night since my nameday that I had slept without my saex in arm's reach.

I went downstairs for breakfast. Zoe hugged me and then clucked at the cuts on my shoulders.

"I'll rewrap those after you get something inside you. Piri, what were you thinking?" She glared at us in full fury and then snapped, "Ragnar!"

Ragnar grinned and followed her. "I do believe I was tellin' you she had a bit of a temper, not like the sweet lasses I was to be growin' up with in the north mind you…" He disappeared into the kitchen and returned a few moments later with plates for everyone. Eirik pushed two tables together, and the six of us ate eggs scrambled with a cheese and onions. Melia plopped in the middle of the table and accepted petting and small pieces of egg with equal expectation.

Her purrs provided the only conversation until Eirik burst.

"What happened?"

Zoe shushed him. I sighed, but at his age, I would have asked too.

"One of the guards wanted me dead," I answered.

"One of the Gropa guards?" His mouth fell.

"Yes. With some help."

"You might say that." Piri chuckled. I glanced at her. Piri smiled and looked at Eirik. "Watch yourself around this one, boy, he's fair to being deadly. The Gropa guard died with at least twenty others in that street, and the Sevener did for most of them."

Eirik's mouth dropped open, "Whaa…?"

"Piri!" said Zoe.

"No, dear one, he's ready to talk, and we need to hear it," replied Piri.

"I suppose. Besides, Ragnar you deserve to know." I gathered my thoughts. "Someone is scrambling for power among the Gropa, and I don't know that Pal is ready for what's happening."

"Who?" asked Eirik.

"Take your pick from their council. Might even be a girl your age. Or someone outside the council."

"Zeus's c—" Eirik stopped with a quick glance at Zoe, who was turning her glare to him.

"Zeus's cock indeed, boy," said Piri. "None of the Mrnjavcevic leaders read the signs the same way. Well, except Vukasin. You impressed him. Go through what you know again."

"Someone went around Pal to get Gibroz to steal the *Notes* for Kristijan. Frano knew who it was, and they killed him so he wouldn't talk. However, I think that same someone also told Katarina. She admitted that someone asked her to waylay Marija and make the text disappear."

I shrugged, wincing in pain. "According to Kristijan, the schism was probably destined to happen, but the loss of the *Notes* guaranteed it would, and that it would be worse than it might otherwise have been. Whoever is behind this used the schism to weaken Pal's position. Katarina would find the schism interesting to watch."

I ate a couple of bites, and thought. "I knew all of this when I went to Pal's. In fact, it's what I told him. Then there's yesterday's attack. I already knew someone wanted me dead, but the only person I'm a threat to is the person behind the attacks here. If I'm right and they're going after Pal, then killing me last night would have shamed Vesela and Pal, since they had pledged to protect me.

I paused, this time without shrugging. "I think the plan was that I would die alongside the members of the escort loyal to Pal and some of the street attackers. There would have been an investigation, of course—Zvono and Kapric were most likely to investigate. I bet they hoped to control them using the normal corruption in the city hierarchy."

"Pal would have accepted that?"

"He might have. He might not have had any choice. The only witness would have been the guard who attacked me. He would have said something like, 'I'm so sorry, Lord Pal, that the foreigner died too, but we did our best. We killed a pile of the buggers that jumped us and we lost three of our own but we just couldn't save him.' All he'd have to do is to keep quiet and no one would know anything different. He wouldn't talk because the new zupan would give him more wealth and status than he could dream of. Or have him killed."

I chuckled. "Pal was pretty upset with me when I left. He might not have minded too much that my blood stained the street." I ate some more of my eggs. "I've known for a while it's someone on the Enchelei council who wronged you, Ragnar. Yesterday proves it. No one knew when I would leave the manor, and because of Pal's anger, I left about two hours earlier than anyone expected. Someone had to not only recruit that guard to kill me, but also be able to change the timing of the attack on the spur of the moment."

"Probably not that difficult in some ways," said Piri. "If I had been arranging things, I'd have had my thugs waiting for the word to attack all evening. Your schedule would always be somewhat unknown. By having them there all evening, all they had to do was wait for you to leave. Not difficult at all."

"Either way. The problem is that I have too many choices. I'm sure it's a member of the Gropa Council, yet I haven't been able to eliminate many possibilities. If pressed, I'd cross Andrija off the list."

I glanced at Piri. "I'd also ignore Agata Kyranna, though she'll hammer the Mrnjavcevic soon enough."

Piri chuckled. "Pal would not conspire against himself. That still leaves four. Of them, I lean against Vesela attacking her father. I think she already possesses too much of the zupan's power for that to be her motive, but maybe the taste of the power makes her want more. It would be a motive for Jeremena, Zacharia, and Davorin, though. I have reasons to suspect all of them, and who knows what other snakes lurk amongst the Gropa weeds."

I paused. I knew my next statement would provoke some outrage. "I need to narrow the field. There's only one person who can do that." Everyone looked at me. "Katarina promised me she'd answer any question I was smart enough to ask her. I think I have some now."

"You're not going to visit her again?" said Zoe. "It's not safe."

"Right now, Zoe, Achrida isn't safe for me. For that matter, I doubt I will be safe in the Great City, even if I'm in the Emperor's Guard. I'll always be a bit of a threat to whomever takes power in the Enchelei."

"He's to be havin' the right of it, love. I've been to be thinkin' about this a mite ever since I was to be hearin' about yesterday." Ragnar smiled a soft smile that seemed odd on his bushy face. "I was to be considerin' lettin' him walk away since things seem to be gettin' deadly, but that'd be no use 't all. He'd not be stoppin' because he'd be sworn to me, and he's not to be the kind to be leavin' that, especially since he's to be bein' a mite upset about Desimir."

Zoe patted my forearm as I stared at my half-full plate.

"And it's not to be matterin' even if he did, they'd be wantin' him dead anyway. I'm guessin' I've a brother and a cousin or two that'd be bein' happier if I was to be dead, but they'd only do somethin' about it if I was to be goin' back to Svellheim. I'm thinkin' the only thin' our lad here's to be doin' is to be leavin' the Empire now and forever, and even that's not necessarily to be makin' him safe."

I looked at him. "So, to Katarina I must go."

"Not alone," said Piri and Zoe simultaneously.

"Are you going to assign Arkady to me?"

"Not at all. I'll go," said Piri.

"You? What about the Pathfinders?"

"Desimir was to be my replacement. Now I have to give the other decarchs some experience. Seems like as good a time as any. Besides, we

Dassaretae have some interest in this, and Vukasin suggested assigning Desimir to you."

"I didn't know that."

"Vukasin's a sharp man."

"I'm not here to create problems with the Gropas, Piri."

"Neither am I. Vukasin gets along with Pal. They have some sort of working relationship, and this mess is hurting business."

I looked at her without blinking.

"I was right, Sevener, you'll do," she laughed. "I give my word to you that I won't meddle. I'll help you as you need and I'll keep you safe, but I won't mess with the Gropas."

"Kapric and Zvono will be showing up soon, and they'll want to talk to me again. Later tonight, you and I will go see what Katarina has to say."

We got up and moved the tables back. This irritated Melia, who showed her disdain by sprawling in a patch of floor warmed by the sun and studiously ignoring us. Piri and I went back to my table, where we waited in silence for the quaesitors to arrive.

Chapter 46
Late Morning, 20 Gersmoanne, 1712 MG

As expected, we did not have long to wait. Kapric had a bundle in his hands when they arrived.

"Here's your sword. We even cleaned it."

"Thank you."

"Let's go over things again," said Zvono, nodding at Piri.

I went through the battle again. My memories had crystallized, and I now described the fight easily, at least the part after Desimir's knife and the spear point.

"You're positive the guard behind your right shoulder attacked you."

"I can't think of any other reason his spear point would be at my shoulder."

"Could he have stumbled?"

"They moved well. They were probably some of the best armsmen the Gropa have. I doubt he'd stumble just walking."

"No, probably not."

We thought for a bit.

"I have some questions for you."

"Thought you might," said Kapric.

"What can you tell me about the attackers?"

Zvono glanced at her wax tablet. "We can't identify them all. Some because we don't know them, and some because we just can't." She glanced at me. "You know your sword-work, eh, Sevener?"

I shrugged.

"Anyway, those who we could identify were either Blazevics or thugs for hire. At least two were cousins of those Blazevics you killed. A couple of the others probably helped kill Frano. All but three lived in the Stracara. The krals had hired nearly all of them before. None of them will be missed."

"But you still have a pile of paperwork."

"Twenty-three different entries, to be exact, if you count all of the guards and the Pathfinder."

291

"Where were they? We'd passed the Stracara, and I must admit I had started to relax."

"The krals are everywhere, so if they want you dead, you're not safe anywhere in Achrida. But for this attack, they hid in a storefront along your path and waited there. A merchant and his family had one of the worst evenings of their lives, but other than a few bruises, they're all fine."

"When did they get there?"

"In the afternoon, long before the merchant usually closed up."

"They were there before I went to Pal's?"

"Yep. They surely watched you go by. Maybe they wanted to identify the guard on their side. Maybe they just wanted foreplay."

"They waited to attack me on my way back?"

"Yes. There doesn't seem to be any reason they couldn't have attacked you on the way."

"It was certainly light enough when they attacked that daylight wasn't an issue either way," I mused.

"Exactly."

"So whoever it was wanted me to talk to Pal."

Kapric and Zvono nodded.

"What did you talk about?" asked Zvono.

I thought about what I wanted to say. I had already told my theory to Enchelei, Dassaretae, and Ragnar. Might as well tell the quaesitors, so I did.

"You're saying that someone is trying to replace Pal?" asked Kapric.

"Yes. Since they waited to attack me afterwards, they must have hoped my meeting with the family would hurt Pal."

"Did it?" asked Zvono.

"Not sure. It may have warned him. It did make him angry. His relaxed face covers a mighty temper."

Kapric snorted. "Every Enchelei knows that."

"Maybe they wanted him angry?" I shrugged. "Too many possibilities right now."

They both nodded.

"Thanks for returning my sword."

"You might need it."

"Yes. Sorry about the paperwork."

They nodded again and got up.

"There'll be more before this is done." Zvono sighed.

"With someone wanting to overthrow Pal and Katarina stirring the pot? Probably."

"Luck of Hermes, Sevener," she added.

I thanked them as they walked out. After they left, I looked at Piri. "Tell me about Zvono," I said.

She looked at me.

"I know she's Dassaretae, and you're of an age. You know at least something about her."

"We spent a lot of time together when we were growing up. We fought as kids. Sparred as teenagers. Beat each other up over the same guys. Her mother is my mother's first cousin. I'm never quite sure what that makes us, but our mothers were close and she was always around."

"How'd she become a quaesitor?"

"Her father was a quaesitor, and it was always sort of expected. She never forgot anything, even as a kid."

"Especially if it's in her wax tablet."

"She's had that thing forever." Piri laughed. "I think her father gave it to her. Said a quaesitor always needed to keep notes."

"She never seems to actually read it."

"Oh, she does."

"So you trust her?"

"Yes." Piri shrugged. "But I don't trust her job. It's always been fucked up because the zupans and the Emperor and the priests and everyone else who can meddles with it. She'll do what she says she will, though. She accepts the hierarchy because she knows she can find ways around it. Not always, of course, but often. She learned a lot of tricks from her father. And she feels someone who's not accepting every bribe has to do the job."

"Kapric takes bribes?"

"No, not him. He's good to his word, too. He's a hard, hard man, though. Not as devious as Zvono, but tougher."

"Then who?"

"There are a couple of dozen quaesitors in Achrida. They're the only two I really trust. There are a couple of others I might trust sometimes, but I can only always count on those two."

"Is that why they handle the murders?"

"I guess. Most everyone agrees that murders are best solved, and no one wants them digging into gambling, theft, or anything that has to do with money." Piri chuckled ruefully.

"How beholden to tribal politics are they?"

"Not much. She'll report to Vukasin and he'll talk to Pal, but both of them ignore specific instructions if they conflict with the job.

"I'd guessed this from talking to them, but it's nice to have confirmation."

"If you do something wrong, they'll hit you as hard as they can. However, they'll not come after you if they don't have a reason. For what it's worth, I think they're glad you're here."

"You do?"

"Yes. They know something's going on. I'll bet they actually know more about this than they hinted at a few minutes ago. But they also know the moment they do anything official something will come down from above."

"So?"

"So, they want this thing ended, and even with all that's happened with you around, there's worse coming if the Enchelei break apart. Maybe not the Sfagi, but bad enough."

"Imagine the paperwork." I chuckled.

Piri nodded and we sat in silence for a few minutes. Eventually, I suggested we visit Gibroz that afternoon, but Piri convinced me to rest.

"You may not feel it right now, but you're still down from the fight. I don't want to visit Katarina unless you're rested."

Even if that advice had not made sense, it reminded my body of its fatigue and I suddenly yawned.

"You see?" Piri laughed.

Zoe came out and rebandaged my arms and expressed herself more firmly. "It's off to bed with you. I'll have a good dinner waiting for you later."

At my best I could not have won a contest of wills with either of them, so I followed Zoe's instructions. I did not fall asleep immediately, but a dreamless nap eventually stole my afternoon.

Chapter 47
Late Afternoon, 20 Gersmoanne, 1712 MG

We met in the taproom for dinner. Zoe had made gulyas again, which had the welcome effect of making me alert.

"How do you eat this?" I asked between gulps of beer.

"I think Zoe added a little bit more paprika, just for you." Piri grinned.

The regulars were laughing at me now. I tried to glare at them, but the constant lifting of my mug to my face made my glares ineffective. Piri waved at Karah, who, with a cruel smirk on her face, brought over a pitcher of lakewater.

"Drink the water, lad," added Piri. "Best you're not drunk for Katarina."

Gradually, as the water cooled the fire in my mouth, I began to appreciate the flavor of the gulyas. I even ate a second helping. Once done, Piri and I decided not to relax, but to head directly to Katarina's.

When we arrived at Tresinova's Treasures, a small, perfectly groomed man greeted us with a flutter of manicured hands.

"Katarina will be so pleased to see you."

One of guards, this time not Katarina in disguise, beckoned us up to the same room Desimir and I had visited last time. Katarina bustled in soon after. She wore a gown black as midnight, and her eyes gleamed like the sun.

"Welcome, welcome, my dear," she squealed in her teenager pose. "It's been so excellent to watch your progress."

I thanked her, not knowing how else to respond. "I'm here to answer your question and because I now know the right questions to ask you."

She squealed again and clapped happily. "So what's your answer, my dear?"

"If I had the *Notes of Naum*, I might be able to make the Gropas sit at my feet. I certainly could if I were Gropa to begin with."

"You think so, boy?"

"Yes, and I think one of the Gropas thinks so, as well. Someone wants Pal sitting before them, either curled up like a dog fed on scraps or as a prized bearskin rug, a trophy to remember the hunt."

"You are learning. You are correct that some of the Gropas feel this way. Yet, you are still so innocent. So straightforward you are."

I looked at her for a long moment. "Straightforward in Achrida terms."

"Yes, dearie." She laughed her full, deep laugh. "And that is your saving grace." She grinned at me. "I do not think that your answer has earned you the right to ask me questions."

"No?"

"Indeed, not. However, your answer has earned something from me."

"And what is that?"

"What I have ached to do since I first saw you."

She looked at me. I noticed she was murmuring something under her breath and her eyes glossed over as they lost focus. I realized she was searching through my life and my emotions.

Searching, however, was a weak description of what she actually did.

She reached into my soul and ripped away my life. Held my faults in her bloody hands and picked through them like a lass searching for the prettiest flower. Dismissed my successes like a butcher disdaining gristle. Laughed like a child running to loving parents at my fears. Criticized my loves as a jeweler sought the perfect stone. Judged me with more care than the Feeder of the Wolf would on my deathday.

Piri grabbed my arm. I had not realized I was drawing my saex.

Katarina shuddered, as if in orgasm, as she had the first time I pulled my steel before her. Languidly, she spoke. "Oh, yes, my dear, this was a much better idea." She shuddered again, screaming in ecstasy and ripping her nails like talons down her arms, tearing bloody tracks in her flesh.

After a moment, the young girl giggled. "I told you I'd demand something from you. Your memories will do nicely."

Blood dripped from a talon. I knew not what to say.

Piri kept her hand on my arm.

"And I can see we shall be great friends. Oh yes. Uncounted shall be the nights I scream your name."

Blood dripped from a talon. I waited.

"I promise you shall think of me when you have captured your beast."

Blood dripped from a talon. She shuddered once more. Closed her eyes. Opened them and stared. "Because now I know how you will track your prey."

Blood dripped from a talon.

"I do owe you your reward," said the haggler. "Are you ready, boy?" She looked at her nails and carefully licked them clean of her blood while we waited. "Your guilt shines like the sun. It called to me. I answered. Yet, now that I have seen it in every way, I tell you, boy, you need to examine, truly understand, the nature of the oaths you have sworn. Then, when you understand the nature of the oaths you have sworn, you can judge others."

She daintily licked off the last drop of blood on her nails. "You will know your prey by the oaths they have foresworn, for you have seen them foresworn by others." She dipped a talon into her flesh and licked one more drop of her tainted blood. "That is all you need."

On our way back to the Faerie, neither Piri nor I wished to speak of Katarina. I suspect neither of us slept well, though Piri might have, for she still had secrets.

Chapter 48
Late Morning, 21 Gersmoanne, 1712 MG

At breakfast the following morning, Piri dismissed all questions by informing us that we would spend the day focusing only on Desimir's memory. That evening, as the sun set, we would attend his funeral.

I tried to follow Piri's instructions, but Katarina's words to me filled my thoughts. *How would knowing the oaths I had seen enlighten me*, I wondered?

I never doubted the truth of her words. She had taken everything from me. She paid me with honesty.

I spent the day examining my guilt. Though the Trickster had helped me break my oath, I still held the shame of oathbreaking. This shame filled me all the more since I had not died to fulfill the oath. Bedarth made me promise to live with that guilt. He made me swear to the World Tree that I would live and fulfill the life written for me in its branches. When I honored that promise, he poured all of his knowledge that he could into me.

In truth, I never really understood why he had done so. He must have known Cynric would never trust me. I could never follow Bedarth as Cynric's advisor, and when Bedarth passed, I was no longer welcome in Cynric's hall.

I blamed Cynric not. I might have done the same. I had, after all, raised my sword against him and slain his thegns. He might have forgiven me, had I fulfilled the oath that had led me to do those deeds.

But I had not.

I lived while my lord, his son, died at his hand.

I lived while my father, his thegn, died at my hand.

I lived while my shield-kin died slaying his.

How could I ever be forgiven?

And now, how could I find out who else had failed in his oath as I had?

What oaths had the Gropas sworn to each other? What guilt could they bear that was as great as the one Katarina told me to seek?

The day passed without me knowing. I presumed lunch had been brought before me. I did not remember eating it. An untouched mug of flat beer sat before me. Piri roused me at midafternoon.

"It is time to send Desimir to Mithra, Sevener. Come prepare yourself."

"What must I do?"

"Put on that bright scale of yours, lad. Tonight we shine for him."

I did so. When I returned, Cvetijin stood behind the bar. Branimira and other women I had seen on the street bustled in the kitchen. The friends of Ragnar and Zoe would ensure the Faerie shined for Desimir as well. It would welcome us home when we returned.

Piri also stood there, immaculate in her Pathfinder armor, waiting for the others. Ragnar arrived first and claimed his sword from its usual spot. He slid it into the sheath over his shoulder. He wore a long chainmail hauberk and had a small axe slid into his belt. His hand rested on a forbidding greataxe. Eirik wore a richly embroidered green tunic. He slid the short sword he kept behind the bar into a sheath at his belt. He looked uncomfortable wearing such finery. I remembered my own discomfort at that age in such clothes. Karah came down wearing a regal silk dress that matched her coloring perfectly. Like Piri, she would never have Vesela's beauty, but I had to wonder how many of the regulars she would have to slap after they saw her.

She went straight to Ragnar. "Oh, Da," she sighed. She went to him and untwisted the baldric that held his sword.

Ragnar grinned. "Where would I be bein' without me bairns? They're to be bein' the light of…"

"Hush, Da," she snapped.

He did, though he winked at Piri and me. Zoe finally appeared.

"Sevener, close your mouth," hissed Piri loudly, with a sly smile.

I glared at her for a moment, then turned to bow to Zoe. I had expected a silk dress from her as well. Instead, she wore a steel chain hauberk. Comfortably. As if it was an old friend. The leather on her semi-spatha's hilt showed the wear of long use. Across her back she had slung a small, round shield. She carried a spear lightly and easily.

She smiled at me. "I've not always been an innkeeper's wife, my dear."

"No wonder Ragnar fears your wrath," I responded.

"Of course," she sniffed. "Are we ready?"

"One last thing," said Piri. She handed each of us an earthenware flask.

"You'll know what to do when the time comes, Edward," she told me somberly.

Piri led the way. She bade me walk at her side. Ragnar and Zoe followed, hand in hand. Karah and Eirik followed their parents.

People knew we were coming. In the Square of Legends they stepped aside for us. Dassaretae looked ready to push back any who did not. The Enchelei bowed respectfully. They would expect it of the Dassaretae when one of their own passed.

A squad of Pathfinders waved us through the Upper Gate, and we climbed the hill to a long wooded plateau where torches flickered through the trees. Amidst those trees, a great slab of darkened limestone held Desimir laying upon a pyre.

Around the slab, a crowd of people chatted amiably, something I had not expected. Freshly oiled armor and weapons gleamed everywhere, even if they no longer fit their wearer as they had years before. Several young lads stammered greetings to Karah. Zoe pushed her amongst them, ignoring Karah's glare. Eirik joined a group of lads his age. They cheerfully began arguing of horses. Piri left to inspect her troops. Arkady and Dmitri must have survived that inspection for they welcomed me with broad smiles. Ragnar waved off acquaintances and remained by my side. Oddly, he stood quietly, except when found reasons to laugh at me.

After a bit, the crowd began shifting its focus to the pyre and the man standing at its foot. He wore Pathfinder armor and held a torch, calmly waiting. I realized it was Vukasin.

"Welcome, my kin," he said. He nodded at Ragnar and me. "Welcome, as well, to those who Desimir claimed as kin."

We bowed slightly. He paused and changed his tone.

"Hecatontarch Piriska, Desimir calls you."

Piri took her place at the head of Desimir's pyre. She also held a torch.

"Did you build the road for his soul?"

"I did."

"Then let his kin judge your work."

She stood there, ramrod straight and waited.

"Bozhidar, son of Cedomir, Desimir calls you."

An old man, proud in his grief, came forth.

"Bozhidar. As his father it is your right to inspect Desimir's pyre. Have you done so?"

"I have."

"Is it laid according to the lines of the earth, the hunger of the fire, the sweep of the air, and the flow of the water?"

"It is." He stepped back.

"Andrijana, daughter of Todor, Desimir calls you."

The beautiful, lush woman took her place.

"Andrijana. As his love it is your right to inspect Desimir's pyre. Have you done so?"

"I have."

"Is it laid according to the lines of the earth, the hunger of the fire, the sweep of the air, and the flow of the water?"

"It is." She stepped back.

"Cedomir, son of Desimir, Desimir calls you."

A young boy stepped forward. He did not understand, I guessed, but he stood there anyway.

"Cedomir. As his son it is your right to inspect Desimir's pyre. Have you done so?"

"I have."

"Is it laid according to the lines of the earth, the hunger of the fire, the sweep of the air, and the flow of the water?"

"It is." He looked at his mom. She nodded in approval and beckoned him to join her and his brother.

"Are there any who find fault with the words of Desimir's kin?"

Silence.

After a time, Vukasin and Piri turned to the pyre.

"Desimir, son of Bozhidar, I send your soul on its path," they intoned together. They slid their torches into the pyre, and it lit swiftly.

The crowd watched as Andrijana and her children stepped forward. They each carried earthenware flasks like the ones Piri had handed me earlier. Andrijana drank from the flask and then emptied it into a small stone basin that flowed under the pyre. When the liquid flared, I guessed it was rakija. She then helped her children do the same. They both coughed at the liquor. Bozhidar was next. Then Piri. Then Vukasin. I realized that the rest of the people were lining up to do the same.

Zoe arrived with Karah and Eirik to chivvy us all into line. We stepped forward into the heat, drank our rakija, and watched Desimir's pyre consume the rest. I was surprised to note that even though we made our toast after many others, Desimir's body had barely started to smolder. It was almost as if he waited to finish swapping toasts with all of us.

I stood staring at the smirk on his face while the universe stopped. *"Of course I waited, Sevener. When did I ever not drink free rakija?"* He clearly said to me.

I tottered away, his laughing face filling my mind. Soon I realized everyone had completed their toasts. The crowd returned to milling sociably.

I found Andrijana and her children standing to one side. People came to them, made their gestures, said their words, and moved on. I moved towards her, and soon realized I stood before her.

"Andrijana…" I started, but I could not finish.

She hugged me. "Cedomir, Vanja. This is Edward. Your father loved him."

I wept as I hugged them.

"I knew the risk, Sevener," she whispered. "Piri told me of the choice he made. Now, he shines in every fire."

I started to speak again, but she reached up and put a finger across my lips. I knew not what else to do, so I hugged them all again and took my leave.

Eventually Zoe herded the six of us together and we joined the crowd returning to Achrida. Once at the Faerie, Piri made me eat dinner.

She also made me drink more rakija. Lots more rakija. Karah plopped Melia in front of me. I stayed, looking at the taproom through the gray light of my soul, until Zoe and Eirik escorted me to my room.

Eventually I slept, despite fire-filled dreams of Desimir and his family.

Chapter 49
Morning, 22 Gersmoanne, 1712 MG

I woke the next morning feeling better than I had any right to expect. The rakija nudged at me, but in a sort of friendly manner. Sort of like Deor nipping at me. I had also slept far longer than I expected. I wondered why Piri had not awakened me to practice. I did not wonder too much though, gratefully assuming she had let me rest.

I dressed and went to the common room. My stomach reminded me that I had eaten little for three days. Zoe recognized the look and began pushing food at me. Gruel with honey, eggs, deer sausage, mushrooms, leftover stew, bread with cheese. I ate it all.

"Feeling better, are we?" commented Piri.

I belched. "Yeah, though I could hardly feel worse."

"This might improve your mood even more. Kristijan sent you a message."

"Kristijan did?"

"Yes."

"What did it say?"

"How would I know? He keyed it to you. It's sitting on the bar where the Naumite who delivered it laid it. No one else can touch it."

"Really?"

She shook her head at my ignorance. I chuckled at her and went to the bar. When I touched the letter it seemed to warm briefly. When I unfolded it, I saw that Kristijan had discovered who had originally spoken to Gregor. The man who had convinced Gregor to send Marija north.

At first, the answer made no sense. Why him? What did he have to do with all of this?

Then I thought about Katarina.

And my guilt.

Suddenly, I understood the coin Katarina had paid me for my memories. Oaths. He had lived up to his oath, but not everyone had. Someone had failed him.

"You will know your prey by the oaths they have foresworn, for you have seen them foresworn by others," she had said. Her words became a mirror, and in the deeds and oaths of the Gropas I could finally see the reflection of the deeds and oaths of myself and my people. For the first time I realized exactly which oaths in my life had been foresworn.

I stood in a tavern hundreds of leagues distant and finally saw the truth of my life in the Middlemarch. I thought about my father. About his face as I slew him. About the smile when he realized that I broke his branch of the Tree of Life. For the first time, I truly understood that smile. For the first time, I knew what he was thinking.

I thought about Bedarth. He had known all along that my own branch of the World Tree had not broken. That I had deeds yet to do.

As I thought of them sitting on benches in the golden halls of the Allfather, laughing at me, I turned to Piri. Katarina's mirror had revealed not only my life but also the prey that awaited me.

"I need help."

"Yes?"

"When I left Pal's manor, he was in a rage aimed, at least partially, at me. I need to return. In fact, you need to come with me." I kept thinking. "And we need to bring Ragnar, Kapric, and Zvono with us. Kristijan, too, if we can convince him."

I sighed. "I'd like Andrijana there, too. She deserves to know why Desimir was killed." I paused. "One more thing. The entire Gropa Council needs to be there. There must be no doubt."

She rocked back. "Kristijan told you something."

I nodded and chuckled. "I have spent much of the time since our talk with Katarina attempting to decipher how the oaths of my past connect to the Enchelei. Which broken oath of mine will unravel this knot? As is often the case, riddles are simple once a person looks at the question in the right way."

"And Kristijan showed you the right way?"

"Yes, with but one name."

"What name?"

I shook my head. "I want to keep this to myself until all those involved are gathered together. Except Svetislav. He needs to know ahead of time."

She nodded. She expected everyone in this city to have secrets, and I could see the wheels of her cunning mind revolving.

"Kapric and Zvono might help." She plotted. "Maybe Kristijan is the key."

"Yes?"

"Do you think you know enough to convince Kristijan to do what I say?"

I thought. "Yes, I do. For a chance to find the *Notes*, I think he'd risk Pal's wrath."

"Will this harm the Gropas?"

I sighed. "Yes, though it has to happen for them to have any chance to heal."

"Can you swear that?"

"I can."

"I assume that quicker is better for this to happen?"

"Definitely."

"Then let's get moving, boy. We have errands to run if we're going to be able to get everything organized by this evening."

I smiled and finished my mug. Piri started by giving Ragnar instructions. We then went to the Pathfinder barracks. There, Piri made more arrangements. Then we went to Heartsquare to meet with Kapric and Zvono.

When we arrived, Zvono worked at a desk in the large room. Seeing us, she motioned to Kapric's office, where he sat behind his desk, upright almost like a statue.

"I need your help."

"We're aware of that, Sevener."

"No time for that, Kapric. I think I know what is happening and I think I know why."

He raised his eyebrows but motioned for me to continue. I explained what I needed.

"That's quite the list of witnesses, Sevener, do you need all of them?"

I nodded.

Kapric looked at Zvono, who shrugged. He shrugged in return.

"Alright, Sevener, we'll help. But if this doesn't work, you'll tell us everything." Kapric's stud-bull look was back. I let his glare pass. I would have demanded the same in his place.

"Zvono will go with you. She will help you as she can. I will see if I can gather the council."

"We need all of them. If you tell them those who do not attend will see the others gather family power at their expense, I suspect you'll have no real problems."

Kapric snorted. "You understand them perfectly, I see."

With that, Zvono, Piri, and I left. We ascended the southern hill to the Temple of Naum. When we arrived, the dark-haired young priestess immediately called for Cassandra, who led us to Kristijan.

"You got my message?" he asked.

"Yes."

"Was it helpful?"

"Yes."

"I fail to see how that answer helped."

"I know more than you." I shrugged.

Cassandra sniffed primly.

"Why are you here, then?" Kristijan demanded.

"I need your help. And you need mine."

"How can you help us?"

"I can tell you who took *The Notes of Naum in His Captivity*. Whether that person still possesses them, I cannot tell you, but I can tell you who took them."

Cassandra and Kristijan stared at me, hope creeping into their faces like the morning sun creeping along the far eastern steppes.

"What will we need to do for you to tell us?"

Piri stood forward. "You need to escort myself, Edward, two quaesitors, a widow, and Ragnar into Pal's manor before the council."

"You should also bring at least one of your priests," I added.

"Impossible. Pal would not allow for any of the Dassaretae to enter their manor. Especially not one so close to Vukasin. And if one of the

308

quaesitors were Zvono, she, too, would be barred."

"Don't forget that Pal would rather kill me than talk to me," I laughed.

"Then we cannot help."

"You can." I laughed. "Think like an Achridan."

Piri smiled. Even Cassandra's frown lightened.

"First, what will happen is important. Piri or another Mrnjavcevic must be there. Vukasin must have a witness. The members of the council, were they to know what I planned, would agree. Grudgingly, but agree they would."

"Go on."

"Ragnar must be there, for all of you owe him this debt."

He sighed. "I see that."

"Andrijana should be there. I owe her this much and more."

He did not know her name, so he shrugged.

"Kapric and Zvono must be there. The Emperor must have his own witnesses, and they, too, are owed a debt."

"Very well."

"Finally, you need to bring one of your priests. And you should pick your escort wisely." His eyes narrowed at my tone. "Gregor should have witnesses as well," I said gently.

"Out of the question," he snapped.

Cassandra and I both started to talk. I gestured to her to speak.

"He is right, Your Grace." He glared at her.

"Imagine, if you will, your reaction if the tables were reversed," I added. "Imagine that Gregor could determine the fate of the *Notes* and could choose whether an ally of yours would be involved or not. Would you allow the schism to end?"

Cassandra nodded. "Master Edward is correct."

Kristijan sat back. "But this is all moot. Even if we accept that all of these must be present, how will we gain entrance?"

Piri explained her plan. Kristijan shook his head but Cassandra nodded.

"We should risk it, Your Grace. And you should bring Zdenko and

Zdeslav."

"The twins? But they're…"

"Gregor's most outspoken allies in Achrida," she confirmed.

Kristijan fumed.

"Your Grace?"

He glared at me.

"I told you it was asking the right question that gave me the answer."

"You did," he muttered.

"Who did you put the question to?"

He paused. "Gregor."

"I thought so. He is the only one who would know."

He fumed for a moment and then sighed.

"You are both correct, he deserves the courtesy. If you truly think this could return the *Notes of Naum* to our church, then we must make the attempt."

Piri spoke. "Send a messenger to Pal requesting the opportunity to meet with his council after dinner tonight."

He nodded and motioned to Cassandra. She left to send the messenger.

"Now what?"

"I will send Pathfinders to escort you and the rest of your representatives to the Faerie for dinner this evening."

Kristijan looked puzzled.

Piri explained. "If you request a meeting with the zupan, whoever it is the Sevener is targeting has the chance to ambush you."

"Ambush priests of Naum?"

"A priest of Naum and her escort have already been slain. Why would they hesitate now?"

Chapter 50
Early Evening, 22 Gersmoanne, 1712 MG

I dressed as I had for dinner with Piri. Blue dragon tunic and sea-green pants. This time I wore the new turnshoes and my favorite winingas, the ones woven in a brown-and-red pattern, with the dagger and sheath strapped inside. I slid on all my arm-rings, including the one given to me by my father that I had not worn since my youth. I kissed the aesc-rune as I lifted the pendant over my head. I belted on my saex but left my sword. I would strike as a freeman, but with my words, not my blade on this night.

I also brought one small, yet heavy bag I had not opened in years.

By the time I returned to the taproom, Kapric had joined Zvono and Piri at my table. Zoe served us roasted goat seasoned with rosemary, with turnips and fresh barley bread and butter. Andrijana, Cedomir, and Bozhidar ate the same at the next table. As we ate, I felt Kapric tense when a new visitor arrived at the Faerie. I looked up to see Sebastijan striding over to my table.

"Brother." He nodded to Kapric, who just glared.

Sebastijan sighed and turned to me. "I am without an employer. You should hire me, Sevener."

Kapric continued to glare while I stared at him. "Why should I do that?"

"I can be valuable to you."

"In what way?"

"My greatest gift is information that you can only get from me. I have many other skills, as well. But I will only give my information or offer my skills to those who employ me."

Kapric sighed angrily, and I looked at the quaesitor who answered my unspoken question.

"Pay him. I've never liked his ethics, but I've never questioned whether he has them. He's here because he knows something."

Sebastijan smiled and leaned back, accepting a mug of ale and giving small words of thanks to Karah. He enjoyed a drink while I thought about

311

his offer. I had not seen him since we met in the streets. His arrival at this moment could not be coincidental, so he probably did know something I needed.

I unwound a golden arm-ring Penwulf had given me after we drove off two ships of sea reavers.

"What will this buy me?"

Sebastijan laughed. "More service than I can give this day, but I could earn it in time."

I held it out to him. He thought for a moment and finally accepted it.

"My last employer insisted on paying me after I served him. He then chose not to pay me at all after I stopped following you."

"Ah, now I understand," came a rumbling voice.

Sebastijan smiled a soft smile. "Yes, Kapric, you do."

I looked at the two.

"My brother is here because his previous employer played him false. He is a believer in consequences."

Sebastijan nodded.

"Who was it?" I asked.

"I will not say."

I nodded.

"I will also not speak of anything else I did in that service. However, I do have things you must know that I may honorably tell you."

Piri angrily slapped her thigh. "Fool!"

Sebastijan nodded. Zvono and Kapric sighed.

"Yes, Hecatontarch, your foe has seen your preparations and will set ambushes in your path."

She nodded. "This Sevener is too straightforward. I did not think."

"Neither did we, cousin," responded Zvono.

Kapric got up and paced back and forth. Five precise steps, a smooth reverse, and five steps back. I watched him for a moment and then turned to Piri with a raised eyebrow. "Explain," I commanded.

"This is Achrida, boy, and the currents always flow. Your foe has set traps along the way for you. And us."

Sebastijan nodded as he drained his mug. "Yes. Your foe cares not for the lives of the quaesitors, nor yours, and certainly not for the lives of these Mrnjavcevics." He belched comfortably. "Nor mine, for that matter."

I turned back to Piri. "You sent a squad to escort Kristijan?"

"Two, actually."

"Where are the rest?"

"There's a squad at each gate. The rest are about."

"Some might be near if need be?"

She nodded.

"Sebastijan, will two squads be enough to guard Kristijan?"

"Probably, though I think that's mostly because the goal is to eliminate you, as well. I'll bet there are enough waiting out there for the entire Pathfinder company and more. Your foe knows as much as anyone that Piri and the Pathfinders will help you."

"We need more blades."

"No, Sevener, we need to think," responded Zvono.

Sebastijan agreed. "Even if you have enough blades to guarantee success, bad things happen. I'm guessing you need a number of these people around when you get to the mansion."

"Yes, I do. How many could they have altogether? There are several ways we could go to the mansion. Can they have blocked them all?"

"No, but they'll watch each route and locate their troops within attacking range of all."

"What do we do?"

"We get them moving one direction and slip behind them."

"A great idea, but how?"

Kapric kept pacing. Piri emptied her mug and refilled it. Zvono pulled out her wax tablet, opened it, and stared silently at it. I glanced at Ragnar.

"Don't be lookin' at me, Sevener, surely yer to be knowin' that I'm not to be bein' smart enough for this crazy place. I'm just to be makin' beer, and whilst me beer is to be bein' the best around, I'm not to be seein' how it's to be helpin' you get to the Gropa mansion and then—"

Sebastijan interrupted Ragnar with a casual "Hmmm." We all looked at him. "I might have an idea. It's tricky. We'll have to see whether Kristijan is up to it. Will he be coming here alone?"

"No, he'll have at least one priest with him. Probably several. And don't forget Andrijana."

He glanced at her. "I don't think she'll matter for what I'm thinking."

"I'll be wherever I can find out who killed my man!"

"Never fear, milady," he interjected before Andrijana could reach a full shriek. "My plan should guarantee all of you reach the mansion safely. A few will have to take a tricky and dangerous path."

"What's your idea?"

"Let's wait until Kristijan gets here. It might not matter. However, my idea only gets us to the mansion. It's usually well-guarded."

"I have a plan to deal with that," said Piri. I looked at her.

"I'll keep my own secrets too, me boy, but you saw me lay the groundwork when we stopped at the barracks."

We settled into a long silence, where we slowly sipped Ragnar's ale and waited for Kristijan to arrive. I sat nervously, wondering whether Kristijan would be killed on the way over.

"Relax, Sevener, your foe wants you dead most of all. Kristijan is secondary."

We chuckled at Sebastijan's words, and soon Kristijan and the Pathfinder escorts arrived. We relaxed with deep breaths.

Cassandra and two other priests had arrived with him. Since these men shared the same long foreheads, pointed jaws, and tense looks, I assumed these were Zdenko and Zdeslav. They stood apart from the archimandrite and examined all of us thoroughly.

I looked at Sebastijan, but Piri spoke first. "Let's talk in the stables." She shrugged at my questioning eye. "It's Achrida."

All the rest nodded.

The priests, the quaesitors, Sebastijan, Piri, Ragnar, Andrijana, and I entered the stables. Piri set her Pathfinders at the doors, and we moved to the back room.

"What's your plan, Sebastijan?"

"Do we have any horses available?"

"I have Deor."

"And we've to be havin' them three as to be ridden here by them's that to have been murdered. We've never to be knowin' just what to be doin' with them." Ragnar pointed at the horses and their tack.

"Excellent. Piri, can you guide a group around the Old Road without much extra light?"

She nodded.

"I have a question for you, Your Grace."

"How may Naum serve you, son?"

"No, Your Grace, I mean you." Sebastijan paused and looked into Kristijan's eyes. "I know what your foe desires and fears. One of those fears is that this Sevener will expose the plan to the family. But the plan hinges upon the current schism among the Naumites. There is a way for you to solve the schism, Your Grace."

"How may I do this? Gregor's policies risk our faith."

Zdenko and Zdeslav muttered angrily.

"Is it more important to you to be archimandrite or to recover the *Notes of Naum*? Especially if Gregor were to compromise?"

"I…" Kristijan paused. "Well…" He took a few steps, not really looking where he was going. After a moment he turned back. "I need not the title, but I do need to see major changes in our path. We have forgotten our own lessons."

"Do you think that you and Gregor could negotiate those compromises face-to-face, especially if you started by expressing your willingness to concede the title?"

"I… don't know. Perhaps."

"Are you willing to make that concession if it meant a much greater chance to recover the *Notes*?"

He sighed. "The *Notes* matter most in the situation we find ourselves. However, I see no good future for us if we do not change our path." He sighed again. "Yes, if it means the *Notes*, I would concede the title."

"Kristijan."

He turned to the twin who had spoken. Both had troubled looks on their faces.

"Yes, Zdeslav?"

"You have betrayed my faith. You know I feel this."

"I know you feel I have."

"Yet, if you are willing to step away from the title in order to improve our chances of regaining the *Notes*, I will believe that you have done so honestly. I would so inform Gregor."

"That might not change his willingness to compromise."

"It would certainly make it more likely."

Kristijan chuckled. "Yes, Zdeslav, it would. He is wrong, but I have no doubt that Gregor is honorable in his own way." Kristijan turned back to Sebastijan. "Your suggestion is that we ride to Basilopolis so that Gregor and I may speak directly?"

Sebastijan shook his head. "No, Your Grace, not exactly. My plan is that you, the Sevener, Piri, one of these twins, and the Pathfinders go to the South Gate, *as if* you intend to ride south to do just that. We leave some of the Pathfinders at the gate to strengthen it from most assaults."

"What does that get us?" I could not see any reason to go south.

"If you all head southward, your foe will see no option but to respond and chase you. You cannot be allowed to end the schism. The men originally intended to prevent your arrival at the mansion must now be used to prevent your arrival in the Great City."

"Ahh," said Piri. "And then I lead us around the Old Road, back through the North Gate, and along the Wall Road to the gate just north of the mansion."

"Exactly," replied Sebastijan.

"What about the rest of us?" demanded Andrijana. "I want to know why my man was killed."

"The Sevener and Kristijan, not any of you, are what his killer fears. You can walk up to the Wall Road and meet the rest once they've come around the city."

"I see that, but all my Pathfinders must escort our group to the South Gate, or the watchers will suspect."

"Yes, Piri, you'll use your Pathfinders to make sure the four of you get to the gate and have a good lead to the Great City."

"I'm not willing to leave Andrijana and these others without some guards."

"No need to worry, Hecatontarch. I will guard them, along with my men. Ragnar and my brother here can help." He chuckled. "And Zvono has her mighty stylus. It would take a concerted effort to stop us, and most will be chasing after you." He smiled broadly. "Do not forget we will remain here for at least two hours waiting for you to take the Old Road. By then, the odds are they will have forgotten about us. We'll just be drinking Ragnar's delicious ale while you risk your lives."

We tried not to laugh at the look on Kristijan's face.

Piri nodded. "He's annoying, but he's right. You two are the key. Separating you from the rest makes them irrelevant. Even if they make it to the mansion, they can't do any damage."

"I still don't know what I revealed to you," snapped Kristijan, peevishly.

"That is one reason I'm not explaining myself. Several things are coming together, and they only make sense when seen all at once. If I tell you now, you'll just think I'm crazy."

"Huh," chorused Piri, Sebastijan, and Kapric.

Chapter 51
Evening, 22 Gersmoanne, 1712 MG

We saddled the horses. Since we were unfamiliar with them, we took our time with the ones from Marija and her escort. Deor sensed the tension and made things easy. He sought action as much as I did. I made sure I firmly attached the bag I needed to Deor's saddle but put it where it would not impede my riding.

I did not know whether Zdeslav or Zdenko joined us, but whichever twin it was clearly had more experience on horses than Kristijan. He had his horse moving smoothly within a few moments of mounting it. Kristijan, however, while he may have known which end was the front of a horse, lacked any other understanding of the art of horsemanship. He sat in the saddle with little comfort and less grace. His horse clearly expected a more skilled rider and initially balked, but Sebastijan calmed it with one of the apples from the basket.

As we made final adjustments, Piri leaned through the door and made several quick gestures. By the time she finished the rest of us, even Kristijan, had mounted our horses. Zvono, Kapric, and Sebastijan approached Piri. The four spoke swiftly. All nodded, and Piri mounted her horse. Ragnar handed her a small piece of smoothed limestone.

"Are we ready?"

Kristijan's jerky nod gave us all a chuckle.

"Yes, Piri," I added. "Let's end this damn thing."

Ragnar gave me a pat on the leg and opened the door. We went out to the Fourth Serpent. Piri's commands had prompted the Pathfinders to clear the street, and we went down to the Square of Legends. Despite the hour, many people seemed to have business in the square. Amongst them were several faces I recognized from sparring at the barracks. The Pathfinders, both those in uniform and out, cleared a path, and we headed southward on the Trade Road.

The Trade Road seemed quieter than the Square of Legends. The calm soothed me. True or not, I took it as a sign that Sebastijan had read the situation correctly, and our foe neither expected nor prepared for our plan. We moved quickly to the South Gate, the Pathfinders trotting next to us. Periodically another face I recognized would peek out and make quick gestures to Piri.

Once we reached the gate, Piri muttered a quick list of commands to the decarch in charge. He started snapping commands of his own. The Pathfinders who had escorted us from the Faerie moved to their own positions around the gate. Piri took one last look and, apparently satisfied, motioned us onward. We headed through the gate.

When we reached the nuraghi marking the Old Road, we moved into nearly complete darkness. The slight crescent of a moon gave just enough light for the horses to see where they put their hooves, but only at an infernally slow pace. Piri took the lead, with Kristijan, the twin, and me following in a line.

I leaned over Deor's head. "Focus on your steps, my friend. I'll keep an eye to our back."

Deor blew quietly in return, and I let him keep the pace while I did my best to watch behind us.

After what seemed like hours of climbing the mountain, I noticed the moon appeared to be slightly brighter. This surprised me, as I had expected the moon to be setting. Then I realized that Piri now held out the small polished rock Ragnar had given her. It glowed with a slightly brighter version of the light that illuminated the Faerie's halls. More work from Ragnar's stonelord, I assumed. Wherever the rock came from, its soft light allowed us to slightly pick up our pace. Surely it helped the horses navigate some of the trickier portions of the road safely, though for me it lit the terrifying drop-offs to our right. In fact, only Piri seemed immune to heights.

When we reached the mountain pasture, Piri let us relax by the stream Deor and I had enjoyed a few days before.

"We've done well."

"Yes, Sevener, we have. I doubt they can catch us from behind."

"But at the North Gate?"

"If they're smart, they'll at least think of the possibility. We'll have the squad guarding the gate and the bulk of my roaming Pathfinders to guard us there. Hopefully, most of the men sent after us tried to force the South Gate and went towards Basilopolis. If they took the bait we'll be fine."

"If not?"

"You may yet wish you had that fancy sword of yours," she answered with a grin.

I laughed, and we remounted the horses. We waited until Kristijan settled himself and continued along the path. The moon had completely set, and now our only light was Ragnar's stone.

We crept along the path. Time seemed suspended as we made our way. Finally, Piri stopped us. She dismounted and walked back to me and handed me the stone.

"Here, take this and keep it under your tunic. We're close to the West Road, and I'm going to make sure we're not walking into an ambush. Hopefully, one of mine will be there to give us a report." With that she slid silently into the darkness.

Kristijan started to say something, but I immediately hushed him.

Nothing is more eternal than a nervous wait with nothing to see and nothing to hear. In my mind's quest for anything to discover, my nose could suddenly smell the mountain grass and the sweating horses. A bird flapped its wings above us. Soon the rock's dim light seemed painfully bright shining through my linen, and I covered it with one hand.

The horses whoofed and shuffled occasionally, but other than that we waited silently for Piri.

Then, with the suddenness of a striking falcon, she was there.

"They haven't blocked the exit to West Road yet, so let's move quickly."

I handed her the stone, and she remounted. She held the stone high, and soon we had passed the crumbling nuraghi at this end.

We took a right turn heading towards the lake, passing a shadowy figure. Piri and the figure made quick gestures at each other. Another figure stepped out when we turned from the West Road to the North Road, and we could see torches at the gate. The light, glittering off of spear points and drawn swords, welcomed us as we entered the gate.

"Sebastijan and the rest will be here in a moment. We can leave the horses here."

I nodded, slid down, and started undoing the ties that held the bag.

"Stay here and protect the others, Deor. I'll be back soon."

He nuzzled me for a moment and then nipped me lightly on the shoulder. Some Pathfinders took Deor and the other horses outside of the gate and tied them up. Kristijan winced as he dismounted, so sad-looking that even the twin took pity on him. He offered Kristijan an arm to help balance him as the archimandrite tottered painfully.

Truth be told, I understood completely. Though well used to riding Deor, my muscles had stayed tense throughout our ride around the Old Road. I could not walk particularly well after dismounting myself. By the time I had recovered, Sebastijan, his large buddies, and the rest of our group arrived.

"Thanks for the ale," rumbled the same grinning hulk who had laughed at me when we had met in the street days ago.

I grinned back. "You're welcome. Better earn it now."

"Damn greedy sheep's dick."

I chuckled and turned to Piri, who told me what her scouts had informed her. "Most of the men set against us went south and haven't yet returned. They forced the gate. We'll have more ceremonies at the Stone Pyre."

She shrugged sadly. "Gave better than they got, though, and I told my decarchs to only hold for so long. Those who have passed through the gate are entirely irrelevant now."

I put my hand on her shoulder. "Was that all of them?"

She shook her head. "No, a couple of troopers think there is at least one group at least the size of a squad left in the city. Maybe two or three. And they're probably close. Getting you to the mansion won't be simple. We'll have our blades and a few of mine to help, but no more than a score or so. I can't leave this gate unguarded."

I nodded. "We'll make do." Piri marched off to finish her arrangements.

Andrijana came to me. "They're still out there?"

"Not as many, but yes."

"I need Desimir's life to matter."

"Me too."

"Give me the bag," she demanded.

"What?" I answered as Piri strode back over.

"Give me the bag you're carrying. Then you can use a spear."

I shook my head, dully.

"Listen to her, lad. Desimir chose her for a reason," Piri agreed.

"Piri…"

"You hold one of your demons in that bag. I know. But, you can't fight the demon if you don't make it to the mansion."

"But…"

"Hush, Sevener." Piri motioned to one of her men, who gave her his spear. She handed the spear to me.

"Give me the bag, Edward."

"Please, Andrijana…"

"I won't look. Trust me, as my man did. Then give him his life back."

Helpless, I did as I was told. Andrijana hugged me.

"Let's go, lad, we've work to do," commanded Piri.

I sighed. "That we do."

We moved onto the Wall Road. Piri had sent several of her troops ahead to scout. Another dozen or so surrounded our group. My mind had started to think again. I realized a group including over a score of people is hard to hide even in a large city. They were going to see us coming.

"Piri, where will they hit us?"

"Not sure. I'm thinking just past the gate at the end of the Wall Road."

That made sense to me, too, but we reached that gate without incident. Several Pathfinders had scouted past the gate and found no one. Piri and Sebastijan looked at each other and shrugged.

"It's going to happen, Hecatontarch."

She nodded to him as Ragnar, Zvono, and Kapric joined us. "Sebastijan, you and your men stay near Andrijana, the priests, and Ragnar. Keep them alive. I'll cover the Sevener's back. I'll extend my troops out. Hopefully, they'll dull the initial blow and give us time. Zvono and Kapric can take care of themselves." Everyone nodded. "Remember, it's all about this crazy Sevener and the damned priest." Everyone nodded again.

She looked at me, hard. "Be smart, boy."

I shrugged. "I'll do my best."

With that, we moved on.

My tension magnified my senses. I kept hearing and seeing things, but none of these things existed or mattered. We rounded the last curve along the lake. The Gropa mansion sat a mere hundred paces away. The torches flanking the manor gates flickered onto the road, making the blackness of night oily and wavy before us.

I will not say that we relaxed once we saw the mansion, but our constant alertness and anticipation had, by this point, dulled. When the rush we had expected finally came out of the liquid darkness, we reacted sluggishly.

Several of the Pathfinders fell in the initial surprise. Others retreated to avoid that fate. Still, they did exactly what Piri intended. They slowed the swift charge and gave us time to react. I settled behind Piri, who had her shield and semi-spatha poised. Zvono and Kapric moved to my back quarters. They each held long knives in both hands. Thus ensconced, I relaxed into the easy, light strikes Hlodowic had drilled into me as a lad.

A slight feint at a rushing face made the attacker stop, giving Kapric time to slide one of his knives into the man's side. From that feint, I rolled my hand over, extending my elbow at the woman behind him. I pulled my spear the moment I felt contact to prevent it from sinking too deeply, knowing her charge would impale her on the shaft.

I withdrew the spear and switched hands as I moved to Piri's shield side. With her shield, she had blocked one attacker into a couple of others. A fourth attacker pressed her and she could not finish off those on the ground, so I started jabbing at the pile. I slid my spear through some ribs, pulled it out and thrust into a leg. I pinned a wrist grasping at a dropped sword, and finally saw a clear shot at a face. Softly, I thrust into the skull. Again, I made sure the point did not stick. I stepped back as Zvono, who had slain the one that had gotten past Piri, reached in with her pair of knives and finished off the rest of the pile.

I tried to move back to Piri's right as another group charged, but Piri had not had a chance to completely regain her balance and their charge knocked her back. Not much, but enough to catch me as I shifted. I staggered backwards, one of the thugs in my face. I tried to thrust at him, but he was too close. I did manage to slow his charge, so his lunging sword slid into my thigh rather than my stomach.

I yelled in pain and fell to my knees. Fortunately, Kapric was there with one knife into the thug's neck and another into his kidney.

I hunched on my knees, holding my spear point outwards, but the rush had ended. After a brief quiet moment, the wounded, including myself, cried out each in their own manner. Mostly, I gasped loudly as I tried to staunch the blood flowing from my leg.

"Dammit, Sevener, let me. I'm not doing the paperwork on you."

Zvono pulled off her belt and tied it around my leg.

I heard Piri snapping something, and I looked up. Svetislav stood impassively at the Gropa mansion gate. He casually tossed a satchel into the road. Without moving he stood watching us.

Andrijana stomped over and grabbed the satchel. She started pulling out bandages and salves. Kapric helped her distribute the supplies.

Zvono took what she needed for me. After cleaning my wound, she applied a salve I thought could make even the One-Handed Lawgiver wince. She stitched the wound roughly and quickly. I nearly passed out from the pain.

"Going to need new clothes, Sevener. Maybe you can find something civilized."

"I'll stick to what I like, Zvono," I hissed.

"You're going to have to get up in a moment."

"Yeah, I know. I'm not looking forward to that. Is Kristijan alive?"

"He's fine, though one of the twin Naumites took a blade and is touch and go. Andrijana is tending to him while the other twin fusses over her."

"Anyone else?"

"A number of the Pathfinders, of course. Kapric's taking care of them."

"Of course," I sighed. "I've brought them nothing but pain."

"Bullshit."

"But—"

"Shut up and listen. We still have work to do. Piri's marshaling the rest of her troops and establishing a perimeter. Ragnar, Sebastijan, and his men are dealing with the remaining attackers."

I shook myself and took stock. My spear lay next to me. Convenient that, as I'd need a crutch. No time to waste, so I tried to rise but could not.

"Help me up."

Eventually, with Zvono's assistance, I stood leaning on the spear. My bag lay near the wounded twin. Close enough for now. I would not argue with Andrijana carrying it.

Piri came when she saw me standing. "How much time do we have?" I asked.

"Enough, I think." She pointed towards Svetislav and the mansion gate. "We only have to go over there."

"What are we waiting on?"

"Well, now that you can hobble, we just have the twin."

"Will he make it?"

"Maybe, but we'll need to get him to a Helper as quickly as we can."

"What are we going to do? Will the other twin leave him?"

"We'll find out. Some of Sebastijan's men can carry the wounded one to a Helper."

Andrijana stood up. Her dress was covered in the priest's blood. I tottered over to join her, the other twin, and a bewildered Kristijan.

"You were right, Andrijana."

"Men! Of course I was."

I stopped her rising rant with a smile and a raised hand. "We have things yet to do. Detail my shortcomings later."

She sniffed. "Indeed."

I turned to the twin. "Are you Zdenko or Zdeslav?"

He shook his head to clear it. "Zdeslav."

"Sebastijan's men will take Zdenko to one of the Helpers, but we must finish this. Gregor will need your eyes. Can you do this?"

"I… I suppose I must. But my brother…" Tears filled his eyes.

"Sebastijan's men will save him if he can be saved." Even as I spoke, one of Sebastijan's men carefully lifted Zdenko. With the help of the others, they slung Zdenko on the back of Sebastijan's largest henchman. Sebastijan said a few soft words, and the four moved off as quickly as they could without jostling Zdenko any more than needed.

Zdeslav helplessly watched them fade into the darkness. I put my hand on his shoulder and he turned and nodded sadly.

I then looked at Kristijan. "What about you?"

He, too, needed a moment to focus. "What?"

"What about you? Are you ready to end this?"

He looked around in confusion at the strewn bodies of our assailants. "There's more to do?"

"These are nothing. The one you need to see sits inside that mansion."

"What Gropa would do this evil?"

"Come with me and find out."

Zdeslav shook his head, sadly. "Kristijan. In the mansion are lessons that we must be taught."

His words finally penetrated. "Of course. You are both correct. This is a lesson Naum would have us learn." He straightened, and we finally saw the confident scholar and priest he had always been.

Ragnar joined us, bleakly cleaning off Eirik's short sword with a ripped scrap of a tunic. "I'm to be rememberin' this day, Sevener. I'm not to be bein' a chosen slain for One-Eye today, though I am not to be bein' what I once was."

The blood of others dotted him. The battle had marked us all in one way or another.

Chapter 52
Evening, 22 Gersmoanne, 1712 MG

Piri strode up alongside me as I approached Svetislav at the mansion gate. He looked at me impassively, as if the events of the evening were normal. The only exception was the drawn sword tapping lightly on his leg. The guardian who had previously granted me entrance stepped out of the darkness to join him. She stared at me with questions in her eyes and magic in her mind. I could feel the rest of us fall in behind Piri and me. I waited until all stood still.

"Yes, Svetislav, this will hurt your family," I said.

He moved not at all, but somehow, his sword seemed sharper.

"I tell you truthfully, though, that should you not allow me passage, your family will fall and not even Agata can save it."

He remained still, but said, "Jaga?"

"He does not lie," came the soft response.

"I could be wrong, Svetislav. You will have to judge me here and now." Slowly, without threatening, I slid my saex out of my sheath. "You know what this means to me?"

"Yes."

"Kill me with it if I am wrong. I have already lived longer than I should have."

I slid it back into its sheath. I unbuckled my belt, slid the sheath and the blade off the belt, handed them to him, and rebuckled my belt. I adjusted my tunic to fit properly.

"I must look properly dressed when I meet the council. Are they all here?"

He nodded.

"How did you get them here?"

"Fish prices."

"Now they're wrangling with each other. Thanks for making sure they're already upset." I smiled.

He chuckled and nodded to Jaga.

"Are you sure, protokarabos?"

He nodded again.

She sighed. "Then so be it."

Svetislav turned, and we followed him through the gate. He led us to the entryway, where I stopped him for a moment to once more admire the swirling green-and-white marble. With a last look at the group behind me, I turned back to Svetislav and confirmed our readiness.

He opened the door, and we entered. The large windows, so joyous in the sun, held only dark emptiness now. At the far end of the room the council yelled so angrily at each other that they did not notice our entrance.

Sanjin, however, despite his surprise, saw our arrival. His head turned so swiftly, he almost mussed his perfect hair. He slithered over like an angry serpent. He would have bitten me if given the opportunity.

"What are you doing, Svetislav?" he hissed.

Svetislav pointed at me.

"Are you crazy? The Sevener should not be here, to say nothing of this Mrnjavcevic and one of her trooper's whores—"

Svetislav stopped Sanjin with a look. I turned and forestalled Andrijana. "Let me take care of this."

She grumbled, but subsided.

"Sanjin, I must speak with the council."

Sanjin started to argue but stopped as Svetislav calmly slid my saex out of its sheath and let the light play upon the water patterns mere inches below Sanjin's nose. Svetislav turned to me, extended his arms, bowed slightly, and with the point of my saex granted us entrance.

I advanced into the fray. The family had finally noticed me, and they started debating about how best to dispose of my body. Svetislav motioned the rest of the group to cluster at my right. He stood behind me within easy striking distance of my steel.

I ignored the ranting and took stock of the room. The council had clearly been arguing for some time. Since none of the council wore any bandages, I assumed wine, not blood, was the source of the new stain on the rug. The servants, who had waited patiently in my prior visits, now stood terrified, except for one who seemed to smile just a tad too happily.

Her eyes gave her away, and I wondered how long Katarina had attended the Gropa Council. I thought about asking her to leave, but I had promised her the show. I decided to let her see the conclusion.

I asked Andrijana for my bag. I undid the knots.

Then I brought silence to the room with a resounding crash.

Chapter 53
Late Evening, 22 Gersmoanne, 1712 MG

A slowly spinning helm and a cloven boar-crest came to rest on the floor.

"What is the meaning of this, Sevener?"

"I am here to claim justice and to fulfill my oaths, Zupan."

"You rudely enter our house to do so?"

"Here is the only place I can face my foe."

"You're here for but a few weeks and you have foes?"

"It is Achrida." I smiled.

Zacharia barked a laugh, and Davorin smirked.

I picked up the remnants of my helm. "I have not looked at these pieces for years. Can you guess why?"

"We have no time for games!"

I laughed. "Of course you have time for games. You all play games and have done so for as long as you have lived. It is my turn to play a game."

"Svetislav, kill him!"

He rumbled behind me. "Not yet."

Andrija gave into his rage and unsheathed his claws, but Svetislav halted the bear. "Not yet," he repeated.

Andrija stumbled and almost dropped his long knife. But he stopped.

"Oh excellent, Sevener, you have exceeded my hopes. You have even corrupted the mighty Svetislav," mocked Davorin. "I never thought there would come a time when I would be more loyal to Pal than Svet. I'd be happy to kill you."

"If you could."

"Oh, I could, but not here, not face-to-face like honorable men."

I nodded. "Well, Pal? Which of your family shall kill me? Or will you allow me the opportunity to speak?"

"I'll grant Jaga what she wishes—"

Before Pal could finish, Svetislav interrupted. "Her lines read him. Truthful."

330

Agata ended it with a voice as young as a soft spring rain. The same soft rain that would ultimately coalesce into a roaring river. "Svetislav holds your knife."

"He does."

"You risk great stakes in your game."

I nodded, and she spoke shyly to Pal. "I would hear him speak, zupan."

Zacharia followed the wishes of his daughter. "Indeed, Pal, I'd like to know what he thinks. After we hear him, then we kill him."

"I agree, though I'd like to have my fun with him before you send him to the deepest part of the lake," Vesela added, smirking.

"You have gained a great enemy today," rumbled Pal.

"I knew I would."

"In that case, say your piece and I will deal with my council later."

I leaned over and picked up the pieces of my helm. I tossed the largest piece to Pal. "Three years ago, the man who trained me in arms from a lad made that cleaving mark on my helm. This"—I held up the remnant of my boar-crest—"and this alone prevented his axe from continuing into my skull."

"Andrija will enjoy finishing the task," snarled Pal. Andrija growled his assent.

"Why he struck me down is relevant, here and now. I had sworn my service to a lord, the son of my father's lord, and the grandson of my grandfather's lord. My lord foreswore his oath to his father and led his thegns in battle. My lord and all of his men were slain, except for me. Much to my sadness, this boar-crest saved my life." I looked at Ragnar. "But now I know why my branch of the World Tree stretched past that day. The Allfather appointed that today I would give Ragnar Longtongue and Andrijana, wife of Desimir, justice."

I shrugged. "Odin led me to this city and, finally, this morning, allowed me to learn the one thing I needed to unravel this tapestry. He showed me my arrogance. I have spent the last three years believing that I had foresworn my oath and killed my father for nothing." I smiled at Agata. "And, my dear, all of this particular game is your fault."

Zacharia spluttered and started to rise.

"Nay, Zacharia, I do not mean that she is the player of this game. She is, in this game, completely innocent. I refrain from claiming any other innocence for her, but of this, there is no doubt."

I started pacing around the room. "However, I get ahead of myself. Let us start with what everyone knows. A priest of Naum with but two companions came from the Great City. She was met on the road by Katarina and her people. They killed her and took her place. Then they made it appear that she and her companions were kidnapped at the Faerie, thus abusing the trust of Ragnar." I nodded at Ragnar. "Ragnar asked me to help remove the stain from his honor. Reluctantly, I swore to him that I would do so, and I started looking around. I started trying to figure out the pieces, rules, and goals of this game."

I turned back to the council. "Ironically, one of the first pieces in this game I stumbled across was Gibroz. He was brought into the game as an afterthought but was useful nonetheless. The player of this game knew that the loss of the *Notes* would be likely to push an already bickering Naumite priesthood into open conflict." I gestured at Kristijan. "Which, of course, it did. Initially, the schism puzzled me. Who gains? Nobody I could think of. Why would they pick this tactic? And why was Gibroz present on the game board? What could he do that Katarina couldn't? Nothing, if Katarina's interest could be sufficiently piqued."

I paused.

"After some time, though, I realized that the schism had to be intrinsic to the game. I could only think of three possible reasons to steal the *Notes*. They could be ransomed for a great deal of money, a collector might desire to possess them, or they could be used to cause a schism within the Naumites. With all of the other things happening, neither of the first two possibilities seemed likely. I soon learned that Katarina would only care enough to participate if she could wallow in the chaos that followed."

I glanced around, carefully avoiding staring at the servants. "Then, in his fear for the safety of the *Notes*, Kristijan asked to have Gibroz steal them and return them to the temple for safekeeping. Kristijan's request must have seemed sent from the gods. Gibroz's presence could only muddy the waters. It worked at first, because all I could see was Gibroz and his thugs who attacked me."

I turned back to the council. "But, in the end, it muddied the waters for everyone, including our game player, who did not want this connection exposed. The connection between Gibroz and the Gropas was a man named Frano. He clearly knew something about the plan, or in this case, the planner, that needed to be eliminated, and he was efficiently assassinated."

I looked at Kapric and Zvono. "His body became another in a line of corpses I have brought to the quaesitors. His death succeeded in blocking my path, but told me that something was wrong amidst the Gropas. There was no other possible reason for Frano to die. I turned my attention to all of you."

I glared at each council member individually. "Now, let's skip forward to the attack planned against me after my last visit. This is the attack that killed Desimir and raised the stakes. Now a Mrnjavcevic had been killed. Piri, Zvono, and Andrijana are here because of his death. The attack also told me, once I thought about it, that I had become a threat. That I had learned most of what I needed to figure out who played this game."

I held up my boar-crest once more. "The rest is not irrelevant, but for this game, these things are sufficient. My master, Bedarth, taught me that I cannot answer without knowing the question. If I wanted to find the player, then the first thing I had to do was define what he or she must be."

I turned around. "The player of this game had to fit five criteria. One, he or she needed to know that Marija and the *Notes* were coming to Achrida and when. Two, he or she needed to be able to pique Katarina's interest, meaning he or she must already understand her tastes and goals. Three, he or she needed to be in the position to work with Gibroz. Four, he or she had to have some good reason to expect that a schism among the Naumites would be useful."

I paused. "Frano's assassination gave me the fifth criteria. When he was assassinated, I began wondering about the blades in the game. I said then that Frano's death was as organized and well planned as any battle I've ever seen. I started thinking about which groups in Achrida possessed the skills and military training to kill Frano in this manner. The skills of the Imperial companies such as the Pathfinders and the Lakewardens cannot be denied. Both tribes have trained and organized household troops. It's possible that one of these units might have murdered Frano, but I do not think they could have without some rumor of the deed becoming public."

I briefly glanced at the servants. "Gibroz and Katarina have their people, of course. However, Gibroz would not care enough to order such a delicate and precise murder. Katarina might, but whoever murdered Frano wanted to reduce his or her risk, not increase it. Katarina would not make that choice. It would be too boring. Hence, neither seemed likely to have arranged Frano's death in that manner."

I looked at Kristijan. "That left me thinking of personal armed retainers. Trained retainers might very well possess the precision and training to eliminate Frano so efficiently. Then, when I remembered Kemal, I remembered how smoothly his attacker had escaped over the rooftops. Whether or not this person was one of Frano's attackers, he too was very skilled. Whoever our game player was must have the resources to keep armed, trained retainers in his or her household. At least a few highly skilled ones, coupled with rental thugs such as the Blazevic family, would provide a solid and useful group of swordsmen."

"Once I defined these traits, I began methodically eliminating candidates. Let's start with the Naumites themselves." I turned back. "Kristijan, for all of Gregor's theological faults, is there any way he would gain from Marija's death and the loss of the *Notes of Naum?*"

Kristijan forestalled Zdeslav with a hand. "There is no lesson Naum would desire taught that would require such a sacrifice."

"I thought not. You are the one who benefited from the loss of the *Notes* and her death. Did you arrange that death?"

Kristijan stared at me open-mouthed and finally sputtered, "No." Even Zdeslav had started shaking his head.

"You see?" I laughed. "Even your foes think you incapable of murdering Marija. However, Zdeslav's willingness to vouch for you means nothing in itself. There are other reasons I know you are not our game player. You could not have organized this deed without help because Katarina would not listen to you. There is no way you could arrange for her to waylay the *Notes*, at least without someone else involved. Nor could you do the deed, unless you had a group of trained retainers."

I looked at Zdeslav. "Could Kristijan have organized supporters in the Naumite temple into a skilled fighting force?"

Zdeslav laughed. "Not a chance."

"Could he have taken money from temple coffers to fund the training and upkeep of scores of trained blades?"

He shook his head firmly. "We are not poor, but not that wealthy."

"I thought not. None of the Naumites fit our criteria. Still, he wanted to ask Gibroz to get the *Notes* back. Knowing this gave me the first step on the trail that led me to the Gropa Council."

Several members of the council muttered and glared at the others. I continued.

"No Gropa would willingly command their followers to steal the *Notes*. It would upset any Naumite followers who served them. They might, however, help Kristijan make arrangements. What Naumite would be enraged by someone helping Kristijan, even with a task as odd as this one? So Kristijan came to the Gropa family, and once Kristijan knew Marija and her escort were coming, he arranged through a Gropa to have Gibroz steal the *Notes* and bring them to him. Kristijan has admitted he did this."

Kristijan shamefully nodded.

"Again, this request provided a perfect distraction. Why would anyone look past the possibility that Gibroz had agreed to steal the *Notes*, realized their value, and decided to keep them to ransom? Even if Kristijan or Gibroz were to point a finger at the game player, neither would trust the other to accept any protestations of innocence. A risk-free bonus to help obscure the plan."

I turned back. "However, by stopping the robbery and wounding one of Gibroz's men, I messed up everything. Now, Gibroz was mad. He couldn't simply just report that Marija and the *Notes* were missing. I might have had them, and they wanted to punish me for wounding one of their own."

I shrugged as I turned back to the council. "This meant that using Gibroz to serve as a distraction failed. By attacking me publicly, everyone saw that Gibroz did not have the *Notes*. Now the normal procedure was not a shield, but an arrow flying directly at the master of the game. Now Frano had to die, and he did, because Frano would not pass on a message from Kristijan without proper instructions. Instructions Frano usually received from Jeremena."

She remained silent, as she had done ever since we arrived. Waves of rage flowed from her, rippling as if I had tossed a stone into her pool of anger.

"In fact, I am sure the original message Frano gave to Gibroz came from her hands. Why change the usual procedure and cause anyone to wonder? Nor would Jeremena care. Her games have nothing to do with the Naumites. There is nothing in this schism and this turmoil that benefits her. No, she has focused on fighting the fish price war, which is why, before we got here, I'll bet she yelled louder than anyone else tonight."

A broad grin erupted on Zacharia's face. "You guessed that right, Sevener."

I smiled back. "I suspect the first message merely arranged a time and place where Gibroz would meet our player. I doubt this would have caused any concern, given that the crazy games you play undoubtedly require an occasional face-to-face discussion to prevent confusion. If the process looked normal, it would seem much more likely Gibroz had seized an opportunity. After all, everyone knows kraljevics are not trustworthy. Any questions asked would be the wrong ones."

I shrugged. "Yet Jeremena would know that Gibroz met with someone in the Gropa family powerful enough that he would listen to whoever it was. That means one of the Gropa Council. No other person would get his attention. She would also, if she sat and thought things through, methodically list which people it could be that met with Gibroz. So here I am to choose among you before she does."

I smiled broadly at the angry faces. "Of course, the possibility exists that Jeremena is our game player. There is no suggestion that she knows when Marija would arrive at Achrida, but she gathers information and possibly could have discovered the time. Obviously, she could work with Gibroz. It's possible she has the armed retainers in her little empire." I looked at Jeremena. "However, she and Katarina cannot get along. Jeremena desires order and Katarina desires... something else. Also, the only reason the Naumite schism could possibly benefit Jeremena is if she wanted to overthrow Pal, which seems unlikely, given her focus on fish prices. Also, while theoretically she could have learned Marija's schedule, I don't think it's likely."

"Get on with it," growled Pal.

I chuckled. "You're probably right, I never liked Bedarth's methodical style much either." I turned to Agata. "The game was for power, my dear. Power that you will one day hold. All know that your talent gives you that destiny and, thus, you are a threat."

She looked shyly at the floor so that her family might still underestimate her. I glanced at the rest of the family.

"Whoever planned these events wanted to limit Agata's power, and the obvious reason for that would be to enhance his or her own. Jeremena has what she needs. Zacharia knows that Agata's rise to power benefits him in the long run. Agata is smart enough to know her time will come. Also, of all the Gropa Council, she is the one least likely to work with Gibroz."

I looked at each in turn.

"So. Which of you seeks to steal Agata's power?"

They looked suspiciously at each other.

"Kristijan supplied the answer when he told me how Marija's journey started. I said that whoever is playing this game had to know when Marija might arrive in Achrida carrying the *Notes of Naum*. The answer to this question is a little more complicated than it might seem initially. Marija had this idea she could connect with the soul of Naum if she could but reach the cell where he wrote his *Notes*. Even for an order well versed in innovative magic, this idea seemed far-fetched, and Gregor refused to allow it.

"In other words, at no time would Marija come to Achrida with the *Notes*, unless Gregor changed his mind. At no time were the *Notes* at risk, meaning that our player could not initiate the schism. Someone needed to convince Gregor to allow Marija to come north. Someone Gregor respected. Kristijan told me who that person was this morning. That's when I finally understood not simply who played the game, but also why Odin had placed me on the other side of the board. I understand oaths and oathbreaking."

I chuckled at their moment of confusion. "None of you understands why this matters, for none of you ever swore an oath explicitly. Nor was one ever sworn to you. However, an oathbreaker betrayed you nonetheless.

I looked up to the sky for a moment. "I've finally realized that I did not break my oath to my lord. The fact that I lived when my lord died did not mean I had broken my sworn word, because my lord had broken his faith to me when he attacked his father, our king. Because of that, I can see who broke his word here." I slowly walked up to Andrija. "You asked Gregor to send Marija, did you not?"

"Yes," he blustered, "But I did not…" He trailed off as he realized.

"Yes, Andrija, the one who requested you ask Gregor is the one who slew her and created this schism."

He was aging as we spoke, years lining his face like rings in a tree.

"You would only make the request for one person. You probably never heard of Marija and had no idea of her research until one person made a seemingly off-hand comment that you, loving as you do, decided to fulfill. You despise Zacharia and Davorin. You distrust Agata's youth. You and Jeremena have sparred for so long that you would only help her as needed. You do not listen to Vesela, seeing her but a shadow of her father's power."

I turned to Vesela. "Oddly enough, the cause of all this was love. Even you know that Agata will take the title of zupan from you when she is old enough. To a certain extent, I believe this relieves you, as you have always enjoyed playing, and the position of zupan requires more than you want to give for the rest of your life. Yes, you want your time in the great seat, but you know that Agata's time will come and you will gladly pass the seat on at that time."

I turned to Pal. "But your father knows her time will come, too. Your father, who loves you, despises Zacharia, and was desperate to prevent you from losing to Agata. Consider the schism and the crisis provoked by it. Consider that the Dassaretae have consistently encroached on your prerogatives and boundaries for some time. Consider the disputes within the council, such as the fixing of the fish prices. You thought Pal preferred spreading the power amongst the council. Instead, he feared the demise of the Gropa and thought that the zupan of the Gropa must consolidate his or her power to be able to face the Dassaretae and regain the family's position. He did this so he could amass that power for himself. With the anger and bitterness spread amongst you in the middle of a crisis, he would have divided you, allowing him to gather all the family power back into the hands of the zupan. Power that he could have handed you when the time came."

I paused and looked at the whole council. "The implicit oath that you swore to Pal to serve the Enchelei and the implicit oath that he swore to serve as the lord of the Enchelei meant nothing to him. Your lord broke faith with you as my lord broke faith with me."

As I concluded my speech, the council members shifted their eyes, one by one, to Pal.

"Father? Did you do this?" Vesela asked softly.

I looked at Pal. I expected I would see him burning with a fire hotter than any forge. Instead, he smiled like a glacier, full of ice and slow, unstoppable hate. Desimir's training paid off when Pal acted, as I shifted as quickly as I could into the Long Guard. However, my wounded thigh betrayed me, though I know it would not have mattered. Pal clearly knew as much as Desimir, and he used my momentum to flip me over his leg and out of the way. I crashed to the floor at the feet of Katarina, who was now moving.

Pal stood amidst the shock and shook his head. "I knew my time as zupan was drawing to a close." As I laid there and watched him, my leg started to bleed again. He looked sadly at Vesela. "I hoped to give you the position you deserved, but this Sevener took your birthright. Forget not the debt he owes you and the Enchelei."

She stood and stared at her father. "I'll remember that. I'll also remember the harm you did to us. How much have the Dassaretae taken from us while you broke faith with us?"

Pal laughed. "My dear, so much you have to learn. Vukasin agreed to allow us to regain what we lost. I told him I had problems within the family I needed to fix that would hurt all of us. I moved him around the gameboard, too. Now, you will have to learn on your own. Farewell, daughter."

He stomped away. Piri, Svetislav, Sebastijan, and the quaesitors started to follow him, but suddenly, Katarina moved next to Pal. Though she wore the clothes of a servant, she now stood in her full power. To that point, I do not think anyone ever realized her true strength.

She laughed her teenage girl laugh. "Oh no, there's still fun in this game. I don't think Pal's quite done playing in our fair city."

She clapped her hands girlishly, and I realized I would feel happier if Pal would leave with her. Somehow I knew we all felt that way. I also knew that feeling was wrong. I could see Piri shrugging angrily at herself. Jaga struggled to use her own magic, but Katarina clearly overmatched her. Katarina's smile broadened as she watched us fail to resist her control of our emotions. She clapped and giggled.

"We'll have so much fun."

And she escorted Pal out.

Chapter 54
Late Evening, 22 Gersmoanne, 1712 MG

Suddenly, Katarina's hold on us lifted. Our anger returned. Svetislav, Zvono, and Sebastijan started to chase after Katarina and Pal, but Kapric and Piri stopped them.

"Waste not the effort," growled Kapric.

"What will you do when you get close?" Piri turned to Jaga. "You can create something to protect us, but that will take time."

Jaga nodded.

"Katarina's probably disappeared already," sighed Zvono.

Svetislav grunted and shrugged. Andrijana came over and started clucking at my wound. She shoved me back down, harder than probably necessary, when I started to rise.

"Lay there, Sevener, I'll rewrap this. Fool to let him knock you around like that."

Kristijan's shouting halted her inspection of the wound. "Edward!" He came over to loom over me. Zdeslav stood at his heels. "What about the *Notes*? What did Pal do with them?"

Andrijana started to yell at them to leave us alone while she rebandaged me, but I halted her. "They need to know, dear." I looked up at them and answered. "I don't know," I said, "at least not positively."

"Oh, no," the two priests blurted simultaneously, looking at each other with horror in their eyes.

"But I know this," I said, waiting for their eyes to turn back to me. When they had, I continued, "I know that Pal had them at one point. Katarina gave them to him. I also know Pal is not the type to toss away a tool unless he was sure he didn't need it anymore."

"What are you saying?"

"I'm saying that I'll bet the *Notes* are hidden in Pal's quarters or somewhere only he could find. He'd want them to end the schism, because once he had consolidated power he would want to restore order to the church. He'd pick one of you to have the *Notes*, thus establishing one of you as the legitimate archimandrite. It would take some time, but your church would settle into place sooner or later."

Kristijan and Zdeslav looked at each other with wild, hopeful eyes and rushed off to grab the nearest servant and begin searching.

I looked over to the council. Vesela stood looking at the rest. I could almost see her gathering the threads of power unto herself, taking on the mantle of zupan. She stared for a while at Agata. I wondered what would become of those two.

Piri slid quietly over to me and smiled. "Vukasin will not be pleased."

Andrijana had finished rebandaging me, and Piri helped me up. I felt lightheaded when I rose and the council swam a bit in my eyes.

"You'll pass on my apologies," I muttered.

"Such as they are." Piri chuckled.

Zupan Vesela turned to me. "Sevener." She paused. "Too much has happened. I don't know if I should order you killed or thank you." She chuckled harshly. "You'll regret not taking me to bed, though."

"I already do."

"In any case, you must leave now," she commanded. "Take these Dassaretae away. The Gropa need their time."

Zvono started to object, as she had already pulled her tablet out to start confirming details with the council. Kapric halted her, but spoke to Vesela. "Zupan, we'll need to talk with them."

Vesela looked at Kapric. "No, you don't. You know what happened. Ask the Sevener if you have questions. He seems to know all the answers."

She sighed, and some of her imperious manner faded. "Father…" She shook herself and spoke formally, "Pal Gropa has broken faith with the Enchelei. We shall no longer protect him. Seek him as you will. Ask him questions in whatever way seems practical."

Kapric nodded. Zvono wanted to ask more, and so did I, but Svetislav had already started to herd us out. Just as well that we left quickly, since by the time we reached the Faerie my wound had started to bleed again and I fainted while Zoe cared for me.

Chapter 55
Afternoon, 24 Gersmoanne, 1712 MG

I suppose there are things Readers will remember of my lost day after the festivities at the Gropa mansion, but not me. I am sure I bathed, ate, and drank. I know Zoe tended to my wounds. In all honesty, though, that day passed beyond my memory.

A full day and a half after transforming the Gropas, Ragnar interrupted my musings of the previous three weeks. "Here's something you'll be wantin' to see, I'm to be thinkin', but I'm to be thinkin' this is to be comin' from one of the Lady of Halves' favorites and I'm sure yer to be knowin' who I'm to be meanin.'"

He held out a carefully folded note, lightly touched with perfume. I did, in fact, know who it came from, and its dainty writing surprised me not.

My dear Edward,

You have given me all that I hoped. Now I have new pieces and a new game.

I wonder how I shall move you next?

- K

I wondered how she would move me, too. I hoped the Emperor's service would prevent me from having to learn that question's answer.

Ragnar glanced over my shoulder and read the message. "Well, now that's what I'm to be expectin' from that one, and isn't she of the line of Loki or I'm to be bein' a Reader, and it's sure that I'm not. I'm to be glad she's to be writin' to you and not to be bestowin' them favors upon the likes of me."

He boomed a laugh. "But I came over not to be simply givin' you that note. I'm to be sayin' what I tried to say yesterday, though none of us

343

was to be bein' mindful of things from all that's to have been happenin'. You've served me and fulfilled yer end of the oath, and I'm to be bein' thankful. Yer to be welcome for some days yet, with bencriht, until you and yer brute are to be makin' the next part of yer journey."

"Thank you, Ragnar, I appreciate that."

I raised the note. "Even knowing Katarina's plans, I will take some time. I stopped here in the first place to rest."

"And you've not been havin' much of that since you've been here. Well, me family, exceptin' maybe Karah, has gotten used to havin' you here, and we'll not be rushin' you out the door." Zoe leaned out of the kitchen. "And yer to be arguin' with Zoe if yer to be decidin' to leave before she's done tendin' to yer new scars."

I laughed at Zoe's look but sobered quickly. "And, well, I need to stay for a few days…"

"Aye, I'm to be seein' that, and yer a good man for that. I'm sure Piri will be by at some point, and to be lettin' us know when her lads and lasses are to be makin' their final march. I'm sure she'll to be appreciatin' you puttin' yer own rakija on the stone."

Kapric and Zvono interrupted our thoughts as they walked in and joined me. Ragnar left to bring full mugs.

"Another whole day without a body, Sevener."

"I'm disappointed too."

Kapric snorted as Ragnar set down full mugs. Zvono flipped open her tablet.

"Not that you care, though you should, we've finished the paperwork on the cases you were involved in. We've determined that the Emperor's service should not pursue cases against you."

"In other words, for now, we'll not arrest you," rumbled Kapric.

I flashed a quick grin at his stone face. "That's very nice of you, quaesitor. By the way, do you know if Kristijan and Zdeslav found the *Notes*?"

"They did," answered Zvono. "Pal had hidden them in a cubbyhole that no one knew about. Fortunately, Kristijan and Zdeslav are both fairly powerful." She chuckled. "I heard they had to combine their power *and* get help from Basil to get past Pal's wards. That must have been interesting."

"Basil? Ragnar's stonelord?"

"Yes," confirmed Zvono.

"When do you leave, Sevener?" asked Kapric.

"Ragnar has given me leave to stay for a few days and relax. I'm likely to take advantage of those days. Don't worry, I don't plan on leaving the Faerie all that much excepting when Piri needs me, and I can't get into too much trouble here."

He raised an eyebrow. "We shall see. I have much more faith in your ability to find trouble."

Zvono closed her tablet with a sly smile. "Damn herd bulls. Stay as long as you need, as long as you aren't making us fill out paperwork."

Kapric nodded with a slight smile of his own. I nodded back. They finished their mugs and returned to work. A few minutes later Sebastijan entered, grabbed a mug from Ragnar at the bar, and sat down before me.

"Your brother was just here."

"I know. That's why I wasn't here sooner."

"Don't like him?"

"On the contrary, growing up, he was always my hero. That I'm different from him doesn't change my love. Still, I see no reason to spend any more time with him than I need. It causes us both pain."

"I'm not sure I'll ever understand this city."

"I think you understand more than you realize."

"Maybe." I shrugged. "So why are you here?"

"Because I owe you, and I pay my debts."

"Yes?"

"You paid me for more service than I have given."

"And if I say otherwise?"

"I will ignore you. I know what I am worth, and I will accept no less and no more."

"How will you fulfill that debt?"

"I will remain your man in Achrida. Even in the Emperor's service, when you are stationed in the Great City, the time might come that you have need of me and my services."

"And your mangy pack of giants?"

"They follow me, and they are in agreement. We have not yet earned what you paid us."

"But, you will."

"Yes."

"Fine. But tell the big one if he calls me a sheep dick again, I'm throwing him into the lake."

Sebastijan laughed. "Oh, I'll definitely be telling him that. Fair dealings, Sevener."

I nodded.

My string of visitors continued when Svetislav joined me about an hour later. "Here for dinner?"

He nodded.

"I'm sorry, Svet."

He shrugged. "We're right."

"Yes, I knew I was. He was the only one with his hands in all the right places." I took a drink. "But, I knew what it would mean for the Enchelei." He simply stared at me. "Yes, I know you know it had to happen. That doesn't make me any happier for doing it."

"Done."

"It's done and you want me to shut up and move on?"

He nodded. I sighed and we both drank, waving Karah over for a pitcher.

Soon after the pitcher arrived, Piri joined us.

"I see you've decided to stay and drink with evil companions."

"Exactly, Hecatontarch. Which is why Karah's bringing over another mug for you."

Piri smiled and sat. "I'm glad you're here, Svetislav. The Pathfinders have agreed that, should you wish, you may join us at the Stone in two days."

He looked at her for a long moment and shook his head. "Honored, but…"

Piri nodded. "I know. We just wanted to make sure you knew we remembered."

"Thank you."

"I'll be there, if it will not offend them," I said.

"We expect you, Sevener. And we hold no grudge against you. The battles we fight are not always so clear, and yet still we die. Next time, it might be the Lakewardens needing to fill some holes."

She looked at Svetislav and laughed. "If you can't take a joke—"

"Stay out of the fucking companies," Svetislav finished.

The veteran warriors chuckled grimly and Piri turned back to me.

"I asked Vukasin about the deal Pal mentioned."

"Yes?"

"Vukasin confirmed it. A favor owed by the zupan of the Gropas was worth more than minor gains for the Dassaretae."

"He might be right."

Piri nodded. "Also, I expect to see you for sparring in the morning. I don't care how wounded you are." Svetislav chuckled as I sighed. She added, "Tonight, I must mess with my company, so I'll forgo Zoe's wonders."

Then she finished her mug and rose. "One more thing, Sevener."

"Yes?" I replied looking up at her.

She responded loudly enough that all heard her.

"I've spoken with Zoe and reserved the room for dinner the night after we take my troops to the Stone pyre." She leaned over the table and looked carefully at me. Her eyes seemed deeper than the farthest bottom of the lake. "Better have your kit prepared and ready for action. Believe me, I'll inspect it thoroughly."

The fact that I had just helped bring down one of the princes of the city did not prevent me from turning bright red.

She strode out as the laughter sang in my new meadhall.

Appendix One – People

Aethelred Aethelwulfson (ETH-el-red ETH-el-wolf-son): Father of Edward Aethelredson. Thegn of Cynric II Alfredson. Killed by Edward in Penwulf Cynricson's failed coup attempt.

Agata Kyranna (AG-a-ta KEY-ra-na): Member of the Gropa Council. Daughter of Zacharia Gropa.

Aglais (ah-GLACE): Minor goddess in the Imperial pantheon. Known for strict expectations of her followers, including abstinence from alcohol.

Aita (EH-ta): God of death in the Imperial pantheon.

Akantha (a-KAN-tha): Black-and-white cat of the Frank Faerie. She normally spends her time in the stables.

Alcaeus (al-KAY-us): Minor god in the Imperial pantheon known for his immense strength and bravery.

Amalija Loncar (ah-MEEL-ya): Retired proreus, or bow officer, in the Lakewardens. Currently owner of the Hillside, a small tavern near the amphitheater of Achrida.

Anastasius: Reader of the Library of Achrida.

Andrejan Gropa (AN-dre-yan): Zupan of the Gropas in the late sixteenth century. He had twin boys who warred with each other to succeed him.

Andreyev Galamdzija (AN-dre-yev): One of Gibroz's henchmen.

Andrija Gropa (AN-dre-ya): Member of the Gropa Council. A renowned warrior in his youth who even in his later years remains formidable.

Andrijana Rakic (AN-dre-yah-na): Lover of Desimir Lukic. Mother of Cedomir and Vanja.

Arkady Zivkovic: Member of the Pathfinder military company.

Basil Vukoja: Gekurios in Achrida.

Basil II Makrembolites: Emperor of the Old Empire in the third century and founder of the city of Basilopolis.

Bedarth Liffrea (bed-ARTH): Zokurios from the Seven Kingdoms and Edward's mentor.

Bisera Tomcic (bee-SAY-ra): Photodotis, or high priestess, of Panteleimon in the Temple of Achrida.

Blazevic (BLAH-tze-vich): Family in Achrida, many of whom are petty criminals.

Bozhidar Lukic (BOW-zhee-dar): Father of Desimir Lukic, son of Cedomir Lukic the elder.

Branimira Jankovic (BRA-nee-mee-rah): Seamstress and wife of Gordan Jankovic. They have a shop on Medusa's Way near the Frank Faerie.

Cassandra Kurelac: Priestess at the Temple of Naum in Achrida.

Cedomir Lukic (seh-do-MEER) (elder): Grandfather of Desimir Lukic, father of Bozhidar Lukic.

Cedomir Rakic (seh-do-MEER) (younger): Son of Desimir Lukic and Andrijana Rakic, grandson of Bozhidar Lukic, brother of Vanja Rakic. Named after his great-grandfather.

Cemil Androic (seh-MEEL): Strategos of the Pronoiars.

Cvetijin Golurza (KA-veh-tee-yin): Chandler in Achrida who frequents the Frank Faerie. Occasionally helps Ragnar out as a bartender.

Cynric II Alfredson (KIN-rik): King of Middlemarch. Father of Penwulf.

Darijo Martinovic (DAH-re-yo): Regular at the Hillside. Known for his skill with throwing daggers.

Davorin Gropa (dah-VO-reen): Member of the Gropa Council. Corrupt but capable and inventive.

Deor (DAY-or): Edward Aethelredson's horse.

Desimir Lukic (DEH-see-meer): Decarch in the Pathfinder military company.

Dmitri Corovic: Member of the Pathfinder military company.

Edward Aethelredson: Former thegn in the Seven Kingdoms traveling through Achrida.

Einarr Ealdwinson: Thegn of Aethelred.

Eirik Ragnarssen (EH-rik): Son of Ragnar and stableboy of the Frank Faerie.

Emilija Stampalija (eh-MEEL-ya): A regular at the Frank Faerie.

Flavian Mouzalan: Cabinetmaker in Achrida who frequents the Frank Faerie. Known for a weird, high-pitched laugh.

Frano Olic: Warehouse worker in the Stracara. Also serves as a courier between the Gropa family and Gibroz.

Gabrijela Yelich (gah-bree-YELL-ah): Erkurios who works for Gibroz.

Gibroz Kasun (jah-BROZE): One of two kraljevics of Achrida. He focuses primarily on gambling, smuggling, and extortion. Usually to be found at his gambling parlor at the end of Metodi Mean.

Gordan Jankovic (gor-DAWN): Tailor and husband of Branimira.

Gregor Daimonoioannes: Archimandrite of Naum in Basilopolis.

Harald (Honker) Stankic: A regular at the Frank Faerie. Also known as Honker Harald for his large nose.

Harald (Little Harald) Stankic: The son of Harold (Honker) Stankic.

Hlodowic Karlssen (HLO-da-vik): Trainer at arms for Cynric. Helped train both Aethelred and Edward.

Ivan Yevgenich (EE-van yev-GEN-itch): Boyar in Zabad Oblast, Periaslavl. Hosted Edward in his izba from fall 1710 to spring 1712 MG.

Jaga Drenovic (YA-ga): Symkurios and door warden of the Gropa mansion.

Jeremena Gropa (YAIR-a-mah-nah): A member of the Gropa Council. Her primary focus is trade and wealth.

Kapric Gropa (ka-PREEK): Quaesitor of the Empire of Makhaira, currently with the rank of tagmatarch. He is the ranking quaesitor in Achrida and is generally tasked with investigating killings. Son of Marjana. Brother of Sebastijan.

Karah Ragnarsdottir: Daughter of Ragnar and Zoe. She helps serve at the Frank Faerie.

Katarina Kopanja: One of two kraljevics of Achrida. She focuses primarily on prostitution and drugs. Usually to be found at her bordello, Tresinova's Treasures.

Kemal Kachar: Member of the Berzeti family used by Jeremena as a courier.

Kristijan Goluza (KRISS-ta-yan): Mandrite of Naum in Achrida. Claims the title of archimandrite, challenging the authority of Gregor in Basilopolis.

Marija Rendakis (MAH-ree-ya): Priestess and zokurios of Naum. She believed she could capture some of the actual thought of Naum if she took the original copy of *The Notes of Naum in His Captivity* back to the cell where he had been held in the Kreisen.

Marko Murcinic: Farrier in Achrida who frequents the Frank Faerie.

Melia (MEL-ee-ah): Fat gray tabby cat of the Frank Faerie. Normally found in the taproom demanding her due.

Mikjal Ekmecic (MIK-yal): Seller of foodstuffs to the Temple of Naum.

Milos Obilic (MEE-lose OH-ba-leek): Ancient hero of Dassaretum.

Naum Gropa (nawm): Prominent Enchelei of the late twelfth and early thirteenth centuries. He created the Glagolitsa script. In a diplomatic mission to the Berzeti, he not only taught the clan to read using that script, but also brought them into the Enchelei tribe as a group. In a different diplomatic mission to the Kreisen, he was captured and held for nearly a year. During this time he wrote what would become *The Notes of Naum in His Captivity*. Upon his death, his admirers kept his memory alive and soon he became one of the many godlings of Achrida. Over the past few centuries, his sect has grown in power and reach, and now he is worshipped through the Empire of Makhaira and in a few places in the Old Empire.

Neven Pochekovic: Most prominent of Achrida's fishing boat captains.

Pal Gropa (pawl GROW-pa): Current zupan of the Enchelei.

Panteleimon Mrnjavcevic (pan-TAY-la-mon murn-yav-CHEH-vich): Member of the Mrnjavcevic family of the tenth century. A skilled gekurios who devoted his time attempting to understand how humanity and light interact. He also studied herbs, drugs, and medicines, preferring to use these instead of magic whenever possible. Since he had two children die during their birth, he also spent many years learning how to make childbirth and pregnancy safer. His deeds were such that he was venerated as god even before his death, and his cult grew quickly. He was named one of the Fourteen Holy Helpers, and he is worshipped across the Empire of Makhaira and in many neighboring regions including the Kingdom of Matara and the Old Empire.

Penwulf Cynricson: Aetheling of Middlemarch. Son of Cynric. Bencriht lord of Edward Aethelredson. Died in a battle trying to overthrow his father Cynric.

Piriska (Piri) Mrnjavcevic (PEER-ish-ka or PEER-ee murn-yav-CHEH-vich): Hecatontarch of the Pathfinder military company. Niece of Vukasin Mrnjavcevic, cousin of Zvono.

Radmila Misimovic: Potter and leader of a coalition of Enchelei tradesmen of many guilds.

Ragnar Longtongue: Co-owner of the Frank Faerie. Husband of Zoe, father of Karah and Eirik. Originally from Svellheim.

Ruzica Gropa (root-ZEE-ka): Seamstress of the Enchelei tribe.

Sanjin Ugrenovic (SAWN-yin): Butler of the Gropa family.

Sebastijan Gropa (See-BASS-tee-yan): Sellsword of Achrida. Brother of Kapric. Has gathered to his service a small group of thugs loyal to him.

Svetislav Kralj: Protokarabos of the Lakewarden military company. He comes from a cadet branch of the Gropa family.

Tanja Nerantzis (TAWN-ya): Member of the Pathfinder military company.

Vanja Rakic (VAWN-ya): Son of Desimir Lukic and Andrijana Rakic, grandson of Bozhidar Lukic, brother of Cedomir Lukic.

Veikko of Haapevesa (VAY-ee-ko ha-ah-pe-VAY-sa): Prominent Reader currently living in Basilopolis. Originally from Svellheim. A correspondent of Bedarth.

Vesela Gropa (VES-sah-la): Current heir to the Zupan of the Gropas. Daughter of Pal Gropa.

Vukasin Mrnjavcevic (VOO-kah-seen murn-yav-CHEH-vich): Current zupan of the Dassaretae.

Zacharia Gropa: Member of the Gropa Council. Father of Agata Kyranna. Cousin of Pal Gropa. Tasked with gathering information for the Council.

Zdenko Mandusic (ZHA-den-ko): Priest of the Temple of Naum in Achrida. Twin brother of Zdeslav.

Zdeslav Mandusic (ZHA-duh-slav): Priest of the Temple of Naum in Achrida. Twin brother of Zdenko.

Zoe Kallikrates: Co-owner of the Frank Faerie. Wife of Ragnar Longtongue, father of Karah and Eirik. Originally from Basilopolis.

Zvono Mrnjavcevic (zha-VOH-no murn-yav-CHEH-vich): Quaesitor of the Empire of Makhaira, currently with the rank of kentarch. She works with Kapric, helping him investigate killings. Cousin of Piriska Mrnjavcevic.

Appendix Two – Places

Achrida (a-KREE-dah): Large trading city north of Basilopolis in the Empire of Makhaira. It sits upon two large trade routes. One route heads north from Basilopolis to Brunanburh in the Seven Kingdoms, passing along the border between several kreisen and western Periaslavl. The other route takes as much advantage as it can of the lakes in the middle of Shijuren. It starts at Lezh in the Empire of Makhaira and ends at Anzhedonev on Lake Kopayev in Periaslavl. From there, several other large trade routes lead farther eastward.

Amphitheater of Achrida: Large open-air theater that shows plays most nights.

Basilopolis: Capitol city of the Empire of Makhaira. Largest city in the world.

Biljana's Springs (bil-JA-na): Small spring fed of mountain runoff water that leads into Lake Achrida.

Brunanburh (BROO-nan-burg): Refers to both the largest city and smallest kingdom in the Seven Kingdoms. The city sits upon the main trade route from the Seven Kingdoms to the rest of the world. As such, it is also the richest city. In the eleventh century the burhealdor, or mayor, of the city managed to use its size and wealth to claim the small area around the city and raise it to the status of a kingdom.

Dassaretum Province (das-sa-RAY-tum): A province in the Empire of Makhaira. It was originally the region where the tribes of the Dassaretae settled.

Empire of Makhaira (mah-KY-ra): Successor to the Old Empire, built around some of the Old Empire's daughter trading emporia such as Basilopolis and Achrida.

Fourth Serpent: Fourth of several small roads leading from Medusa's Way.

Frank Faerie: Tavern and inn in northwestern Achrida. Owned by Ragnar Longtongue and Zoe Kallikrates.

Haapavesa (ha-ah-pe-VAY-sa): City in the farthest north of Svellheim.

Heartsquare: Central square of Achrida. On its corners are the main administration buildings of the Empire and the city. Also, many of the wealthiest merchants of the Empire have offices for their factors within a block.

The Hillside: Bar near the Amphitheater in Achrida.

The Kreisens (KRY-zen): The overall name for all of the kreisen. Because of the constant competition between kreisarchs, the area is known for its conflict and strife.

Lake Achrida (a-KREE-dah): The westernmost of five large lakes stretching across the central portion of Shijuren. Rivers and relatively small portages make up a busy east-west trade route. The city of Achrida is its primary port.

Lezh: City in the Empire of Makhaira. It is located just to the west of Achrida on the coast of the Middle Sea.

Markanda (MAR-kan-da) Trade city in southern Markanda. Known for making paper.

Matara (ma-TAH-ra) Kingdom far to the south, known for its cotton and textile production.

Medusa's Way: A road leading out of the Square of Legends. A series of roads called the serpents leads from it.

Metodi Mean: Short street, more of an alley, in the Stracara of Achrida. It starts at Samiel's Way and ends at Gibroz's main office.

Middlemarch: One of the Seven Kingdoms.

Milos's Mare: Inn in Achrida.

Old Empire: Remnants of the first major empire of the west, the Empire of Sabinia.

Old Road: A road around the west of Achrida connecting Crownstreet to the Trade Road south of Achrida.

Periaslavl (PEAR-ee-ah-sla-vel): Country laying to the north. Ruled by the Velikomat, the Great Mother who lives in Medvedgorod.

Samiel's Way (sa-MEEL): Street running through the Stracara in Achrida.

Seven Kingdoms: Group of small kingdoms of similar culture and language situated in the northwest.

Shijuren (shee-YOU-ren): Imperial and Old Imperial word for the world. In Sevenish, the word is spelled Sciuren. There is a cognate of this word in every major language in the world.

Square of Legends: A square in Achrida. The Trade Road goes through it. Medusa's Way and Hydra's Way lead out of it.

Stracara (strah-KA-rah): Poor area of Achrida, filled with crime and violence. Gibroz has his main office here.

Svellheim: Jarldom between the Seven Kingdoms and Periaslavl. Also called the Northlands.

Tresinova's Treasures: Brothel slightly to the outside of the walls of Achrida owned by Katarina.

Appendix Three - Glossary

aesc (ash): One of the letters of the Sevenish alphabet. Also used as a token to represent all the gods in the Sevenish pantheon of gods.

aetheling (EH-tha-ling): Prince or noble in the Seven Kingdoms.

ajvar (AY-var): Spicy relish of peppers and garlic often spread on bread.

Akritoi (AK-ra-toy): One of six military companies in Achrida. Most of its members are from the Enchelei tribe.

Allfather: Epithet applied to Woden, the leader of the Northern gods.

Altmezzers (ALT-metz-ers): One of six military companies in Achrida. Their membership includes a high percentage of immigrants from the Kreisens. The rest come from the Dassaretae tribe.

archimandrite: Imperial term for a leader of many religions in the Empire of Makhaira.

atramentum librarium: Type of valuable and rare ink. It is rare because it is illegal to make in the Empire of Makhaira except by a small number of producers licensed by the Emperor. While anyone able to afford the price may use this ink, all Imperial documents are written using it. Practitioners of Land magic are able to determine whether a document has been written using this ink, limiting forgeries.

baka: Imperial term for grandmother. Connotatively, it identifies the matriarch of a clan or family.

bakica: Essentially the same as "baka." It is another Imperial term for grandmother, however, it does not have the same matriarch connotation.

bencriht (BENCH-rikt) Sevenish for, literally, "bench-right." An agreement in the Seven Kingdoms and Svellheim between a lord and a retainer. The retainer promises his service to the lord in whatever capacity they agree, while the lord in return promises a seat on the benches in his hall. This also implies that the lord will feed, clothe, and shelter those who have sworn to him.

Berzeti (ber-ZAY-tee): Group of horse nomads who crossed the steppes from east to west. In the thirteenth century leaders of Achrida sent Naum as a diplomatic envoy to these nomads. His mission was so successful that they entered into the Enchelei en masse as a clan. Many Berzeti serve in the Pronoiars, the military company that serves as the city's cavalry.

Black Dog: Mythological beast that foretold a bloody death.

carl: Sevenish term for a trained warrior.

Child-Eater: Epithet for Aita, the Imperial God of Death.

clikurios (klee-KOO-re-ose): Imperial term for a person skilled in the Lore Stream of Magic. The plural form is *clikurioi*.

Dassaretae (DAS-sa-reh-tie): One of two competing tribes in Achrida and the surrounding environs. They compete against the Enchelei. The tribe has lived in the area of Achrida for at least two millennia. They lent their name to the Imperial province of which Achrida is the capitol, Dassaretum. Their primary clan is the Mrnjavcevic family.

decarch: Military rank in the Empire of Makhaira. The word literally means "leader of ten" and is bestowed upon those who lead a unit of approximately that size.

dinar (DEE-nar): Main unit of currency in the Empire of Makhaira. It comes in bronze and silver versions. The silver dinar is worth two bronze dinars. Ten silver dinars are worth one solidi.

dromon: Main style of warship in the Imperial Makhairan Navy. Their design signaled the end of ramming as a naval tactic because their hulls were sufficiently sturdy to withstand ramming while retaining the flexibility required to handle medium-sized seas. They include a full upper deck, allowing for more and larger missile weaponry. They also possess a lateen sail.

ealdmodor (eld-MO-der): Sevenish for "grandmother." Though the word does not necessarily carry the connotation of matriarch that the

Imperial word *baka* might, grandmothers in Sevenish society are the keepers of wisdom and history, meaning they are well-respected.

elatos (EL-ah-tohs): Term given to rowers in the Imperial Makhairan Navy.

Enchelei (en-ka-LIE): One of two competing tribes in Achrida and the surrounding environs. They compete against the Dassaretae. Though they arrived in the area in the second or third century, they arrived after the Dassaretae. Their primary clan is the Gropa family.

erkurios (air-KOO-re-ose): Imperial term for a person skilled in the Love Stream of Magic. The plural form is *erkurioi*.

Father of the Slain: Epithet applied to Woden, the leader of the Northern gods.

Feeder of the Wolf: Epithet applied to Tyr, the Northern god of law.

Feroun (FAY-roon): Imperial for "bears." One of six military companies in Achrida. Most of its members are from one of the families of the Dassaretae.

Five Streams of Magic: See Appendix Five – Magic in Shijuren.

The Fourteen Holy Helpers: Group of gods and goddesses known for the ability to heal.

gekurios (gay-KOO-re-ose) Imperial term for a person skilled in the Land Stream of Magic. The plural form is *gekurioi*.

gestriht (GUEST-rikt): Sevenish for, literally, "guest-right." It is the implied agreement in the Seven Kingdoms and Svellheim between a lord of a hall and a guest in that hall. Like many such agreements in that part of the world, it implies many responsibilities upon both sides. A guest must act respectfully to the host and his people, goods, and gods. A host must in turn protect the guest against any harm, whether from the host's retainers, someone else, or forces beyond the host's control.

Giants: Race of beings who kept humans in slavery until defeated more than seventeen centuries ago. The current era, MG, dates from the time, years after their defeat, when humans had recovered some semblance of civilization. Giants, as their name implied, were physically larger than humans. Nearly everything else that was once known about Giants has faded with the centuries, with the possible exception of records held by the Readers.

Glagolitsa (gla-go-LEET-sa): Script invented by Naum, now used rarely outside his order.

gospodar (go-spo-DAR): Imperial for "lord."

Gropa (GROW-pa): Most powerful of the clans within the Enchelei tribe. Nearly all of the leaders of the Enchelei have come from this clan.

gulyas: Thick, stew-like dish heavily spiced with peppers unknown in western areas such as the Seven Kingdoms, Svellheim, the Old Empire, and the Kreisen.

hacksilver: Form of payment given by lords in the Seven Kingdoms and the Kreisen to their retainers. Essentially, they are chunks of silver hacked or chopped off of a larger piece of silver. That larger piece is scored so that each piece that is hacked off is approximately of the same weight.

Hanged God: Epithet applied to Woden, the leader of the Northern gods.

hecatontarch: Military rank in the Empire of Makhaira. The word literally means "leader of one hundred." Despite its literal meaning, it actually refers to the person in charge of day-to-day command of an Imperial company, whatever its actual size.

The Helpers: See the Fourteen Holy Helpers.

Imperial: Language spoken in the Empire of Makhaira.

izba (EEZ-ba): A small community in Periaslavl. Generally it consists of a lord's hall, family homes, and communal production facilities.

jebi se (JEB-ee seh): Essentially, "fuck off" in Imperial

kentarch (ken-TARK): Civilian rank in the Empire of Makhaira. It is applied to a relatively low-level but nonetheless vital member of a particular bureaucracy. A real world equivalent would be a Sergeant on a police force or the administrative assistant of a major bureaucrat.

koryfoi (ko-re-FOY): People of Achrida who are not affiliated with a kral.

kral (krawl): Term for a major criminal gang in the Empire of Makhaira.

kraljevic (KRAWL-ya-vich): Essentially, Imperial for "Prince of Crime." These are the bosses of krals. As of 1712, there are two kraljevics in Achrida (Gibroz and Katarina).

kreisen (KRY-zen): Term that refers to a tribe or region of the same clan or culture in the broader area known as the Kreisens. There are hundreds of separate kreisen of various power, each controlling whatever area they can.

kreisarch (KRY-zark): Lord or chieftain of a kreisen. Each kreisarch competes constantly against his neighbors, routinely raiding each other or making alliances of convenience as seems practical.

The Kreisens (KRY-zenz): Overall name for all of the kreisen. Because of the constant competition between kreisarchs, the area is known for its conflict and strife.

Kreisic (KRY-zic): Language of the Kreisen.

kuja: (KOO-ya): Achridan slang for "bitch."

kurios (KOO-re-oy): Imperial word for a person skilled in any of the Five Streams of Magic. The plural form is *kurioi*.

Lady of Cythera: (KY-the-ra): Epithet of Chryse, the Imperial goddess of love and beauty.

Lakewardens: One of six military companies in Achrida. Most of its members are from the Enchelei tribe.

leorner: Sevenish term for a person skilled in the Line Stream of Magic.

Lezhans: People from the city of Lezh. Lezh is just west of Achrida and is the terminus port of the east–west trade route that goes across Lake Achrida and the city of Achrida. Lezhans and Achridans routinely compete for a greater share of trade profits on this route.

liffrea: Sevenish term for a person skilled in the Life Stream of Magic.

Luckbringer: Epithet for Hermes.

M.G. or MG: Dating of the current era. It is an abbreviation for the Imperial words *metagigantes*, which means "after the Giants."

Mithra: Major god of the Empire of Makhaira. Most soldiers worship Mithra to some degree or another.

Mrnjavcevic (murn-yav-CHEH-vich): Most powerful of the clans within the Dassaretae tribe. Nearly all of the leaders of the Dassaretae have come from this clan.

nobilissimi (no-be-LIS-se-me): Imperial for, literally, "most noble." This is the Imperial class of the greatest and most powerful nobles in the Empire of Makhaira.

The Notes of Naum in His Captivity: Long collection of thoughts and philosophies written by Naum when he was imprisoned in the Kreisens.

nuraghi (noo-RAG-hee): Imperial term for an ancient ruin. Many nuraghi are thought to have existed since the time of the Giants. Some are speculated to be even older.

Old Imperial: Language once spoken in the Old Empire, also known as the Empire of Sabinia. Its descendants are spoken in various areas that the Old Empire controlled. It is also used in the Empire of Makhaira primarily as a language of the intellectuals and aristocracy.

One-Eye: Epithet applied to Woden, the leader of the Northern gods.

Pathfinders: One of six military companies in Achrida. Most of its members are from the Dassaretae tribe.

photodotis (foe-toe-DOE-tees): A rank within the hierarchy of Panteleimon. Generally the highest-ranked member at a given temple.

Pismenech (peez-MEN-ek): Holy text of the Naumites based in part upon writings in *The Notes of Naum in His Captivity*, as well as a description of the creation of the Glagolitsa and his work teaching the Berzeti how to read in that script.

Pronoiars (PRO-noy-ar): One of six military companies in Achrida. Most of its members are from the Berzeti. It is the cavalry of Achrida, and its members are known both for their horsemanship and arrogance.

proreus (pro-RAY-us): Naval rank in the Empire of Makhaira given to the bow officer, whose primary responsibility included organizing the watch for other ships.

protokarabos (pro-to-KA-ra-boess): Naval rank in the Empire of Makhaira given to highest-ranking noncommissioned officer on a ship.

quaesitor (KWAY-za-tore): Member of the Imperial bureaucracy. Quaesitors are tasked with investigating and eliminating crime within the Empire of Makhaira.

rakija (RA-key-ya): Type of brandy that can be distilled from many different fruits and is quite popular in the province of Dassaretum.

Reader: Not simply the noun for a person who reads, rather it is the proper noun for an order of lorekeepers and Lore magicians. The order always strives to learn everything it can. It will dispense that information to anyone who asks, as long as doing so does not violate their complex oath. Essentially, they will not tell anyone any information that gives the recipient an unfair advantage. The definition of "unfair advantage" is entirely up to the ranking Reader available at any given moment. The goal of the Readers is to gather knowledge, not to influence events. Not every Reader is a practitioner of Lore magic, but many are.

saex (sahx): Type of knife used in the Seven Kingdoms. Also the symbol of a free man in the Seven Kingdoms, and its bestowal and ownership is surrounded by many customs and traditions.

scop (shope): Sevenish word for "performer" or "bard."

Sevener: Epithet used to denote someone from the Seven Kingdoms.

Sfagi (sva-GEE): Imperial for "slaughter." In Achrida it is also the name for a particularly bloody moment in the competition between the Dassaretae and the Enchelei. Nearly every leader of both sides ever since has attempted to avoid a recurrence.

shopska (shope-SKA): Type of salad common in the Empire of Makhaira. It consists of chopped cucumbers, onions, a vinegar dressing, and an extremely salty goat cheese.

stola: Cloak-like garment in the Empire of Makhaira. Generally it was only used by members of one or another religious hierarchy, though its use has fallen out of favor in the seventeenth and eighteenth centuries.

stonelord: Sevenish term for a person skilled in the Land Stream of Magic.

strategos (stra-TEE-gose): Military rank in the Empire of Makhaira given to generals and leaders of armies. In Achrida, the Pronoiars use the term for their commander.

symkurios (sim-KOO-re-ose): Imperial term for a person skilled in the Line Stream of Magic. The plural form is *symkurioi*.

tagmatarch (tag-ma-TARK): Civilian rank in the Empire of Makhaira. It is applied to a bureaucrat in charge of some division or section.

thegn (thain): Retainers who have sworn bencriht to a lord in the Seven Kingdoms.

Thunder God: Epithet for Thunor, one of the Northern gods.

Trickster: Epithet for Loki, one of the Northern gods, famed for his mischievous tricks.

Trollsbane: Epithet for Thunor, one of the Northern gods, famed for his antipathy towards trolls in the Northern sagas.

turnshoes: Type of shoe constructed by sewing the shoe inside out and then "turning" it right-side out. This method both protects the primary seams from unnecessary damage and helps keep water out of the shoe.

vranec (VRA-nek): Means "black" in the Dassaretic dialect of Imperial. It usually refers to a type of grape grown in Dassaretum. Makes a wine that is such a dark red it is often called "black wine."

Wealthtaker: Epithet for Aita, the Imperial God of Death.

White Bull: Epithet for Zeus, the leader of the Imperial gods. So named because Zeus was known to take the form of a White Bull.

winingas: Sevenish term for strips of cloth used to wrap around the foot and calf.

wizard: Old Imperial term for a person skilled in the Lore Stream of Magic.

Wolfsbane: Epithet for Tyr, a Northern god.

World Tree:, The World Tree held a branch bearing the life and death of all things and all lives in the Northern religion.

zokurios (Zoe-KOO-re-ose): Imperial term for a person skilled in the Life Stream of Magic. The plural form is *zokurioi*.

zupan (ZOO-pawn): Clan or tribal leader in the Empire of Makhaira. In Achrida, the Enchelei and Dassaretae tribes each have their own zupans, who essentially compete for control of the city.

Appendix Four – Calendar of Shijuren

The current era is dated from the civilizations that rose after fall of the Giants. The abbreviation *MG* comes from the Old Imperial word metagigantes.

Days of the week

Six days of the week, five weeks per month.

- **Helimera** (HELL-ee-mair-ah)
- **Selenemera** (se-LAY-na-mair-ah)
- **Aremera** (ARR-ee-mair-ah)
- **Hermoumera** (hair-MOO-mair-ah)
- **Jovimera** (YOE-vee-mair-ah)
- **Kronomera** (KROW-no-mair-ah)

Months of the year.

Each month is 30 days long, plus five additional days (sometimes six).

Styrtendeniht (stir-TEN-de-nikt): New Year's Day. Every four years, the New Year is celebrated with two days.

Foarmoanne (FORE-mo-an-nah): Corresponds with late January, early February.

Sellemoanne (SEL-la-mo-an-nah): Corresponds with late February, early March.

Thunorsniht (THOO-norz-nikt): The vernal equinox.

Foarjiersmoanne (for-YEARZ-mo-an-nah): Corresponds with late March, early April.

Gersmoanne (GEHRZ-mo-an-nah): Corresponds with late April, early May.

Blommemoanne (BLOW-muh-mo-an-nah): Corresponds with late May, early June.

Wodensniht (WOAH-denz-nikt): The summer solstice.

Simmermoanne (SIM-mer-mo-an-nah): Corresponds with late June, early July.

Heamoanne (HEY-ah-mo-an-nah): Corresponds with late July, early August.

Rispmoanne (RISSP-mo-an-nah): Corresponds late August, early September.

Wyrdsniht (WEIRDZ-nikt): The autumnal equinox.

Hjerstmoanne (ha-YERST-mo-an-nah): Corresponds with late September, early October.

Wynmoanne (WIN-mo-an-nah): Corresponds with late October, early November.

Slachtmoanne (SLAWKT-mo-an-nah): Corresponds with late November, early December.

Helsniht (HELZ-nikt): The winter solstice.

Wintermoanne (WIN-ter-mo-an-nah): Corresponds with late December, early January.

Appendix Five – Magic in Shijuren

Magic in Shijuren is both a talent and a skill. Approximately one out of ten people has the mental capability to manipulate energy to some degree. There are many names for such people, but the Imperial term *kurios* (pl. *kurioi*) is known across the world. With training, the most talented can perform great feats, while those with lesser talent can do many useful things depending upon the type of magic they use.

There are five types of magical energy in Shijuren: Life magic, Love magic, Lore magic, Land magic, and Line magic. These are the Five Streams of Magic. The traditional rhyme used to remember the Five Streams is:

To change nature's guise

One needs loves or lives

Stone's laws or sharp lines

Or lore of the wise

Kurioi are limited by several factors, including raw talent, distance, type of magic, and difficulty of the magic. As noted, magical talent varies in the person. Some kurioi can cast spells seemingly without rest, while others fade quicker but are especially powerful. In general, the greater the spell the greater the resulting fatigue.

The only known way to regain magical power is food and rest. Magic power can restore physical energy but cannot restore magical power. Certain foods, such as liver, are more effective in restoring power, but all food helps.

Generally, kurioi can only affect things near them. They do not have to see their targets, but seeing a target makes the magic more efficient. Some kurioi can reach longer distances, and the most powerful can reach far indeed. However, their power attenuates the farther they reach.

With few exceptions, a kurios can influence only one type of magic. Furthermore, within the type of magic, some things come more naturally to a given kurios than to another. In other words, though kurioi fall into these five broad categories, each is different from every other.

There are tools to enhance magical power, generally differing for each type of magical energy. Pitchblende and Mavric iron are notable as the only known substances that can enhance all types of magic. Mavric iron is created by powerful gekurioi who focus their power upon pure chunks of pitchblende. Once created, Mavric iron can be forged liked any other metal, though tends to be brittle and is often alloyed with other metals.

Unfortunately, both pitchblende and Mavric iron are extraordinarily harmful to anyone who uses them. Their minor effects are rashes, burns, and a pallid appearance. Nearly every kurios who uses these substances records nausea and headaches. Kurioi who have survived prolonged use report suffering from wasting diseases and headaches so powerful they prevent magic use. In truth, however, most who use these substances die quickly.

Each type of magic has other, safer methods to increase power, such as location or items that focus magic. Also, kurioi can collaborate to create increased power or store power in other objects. An erkurios could work with a zokurios to increase the emotional power of a plant. For example, certain flowers enhanced in this way increase feelings of love in a couple. A zokurios and a gekurios could imbue healing power into a crystal or another object, giving it the ability to heal someone, such as a wounded soldier. The possible collaborations are truly limitless.

A larger description of each type of magic follows, but even more information can be found on the wiki at www.robhowell.shijuren.

Land Magic

Land magic, or gemejea, manipulates the nonliving energy and matter of the universe. There are many names for Land magicians, but all Shijuren accepts the term *gekurios* (pl. *gekurioi*).

Land magic is the least subtle of all of the streams. Since matter is energy and energy matter, gekurioi can manipulate any type of energy or matter to some extent. They can even affect light, depending upon power and aptitude. Theoretically, a gekurios could liberate all the energy of a thing, though no one has ever come close to that capability.

Not surprisingly, Land magic cannot affect living beings, except when a gekurios manipulates an object around a creature or plant. For example, Land magic cannot induce blindness by changing a creature's ability to see, but it can stop light from traveling in an area.

Minerals, especially in crystal form, can enhance Land magic. The type of mineral or crystal that is most effective depends entirely on the gekurios. Some require diamonds to enhance their power, and some need sapphires or rubies. Others do better with simple quartz.

As mentioned, some gekurioi can convert pitchblende to Mavric iron. It is always worth remembering the health costs of working with this material, and few gekurioi are willing to make that sacrifice. Mavric iron is thus extraordinarily valuable.

Life Magic

Life magic, or *zomejea*, manipulates the energy of living things. There are many names for Life magicians, but all Shijuren accepts the term *zokurios* (pl. *zokurioi*).

Zokurioi see energy fields around living things and can draw from or influence those fields in many ways. They can heal or harm living things, but they do not have much power over nonliving things unless a living thing can affect a thing. For example, a zokurios could not affect a boulder. However, if the boulder was near a tree, he or she could influence the tree's roots to grow swiftly and shatter that boulder.

The greater the number of living things around a zokurios, the more powerful the magic he or she can perform. A zokurios is especially powerful in a jungle, for example. Zokurioi can imbue extra personal power in a place, such as a garden or a grove, which enhances their individual power. Furthermore, certain items, such as a staff cut from a tree in that grove, can allow a zokurios to carry stored power with them, though that power is much reduced compared to actually being in their home.

Line Magic

Line magic, or symmajea, manipulates runes, writing, and symbols. There are many names for Line magicians, but all Shijuren accepts the term *symkurios* (pl. *symkurioi*).

The most versatile of the streams, symmajea can do anything if a symkurios can create a pattern they can recognize as a symbol. Not every symbol works for every symkurios. For example, some use runes, others use music, and still others have their own symbolic vocabulary.

Nevertheless, some symbols can be taught. For example, one of the first symbols taught is some version allowing the symkurios to determine whether or not a person is speaking truthfully.

As symkurioi become more experienced and their symbolic vocabularies become larger, they can increasingly create new symbols to shape influence.

Many types of symbols can achieve similar effects. For example, a symbol on a banner can increase the military might of a unit, but so can a particular song.

The materials a symkurios can use are as varied as the symbols themselves. Charcoal and pen can create symbols. Tattoos, either permanent or in henna, are often used to imbue magic on a person. Symbols can be embroidered on cloth. Each of these methods affects the magic subtly. Henna tattoos, for example, become less powerful as they fade. Tattoos in general are a constant drain on a symmajea, and permanent tattoos, while powerful, tend to shorten their bearer's natural lifespan.

Lore Magic

Lore magic, or climajea, manipulates the power in knowledge and history. There are many names for Lore magicians, but all Shijuren accepts the term *clikurios* (pl. *clikurioi*).

The past influences the future, and a clikurios shapes that energy. Working with the most subtle of all the Five Streams, clikurioi tend to think in longer terms than nearly anyone else. They manipulate potentialities in people and items. Each potentiality is called a *kairos* (pl. *kairoi*) and clikurioi create chains of kairoi to make a desired outcome more likely. This magic often takes significant time and no outcome is sure.

The more knowledge a clikurios has, the more they see and understand kairoi, and hence the greater his or her influence. The most prominent collection of clikurioi in Shijuren is the Readers. Though not every Reader is a clikurios, climajea is the clear focus of the order. This means that their strongest kurioi have at hand a great pool of knowledge, making them extraordinarily powerful. It is this power that prompts the Readers to take and live up to obscure oaths that guide their decisions.

In many cases, clikurioi do not even need magic to influence events. They are in great demand as advisors and can change the future simply through normal influence.

Love Magic

Love magic, or ermajea, manipulates the nonliving energy and matter of the universe. There are many names for Love magicians, but all Shijuren accepts the term *erkurios* (pl. *erkurioi*).

Though it is called "love" magic, ermajea is a magic of all emotions. Erkurioi see and manipulate tendrils of emotion flowing from people and creatures. An erkurios may also be able to influence animals, but as animal brains get smaller and less emotional, this becomes less likely. Unlike zokurioi, erkurioi cannot influence plants at all, nor can they influence nonliving things unless they can convince a creature to do so.

Emotion feeds emotion, so in places where there is a great deal of emotion, such as in a large crowd, an erkurios has access to more power. Also, friends and family can feed emotion to an erkurios, which is especially effective because of the added emotion of their relationship. For example, the Velikomat of Periaslavl chooses three husbands in part for their ability to love her. They help her perform great feats of magic.

It takes less power to enhance an existing emotion than to create an emotion, and one needs more power still to override an existing emotion. So, while an erkurios can, for example, change a person's love to hate or vice versa, it takes a great deal of power to do so.

Appendix Six - Gods in Shijuren

Divine creatures and things do exist in the world of Shijuren. These gods and godlings are by definition symbols; hence, most religious magic is Line magic. No matter what other aspects a god or godling may have, it will provide magical energy to Line magicians who follow it.

Religions tend to attract magicians who fall into one of the other types of magic. For example, the church of Naum, a scholar, tends to attract Lore magicians. The church of Mithra, whose following consists primarily of soldiers, tends to attract Life magicians, both those who heal and those who slay. The church of Panteleimon is unusual because while Panteleimon was a Land magician, he was also a great researcher. Hence both Land magicians, especially those interested in light, and Lore magicians, especially those interested in herblore and medicines, are attracted to his church.

Divine beings require two things to become divine. First, enough of their essence must exist to provide a framework for power. For example, the history or lore of a person or thing must be remembered by many. The life force of a person or animal must be so abundant that it endures after death. Extremely strong emotion can remain after it is expressed. If a nonliving thing becomes suitably symbolic, it too can gain a following. Whatever the method, a powerful essence must remain to anchor divine energy.

Second, whatever the source, an essence must then also be sufficiently worshiped to provide that essence with the power to become divine. Worship by a great many people can provide that energy, but so can relatively few but especially devout disciples. However, without the framework provided by an essence, no amount of worship can create a god.

A Line magician cannot *create* a god per se, but he or she can affect the power of a potential god's symbols. Since one of the requirements is sufficient worship, if a Line magician can influence enough people to worship with enough intensity, then a god will come into existence, assuming enough of the target's essence remains. One does not need magic to influence a potential god's symbol. A particularly effective speaker can do much the same without using magic.

Once an essence is combined with worship, its symbolic power becomes divine power and the essence becomes a god or godling—that is, a being in its own right. Gods and godlings are immortal and can never completely die. However, without any worshipers, a god or godling is merely a shade with no power to speak of. Many worshipers, in contrast, can make that god extremely powerful and its symbols extraordinarily influential.

The only real difference between a god and a godling is the number and devoutness of worshipers. A person can easily worship more than one god or godling, and most people in Shijuren do. Logically, a god receives whatever amount of energy is focused on it, while energy focused on other gods goes to that god instead. Few people give divine beings the full amount of energy they are capable of producing, as most people expend their energy on the world around them.

Many familiar names appear among the gods and goddesses of Shijuren. Once an essence has become divine, it is not limited to the universe in which it originated. As a god loses power in one universe, it may very well seek followers in another: as the Germanic and Greco-Roman pantheons lost influence elsewhere, both migrated to Shijuren. They joined many other gods and goddesses of purely Shijuren creation, most from the eastern and southern portions of the world.

Sample from *The Eyes of a Doll*
Book 2 in the Adventures of Edward Aethelredson

Chapter 1
Late Afternoon, 29 Gersmoanne, 1712 MG

I felt better than I had in many years.

One reason was the table sitting before me. It had become my standard table in the Frank Faerie, which had been my home for most of the past month. The family who ran the Faerie had welcomed me with open arms. In the nearly six years since my lord had been slain, no place had seemed so comfortable. Not even the izba in Periaslavl where I had spent much of the previous three years.

The full mug of ale upon that table was another reason. The Frank Faerie's brew tasted as good as the owner boasted. Ragnar would not tell me all of his secrets, but he admitted the crisp, cool water of the lake sitting next to this strange city of Achrida improved his ale.

The food that would soon appear was a third reason. Ragnar's wife, Zoe, could work magic in the kitchen, maybe not true magic of the Five Streams, but near enough. The aromas from her kitchen could not fail to brighten anyone's mood. I happily awaited that night's creation.

Melia, the gray tabby who ruled the Faerie, also awaited that night's food. I rubbed her belly as she stretched out with no shame or propriety. She responded to my petting with rhythmic purring. Every once in a while she would get up, butt my hand with her head, turn around two or three times, and resume lounging in exactly the same position.

I stretched back and took stock. During the previous month I had earned a series of wounds, one in each shoulder and another in the meaty part of my thigh. Zoe had tended to them with the ease of much practice, and only the thigh wound continued to hurt. Well, much, at least.

With my feet sprawled before me, I considered when I would need to continue my trip to the Great City and my future. Achrida was simply a stopping point on my way to join the Emperor's service, but somehow I had gotten caught up in the politics of this crazy place and stayed here about a month.

The month had given me lessons, as well as wounds, friends, and enemies that I would not soon forget. Nevertheless, though the Frank Faerie and Ragnar's family had become more of a home to me than any since my lord's meadhall, I could not stay here forever.

As I planned my future, Honker Harald, one of the regulars in the Faerie, came over shyly.

"Master Edward."

"Honker, we've drunk too much ale together at this point for you to be calling me master."

He nodded, but stayed there standing nervously.

"Please, Honk, sit down. How can I look past your nose and see your eyes when you're standing up?"

That got a short laugh, and he sat down, clearly still not at ease.

"Well, it's just this, Sevener..."

He paused and started to rise.

"Never mind, it's silly."

"Wait. At least tell me what it is. You can't make me curious and not tell me. Besides, you're disturbing Melia."

He hesitated again, glancing at the cat, who was now sitting up in curiosity.

I called across the taproom, "Karah, bring Honk a mug of ale and tell him he can't leave my table until he drinks it."

"Stop shouting at me or I'll pour the mug in your lap."

A glare followed the angry shout, but so did a mug. The regulars in the Faerie laughed quietly and kept their heads down, lest she turn her flashing eyes at them.

Honker took the mug and drank most of it immediately.

"What's bothering you, Honk?"

"Well, it's just that... I mean, it's nothing, but... Well, me daughter's lost somethin' and, well, I haven't the time... and, well..."

He finished the mug and started to rise.

"Wait. Your daughter lost something and you don't have the time to get it, and you want me to get it back?"

"I said it was stupid."

"What did she lose?"

"Well, me daughter's but six, and she had this doll I made for her last birthday."

"And she lost her doll?"

He hung his head. "Yeah. We were visiting the springs."

"Biljana's Springs?"

He nodded.

"I don't blame you a bit, Honk. Svetislav took me there once. It's beautiful. The water tastes amazing, and it's so cold."

He nodded again, this time with a smile.

"So you and your family spent an afternoon by the springs, and your daughter lost her doll. You want me to go look for it because you don't have the time it will take."

"Yeah... I mean, I'm sorry to have bothe—"

"Oh, don't be silly, I wouldn't mind going to the springs. This is as good a reason as any. I'll be happy to take a look."

"You don't have to."

"Of course not. But really, I'm happy to help you. You've picked up a cudgel to stand at my back when I came bleeding into the Faerie a night or two. You didn't have to do that, either. I might not find it, but I'll enjoy the trip. I'll do it tomorrow morning."

Honker got up with a smile bigger than his mighty nose and nodded his thanks.

"Wait, what color is it?"

"Oh, right. Well, Sevener, it's got a dress of a white scraps where me wife embroidered small blue waves on the hem and cuffs."

"Excellent, I should easily be able to recognize it."

He returned to his normal table with Marko and Flavian. I heard Flavian's weird laugh as they teased Harald about seeking my help with a doll.

Karah came by for his mug and gave me a slightly less angry sniff than was her wont.

I finished two more mugs while Zoe worked her magic for the evening. As Ragnar brought dinner out, Melia jumped off of my table collect her tithe from all those eating Zoe's feast.

"Well, Sevener, I'm to be seein' that yer to be havin' yet another job here in this fine city. And I'm to be bein' certain it's a might less of a hunt than all them's writin' of the Naumites. Yer a fine fellow, I'm to be thinkin' and it's a good thing yer to be doin'."

Ragnar plopped down the night's meal in the midst of his torrent of words. Gulyas. I sighed.

"It's to be bein' yer favorite, I'm to be thinkin'." He laughed as he walked away.

In truth, I enjoyed gulyas though it made my mouth burn. The Empire had spices unknown in my homeland in the Seven Kingdoms.

I stopped Ragnar when he came over to retrieve my plate.

"I'm not sure I can ask Svetislav to row me over to the springs after all that has happened recently. I assume there's a road or path around the lake where I can reach the springs?"

"Oh, aye, it's to be bein on the part of the Kopayalitsa. There's not but a few caravans headin' east or west from Achrida on accounts that boats are to be bein' so much faster and safer, but Achrida's not to bein' always here, and there's always to be bein' some as to not be likin' boats. Yer to have passed it on the Trade Road north a' the city when you were to be comin' here before all this were to be happenin'."

I marveled again at Ragnar's ability to say so much in one breath while simultaneously clearing plates, stacking mugs, acknowledging orders, and never missing anything happening in the rest of the taproom.

"So I could be ridi..., errr... ride Deor over?"

"Oh, aye, it's to be bein' old and them as to be keepin' up them roads don't be spendin' too much time there, but it's to be bein' better than the Old Road even if it's to be seemin' not so good at first."

"Excellent, thank you."

"Yer to be wantin' me to be havin' me boy saddle yer lad in the mornin' then. I'm to be tellin' him, and he'll be bein' happy…"

He wandered off before I could say I could saddle my own horse, thank you, never stopping his conversation though I could not hear all of it. At least Deor never bit Eirik. He even let Eirik tighten the saddle properly where I would have to punch him in the stomach first.

I settled in for a relaxing night, anticipating a pleasant ride in the mountains.

Chapter 2
Morning, 30 Gersmoanne, 1712 MG

Over the past week Branimira, a seamstress recommended by Zoe who lived just down from the Fourth Serpent on Medusa's Way, had repaired the rips and tears that various knives had added to my tunics. I chose the one with the lightest linen, dyed light brown with walnuts, and shrugged it on over heavier linen riding pants of woad blue and my old, comfortable riding boots.

I always wore the saex my father had given me as a lad that identified me as a free man. I also carried a small dagger that once had been thrust into my left shoulder. Eirik had made a sheath for it that fit inside either my boots or winingas. By this point it seemed odd not to have it strapped to my calf.

I decided to wear my sword, even though few people walked around Achrida routinely with one. No longer could I roam Achrida without worry, given the enemies I had made. I made sure I could slide its water-patterned steel out smoothly and swiftly.

I hesitated, but finally chose to bring my shield as well. Better to hang it off my saddle and have it with me than wish I had it should Katarina, Pal, or Gibroz decide to deal with me.

I went down to the stables to find Eirik feeding Deor one of the old apples they kept in a bucket there.

"I see you're spoiling him."

Eirik laughed shyly. "He likes them."

"That he does."

As we chatted, I double-checked that Eirik had saddled Deor properly, also taking the time to check his hooves and legs. Not surprisingly, Eirik had made no mistake.

"You're doing well, old friend," I said as I patted Deor's side.

He showed his agreement by nipping at my arm, but I knew him well and dodged the bite and slung my shield on his saddle.

Atop the stable wall, in her normal perch, Akantha watched with heavy-lidded eyes. With a great yawn, she dismissed us and curled up under the rafter.

Eirik opened the stable doors and waved at us as we went down the Fourth Serpent to Medusa's Way. That led to the Square of Legends, where I turned north up the Trade Road.

The guards at the North Gate surprised me slightly. The Pathfinder Company had served as gatewardens all of the time I had been in Achrida. However, as I thought about it, the change made sense, with over a dozen Pathfinders slain and at least as many badly wounded helping me with the Gropa Council.

Their dead included my friend Desimir. I sighed, remembering his smile.

Despite the fact that the guards at the gate belonged to a company other than the Pathfinders, they recognized me as I rode up.

"Gospodar Edward," called their leader, a small but powerfully built, balding man.

"Greetings."

"I am Vojin, a decarch of the Feroun."

"And the Feroun have gate duty."

"Hecatontarch Piriska asked us to take over for a while. The Pathfinders need a break and the Enchelei companies seem to be distracted."

His smirk reminded me that the members of the Feroun also generally came from the Dassaretae.

I would never understand this city, but I had learned about the rivalry between the Enchelei and the Dassaretae tribes. In fact, my deeds of the previous month had thrown the Gropas, the main family of the Enchelei tribe, into disarray. I supposed that Vukasin Mrnjavcevic, the leader of the Mrnjavcevic family and hence the zupan of the Dassaretae, would have preferred something a little less dramatic, but the rest of his tribe undoubtedly were enjoying the damage done to their ancient enemies.

"I'm headed up the Kopayalitsa to the springs for Honker Harald."

"Is his nose as big as they say?"

"Come by the Faerie and find out," I laughed.

The Feroun made a pathway through the gate for me, and I ignored the glares of the others who waited in line. Once past the cluster awaiting entry, I let Deor trot up the road past Crownstreet to the overgrown smallish path that Ragnar had called the Kopayalitsa.

As we pushed through the branches, I realized a lack of upkeep created an illusion of the road's small size. Once, the Kopayalitsa had spread wide enough for two wagons to pass easily. Now, with the brush growing on the uphill side and the roadbed crumbling away on the downhill side, the road only allowed a single wagon to pass precariously along the mountainside.

The day shone gloriously, though much warmer than I liked as we approached Wodensniht, the shortest night of the year. The deep blue of Lake Achrida sparkled below us, and as we progressed I could look back at the city. From here, Achrida gleamed, a town of white limestone and red ceramic roof tiles. Looming above it all sat its fortress.

Now that I knew what to look for, I could pick out the domes and symbols that dotted the rooftops, denoting various shrines, churches, chapels, and wherever else anyone decided to pray. I had been told a person could worship with a different god or godling each day of the year in Achrida. I would be surprised if that were not true.

I nudged Deor down the path leading down to Biljana's Springs. Honker said the family had picnicked near a copse of pines that extended shade into a relatively flat, grassy area just above where the water poured from the mountainside. Though no families sat in the long, soft grass on this day, I recognized the copse easily and urged Deor down the last section of the path.

I slid off Deor's back once we reached the springs. I had remembered to bring a mug from the Faerie. With Deor lapping noisily and me dipping the mug in the springs, we drank our fill of the blissfully cold water.

I then led Deor up into the grassy area and let him nibble as he wished while I searched for the doll.

I hoped that the white dress would make it easy to spot, but a systematic stroll up and down the edge of the copse and into the field showed me nothing.

I decided that Honker's daughter might have gone into the copse itself, even though the pines had grown up tightly together. A small girl could easily crawl underneath the branches. For a grown man, however, its branches and needles poked out like spear tips from a shieldwall. The light tunic I had chosen had helped keep me cool on the trip, but provided little armor against the green barbs marshaled before me.

No help for it, I thought, wincing as I shouldered through the sharp needles stabbing through the light linen of my tunic. Past the first rank of branches, I found some small gaps among the trees and wove through them. Finally, close to the mountainside, deep amongst the tree trunks, I thought I saw flash of white.

I got close enough to realize that I had found the doll.

I also realized I had found something else.

Kapric and Zvono were not going to be happy with me.

A loud whinny from Deor disturbed my reverie. He only did that when—

I had my sword in my hand as I burst out from the copse. About ten yards away, two men with prominent brows rushed at me. Their drawn swords suggested they were not here to chat about the loveliness of the springs. They also had small round shields.

Had this happened but three days before, I might not have done so well. My leg wound still bothered me, but it had definitely gotten better. Also, the day before yesterday I had taken the time to spar with Piri's Pathfinders, and I felt free and loose.

Without my shield, I decided to use theirs. I feinted slightly to my left, and once they reacted I took two quick chopping steps to my right. Their momentum carried them forward until I stood even with the shield held by the man to my right.

I grabbed the bottom of his shield and yanked up, taking the opportunity to thrust my blade into the side of the shield's owner. I had heard that squishy sucking sound many times before, so it did not bother me as I withdrew my sword from his guts. Or, at least, not enough for me to lose track of the fight.

I pushed him and his shield at the other man, moving back to give us more space. Though we were of about the same height, my longer sword gave me a reach advantage. I tried to keep him away while nicking at his hands, legs, or anything else I could aim at around his shield.

I found myself slipping into the wrestling Long Guard that Desimir had taught me some weeks ago. It also tried to keep a foe at distance while channeling their rush when it came. Now, instead of keeping my hand out, I held my sword tip in that position, but the new footwork Desimir had drilled into me adapted itself well to this fight.

A quick jab put a small cut on his sword arm. He was barely aware of the cut, but was a touch nonetheless. I added another touch as a flip of my wrist allowed me to slash along his advancing thigh.

This combination of stance and length counteracted his extraordinary quickness, and the fight seemed to slow as we each probed for new lines of attack.

Suddenly, he charged. I stepped back, slashing downward to clear the space and keep the range. I realized, not quickly enough, that his charge was merely a feint. My reaction gave him the space he needed to run to his horse.

I had no chance to catch him before he mounted, so I ran to Deor. Unfortunately, Deor was near the springs while the man's horse sat near the road, and by the time I had mounted, the quick swordsman had already pounded up to the Kopayalitsa and ridden off to the east, away from Achrida.

I gave Deor his head while I tried to keep my eye on the fleeing swordsman. After about a quarter of a mile, I realized that I probably would not catch him. Worse yet, I might catch him at the time and place of his choosing. I pulled Deor up.

There seemed no help for it, so I cleaned my sword off with the inside of my tunic and sheathed it. Better a stained tunic than a rusty sword. Then I turned Deor around and told him to get us back to Achrida as fast as he could.

As we rode up to the gate, I shouted for Vojin. He emerged and I led him to the side.

"Do you know Kapric and Zvono? The quaesitors?"

"I know Zvono."

"Excellent, I need to get a message to them. Tell them to come to meet me at the springs."

"You have a reason I should tell them?"

"Just tell them it's me and they'll probably know."

He nodded and marched off, detailing a couple of men to the task.

I wheeled Deor around and we returned to Biljana's Springs as quickly as we could.

78026863R00216

Made in the USA
Columbia, SC
07 October 2017